ANTIPODES SERIES BOOK 1

PROJECT HEMISPHERE

ANTIPODES SERIES BOOK 1

PROJECT HEMISPHERE

T.S. SIMONS

4 Horsemen
Publications, Inc.

4 Horsemen Publications, Inc.
1497 Main St. Suite 169
Dunedin, FL 34698
4horsemenpublications.com
info@4horsemenpublications.com

Typeset by Sydney Wilder
Cover Design by Jen Kotick

Library of Congress Control Number: 2021947594

Ebook ISBN: 978-1-64450-370-6
Audiobook ISBN: 978-1-64450-369-0
Print ISBN: 978-1-64450-371-3
Hardcover ISBN: 978-1-64450-532-8

For my family—thank you for believing in me

Would YOU be chosen?

AFTER A GLOBAL OUTBREAK that threatens to decimate the planet, Australian scientists select a group of highly skilled young people to establish a sustainable island community built on the modern values of equity, diversity, and inclusion.

Lonely and homesick, Cam Mackintosh overcomes his anxiety and finds belonging, passion, and friendship in his new life before his dreams are suddenly ripped from his grasp. Sent hurtling on a journey of discovery, he finds friendship and acceptance when he encounters other communities like his own, but he is forced to make a decision that will ultimately change everything.

Kerguelen Islands

Melbourne

August Island
Auckland Island
Bellcamp Island

CONTENTS

ACKNOWLEDGMENTS

SOMETIMES IT IS LESS than pleasant events that set you hurtling toward a dream you had neglected. It is during these challenging times that you realize who are your loyal friends and supporters. To everyone who has encouraged and supported me–thank you. Rob, thank you for supporting me in my many hare-brained schemes over the years and not rolling your eyes at me too much. Thank you for sharing this crazy ride (and zoo) with me. To my family, thank you for the love, support, education and always caring for my fur-kids. Maxine, we have been friends for more than half our lives, and I can't tell you how much you mean to me. Thank you for being my beta reader and always being there for me. I wish your mum was here to see this. Isabelle, thank you for being a wonderful friend and always supporting me. I always value your input and perspective, even when I am exhausted, and you are always cheery. Kelly, thank you for being a wonderful colleague and friend for so many years. Melissa, thank you for being the best boss I ever had and believing in me, even when I didn't believe in myself.

Roslyn, thank you for your patience and kindness (and being a genius with editing). To everyone who reads this book or recommends it to a friend, THANK YOU. All books are important, and authors put years of effort into writing them. If you enjoyed this book, it would mean a great deal to me if you could spare a few minutes to write a review on Goodreads or any other platform.

PART ONE

CHAPTER 1

THE LOW DRONE WAS relentless, reverberating through my skull. I dared to crack open one eye, and a beam of white light crippled me, forcing me to curl into the fetal position. I groaned as I heard the sound, someone vacuuming a particularly dirty section of the hallway rug right outside my bedroom door. I recognized the masterful handiwork of my mother. Mum derived a perverse sense of pleasure in torturing me when I was sick—especially if it was of the self-inflicted variety. The subterranean growl my inebriated brain thought I heard while failing to sneak in at 3am and tripping over the cat clearly meant that I had indeed woken her when I fell full force into the hallway wall.

Merlin had gleefully registered someone awake as breakfast time and yowled at the top of his lungs. That cat has no off-switch. My choices at that point were limited: clatter around the kitchen feeding him or allow him to follow me to bed, purring like a chainsaw, walking on my belly, and pushing random items off the dresser until I succumbed. Like all rescue cats, Merlin considered himself a black furry god, so like a good servant, I shuffled around the kitchen in the dark to open the noisy pest a can. Wafts of tuna atop a bellyful of beer and kebab made me gag, so I bolted. Loud rumbles of contentment echoed down the hallway as I shuffled to my room, trying not to wake my family in that exaggerated way one does when extremely intoxicated.

Thus, the excruciatingly loud vacuuming at stupid o'clock on a Sunday morning.

Still trying to avoid the bright light from my window, I glanced at my watch: 8:05 am, an indication Mum was not impressed at being woken. Ten minutes later, Mum still hadn't managed to dislodge that stubborn bit of dirt from outside my room. I knew the futility of avoiding my fate.

Mum was born and raised in a small community on Lewis, a remote island in the Outer Hebrides off the north-west coast of Scotland. The determined Scots streak in her had never waned despite living here for more than twenty years after she met my Scots-born, Australian-raised Dad while he was backpacking and visiting his relatives in Scotland. Mum readily admitted that at the time, she was desperate to escape her small-island, small-town existence. The occasional subtle dig from my father indicated Mum was a wild child and left some carnage in her wake before she met Dad and moved to Australia. Small town living was clearly not suited to her.

When we were young, Mum returned to university and completed her teaching degree. Now that she was a principal, I had no doubt that the kids at her primary school were absolutely scared shitless of her. Despite her heart of gold and inability to walk past a person, child, or animal in need, she still hadn't lost the sharp accent, acerbic wit, nor the ability to reduce a fool stupid enough to take her on to a withered mass within minutes. If eyes were the window to the soul, they also expressed a spectrum of emotion. Mum possessed an arsenal of rather creative tactics to express her displeasure. Nothing as mundane as yelling.

Since no torture felt worse than those moments spent lying in bed trying to decide whether to get up and go to the bathroom or continue lying there, trying to sleep, but desperately needing to piss, I finally got up.

"Morning!" Mum chirped over the vacuum's roar as I staggered past, misjudged the corner, banged my elbow, and finally closed the door to the bathroom firmly behind me. Dropping my head, I groaned loudly, my long fringe falling across my face. Torture tactic number two had commenced: excessive chirpiness until I told her where I was last night, who I was with, and what I did. At least she had the decency to turn the vacuum off.

"Ah, Campbell. You have finally graced us with your presence. What are you up to today?"

The prying questions continued as I shuffled from the bathroom to the kitchen, aspirin in hand. Trying to respond but unable to dislodge the dry furry throat without a drink, I ended up grunting a monosyllabic response in her general direction that came out remotely like the desired word: sleep.

Sorcha was sitting on the bench at the dining table. Her back to the window, she had a cup of coffee in hand and an empty cereal bowl to the right of the newspaper she was reading. Despite paying bills, shopping, and performing most day-to-day

5

transactions online, my parents were old school in that they still enjoyed having the weekend paper delivered. Facing the kitchen door where I entered, my sister was engrossed in the paper and barely registered my existence. We had never been close, not since we were young. Contemplating cooking a breakfast to settle my throbbing head and queasy stomach, I realized I would need to clean up afterward. Rather than face the chore of scrubbing a greasy frypan, I settled for toast and coffee. The coffee machine whirred as it ground the beans, and I cringed as the noise pierced my skull, making me clutch my head, grimacing in pain. Filling a glass of water from the tap, I gazed blearily at the painkillers in my hand, wishing they could alleviate the pain by osmosis as I waited for the toaster.

Funny how two tiny white tablets can ease so much.

Tilting my head back, I dropped them into the back of my throat, washing them down with a gulp of the water.

Cup and plate in hand, I finally flopped into the chair opposite Sorcha. *Toast and coffee should be granted official medicinal status,* I thought absently. *There is absolutely no situation that cannot be improved with the addition of hot buttery toast and strong coffee.*

"Where's dad?" I asked Sorcha between mouthfuls, the coffee reviving me into some semblance of humanity.

She wrinkled her nose at the interruption but responded without glancing up, "The block."

Dad had always loved taking us camping. Dad was a different person in the bush—he just blended in. It was like Dad fit somehow, evolving into something different. Dad loved it all: fishing, cooking on open fires, hiking in the mountains—and he had loved teaching us how to be self-sufficient. For years, he refused to own a smartphone, responding with "smartphone, dumb user." Nothing could be further than the truth. He had an immense knowledge of medicine, history, and obscure topics that made him an interesting man to talk to. Often I wondered why he had chosen a career as a paramedic in the city when he was so clearly better suited to farming or rural life or even a career in academia. Dad had immense knowledge and interest in World War One history and had allegedly dragged Mum all over Europe to see historical sites like the Menin Gate, the Somme, and Villers-Bretonneux on their honeymoon.

Despite sharing his love of history, Mum's particular area of interest was Celtic and Pict archaeology; Mum was a city creature. She loved shops, cinemas, and people. Mum couldn't stop by the supermarket to buy milk without striking up a conversation with a stranger about some arbitrary topic. Shopping with her was a veritable nightmare as she would try to draw me into the conversation, and I ended up being forced to share highly embarrassing anecdotes from my childhood. I refused to shop with her when she regressed to chatting with people who adopted her as a kindred spirit in the pet food aisle. That whole section between cat food and laundry liquid was a quagmire best avoided.

Most years, Mum would invite strays to join us at Christmas dinner. Random people: those new to the city with no family, homeless people she harassed into coming along. Goodness knows where she found them. Probably buying cat food with a solitary Lean Cuisine in their trolley, the beacon of a lone dweller.

Mum could spot a lonely person a mile off. Mum was the type of person who, if someone arrived during dinner, would take a small portion from everyone's plate until she could feed them. Refusing to get rid of old coats, she would run a collection donating winter jackets to those in need every year. Warm, caring, cajoling, or blatantly manipulative, Mum had a way of getting what she wanted. But people loved her and said she had a heart of gold. My pounding head, eardrums still vibrating from the vacuum cleaner, wasn't convinced.

Sorcha, three years older than me and now in her final year of a postgraduate medical degree worked part-time as a university tutor. She claimed she didn't have time to go camping anymore. But she had never really enjoyed it. I had long suspected that Dad had always known that, but being the eternal diplomat, he never said a word. He welcomed her and enjoyed her company. He nodded sagely when she finally plucked up the courage and told him she didn't want to spend her weekends at our bush block [1]anymore.

The Block, as we had called it, from the time my parents had bought it twelve years ago, was five acres of blue gum and candlebark trees just over three hours' drive from our Melbourne home in the middle of nowhere on the back road to Mount Buller. We had debated names for hours, arguing over the merits of each but couldn't reach a consensus. Mum finally ended the debate by stating that the property would name itself, and the name would become apparent when it was time. It hadn't. Now it was just

---

[1] In Australia, bush is native forest, undeveloped land, often with native wildlife.

too embarrassing to try. I had long suspected that no one else wanted this particular piece of bushland when my parents bought it, dead cheap, at the end of a dirt track over a kilometer off the nearest road and surrounded by state forest. I was ten when they made the purchase, old enough to roam the forest for hours on a trail bike during my school holidays and long weekends—making slingshots, climbing trees, and enjoying bushfires at night with toasted marshmallows. For Dad, it was his nirvana, and he loved being there like nowhere else on earth. Despite the years we had owned it, the lot was still mostly native forest with a small two-room cottage we had built from scratch.

Surrounded by a forest of eucalypts[2] with soaring tree ferns, bracken, and ground cover, over the past few years, Dad had begun more clearing and had planted a mixed orchard and a decent-sized vegetable patch. He was still working out what grew well and what didn't. Keeping the local wildlife from snacking was an ongoing issue, requiring creative fencing solutions. Wallabies, wombats, and koalas, even deer, regularly came to help themselves to dinner. The possums got most of the cherries, even with sheets of metal clad around the trunks to hinder their climbing, so after two seasons of failure, he finally gave up with them, letting the possums have them. There was no point in ripping them out, after all. Stone fruit grew well, but he simply couldn't get lemons to grow. Finally, Mum had said acerbically, "You could have bought a lot of lemons with the money you spent on citrus trees."

---

[2] Eucalypts – collective term for eucalyptus trees, of which there are more than 700 species

Dad rolled his eyes and said nothing, but I noted he stuck to stone fruit after that. I'm still unable to describe why, but I loved it there so much. Like Dad, I felt a bond—a connection to the peace of the bush, the sounds of lyrebirds calling, the wind in the trees. I always felt a lingering sense of sadness when I left.

Seated at the kitchen table, food in my stomach, I pondered what to do with my Sunday. My head still throbbed from the previous night's adventures when I celebrated my twenty-third birthday with my agricultural science friends from Melbourne University. Although I wasn't a massive fan of noisy clubs, I knew I needed to do what normal people did, so I went along with the plan. I was now in my honors year and contemplating what to do next: look for a job? Postgrad study? Or my usual course of action, wait and see what landed in my lap? We had been back at university for a week, and I enjoyed catching up with friends and acquaintances after the summer holidays before knuckling down to my thesis. Most of us had jobs to help fund the reality of undergraduate study. I considered myself lucky that I still lived at home and didn't pay rent or bills but working part-time at a wholesale plant nursery helped provide a much-needed source of disposable income, plus a staff discount that Dad regularly put to good use. Working with plants was therapeutic and one of the reasons I was seriously contemplating a career in global food security, despite not knowing how to make that idea a reality. Time for those decisions in a few months.

Last night, copious amounts of alcohol had been consumed as well as the obligatory late-night kebab on my way home. Glancing down at my empty coffee cup, I pondered the merits of a second.

Sorcha looked up from the newspaper, belatedly acknowledging my existence, and asked if I had seen the news. My general policy was to avoid the news as I found it highly political and, thus, boring. Shaking my head, I knew where this was going. She had the look—the derisive way her eyes narrowed and nostrils flared indicated she was about to launch into yet another monotonous academic lecture about the merits of some obscure scientific theory, spotlighting her vast medical training while simultaneously proving, beyond doubt, to the world at large that I was a complete moron.

To my surprise, instead of lecturing me, Sorcha folded back the paper to expose the front page. A large headline loomed at me: *Unknown Virus Kills Hundreds*. Squinting through my headache, I scanned the slightly blurred first paragraph. An unidentified epidemic was spreading across several countries in Europe, killing people, animals, aquatic life, and plants. Continued page three.

Looking up, I shrugged at her. "So?"

"Don't you get it?" she sneered, unable to contain her incredulity. In the space of fifteen seconds, I had proven myself to be the cretin she evidently believed I was. "You do study biology, right? Remind me to have a chat with Carter about reviewing your grades."

"Well, clearly not to the same level as you, *Doctor Mackintosh*," I retorted. "Planning to enlighten me?"

Rolling her eyes in exaggerated exasperation, she adopted the tone one uses when speaking to a child or an idiot. Both in this case. I wondered if she talked to her recalcitrant students like this, doubting it would have much effect on them either.

"The virus is in the water," she explained—very slowly so the stupid among us could catch on.

"Okay," I replied hesitantly. "So..."

"Hmmph. It is spreading," Sorcha sniped caustically. "Rapidly."

"Okay, but it is in Europe," I countered sarcastically. "Not exactly next door. Surely it can be contained."

"That is precisely the problem. How do you contain something in waterways? The World Health Organization is saying that it started in the Danube, and within a few weeks, it's killing people all over Europe. Did you learn about Brownian motion at school? You know, particles suspended in liquid spread and move randomly?"

"Sure, but then it dilutes, right?"

"Well, that is where this one is different. This epidemic, they are calling it the Vienna Virus, by the way, because that is where the first known death occurred, seems to multiply, and scientists yet can't work out how. There are hundreds of people dead already, and many more than that infected. None of them survive once infected."

Though I desperately wanted to needle her, I didn't have the energy. "Look, I get I need to read the article, but tell me the basics. I mean, we have survived swine flu, avian flu, SARS. How bad is it, really?"

Glancing back at the paper, she read, "2850 kilometers of waterways and crosses eleven countries. If it spreads into all of those countries' waterways and eventually into the ocean, it will end up in the Black Sea."

"Well, that isn't too bad, is it?" I countered, my limited geographical knowledge kicking in. "Isn't the Black Sea the one that is fully contained?"

"Nope. The Black Sea is navigable to the Atlantic Ocean."

"Ohhh." The word came out like a deflating tire. I had nothing to say to that. I sat and stared at Sorcha, dumbfounded.

"Some critics are saying this is Malthusian theory in practice."

Scratching my still aching temple, I tried to recall who Malthus was, not wanting to appear a bigger idiot in front of my judgemental sister.

"That was the guy that said that the population increases at a faster rate than its ability to feed itself, right?"

"That's him. He also said that unless the population is kept in check by moral restraint like celibacy, or by disease, famine, war, or natural disaster, then the population will continue to experience widespread poverty and will never achieve utopia."

"Happy bloke," I commented cheerily. "Must have been great fun at dinner parties."

The door to the kitchen opened, and Mum backed in, dragging the vacuum behind her. As she turned it on and it roared into life, this effectively prevented any further conversation. Sorcha returned to her newspaper, and I decided a second cup of coffee was warranted, the noise of the grinder no longer an impediment. Going back to bed wasn't an option. Nor was continuing to endure Mum's interrogation. Years of experience told me she was not finished with me.

Mum finished up the floors in the kitchen as I was steaming the milk. Wiping down the machine after years of being nagged into cleaning up as I went, I watched Mum move into the lounge room, and I firmly closed the door behind her, sitting down with my now full steaming cup and placing the second in front of Sorcha. She looked at me with surprise but smiled her thanks. Sorcha and I sat in silence for several more minutes before she looked up again.

"Well, are you going?"

"Going? Where?"

Another loud and overly exaggerated sigh responded, before she pushed the paper in front of me, displaying a half-page advertisement. My head still hurt, and I couldn't focus my eyes on the slightly blurred fine print, so I pushed it back.

"Call me stupid. Summarize it for me."

Sorcha rolled her eyes. "This is everywhere. Papers, TV, email, through the university faculty. I must have received it six times already. Don't you have a phone? Check your email?"

A lightbulb went off in my head. Remembering that my phone had gone flat the previous night, I stood and picked it up from the bench where I had dropped it with my wallet and keys the night before and plugged it in. Within seconds, the distinct pinging sounds of messages, email, and SMS reverberated around the kitchen.

"Just tell me," I wheezed with exaggerated drama as I fell back into the chair opposite her.

Sorcha took a deep breath and read. "It is an official announcement from the Commonwealth Department of Innovation and Science. They are seeking people to attend a briefing at their primary site in Melbourne. Very specific skills. Set age ranges. You need to register online."

Misreading the cues, I asked, "Do you want to go together?"

"I'm busy," she snapped. "I have a class at nine o'clock. *You* don't have classes until the afternoon, so you should see what it is all about. You meet the criteria. Well, apart from the not being an idiot part which they neglected to mention as a deal-breaker. So you go, then you can call me. There are multiple session times, anyway. I will go to the evening one *if* it isn't wasting my time."

Ignoring her taunt, I clicked on the link in one of my countless messages, registering my expression of interest. An automated reply pinged back, noting my booking for a bus departing the university campus at 8:30 am. Excellent. I could go and be back in time for my afternoon class.

CHAPTER 2

A CONGA LINE OF UNMARKED white buses lined the gated entrance, each filled with hordes of confused-looking candidates peering from the windows. There was already a long queue when I arrived. With an entire lack of ceremony or conversation, my name was checked, and I was shoved on the first bus—with two more empty buses patiently waiting behind. *Perhaps choosing the earliest time slot was a sensible choice*, I mused on the twenty-minute bus journey while seated next to a tall skinny guy with horrendous body odor. I couldn't imagine what the later queues would be like, not to mention the smell of sweating people crammed on buses, sweltering amidst a typical Australian summer.

We approached an enormous secure complex with guards on each gate, their backs to the high fencing topped with vicious-looking barbed wire. Security cameras pointed in every direction. Even an invading ladybug would be captured on film here. I studied the entrance as I entered, still holding my breath as much as possible to avoid the sensory assault from my neighbor. Walkways, most undercover, connected looming multi-story, austere, gray concrete buildings. Small windows were set high in thick concrete walls, all with security grilles. Doors were guarded or solidly bolted. It reminded me of some of the high-security military bases I had visited with dad looking at World War II aircraft and tank displays. Staff stood in doorways, looking official, while others rushed around like they had a purpose. A feeling like I was misbehaving just by being there washed over me, that irrational fear that someone was going to tap me on the shoulder and evict me for trespassing. I didn't belong here.

How did I let Sorcha talk me into this?

Muffled announcements were made outside the bus, but even straining, I couldn't quite hear what was being said.

Not good with crowds, I dashed for the exit as soon as the bus came to a stop. As I stood on the crowded driveway, blinking in the sunshine, the announcements became audible. A woman on a loudspeaker was instructing us to report for registration and remove all belongings from the bus. This audio message kept repeating every thirty seconds to catch all the newcomers. Looking around, I noticed the large, printed sign—Registration.

Registration consisted of an eternity of waiting in clearly defined lines marked with tape attached to shiny silver bollards along with hundreds of people, then finally filling in pages and pages of electronic forms when a computer terminal became available. The wait was horrendous, and it was impossible not to continually count the people ahead of me.

Fidgeting, coughing, smelly people crammed into the narrow space.

Closing my eyes, I tried to focus on my ecology class that afternoon. It had been several days since I completed the prescribed reading. Being crammed into a crowded space was one of my primary hates. People were shuffling, sniffing. In a futile attempt not to envision all the germs floating in the air, I tried to minimize my breathing. After more than an hour, I finally made it to the front of the line. I groaned when I saw the survey. They wanted to know everything: education, religion, medical history, what I studied at university, hobbies, and skills.

Seriously, they will ask my favorite food next, I thought snarkily as I clicked to page eighteen of what seemed an endless online form. I snorted. Allergies. For fuck's sake. Couldn't they have asked all of this in advance? The document finalized, I stepped away from the terminal and looked around as the next grateful person rushed to the terminal.

There were people as far as I could see, waiting in an enormous line, much like the entry to a theme park. From the mob, they were being channeled into distinct ten lines. One person at a time passed through the gates, each manned by a security guard. Looking past the crowd, I could see another area, farther away, where more people were channeled into another set of gates. I didn't have time to look further before I was physically moved on by a man in a khaki uniform and hustled to a desk where a bored woman sat.

"Watch and phone," she droned.

"Huh?"

She pointed to a sign on her desk. "All electronic devices are to be confiscated until your departure," she replied in a monotone that indicated that she had already said this a thousand times. Her distinct lack of enthusiasm indicated that she knew she would say it several thousand more today. Instinctively, I took a last glance at the 21st birthday present from my parents as I unbuckled it from my wrist and handed it over: 11:15 am. Feeling an unexpected surge of regret, like I was saying goodbye to an old friend, I watched apprehensively as my watch was unceremoniously dropped into a large white envelope with my phone, then carelessly tossed into an enormous plastic container containing hundreds of envelopes, identical apart from the barcode. I had been here for two hours. Hopefully not much longer. I wanted to get to my class at 1:30 pm. Following the horde, I moved past and out into the open asphalted space beyond, where yet more crowds stood.

I waited. And waited. In that bizarre fashion when you have no concept of time, it could have been one hour or three. With nothing to do and nothing to focus on, time passes in a way that is difficult to measure. I found a quietish spot against a wall and sat, trying to avoid the interrogation of the midday sun in my eyes as I wished I had worn a cap or sunglasses. At first, I looked actively at the people passing and lingering, mainly in singles, but some in small groups chatting quietly. All looked unsettled. As I glanced around, it occurred to me that what I was seeing was a mix of society, male and female, and all cultures and sizes. Despite the limited age ranges, this was a true microcosm. I found this quite fascinating.

Losing interest in people watching, I closed my eyes, listening to the chatter at a level that was audible, but with so much noise, I couldn't quite pluck one conversation out of the din, no matter how hard I tried to focus. Periodically, I was jolted from my trance by names being called, but never mine. The sun was part-way down the sky when my name was called, along with a group of roughly a hundred others. We streamed into a room looking like a large university hall for our final exams. But rather than empty desks, this huge high-ceilinged room had rows and rows of computers at individual workstations. It looked like one of those old photos of factories during wartime or a sweatshop with underpaid migrant women being exploited on industrial sewing machines. Long strips of fluorescent lights in the roof reflected off the screens, cables drawn neatly into the ceiling and following large tracts of conduit to a central point. The floor was filthy, showing clear imprints of fresh footprints. This room had seen a lot of traffic or just really shitty cleaners. Officials were walking up and down the aisles, looking irritated. The previous group was still exiting from the door at the back as we were led in from the front entrance; they were pumping candidates through as fast as possible.

With some contortionism, I wedged my long legs under the tiny white desk I was allocated, complete with unidentifiable stains on the top. Being one of the first to enter from my group, I had a few minutes to look around the room with interest. A large digital clock showing 4:00 was on the wall at the top end of the room, along with a long table with eight chairs.

Goodbye, ecology class. I just hoped that there wasn't any homework. Professor Kareem wasn't keen on me since he had been my biology lecturer in first year and would take the utmost pleasure in failing me.

The people behind the long table were murmuring, pointing at their screens.

A dark-haired woman who strongly resembled a bird stood up from one of the chairs and stepped to the front of the table. She was tiny, but the pointed chin, small, pointed nose, and black-rimmed glasses completed the bird-impersonation. The mid-blue of her suit with a white shirt didn't help her cause, and I smiled as I thought of my elderly neighbor's beloved blue budgie, Luigi. Perhaps she would tweet too? I nearly fell off my chair when she spoke with possibly the loudest voice I had ever heard.

"*Candidates!*" she boomed. She got our attention alright. Everyone gaped at her in astonishment. It wasn't just the volume. It was the tone. An author-itative, commanding tone. This was a woman who was used to getting her way, and heaven help anyone who didn't obey. She must have been military with the straight carriage of her posture, hair pulled back into a bun with not a hair out of place, and sensible shoes. Closing my mouth, which had fallen open in shock, I couldn't believe that such a colossal voice could come out of such a tiny person.

"Candidates! You have exactly two hours. Answer as many questions as you can. If you cannot answer a question, move to the next question. There is no right or wrong answer. You may not leave the hall for any reason. You have water on your desk. It is recom-mended that you not drink it all at once as we will *not* be permitting toilet breaks. Your time starts... *Now!*"

Recoiling like I had been yelled at for an hour by an over-enthused boot camp trainer, I dragged my attention to the computer screen. It wasn't diffi-cult—just lots of what-if questions and asking your preferences. I had completed psychometric testing before: those tests trying to get a profile of someone's character, capabilities, and style, your responses in different scenarios. I figured that a team of psychologists had derived this test, and they knew what they were looking for, so I had nothing to worry about.

Glancing up at the clock, I noted that there were thirty minutes to go. Shit. I felt like I had barely started. I looked up and saw supervisors patrolling the aisles looking no happier than they had as I had entered. Maybe they were hungry. I was. My stomach growled to punctuate this point.

Fifteen minutes to go and I was still nowhere near finished. I could feel my anxiety increasing. My stomach was in knots and my palms so slippery that I found it difficult to control the mouse to click on the next question. My mouth was dry. I wanted to drink but was scared I would need to nervous pee. Shit. Now thinking of water made me want to go.

Five minutes to go. *Fuck...*

"Stop *now* and stand up!" military budgie boomed. "Do *not* touch your computer."

The sound of a hundred people simultaneously scraping metal chair legs across the hardwood floors was deafening, and I winced. The supervisors began herding people using wild arm gestures toward the back of the hall where a set of white double doors with blacked-out windows were held open, and the group shepherded out. As I was jostled and pushed, I was knocked sideways, my head turning enough to see the next group entering, looking bewildered and lost. Booming behind me indicated the budgie had started again.

Transferred into an enclosed room, we were told to wait. The air was hot and thick with the smell of fear, sweat, and anxiety. I wondered if I could find an exit and just leave. Feeling very over all of this, I looked around for a door that wasn't back into the room we had just left, where I could now hear the budgie barking instructions at the next group of hapless candidates. A tall, featureless man stood in one corner, clearly listening to the earpiece in his left ear. Lifting a screen, he started calling names in a monotonous voice, hard to hear over the din:

Abeysinghe, Nalini
Cheung, Calliope
Christian, Liana
Hochstatter, Gretel
Ibrahim, Abdullahi

I zoned out. The heat. The noise. The hordes of people. The smell of sweat. I tried to focus on my breath, to withdraw into myself, to deal with it all. It was too much. Too noisy, too crowded, too...

Jangra, Priyanka
Katwala, Shaminder
Li, Guan Hua
Mackintosh, Campbell

I jolted back into my body. *Shit. Did I just hear my name? I wasn't paying attention.* But it was too late. He had moved on.

Martini, Matthias
Miller, Bertha

Shiiiiiiiiiiiitttt! What do I do? Did I hear my name? Did I just think I heard my name?

Do I just leave? What do I do?

Waiting until monotone-man finished calling out his list of names, I considered walking up and asking him to confirm. Maybe he would give me a hint, like "you twenty" when he finished, and I could count people heading toward him. But no. No such luck. Why would this be easy?

The reverberation was hurting my ears. I cringed again. I just wanted to get out of here. I was done. I no longer cared why I was here. I just wanted to go home.

"Those whose names have been called, please come to the front. The rest of you may leave via the rear doors. Thank you all for your time."

The frantic crush started. Hundreds of sweaty people surged toward the exit, worse than any Boxing Day sale. Concerned I would be swept along and knocked to the ground, I managed to keep my footing. At times like this, I was eminently grateful for my six-foot height and solid build inherited from my father.

"Umph!" I grunted after a blow to the stomach as one man elbowed his way out.

"Oww!" As another stood on my foot. Adopting a warrior stance, I used my arms to protect my torso from random, flailing limbs. After what seemed an eternity of being thumped, knocked, and trodden on as people pushed past in a rush to escape, they were gone. It was preternaturally quiet, and I managed to make my way to the front with those called. A quick glance around the group confirmed what I had suspected. We were all shitting ourselves. We had been chosen for something, but what?

A woman with a matching tablet and a stylus approached me with what could have been a smile but honestly looked akin to a tiger baring its teeth. Flinching as she glanced at me, she barked, "*Name?*"

"Ahh, uh, Mackintosh. Campbell Mackintosh."

She quickly scanned her list. "Mackintosh." She used her stylus to make a mark next to my name. Phew. Relief washed over my face. I hadn't misheard then.

Efficiently, she marked all of us off her list, then turned on her heel, clearly expecting us to follow. We did, like well-trained golden retrievers. Looking down at our feet and shuffling along behind her, no one spoke a word. *Prisoners.* The word just popped into my head for no reason. Being led on a death march to an unknown fate.

We followed her single file into a narrow, feature-less hallway with numerous doors leading off each side. Each door was identical with no markings except a solitary discreet number. Entering number seven, she moved through a small central space with four rooms located off it. We were subdivided into four smaller groups and directed into one of the smaller meeting rooms. Dutifully, I followed my allotted group into a white, sterile room with no wall dec-orations and basic white plastic chairs that were a chiropractor's dream. No tables, no reading materials. Just a tiny room with artificial lighting and twelve horribly uncomfortable chairs set against the walls of the small room, crammed so close it was hard not to brush up against each other. We each sat and watched the door closing as she walked away, trying not to lean on the armrests and be in each other's personal space. *Like an airplane,* I thought, *shared armrests and that awkward social interaction where you want to max-imize your allotted space but not invade someone else's.*

We looked around the room, feeling much like pris-oners on death row. One person, a beautiful woman of African/Asian appearance with sparkling dark eyes and long straight dark hair seated directly opposite me, smiled at me and said, "Hi, I'm Callie."

"Campbell," I replied, but with my dry mouth, it came out as "wggg." I cleared my throat and tried again. With no water, it was thick and furry. "Cam," I said with more forcefulness and tried to smile. I'm not sure it came out as a smile, but she didn't seem to notice. We smiled awkwardly, but with everyone else looking at their feet, we reverted to silence.

CHAPTER 3

AN UNMEASURABLE PERIOD PASSED sitting in that soulless, artificially bright room. We slumped and squirmed in our uncomfortable rigid plastic chairs, trying to sleep. A process made even more difficult by the glaring lights piercing our eye sockets like lasers. Eventually, my eyes grew weary and drooped, finally feeling the heavy waves of sleep overtaking me despite the aching cramp in my lower back and stomach rumbling audibly.

Boom!

I jerked awake, blinking like an owl rudely awakened from sleep. Struggling to focus, the open door revealed three people in lab coats, one man and two women.

"*Follow*!" one of them barked and walked away before we had even registered their presence. Staggering out of our uncomfortable stupor, we sluggishly followed. Callie and I were the last to exit the room.

"Have you noticed no one says please here?" I whispered to Callie, who giggled a fraction too loudly, attracting a glare from one of the lab-coated women. She subsided, but I could see that hilarity from sheer exhaustion and nerves were still close to the surface. I resolved to keep my mouth shut—many times over my lifetime, my big fat trap had got me into trouble that could easily have been avoided. We were split into three groups of four. Callie was placed in a different group. Deliberately no doubt. Smiling wanly at her as she was pushed into a room, I was moved past and farther down the corridor.

As directed, I followed the man in the lab coat, wondering how many people worked here. It seemed to be a well-organized facility but with a distinct air of urgency. People were rushing around clutching tablets or clipboards, speaking in hushed tones, and generally looking busy. There must have been quite a few assessments taking place today.

Once again, I wondered why I was here and what I had signed up for.

Bloody Sorcha, I thought uncharitably. *This is entirely her fault.*

I was shown into a small room with a chair and a silver trolley holding needles, test tubes, and a rack holding the tubes. Evidently, I was the first victim. I sat down and glanced at the technician, who looked exhausted and paid no attention to me whatsoever. I could have been a slice of bread he was toasting for all the attention he paid.

"Arm," he droned as he picked up my limp left arm without consent, deftly swabbed it, and inserted the needle. I flinched slightly, mostly from surprise. Aside from the initial sting, it was uncomfortable rather than painful. He didn't seem to notice. Or care.

"What is it for?" I asked curiously.

Without taking his gaze from the filling vial, he sniffed. "Screening."

It was evident that asking Mr. Chatty any additional questions would result in no further information. Instead, I watched, intrigued, as he kept changing the vials as they filled with my bright red blood, rapidly applying labels to each tube. He took ten glass vials, all coded with different colors and evidently for various purposes. Blood always looks thicker and more viscous in those transparent tubes, but thinner when you cut yourself or have a bloody nose. I was mesmerized by the flow of blood up that tiny little needle. Well, it didn't feel tiny embedded in my arm. But the needle was small compared to the startlingly large volume of blood I could now see in filled, labeled test tubes, lined up neatly in a clear plastic rack with corresponding labels and barcode.

"Open," he droned, and I looked at him blankly.

"Your mouth. Open it," he repeated, alerting me to the fact that, just in case I was considering it, being a lab tech was an indeed highly stimulating and enjoyable career.

Confused, I opened my mouth and was rewarded with a metal spectrum scraping cells from the inside of my cheek. It wasn't painful, but not exactly pleasant either. A jerk of the head toward the door economically indicated he was done with me.

No closer to understanding why I was here, I stood awkwardly, moving hesitantly to the door, and turned back, waiting to be told what to do next. Mr. Chatty made shooing gestures as the next of my group was shown in to see him.

The assistant who had brought in my former companion from the room of boredom now escorted me down another long white corridor to the swinging double doors of a cafeteria and left me there. It was a large, well-lit room with... shock! Natural light! My body shivered with the touch of light on my arms after hours of being cooped up in confined, airless spaces.

Uniformly spaced tables, each with four chairs, filled the room, and a long wall ran along one side, holding several trestle tables covered in crisp white tablecloths, the ironed folds still clearly visible. Closer inspection revealed that the tables held jugs of water, juice, tea, coffee at my end of the room, but the far end contained a variety of platters holding a vast selection of cakes, biscuits, petite quiches, and sandwiches.

My stomach emitted a loud growl, and waves of embarrassment washed over my face as a man glanced at me, startled. I realized it had been hours since I had eaten. As I looked down at my empty left wrist, I had no concept of what time it was.

"Fattening us up for slaughter."

Startled, I jerked up from the platter of cakes I was surveying to see Callie grinning at me, showing a mouthful of perfect white teeth in her tanned face. She was holding a plate loaded with cakes and sandwiches. I didn't doubt that she had the right idea. Who knew when I would see food again? Besides, it looked delicious.

Loading up one of the white dinner plates and trying to juggle the overloaded stash of goodies, I followed her to a table by the far wall, well away from the chatter.

In between mouthfuls, we got to know each other. Callie was also twenty-three and in her final year studying electrical engineering. Originally from Mauritius, she wasn't from Melbourne but had been bussed here from Adelaide along with fifty others. She had done initial testing in Adelaide but had been told that Melbourne was the final testing center for candidates. That took me by surprise, and I said so.

Tentatively, I broached the subject of why we were here. Callie looked around cautiously before answering. "I don't know exactly. But I know it has something to do with the water virus in Europe."

"I guessed that, but what do they think *we* can do to help? We are half a world away. Are they looking for more lab technicians? It isn't my field. Yours either, come to think of it. Electrical engineers rarely solve biological problems. Besides, why take my blood for that?"

"I have been wondering if they are looking for people with a natural immunity," Callie said quietly. "You know, so they can develop a vaccine."

I pondered that for a moment. "But why be so secretive about it? Why all the psych testing?"

She shrugged but responded, "Perhaps to avoid mass panic? Let's face it: if you thought everyone was going to die but a select few, you would, one—want to be tested, and two—want them to hurry with a vaccine."

That makes sense, I thought as I chewed industriously.

Two young women at the next table stopped talking and discreetly moved their chairs to sit with us. Introducing themselves as Ivy and Mai, they were both medical students from Brisbane. They were the last two left from their group and had been here for two days.

During those days, they had been in and out of this cafeteria and had spoken with many people. Callie and I looked at them expectantly.

Gossip among the shortlisted was that they were looking for a specific set of people: half male, half female; all aged twenty to thirty; in excellent health with compatible blood types; and possessed of skills conducive to a challenging environment.

What challenging environment could they possibly be referring to? I wondered as they spoke. *Surely high school doesn't count. Surviving that was quite an achievement.* I got little chance to contemplate this as a bored-looking man in a lab coat called my name from the double doorway, and I was dragged away to further my tests. With no time to stuff my pockets with food, I hurriedly crammed a final sandwich into my mouth as I followed the officious lab coat out of the room. I turned and smiled at Callie.

"See you later," I managed to mouth between exaggerated chews of ham and inconveniently crusty bread.

Escorted to a room that looked remarkably similar to an austere dentist's office, yet another exhausted technician indicated via hand gestures and without looking up from his screen that I was to sit in a chair as an oxygen mask was placed securely over my face. Looking up as I inhaled, I noticed a strange white pod suspended from the ceiling. Feeling woozy, I inhaled again, trying to focus. My head fell backward, and the world went black.

Something was wrong. Dread overtook me, making me shudder. Sweat beaded on my face, and my heart pounded in my chest. Something was seriously wrong. I could feel my exhaled breath bouncing back onto my face. I was trapped. Moving my hands and using the minimal range of motion available to me, I ascertained I was enclosed, laid flat in the form-fitting chair. Reaching out, I could feel that the circular walls were only centimeters from my face and surrounding my body. Remembering the panic I had experienced when trapped in the MRI machine I had been forced to endure when I had a skiing injury at sixteen, the alarm continued to well up inside me. My heart raced. Rivers of sweat ran down my neck and chest, but being so restricted, I couldn't move with enough range to blot it.

Where the bloody hell am I?

I wanted to hammer on the inside of the tube, but unable to bend my elbows, I couldn't get enough space to swing my arms. Unable to see anything in the utter desolate blackness, I tried to raise my hands to chest height by maneuvering my elbows behind me. My feet could tap the surface but without enough range for a loud kick that might alert someone. My breathing was getting louder and faster. I couldn't breathe; I couldn't see; I couldn't hear. Then the notion popped into my mind—*this must be what being buried alive feels like*. Closing my eyes, I started to consciously focus on my breath like I had been taught in meditation: focus on the in-breath and focus on the out-breath. In. Out. Deep, slow breaths.

But my heart was thundering like a jackhammer in my chest. Every molecule of my being was screaming at me.

This is it. You Are Going to Die. Suffocated to death in a plastic tube.

A voice. I could hear a voice, a scrabbling noise, and then light blinded me. Instinctively closing my eyes, I turned my face into my shoulder as it went from pitch darkness to the brilliance of artificial white light stabbing me painfully in the eyeballs. Slowly opening my eyes, I needed to close them again to adjust to the sudden onslaught of brightness. Blinking madly, I tried to focus my eyes as I rolled, falling out of the full-length MRI-type machine which was retracting into its place on the ceiling.

"Sorry," a man breezed as he rushed past. "It is easier if you aren't moving."

Noting that I was wearing a hospital gown, I scanned the room for my clothes, locating them on a nearby shelf. Trying to steady myself, my body, and my nerves, I was done. Feeling violated and furious, I looked around for someone to talk to, demand that I was released, rescind any permission I had granted to be here.

Without even a chance to catch my breath, the second I was dressed, I was forcibly steered through one of two doors, each at opposite sides of the room. Natural light radiated from the other, but mine led into a hallway. I was shuffled, along with other equally scared-looking young men and women, into a lecture theater. Frantically looking around for an exit so I could leave this hellhole, I couldn't find one. Rows and rows were slowly filling up, rising from the stage at ground level where I had entered to rows so high against the ceiling at the back of the room that I could barely see them.

Whispered apologies filled the space as people pushed past to take all vacant seats. Looking ahead, I could see that the hall was enormous, and it was filling fast, everyone looking apprehensive and more than a little scared. Fearful that I may need to stand through the next installment of torture as waves of post-anesthetic nausea continued to wash over me, I chose a seat a few rows up. Not too close to the stage—the last thing I wanted was to draw attention to myself. But not so far from the lectern that I couldn't hear. I sat quietly and waited. I was still trying to slow my heart rate.

The shuffling of feet, muffled coughs, and mumbled small talk kept the room noise at a low steady buzz. A nondescript, tall, slim man with sandy-colored hair and beard walked from the wings onto the stage, adjusted the microphone, and took his place at the lectern. He waited as the room quietened, and people took their places. The usual situation occurred when a large group was trying to pay attention to a single speaker. Most people shut up, ready to listen. Some keep talking, assuming that they don't need to be quiet until told to do so, and a third small group of people take it upon themselves to shush everyone else and make more noise themselves in the process.

"Thank you," he started, and people quietened down. "I am Professor Ashton, and I am the head of this project. I know the last few days have been rigorous and stressful for you all. Above all else, you will probably want to know *why*. Why you are here, why *you* were each chosen and why the secrecy. We can finally answer all of your questions. There are two main topics I will speak about today—one, the issues we are facing, and two, why you are here. I know you have been put through a lot, but I ask for a little more patience and that you keep your questions until the end of my presentation."

Turning in my seat, I scanned the room for Callie but couldn't see her long, dark hair anywhere in the low light. Maybe she hadn't made it this far?

My attention snapped back to the presentation when an outline map of the world with colors indicating the world's waterways flashed up onto an enormous screen. Ashton cast a tiny shadow against it.

"Despite our best efforts to keep it from the media and prevent mass panic, there has now been widespread coverage of the water-borne epidemic that has been spreading through the rivers and waterways of eastern Europe. This is nothing new. But this particular virus, which is a new variant of enteric protozoa, is actually not a virus at all."

He clicked to the next slide.

"As you know, people are getting sick. *Dying.* He emphasized that word and paused to ensure we understood. We know they are contracting the illness through water sources. At present, we have no means to track how far the protozoa has spread, control the spread, nor treat the infected. But it is looking increasingly likely that it will become a full-blown pandemic and affect all countries and regions."

Gasps from the audience made him stop and wait until he had full attention again.

"Briefly, water-borne illnesses are generally caused by one of three things: Viruses, Bacteria, or Enteric Protozoa. This contagion is actually the third of these things, but a protozoon that has never been seen before. It managed to escape detection mainly because while developed countries have established epidemiological surveillance systems, there is still no international agreement on the reporting structure. European epidemiological surveillance systems are used to determine national *infection* rates, not regularly testing for water-related diseases. In simple terms, this means they didn't find the source nor cause of the infection fast enough, and so now it has spread beyond their borders. I know that a significant percentage of you have scientific training, but for those who do not, there are several types of protozoa. This type is called free-living protozoa. Protozoa are commonplace and live in fresh, brackish, and saltwater as well as other moist environments. Some species even survive in extreme environments such as heat, salt, and ice. They reproduce via multiple fission, meaning they divide and continue to divide. Frustratingly for us, they are now dividing at a rate of once every twenty-four hours in ideal oxygenated environments. This means that the contagion is spreading faster than we can control it."

I inhaled sharply. Now in my fifth year of scientific study, I knew this was bad. Seriously bad. For a protozoon to adapt to different environments, survive at different temperatures, and divide so rapidly meant it was a genuine threat.

"Scientists have categorized these new protozoa as P4365, or the Vienna Virus as it is now, most unfortunately, being referred to in the media. It has now been detected in most European waterways and has spread into the Black Sea and the Mediterranean Sea. It is only a matter of time before it reaches the Atlantic Ocean, and after that—well… the world's oceans will all be infected. A true pandemic." The footage on the screen showed an orange spot in a river in Austria. As we watched, mesmerized, the orange splodge spread down the blue waterways of the map and into the oceans. Soon, the orange began to overlay all the blue on the map.

"Seventy percent."

There was a collective intake of breath as we drew our attention from the orange slide back to Ashton.

"Seventy percent," he repeated. "That is how much of the earth's surface is covered in water. But of this water, only ten percent is drinkable."

We had all undoubtedly seen the media coverage, yet I suspect that many, like me, had not realized the extent of the problem. I felt foolish. Here I was, working toward a career in a scientific field, yet I hadn't even come close to grasping the magnitude of the problem facing us all.

Ashton raised his hand to quell the outbreak of chatter. He raised his voice slightly to be heard over the commotion.

"I *know* that this is confronting. The finest scientific minds across the world are working together on this issue. In fact, this may be one of the very first projects that have seen a truly united global team working on it. Dedicated teams are trying to slow the spread, work out what conditions it thrives in, what conditions slow the division. We are working on how to contain it and also how to eliminate the virus altogether. One of the great hopes is that we *are* all working together."

He paused, but we were all too stunned to say anything.

Ashton continued, trying to listen to the questions. "The infection started in fresh water. We had hoped that once the protozoa hit salt or brackish water that it would slow or stop it from spreading. Unfortunately, we received word just over a week ago that this was not the case. In fact, our worst fears were founded, and the protozoa have continued to multiply. Like most protozoa, they appear to need oxygen, so we hope that only the top part of the ocean, that part that is oxygenated, will be affected. But currently, it is too early to tell."

Shit, I thought. *How long do we have?*

Ashton continued as though he had read my mind. "The logical questions now are how long and what are we doing about it. How long until all the world's water is infected, and most importantly, drinking water? The short answer is—we simply don't know. Without going into the science, which is complex, there are simply too many variables. What allows the fission to occur faster or slows it down? There are many theories in the scientific community at the moment, and opinion is divided. It will certainly be at least several months. Possibly as much as a year. Perhaps it will peter out on its own, although I have to say at this stage that is looking unlikely. We just don't know. Water is found everywhere—ice tundras, deep ancient artesian basins, wells, mountain streams from snowmelt, rain clouds.

The second part of this question, what are we doing about it? Well, frankly, everything we can. Scientific teams from all over the world are working twenty-four hours a day on this problem to slow or halt the spread. Teams have been reassigned from different research projects, and everyone is working on this. Governments are committing millions from their budgets to the cessation of these protozoa and treatment of the infected—people, plants, animals. But every additional day this takes, hundreds of thousands more are infected."

Ashton ignored the chatter that started up again and continued as he changed the slide on the screen to one showing a human outline. "The effects of the infection are quite simple: it extracts water from its host—cellular dehydration. Once infected, the host, be it plant, animal, or human, simply dehydrates, and no amount of non-infected water will reverse the dehydration process. In short, dehydration occurs when you use or lose more fluid than you take in, and the body just doesn't have enough water to function. Fluid flows from the cells to the bloodstream, tissues of the body dry out, and cells shrivel and malfunction. This protozoon appears to release a chemical that prohibits the body from allowing cells to rehydrate. Initial symptoms are extreme thirst, fatigue, dizziness, and confusion."

I felt sick. I knew what he wasn't saying to spare us the graphic reality. I remembered the rule of threes: three minutes without air, three days without water, three weeks without food. Within a day, blood pressure would increase, the kidneys would shut down, seizures occur, and finally, an excruciatingly painful death. Every living thing on earth requires water—animals, people, plants. They require water in differing amounts. Cactus and desert-dwelling animals require little. Humans need water far more frequently to survive.

Ashton was speaking again. Leaning forward in my seat to listen better, I struggled to hear what he was saying over the chatter.

"That makes the scale of this problem quite simply catastrophic. I do not use that term lightly. Imagine a world where every plant, animal, and human cannot survive. That is what we face."

Ashton took a breath and looked around the room at the shocked faces. We all sat in silence now, trying to absorb the magnitude of what we had just been told. We were all going to die.

Game Over.

Ashton cleared his throat and spoke in a gentler tone. "I know this is a shock. Shock doesn't even come close to covering it. The scientific community has had weeks to come to grips with this and activate contingency plans. I can't imagine what it is like to have it dropped on you in the space of a few minutes. But sadly, time is something we simply don't have." Ashton exhaled audibly.

"This brings me to why you are all here. Why we have spent the past days putting you through a battery of tests. Interviews will come later, but for now, you have all been chosen. Today, we are making you an offer. We are working relentlessly to slow or stop the spread, but we have also made contingency plans. What happens if we can't stop it? How do we prevent people from becoming extinct?" He paused.

"We build an Ark."

I snorted. I didn't mean to. It just slipped out. The woman seated to my right looked at me, shocked, then giggled softly at my horrified face.

Ashton was still speaking. "A modern-day Ark. We place selected plants, animals, and the healthiest people," he paused as he looked around the room, "and contain them in an uninfected area. As silly as it may sound, an island is what we are planning." He raised his hand to quell the noise. "Yes, I am well aware that islands are surrounded by water. But they are also self-contained. There is no freshwater flow to islands. This is good. Yes, the ocean will be infected, but that only affects the edge of the island. What we have sought is an island where the natural water source is lakes or dams, or where rivers flow *to* the sea.

Around the world, there will be a total of twelve project sites, with the possibility of more—if there is time and if the initial pilot sites are successful. One will be here in the southern hemisphere. We are partnering with our colleagues from New Zealand to find the best candidates for the project. One of the fortunate things about the geography of Australia and New Zealand is the distance from other major countries of the world. Our distance from Ground Zero is highly beneficial. The infection is not here yet. We have a little time.

The island we have selected for our community is in the southern ocean. Its location is and will remain secret for obvious reasons. We plan to place a permanent geodesic dome, or PGD, over the island, completely encasing it and isolating it from the rest of the world. Air will filter through, but not water. Much like a breathable terrarium, for lack of a better description. Water will evaporate from the freshwater currently on the island, as well as plants and soil releasing water vapor. It will fall again as rain, essentially recycling the water. Drinking water will be filtered through a range of filters, including ultra-violet, carbon, and ozone, keeping it uncontaminated. You may recall from high school biology that plants undergo a process called photosynthesis. Even though plants use oxygen, they also produce oxygen, but they need sunlight to do so. We have carefully calculated the freshwater supply on the island, the arable land, and the number of plants required to sustain life indefinitely, along with how many people they will support."

I nodded along, understanding. This was something I knew a bit about.

"This is where you all come in. You will have noticed that you are all young. Our criteria for these communities are relatively simple—young, healthy, no children, and with skills that would enable you to thrive in this environment. We seriously considered staffing these sites with experts—scientists, doctors, engineers. But ultimately, that skill comes at a price. Most are married, have families, and honestly, their skills are now required here to help deal with the situation we will soon face. A large percentage of you have recently completed, or are nearing completion, in tertiary[3] study in these fields, and this is, in part, why you were chosen. Some of you have valuable trades. You possess some knowledge, and if you decide to accept this offer, we will spend the remaining time giving you all the information we can to assist you and the team. There will be one final interview with a panel, if you accept, prior to your departure. That is a final assessment to ensure that you are suited to the conditions you will face, and that you understand fully what you are signing up for.

You may note that I used the word offer, and yes, it is an offer. You are not being forced to go. Most of you will find the idea of being taken away from your homes, families, and friends in a time of crisis too much to bear. No one will judge you if you choose to opt-out. This is a monumental undertaking. But this pilot project may be responsible for the survival of the

---

[3] In the Australian education system, education is categorized as Primary, Secondary and Tertiary (usually university or technical training post high school)

human species. Not trying to put any pressure on you." Ashton smiled, but it didn't reach his eyes.

Even from a distance, I could see that he was desperately tired. I wondered how many times he had given this presentation. To how many people? How many would accept?

Again my runaway brain was interrupted, and I tried to focus on what he was saying despite the questions swirling through my head.

"All essential equipment will be provided. Still, what we are proposing will be incredibly difficult for most of you. There will be limited technology as it needs to be maintained, and in a small community, you will be unable to maintain large amounts of infrastructure. You will need to be self-sufficient. Maintaining an equilibrium will be essential, especially given the limited space and resources. We will do our best, but make no mistake: this will be hard work."

Ashton wilted visibly, then took one step to the side of the lectern, still holding the microphone. Evidently, it was question time. One... two... three seconds of silence, and then the auditorium erupted into a cacophony of chatter and questions.

A man and woman, both wearing suits and glasses, walked onto the stage from the wings and flanked Ashton at the lectern. The woman was military budgie, the man I hadn't seen before. They had that no-nonsense look of senior officials—people who were respected and knowledgeable and who didn't tolerate time-wasting.

Roving staff with microphones appeared up each aisle and handed them to individuals who had raised their hands with questions.

"How long do we have to decide?"

"We need final responses by 5pm Friday." It was the man who had spoken. A clipped, slightly British accent made it sound somewhat harsher than I am sure he intended. The problem was, I had no idea what day today was. I had come here on Monday. Was today Tuesday or Wednesday? Two days, maybe three, to make the most monumental decision of my life.

"When would we need to leave?"

Monday morning. But two weeks of quarantine in Melbourne before we left to ensure that we were not carrying any illness plus cramming of essential survival knowledge. Arrival on the island in late February.

"What could we take with us?" A small number of personal belongings. Everything else would be provided, including clothes, linen, furniture.

"What happens if we change our minds?"

Ashton took this one and spoke slowly, clearly, and concisely. "Let me be crystal clear. This is a one-way trip. Once you arrive on the island, there is no going back. There will be absolutely no way off the island once it is sealed. This is for your own safety and for that of the project."

Collective gasps rose at this. Ashton continued, unperturbed. "I cannot stress enough the importance of what we are doing here. The world is facing the biggest crisis it has ever seen—plagues, natural disasters, world wars. Nothing, absolutely nothing, comes remotely close to the absolute risk to the ongoing existence of the human race that we face right now."

Silence.

A quiet male voice asked, "Will there be communication with the outside world?"

"Minimal and inbound traffic only."

"What happens if we get sick?"

A pause at this. The man to Ashton's left responded. "Some of you are medically trained, or at least partially so. But the reality is there will be no hospitals as you know them, although we will do our best to ensure that we provide the best equipment and supplies we can. This is why we are choosing the best possible candidates to ensure the survival of humanity. You are in the prime of your lives. You are fit, healthy, and of reproductive age. But..." he paused, "we all need to acknowledge that accidents and illness will happen. Not transmittable viruses, hopefully, as you have all been screened, and you will be isolated from the rest of the world. But we cannot control all eventualities. Make no mistake—this is no tropical holiday. This will undoubtedly be the hardest thing you have ever done in your life. You will be assigned responsibilities, and you will work. Hard. For many of you who have never lifted anything heavier than a pen, this will be a very steep learning curve. But this is our best chance of survival. We are relying on these projects to be a success. You have been chosen. What you need to decide is if this is for you. Ask yourself... can you do this?"

Questions flew hard and fast. Zoning out after a while, I contemplated the enormity of what was being laid out in front of me. Could I leave it all—my family, my home? Everything I enjoyed? Then the reality hit. What if the virus spreads to Australia? According to Ashton, it would, and it would only be a matter of time. Will we all die anyway? Does it matter if we *all* die? Can I possibly accept the offer and go, knowing that my parents, my sister, will most likely perish?

Growing up, Mum always told me I wasn't special. I was *lucky*. I wasn't special, as I didn't deserve preferential treatment. I was lucky as I had a family who

believed in me and had the capacity to give me opportunities—overseas holidays, sports, pets, a university
education. But they raised us with no sense of enti-
tlement. I wondered if that was why I felt so uncomfortable now, feeling like I had been singled out.

Filing out, shellshocked, we were forced to sign a
non-disclosure agreement that permitted us to speak
about the project only with our immediate families,
then handed a simple white business card containing
a single discreet telephone number but no text. We
were to use this for any inquiries and our response.
Shown out through a secure back exit into the dawn
light, we were separated into geographical areas,
pushed onto mini-buses, and taken home. Everything
after the lecture theater was hazy. Wondering if I was
in a dream, I looked around the bus, seeing everyone
else in a similar state of silent disorientation. Who
would go, and who would stay?

CHAPTER 4

UNLOCKING THE FRONT DOOR, I fumbled with the key, unable to keep my hand steady. As I half walked, half fell through the door, Mum flew at me.

"I thought ye were deeeed!" Mum's Scots accent always came out more forcefully when she was emotional. Evidently torn between wanting to beat me senseless and hug me, she came up short when she reached me. She hadn't slept. She looked terrible: her usually neatly tied back long ginger hair in a mess, her clothing worn for days judging by the wrinkles and stains. I glanced over at dad; he was in no better shape. Exhausted and tired, looking older than his fifty years. Enormous bags hung beneath his bright blue eyes, his face bearing several days of stubble under unbrushed dark hair. His skin was gray and ashen.

Clearly, they had been worried sick about me. Looking closely at my father, I assumed this is what I would look like in thirty years. *Hadn't they left the house at all?* Guilt consumed me for even contemplating accepting. *How could I even consider leaving them? Had I been swept up in the testing, the magnitude of the issue? My responsibility was here with my family.*

Mum had obviously intended to berate me but stopped, her mouth slightly open. She shoved me toward the leather couches where Dad was sitting, too exhausted to get up and greet me. I sat on the couch Merlin scratched up as a kitten, hiding behind them and then pouncing out at us as we walked past, scratching up the arms in the process. Mum always said that she would replace these couches when she no longer had pets, only that never happened. I may well be sitting on this couch for the last time.

I sat and stared dazedly at the photos on the walls that captured our family history, really *looked* at them in a way I hadn't in years. The staggered display of matching frames: Mum and Dad's ancient wedding photo with awful hair and dated clothing. Several of Sorcha and me as kids: staged school photos, some with front teeth, some without, all in appalling school uniforms. One primary school picture had red tops and green shorts, which made Sorcha with her red hair look very much like a Christmas tree—just add tinsel. Photos of sporting triumphs. Holidays. Graduations. The worst was a hideous posed studio photo of us all, me aged five and Sorcha at eight, that I had always hated and could have sworn Mum kept it on display to torture me in front of my friends. Mum and Dad seated on old-style dining chairs. Sorcha standing next to Dad and me next to Mum to split up our coloring. Posed and awkward with fake smiles.

Now, those awful photos with my dark hair in a pudding bowl haircut and wearing what Mum liked to call nice clothes may be the only things left of me. Suddenly, the matching shirts she had forced us to wear and had terrible itchy tags didn't seem so awful. Funny how your perspective changes when something catastrophic happens.

I didn't know where to start, so I just sat there. I could see they were bursting to ask questions, but instead, they waited. They knew me well enough to know that I needed time. I started tentatively, explaining where I had been, the testing process, why it was necessary. The pandemic. Then the words flowed in a torrent I was unable to stop. The pressure, my fears. Why me? Why was I chosen? What if I wasn't suitable, failed? How would I be part of a community where there was no escape if I offended someone? How *could* I...?

The steam ran out of me as quickly as it had started, and I slumped in the chair, running out of words mid-sentence.

Mum glanced briefly at Dad, looked back at me, and said, "Eat, then sleep." I looked up at her, dazed and confused. The watch on my wrist that had been returned as I had lined up for the bus showed it was barely midday.

"Eat," she repeated firmly. "Then sleep. You can't make an important decision on an empty stomach. It isn't like your study is the most critical thing in the world anymore, now is it?"

Mum steered me into the kitchen. She pushed me into a chair and started making pancakes. Fluffy buttermilk pancakes with maple syrup. My comfort food from the time I was young.

"Is there vanilla ice cream?" I asked hopefully.

She gave me one of those all-encompassing Scottish noises, deep in her throat, that conveyed so many emotions. In this case, I knew it meant *well of course* as she opened the freezer and plonked a tub of ice cream on the table.

Ice cream. I sat and looked at the familiar tub, the colors, the label. Touching it, the crystals formed on the outside. Clear spots appeared where my fingers held the tub. *What if this is the last time I eat ice cream?*

"Mum?"

"What is it?"

"Do you know how to make ice cream?"

To my surprise, Mum laughed. "Aye, and a great deal more!"

Throughout my childhood, Mum had tried to tell me countless times about her own upbringing on a small farm on Lewis. Mum and her sister Angela had been raised by their grandparents after the death of their parents when the ferry taking them to the mainland had capsized in a storm. Helping milk the cows, making butter, cream, and evidently, ice cream. Collecting eggs. Shearing sheep and helping to spin it into wool, which was sold to the Harris Tweed co-op. As a kid, it seemed dull, some far-off boring place, although I had been there several times. Now, as I ate, she regaled me with tales of life on the farm. I forgot where I was and just listened. She spoke of her daily chores: collecting water from a well, weeding vegetable patches, helping a favorite cow give birth. Her eyes misted up, and she sat, staring into space. She was back there on her grandparents' croft.

I asked in a voice barely above a whisper, "Do you miss it?"

Mum sighed. A deep sigh, like all the life was oozing from her.

"Aye," she said simply. "I do."

We both sat in silence for what appeared to be an age. Dad wandered in and looked at us both, slumped at the table, staring into space.

"Mum, why did you come here?" I asked.

She refocused her eyes and looked at Dad, then at me.

"For your da," she said simply, "for you and your sister. Then, well.... Life... just happened."

"Would you ever go back?"

"In a heartbeat. But you know, my life is here now." She looked me directly in the face and held my gaze before delivering her order. "This is a remarkable opportunity you have been given. Consider it carefully. Now. Off to bed with you."

Stumbling like a drunk into my room, I stood in the doorway and took in the grand sum of my life. All around me was crap I had collected from when I was a kid, and Mum had never made me throw it out. *Why? Why hadn't she made me clean up this shit years ago? The world was going to end. Everyone was going to die.*

Picking up the snorkel mask from a shelf, I snorted– what a joke. No one would ever snorkel again. The last time I had was off the beaches of Ile de Canard in Noumea. There were gorgeous tropical fish that would brush against you as you swam in the warm turquoise ocean adjacent to pristine white beaches. Soon, they would all be gone. How could this be happening? *No.* I reasoned. *Someone would work it out and find a solution. There would be news conferences and events. Everything would go back to normal.* As I lay on my bed, I took in the posters, pictures, shells, bits of useless crap. My crap. My life. But deep down, I knew. This was no Hollywood movie.

Whether it was waking drenched in sweat or my head pounding, I knew as soon as I came to my senses that I wasn't going back to sleep. I squinted at the clock—2 am. Crap. Too early to get up. I lay there, willing myself to sleep. Watching the clock mark the half hours finally pissed me off enough that I got up and padded down the hallway. Painkillers were my focus. I headed to the bathroom to seek relief. Swallowing them with a glass of water, I pondered the complexities of running water. Some engineering genius had clearly worked out how to get water from a river, through pipes, suburbs, and individual houses. Filtered, heated. All I had to do was turn on a tap. I stood there, turning the tap on and off. On and off. Would there be running water? From what Ashton had said, I doubted it. I imagined a shack, not dissimilar to ours on the block. Then I relaxed somewhat. The block wasn't so bad. We cleared that land by hand, albeit with a chainsaw. Fairly sure the government could provide a chainsaw. I relaxed a little. There was no running water, gas, or electricity. But we had tank water and a wood heater. I could survive with that. The real question was, did I *want* to?

Knowing from experience that there was no value in returning to bed unable to sleep, I sat and watched television with the volume as low as I could keep it to hear it myself, but without waking the family. Hearing me up and about, Merlin appeared from somewhere and settled himself on my lap, kneading me like bread.

Sorcha's bedroom door, visible from the lounge, was closed. I hadn't watched TV like this in years. Just turned it on, sat, and absentmindedly flicked through channels. Between online news, news on demand, podcasts, and even listening to the radio in the car, I never watched TV news anymore. Bizarrely, I found the mindless channel flicking was actually therapeutic.

Merlin purred loudly as I scratched him under the chin, along his cheekbones, and around his neck, pushing his face into my hand in ecstasy. Merlin had flatly refused to wear a collar and had promptly lost the several we had bought him, never to be seen again. We gave up buying them, and clearly, he was happy that we had finally worked out that he was in charge.

The news ticker was scrolling—nearly all headlines were related to the spread of the virus in Europe. Images of piles of dead fish, birds, animals rotting in fields. Yet the rivers themselves looked clean and pristine. How could something so beautiful be so deadly? The death toll stood at several thousand now. Interviews with scientists with lengthy official-sounding titles and degrees. Politicians were promising that something would be done, pledging funds, and advising people not to panic. I knew better. I knew that there wasn't much that could be done. The best minds in the world were working on this and couldn't solve the problem. How scared must they be if they were simultaneously planning to set up communities on isolated islands across the world? I considered all the puffed-up self-important politicians, millionaires, and celebrities who all undoubtedly believed that *they* were important enough to be a candidate.

For the millionth time, I pondered the question, *why me?* Why would they even consider that I had a smidgen of the skill required to be part of a project that could save the human race from extinction? I stewed over those words for a minute. Extinction.

Human race. Ended. Finished. Obliterated. Wiped from the earth.

The repetitive news had become unbearable. Merlin, sensing my intention to move, saw this as an opportunity for his first breakfast and stood upright on my lap, purring loudly. Scratching his head, I carried him to the kitchen and fed him, then returned to the family room. Unable to settle in, I wandered around the room, picking things up and putting them down without really looking at them. Mum used to get grumpy at me for doing this.

Wandering around aimlessly, she called it. For a split second, I wondered if I would forget my mum if I went, then berated myself. Of course not. People don't forget their parents if they die. But this was different. This was leaving my family behind, knowing that *they* would die, but that I wouldn't—an immense burden and honestly not one I could see myself living with.

A light breeze blew through the house, rattling the blinds. I glanced up to see Sorcha standing in the doorway. She was watching me intently, sadness in her eyes.

"You know." It was a statement, not a question.

"Yup."

"Well? You have always given me your opinion whether I wanted it or not."

"No, I...." she trailed off. "Okay. Well... maybe that is true. First-born privilege and all."

"What are you thinking?"

"I'm thinking..." Sorcha said slowly, "... that it must be a hell of a decision to make."

My head dropped as the muscles in my neck gave way. She got it. Finally, someone who understood. I sank into the couch, head in my hands, trying not to lose it altogether. I felt the sofa move slightly as she sat beside me.

"What would you do?"

"I have spent the last few hours stewing over precisely that question," she admitted. "The truth is, I have absolutely no idea."

Seated on the couch beside me with her head rested on my shoulder, conversation flowed between us in a way that it hadn't in years. About nothing in particular. Family trips. Our Scottish granny who had called us wee and bonny and had regularly had us in fits of laughter. When Merlin returned for more attention, the conversation turned to old pets. Oscar the cat, who had lived to the ripe old age of seventeen. Memories.

Finally, she looked at me and said, "You know you have to go."

"I'm not sure I can. How do I... go? Knowing what is to come? What could happen... to you. To you all. I keep asking myself—Why me? I'm not special. I am no different from you, or anyone else. And on that note, why not you? You are the smart one!"

Sorcha laughed. A genuine, deep laugh. I hadn't heard her laugh like that for a long time. Smiling at her, I said, "It's so good to hear you laugh, Sorcs. It has been too long."

"Funny, isn't it? Suddenly all the shit you stress about, lose sleep over: boyfriends, exams, people gossiping, having enough money for something, paying a bill. None of it seems important any- more—does it?"

The loss was still weighing on her, but I didn't probe.

Quietly she spoke, "I'm not the smart one. You are really. You just don't believe in yourself. Ever since you were little, you didn't believe that you were worthy. But you are. You have always been bril- liant, especially in math and science. Now it has been proven. You were chosen. I wasn't."

Looking at her face, etched with sadness, I started to speak, tell her it must have been a mistake, but stopped when I saw the sorrow in her eyes.

"Asthma."

It was like a resounding slap to the face. Asthma. The truth was that I had forgotten entirely as it wasn't how I saw her. It was just something that happened *to* her. It wasn't who she *was*. She was a strong, deter- mined woman, so much like Mum. Sorcha hadn't had an asthma attack for years, but I still remembered the scared pale faces of my parents as they stood over her in a hospital bed as a child, watching her with an oxygen mask attached to her face, struggling to breathe. Years of never leaving the house without an inhaler. Ambulances called by the school to come and get her as she was having difficulty breathing. The real question now was, had asthma saved her life—or mine?

Sorcha shifted her weight to get comfortable. My shoulders were stiff from holding the weight of her head, Merlin curled up on my lap, but truthfully, I was grateful for the physical discomfort to parallel my emotional turmoil.

"How do you think you will cope? I mean, it is a big change."

I looked at her. Change. She knew full well that it was something I wasn't good with, and for her, she was actually trying to be diplomatic. Diplomacy had never been Sorcha's strong point. Like Mum, she was as subtle as a sledgehammer. You knew precisely what she was thinking the minute she thought it—no niceties or tiptoeing around.

Change made me feel tight in the chest and tense all over. When I was little, I had what Mum called meltdowns over unexpected change. Over the years, I had learned to cope, but I still didn't like plans changing without time to process it. But there it was. Logically, I knew change was coming regardless of what I thought. Big, massive change. Change happened, for better or worse. I know I didn't cope with it well. But at least I had strategies now.

"Honestly, I am trying not to think about it."

"Probably a reasonable approach."

"Should I tell them?"

"What makes you think they don't already know?" she asked incredulously. "Privacy principles likely go out the window when facing an international crisis of this magnitude, and all government departments share whatever data they have for the advancement of the cause. Besides, they had access to *my* medical and academic records." She smiled wanly.

"Would you really want to have gone?"

"And escape that dress in my wardrobe? All the memories that go with it? Yes," she said quietly. "I would go."

"And you will too."

I looked up to see Mum and Dad in the doorway. I sighed. Seriously, what is it about my family sneaking around like cats? The cat isn't even as stealthy as my parents.

"I'm not sure."

"Of course, you aren't, Campbell. You are kind and caring and are thinking of everyone else but yourself as you always do. But you *are* going. You were chosen. We..." she looked at Dad for support as the words choked her a little, "have discussed it, and we want something to be left of... us."

Instinctively, I tried to argue, but at her words, I knew. That was the end of it. Mum had decided. No sane person went up against a five-foot-nothing fiery redheaded Scottish woman when she had decided. For years I had watched, equal parts mortified and entertained, as people took her on thinking that because of her small stature that she would be a pushover. Watching as she cut them down with her acerbic tongue and sharp wit. This time, I was grateful. I would have spent days stewing over it, tossing up the pros and cons, and as a result, the deadline would have passed.

With my parents flanking me, I called the number I was given, gave my name, and a yes when asked for my response.

PART TWO

CHAPTER 5

"TEAM." ASHTON PAUSED, LOOKED up from his pile of papers. He was conflicted. The turmoil showed plainly on his face. Pushing his notes aside, he sighed. "I had an entire speech prepared, you know, motivational stuff about how important this mission is. How your roles here will secure the future of the human race. But there is absolutely nothing I can say now that will make the slightest difference. I have some idea of what you are all feeling because we—he waved around the room to encompass all the staff who had come to the final departure briefing—we all feel it too. All I can say now is… good luck."

Fourteen days of interviews and meetings, training and cramming with barely five hours of sleep per night had come down to this. We had not been permitted to meet with the other candidates chosen. Quarantine, they said. But part of me wondered if it was to ensure that we didn't scare each other off the project.

The first day had been filled with panel interviews, one final assessment to ensure that we knew what we were getting into. I wondered why there had been no interviews in the original assessments. So, I had asked.

"To ensure that the selection of shortlisted candidates was based on fact and not perception," I had been informed. As scientists, they were well aware of human factors. They weren't assessing how well we interviewed, recognizing that they didn't want one person's bias, personal values, or perspective to influence the decision of who was chosen and who was not. The short-listing was all about data. Interviews were only held now to ensure we fully understood what we were accepting—a one-way ticket. The hardships and limitations, but also the opportunity.

Boarding the helicopter in the dark with my cohort, I tried to capture the colors, the smells, the *feel* of home. Deep down, I knew my journey had just begun.

We watched the sunrise, glaring and orange over the horizon as the helicopter slowed upon approach to an island. The island looked like something out of a glossy travel brochure: pristine white beaches edged with sheer rock-lined cliffs rising into beautiful green hills, two prominent peaks covered with lush green forests towering over the valleys between. Several bays were visible along the coastline, large enough to accommodate small towns. At one end of the island, a narrow peninsula opened out to a flat green space at the end in the shape of a lollipop. Almost another island, but not quite. A multiple-level terraced area was cut into the earth slightly below the village area, evidently for food production. While the landscape was undulating in appearance, there was undoubtedly a lot of fertile grassy area, room for us to expand into.

As the helicopter slowed for landing above a floating pontoon moored adjacent to the island, I peered out of the windows with my fellow settlers. The trip had been loud, making holding a conversation difficult, which I was secretly pleased about. From the window, I could see neatly organized rows of long gray buildings, perfectly symmetrical, surrounding a central grassed area. Suspecting these were the dormitories, they looked suspiciously like university accommodation surrounding playing fields. Slightly farther off were several buildings in a cluster connected by covered walkways. Likely they were the common areas we had been briefed on: a community hall, dining room, and central kitchen. The rising sun glinted off an enormous bank of solar panels mounted onto the hillside overlooking the township and covering the surface of every rooftop. As we made our final descent, I cast my eye wider. There were freshly graded unsealed roads around the settlement, and I could see various sheds scattered around the island, all equipped with water tanks and solar panels. It was far more polished than our cabin at the block. Clearly, they had spared no expense for this experiment. Despite the utilitarian appearance of the buildings, it looked idyllic—for a holiday, perhaps. Conflicting emotions surged within me as we came in to land.

The fifty of us in my cohort were classified as number six. Six groups. Three hundred strangers to inhabit a small island. Hoisting the single backpack I had been permitted to bring, I followed our guide, Derek, ashore onto those pristine white sandy beaches. All guides would be evacuated by the end of the second day after they had oriented us. After that, the permanent geodesic dome would be fixed in place, and... that was it. Hello, brave new world. Making my way from the pontoon along the neatly paved path behind a small dark-haired woman, I pondered what personal possessions everyone else had brought in their bags.

We had each been allocated one primary job function, and it was in this area that we had been provided with our intensive pre-departure training. Some people, such as those earmarked to be teachers, had an immediate role before the second one was required. Mine, specializing in agriculture, was horticultural farming: producing an enormous range of food for the community in both vegetable gardens, orchards, and greenhouses. Initially, we were trialing what would grow well here as we had an abundant supply of food to get us started. After that, we would need to have finessed what suited the environment. With the dome in place, scientists weren't entirely sure what impact it would have on the local climate and what could be grown successfully, so the first years would be trial and error.

As we walked, Derek told us that there would be no natural rainfall because of the dome's waterproof construction. That was probably just as well, considering the reason for us being here. There were several clean water reservoirs on the island for drinking and showering, then that water was recycled and used for agricultural purposes and clothes washing. Crops would require no additional watering. Like a terrarium, the water we used to water plants would evaporate as the sun penetrated the dome. It would condense and then fall again each day as rain. The water in the reservoirs would be filtered using various methods before use, so we were continually protected. With no accurate test, no one was sure if our water supply would last indefinitely, so we were cautioned about using too much water.

The scientists who had chosen this island had estimated that there would be enough water for hundreds of years *if* we were careful about its use and didn't let the population outgrow our capacity to grow food. *It is Malthusian theory*, I considered, remembering Sorcha and our conversation in the kitchen that day. I couldn't help but visualize the terrarium we had built out of old plastic bottles at school and me as the tiny Lego figurine we had placed inside it.

One of the compulsory briefings we attended in those first two days was about the dome's structural integrity. The structure permitted air to pass through, but not water. Never water. Like most, I suspect, I was fascinated by the dome and felt the need to touch it, run my fingers along the slightly thicker angular seams where two triangles joined around a lightweight frame. Expecting it to be hard, I was surprised when I found it pliable. A sample was handed around in the briefing session, allowing us all to become familiar with the structure that would protect us. A transparent thick fabric composed of rows of triangles, then inverted triangles, that was designed to enclose us completely, each triangle roughly three meters along each side. The material was drawn tightly in places, but there was room for the dome itself to move slightly in the breeze without catching it like a tent and blowing off in a decent storm.

"So, how does air pass through but not water?" someone asked. "That is quite new technology, isn't it?"

"Not at all," said Derek. "You have all heard of Gore-Tex fabric, haven't you?"

Most people nodded in agreement.

"The manufacturers of Gore-Tex have been working on this for a very long time. It is the next generation, I suppose you could say. Like Gore-Tex, it is breathable, we don't want you to suffocate, but this is completely waterproof. It is stronger too, much stronger. It will withstand cyclones, hurricanes, even fire. After all, the original Gore-Tex fabric was invented in 1969. What do you think they have been working on all this time?"

"As it is fabric, can it be cut?" I asked, concerned that some suicidal nutjob might sacrifice us all. In my initial briefing, I had envisaged the dome as a hard, impermeable plastic. I was a little perturbed to find it a soft fabric.

"Try."

Derek held the sample triangle taut against its frame. Pulling my newly issued pocketknife from my jacket pocket, I tried cautiously to make a hole. Surprised that it was exceedingly strong, I tried again. This time I stabbed it with a great deal of force. The sharp knife tip bounced off the fabric like it was impacting sheet metal. I was relieved but also intrigued. Others wanted to try, stabbing madly, and slashing at it with various implements. Again, nothing, to my immense relief.

Derek was standing back, smugly smiling at our vain attempts.

"How was it made?" I asked.

"That part is secret. But I can assure you that you are safe. We are positive that there is nothing here that can cut the fabric."

Nodding, I asked my next question. "Will it disintegrate or degrade over time with sun or oxygen exposure?"

He nodded at my question. "Laboratory tests have indicated that it will last about 500 years, much longer than any of you!"

Nervous laughter rippled through the group.

"We are also working under the assumption that the pandemic will be controlled well before that time."

"What are the frames made from?"

"Reinforced fiberglass, basically thin, light, but extremely strong frames. Protected by the fabric, they too should not degrade to any extent where it impacts the integrity of the dome."

"You said it was fireproof. Will smoke escape?"

Derek nodded at the question. "That was going to be my next point—risks. No, smoke cannot escape, and that is something I need to press upon you all. Smoke is the single biggest risk factor here. There are to be no fires, and every precaution must be taken to avoid bushfires. There is no risk of lightning impacting the dome as it is not a conduit, so other causes are all you need to worry about. Remember that steam differs from smoke. Steam is pure water vapor, which will happen naturally when the water evaporates from the ground with the sun's heat, so you don't need to worry about boiling pots and kettles. Smoke is a different matter. Smoke contains soot, ash, and other particles. That is what will build up on the dome fabric and stop it from allowing air through."

A moment of silence as we absorbed this news. Smoke = bad.

"Is there a way out?"

"Nope. Once you are in, you are in." This had been pressed upon us several times per day for the fourteen days we were in training. At lunch, the principal topic had been that two people had allegedly freaked out on the way here in one helicopter, forcing that cohort to return to base, leaving our number at 298 and making one group miss the first of the on-site briefings.

The following morning, 20 February, our lives changed forever. The guides and mentors who had oriented us waved goodbye as they departed on the final helicopter off the island. The entire community lined the cliff edge to watch the custom-made dome, which wasn't uniform in shape, carefully maneuvered into place by a team of skycranes, those fascinatingly big and ridiculously loud helicopters. Birds flew squawking from the island, never to return. Others were trapped, and we watched helplessly as they repeatedly slammed into the fabric.

It was equal parts thrilling and terrifying. Fascinating to think that such a comparatively thin piece of fabric could keep us safe from something so catastrophic. Equally, it felt so permanent, yet not claustrophobic. Shut off from the rest of the world. But the transparent nature of the fabric and the fresh air didn't make me feel trapped, as I had feared it would. We watched as engineers drilled the irregular frame several meters into the earth from the outside, deep enough to ensure we couldn't accidentally dig under it—an rappelling team locking the pieces in place. Watching the sky cranes fly away with the last of the settlement team, I felt utterly alone. People surrounded me, but they were all strangers.

My thoughts turned to my family, friends, acquaintances. Had anyone missed me yet? My immediate family knew where I was, but no one else. I wondered how long it would be before anyone came looking for me. Did the university know? As I left, Australia hadn't been in a complete panic over the viral spread. Most people still had that feeling of being safe, being so far away from the rest of the world. But it would come. If it didn't, then I assumed someone would come and collect us. Surely they wouldn't just leave us here?

A gut-wrenching concept crossed my mind. What if *we* were the experiment? What if this was like the Biosphere 2 experiment, the group of eight scientists locked into a controlled environment with different biomes in Arizona for two years in the 1990s? Famously, they hadn't lasted because of conflicts and politics, and the experiment was cut short.

My thoughts turned to Derek, my guide to the island. Hundreds of people must know the location of this place. The government officials who had tested us, chosen us, designed and manufactured the geodesic dome. The guides who came here, people who had built the housing, the water supply system, the renewable energy systems, even the helicopter crews. Would any of them try to return here when Australia was eventually infected? How traumatizing to know that you are helping a group of strangers survive, yet you can't even save your own family? A fresh wave of guilt washed over me as I followed the community back to our dormitories for our first house meeting, and tomorrow night, a full team meeting.

Each of us had been allocated a small room in a bunkhouse with shared common areas. Each identical bunkhouse was made of gray prefabricated wall panels, a roof constructed of solar panels and windows along each side with an exit door at either end. Ten small bedrooms, five down each side, each identically equipped with a queen bed, a wardrobe, a small desk, and a chair. Sighing in relief, I was eminently grateful for the larger size of the bed. At six feet, my feet would hang out of a single bed, making decent rest impossible.

Meals would initially be taken in the main dining room in shifts, attached to a large recreation hall. Logically, the population would expand over the next few years before balancing out a bit. This hall would be used for meetings, movie nights, information sessions, and social events. I winced slightly as they discussed social events, but logically knew that I would know each of the strangers in this community soon enough.

Arriving last at my house meeting, it didn't appear that they had been waiting long as people quietly chatted among themselves. We were a mix of five men and five women, all working in different areas in the community. Lengthy training and briefing sessions had been provided over the past two days, so we hadn't met as a group until now, although I had passed some people in the hallway for a quick chat.

The community planners had deliberately spread out each role: engineer, plumber, builder, cook, vet, and even a seamstress, miller, and artisans who knew how to make pottery and even cutlery. A cutler, I was surprised to learn this latter role was called. No two people of the same occupation group lived in the same dormitory, a deliberate attempt for people to keep home and work separate, but also to maximize our exposure to other people in the community, Derek had advised. Thus, I was the only one engaged in horticulture in this dorm and was asked several questions about what I planned to grow. With the rest of the agriculture/horticulture team, I had already attended extensive briefings about the mind-blowing array of tools, equipment, seedlings, and trees that were here for our use. We even had our own seed bank. I was surprised to realize that I was looking forward to starting in the morning despite my reservations about being here.

Following the house meeting, which had focused mainly on introductions, getting to know each other, and agreeing on basic courtesy and house rules, I returned to my allocated room and gratefully closed the door. It was solid timber and blocked most of the chatter still filtering down the hall from the living room. After the meeting, a few residents on early shifts had retired to their rooms. I was grateful that I could escape the social chitchat. There would be ample time for that later. After all, time was something we had no shortage of.

My belongings, as well as my allocated clothing and linen, had been placed in this room with my name on the door when I had arrived two days ago. A great deal of planning had gone into ensuring that we had enough high-quality clothing and supplies to last a very long time.

The first day at work comprised a team meeting where we drew up a plan of what we would tackle first and divided up the tasks. The greenhouses had already been built, but none of the fruit trees, vegetables, or herbs had yet been planted. Some fruit grew in greenhouses only, as they weren't suited to the island's cool climate. The team—Kelly, Diana, Anneliese, Farid, Jamie, and I quickly found that we were treated with special reverence.

Diana, Jamie, and I had chosen to work the early shift, six days per week with a rotating day off. As a team, we drew up a plan for the season, broken down into weekly tasks. Despite being cooler here than Melbourne, it was still late summer, so we had limited time to get our crops in before winter, and no actual knowledge of what winter here might look like. Kelly, a pretty blonde, was happy, vivacious, and chatty. Originally from the Goulburn Valley, the food bowl of country Victoria, she had grown up on a large commercial orchard and knew a great deal about various fruit varieties. We sought her advice on what to plant where and in what order. We were still in the planning phase, but knew that establishing the orchards quickly was critical as several species would not be productive in the first year. Knowing that we needed to get them in the ground fairly quickly, as well as being able to maintain them, we espaliered[4] some trees to maximize their exposure to the sun and

---

[4] Espaliering is a horticultural practice of training trees into flat two-dimensional forms. In a temperate climate, espaliers may be oriented so that they absorb maximum sunlight by training them parallel to the equator. This allows the season to be extended so that fruit has more time to mature.

cropping. It would also enable us to manage their size. This meant building a long fence with trellis wire to train the branches along. Farid volunteered to construct the espalier fencing as Kelly and Anneliese planted the trees. That left Diana, Jamie, and me to establish the vegetable gardens. Herbs were generally quick growing and would be planted in between.

Diana was of Chinese descent, although to listen to, she sounded more Aussie than any of us, regularly having Jamie and me in fits of laughter as she impersonated her domineering Chinese grandmother. Her parents had owned a market garden west of Sydney, so her expertise was in vegetables. Companion planting was her particular area of interest. We discussed the benefits of growing tomatoes with basil and broccoli with beans and planned garden beds, soil improvement, and crop rotation. We knew that in time we would need to have extra garden beds as we would need to rest them in cycles, but fortunately, we didn't need to do this yet. Bugs and pests were not a significant concern here, although there were some. No natural wind caused interesting issues, but fortunately, not pollination. There was a vet here who had a particular interest in beekeeping, so there were bees. Derek had told us that an artificial wind turbine was on the island, but I had not had the chance to see it in action, although I could feel the slow, steady breeze at various points of the day.

Food security, basically ensuring sufficient quantities of good quality, nutritious food that met people's dietary needs and preferences, was my responsibility. Allowing for a reasonable margin for crop loss, planning crop quantities kept me busy, and I regularly took plans home to update my seasonal planner. Too much food was only slightly better than too little. We didn't want waste, but at least most things could be preserved in some way.

Jamie was a quiet, unassuming man. I didn't hear him speak for the first few days we were working together. Assuming he was homesick or merely struggling to adjust like many here, I gave him a wide berth. When I needed to talk to him on our fourth day about the crops planned for each garden bed, I discovered he was from New Zealand—one of the many Kiwis here. He was intelligent and articulate, and I soon found him a great source of information about various topics from music and film to archaeology and history. We spent hours laughing about the quirks of our parents as we worked. His father had migrated from Aberdeen, and he had me in stitches teaching me crude Aberdonian Scots as we dug and planted. Friendship with Jamie and Di made the new reality of my life much easier to bear, and I looked forward to seeing them each morning.

In the fields next to our terraced gardens were the animals. There were herds of cows, so fresh milk, cream, and butter were already available. Flocks of chickens of several breeds squawked happily and rolled in the single patch of dirt. I smiled, half-watching them as I spent the afternoon digging new vegetable gardens.

Naming our community had been left to us. On our second Friday evening, we gathered in the community hall to agree upon a name. After a community meeting, listening to the broadcast from Australia and New Zealand, we all were offered the opportunity to present one name and explain our reasoning. A shortlist would be compiled based on agreement, and a vote taken. There was no appointed leader here yet. The designers of this project had clarified that the community would make its own rules and set its own values. But as always happens, a natural leader, or several, invariably tries to control the group.

Utopia. This fairly ambitious choice was met with much eye-rolling and groaning. Beautiful it might be—utopia it was not.

Arcadia. This received a similar response.

Hawaiki. This from one of the New Zealanders, of which the meeting tonight confirmed made up around one-third of our nearly three hundred strong community.

"What does it mean?" an Aussie asked.

Much discussion among the Kiwis ensued. Eventually, it was established that Hawaiki was the traditional Māori place of origin. In Māori mythology, Hawaiki is the place where the supreme being created the world and its first people. It is from where each person comes, and it is where each will return after death.

Much discussion took place after this revelation. People considered the name was too similar to Hawaii. Some said that the name was not as culturally relevant to the Australians. A tall, bronzed, blonde woman with a booming voice named Erika, who fancied herself as a leader, tried to bring the group back to order by insisting we continue around the room.

My turn came. With nothing to offer, I shrugged and looked at the person to my right. Increasingly people were skipping their chance to provide a new option.

Gilligan's Island. Lots of laughs at this one.

Hope Island. More groans.

Azkaban. A few sniggers from some. Puzzled stares from the rest.

Twin Peaks. A few maybe looks. We could all see the two prominent hills from the village. But perhaps the associations were not great.

Two very long, excruciating hours later, there was a shortlist. I would have preferred them to stab me in the eye with a red-hot poker than sit through this bullshittery. What difference does it make what we call the place? Exhausted after a long day of digging and planting, I just wanted to go to bed but knew this was important and that all residents were needed for the final vote. I wished they would hurry up.

It was evident that many others were also feeling frustrated about the conversation going around and around, and the blatant lack of progress. As is usually the way when there is a large group trying to nego-tiate a democratic outcome, there were a few distinct groups at play here. A relatively small number of very vocal people led the argument, vigorously trying to sway others to their way of thinking. The next reason-ably large group was interested in the discussion and engaged, but not contributing to progressing it. The remainder, like me, were bored and disinterested and just wanted to vote so that we could go home.

"Well, it would help if we knew where we *are!*" Phil chimed in, for what was likely the seventeenth time that evening. "Then we could choose a landmark, a historical or cultural name."

Lots of audible groaning and facepalming ensued.

"Oh, for fuck's sake!" bellowed George, a large man of Greek heritage who had clearly had enough of Phil. "None of us have any idea where we are! We are all dumped here on a nameless sodding island, trapped in the middle of the bloody ocean, halfway between the ass-end of the earth and the fucking *moon!* What difference does it make where we are?! For all I know, we could be halfway between Easter Island and fucking Christmas Island!"

"Then name it August Island!" came a raucous call from the back of the room.

A long pause, then the hall erupted into laughter as the penny dropped. The hysterical kind that happens when people are exhausted and have had enough. Ten minutes later, when the room finally calmed down, a vote was taken.

August Island it was.

CHAPTER 6

RISING AT SUNRISE, I attended the early breakfast sitting with those who needed to be up and out early. Breakfast was usually quite simple. Tea and coffee were a limited resource and rationed to one cup per person per day, a difficulty quite a few of us needed to adapt to.

Knowing that our supplies were limited to one year, I felt immense pressure to ensure that the tea and coffee plants were successful. We planted them inside the greenhouse and outside in an appropriately sunny spot, hoping one may prove more successful than the alternative, enabling us to expand the planting space in the following year. In the meantime, I savored my daily cup of coffee. Fortunately, we had a decent industrial machine, a roaster, and enough raw beans to get us through a year.

Diana and I chatted about the day ahead. Over the weeks we had been here, she and I had developed a routine of breakfasting together and drinking our coffee on our walk to work. I watched the steam rise from the coffee machine with interest.

"Jenny?" I called to the head cook, who took no nonsense from anyone. She was refilling the food table in time for the second sitting. Jenny and I had already consulted extensively about varieties, stocks, delivery times, and menus, so we had an amicable relationship.

"How do you cook without generating smoke?"

Jenny gave me an all-knowing look. "Come with me," she beckoned, scooping up the large bin containing food scraps effortlessly.

Picking up my mug, Diana and I followed her across the dining room and through the double barn doors into the kitchen. Unlike most people who were not permitted in the food preparation areas for hygiene reasons, I came into the kitchen all the time, but usually dropping off freshly picked supplies to the cellars below the kitchen. Cautious not to impede the cooks, I followed Jenny through. A few days prior, I had needed to dash out of the way as a large pot had been moved from the cooktop to a bench. In my haste, I accidentally placed my hand on a cooktop, burning the edge of my palm. After that episode, I made a greater effort to drop and go.

But Jenny didn't stop in the kitchen, instead beckoning me out the back doors, still carrying the bin of scraps. There were two sets of doors at the exit to prevent flies and insects from getting in, a small airlock in-between.

Cooking, she explained, was undertaken in enclosed ovens, fired by biogas[5], and completely enclosed. Cooktops, also fueled by biogas, had range-hoods with large fans that extracted any smoke or steam. Ovens had a window built into the back that captured the smoke and allowed the water particles to escape. Smoke consists of a suspension of water vapor and solid matter. In cooking smoke, the solid is mainly vaporized vegetable oils and animal fats. These were collected via filters and cleaned, not released into the atmosphere. But it was the biogas setup that fascinated me.

Although I had learned about the theory of biogas at university, our studies had focused on the large industrial setups, such as running buses and heavy machinery. I had never seen this type of biogas equipment before and found the concept remarkable. Effectively an enormous soft bag that mimicked a stomach, you fed it waste through an inlet funnel. Anything that was once something living could be digested, including our food scraps, green waste, plant material, or manure. Even meat scraps, I was amazed to learn.

Then, the expanding bag effectively digested them. I suddenly felt a lot less guilty about not eating the crust on my toast that morning as I watched Jenny tip the waste bin into the inlet funnel. The unit operated without oxygen but required micro-organisms to perform anaerobic digestion. The by-products were gas,

---

[5] Biogas is a renewable energy source produced by organic matter in the absence of oxygen. Biogas can be produced from raw materials such as plant material, sewage, green waste, or food waste.

an energy source used to fire the kitchen ovens and cooktops. The second by-product was a fabulously rich liquid fertilizer we could use on the gardens.

Jenny proudly displayed the multiple rows of biogas set-ups which astonishingly didn't smell. She also told me we had additional units waiting to be set up when the community needed them and would be connected to each of the new homes being built. The kitchen scraps of vegetable and fruit peelings would be fed to the chickens, goats, and livestock, and all remaining waste from the dining room was fed to the biogas units. It was reassuring to know that we wouldn't need a rubbish dump anytime soon. That was one part of a civilized society we were all pleased to leave behind.

Farewelling Jenny back to her kitchen and preparing to leave, I picked up the basket I carried the daily fruit stock in. The handle of the basket inadvertently pressed on the burn on my hand. Grimacing, I switched the basket to my left hand.

While Jenny showed me the biogas setup, Diana had been chatting to another lady just outside the kitchen door. Waiting patiently for her to finish her conversation, Diana introduced me to Jacinda, one of her housemates, a New Zealander with evident Maori heritage, including a stunning tribal tattoo around her upper arm. Jacinda was tasked with making the cleaning products used on August, Di told me. It was Jacinda's role to ensure that all soaps, shampoos, detergents, and cleansers were all-natural and biodegradable. Smiling politely as my back ached from yesterday's digging, I considered that perhaps a soap maker was one of the easier roles here on August. Listening intently as she described how she collected oils, herbs, natural fragrances to make her formulations, and how they all had medicinal properties, I realized how passionate she was about her craft. She was also making reusable beeswax wraps for the kitchen to keep food fresh in place of plastic or foil. When she started describing the lotions and salves she had been asked to make to support the medical teams for rashes, burns, and allergies, I rapidly revised my opinion, realizing that I had been quick to judge. Recognizing that the agricultural team would need to grow the crops to produce these oils, trees that took some years to produce a good supply of fruit, this was something we would need to plan for. Three hundred people, all washing their hands several times a day, would use a lot of soap. Not to mention clothes washing, which was done in low water, low power machines that pumped the gray-water into a tank to re-use and recycle onto home gardens.

Jacinda had seen me grimace as she spoke to Di, and without asking, turned my hand over and looked closely at the blistering red sore, which admittedly was looking a touch green around the edges. Leading me back into the kitchen, she pushed me into a chair and got some honey, which she soaked into a dressing and applied to my hand.

"Honey?" Di asked jokingly. "Is Cam trying to attract bees?"

Jacinda laughed. "Actually, honey is a natural antiseptic and was used for years on wounds, cuts, and sores. It should stop the burn from getting infected. The viscosity of honey also helps to provide a protective barrier against infection and promotes moist wound conditions which are preferable for healing."

I looked interestedly at my now wrapped hand, and then at Jacinda. "Really? Honey? How did I not know this?"

"Garlic also has antibacterial properties. Lots of natural healing is effective, albeit a little messy. Many common drugs and medicines we take now originate from natural sources. You would know that penicillin was originally discovered as a mold spore on an uncovered Petri dish? And that aspirin originates from willow bark?"

I nodded, fascinated.

"Well, we have come a long way as a society only to return to ancient knowledge."

"Chemist?" I questioned curiously.

"Compounding pharmacist," Jacinda smiled back at me, "with a side interest in naturopathy."

As Diana and I prepared to leave, I asked Jacinda to write me a list of all the plants she would need to be grown and the approximate time in which she would need them. Growing food would not be our only priority.

"The designers of the community really planned this out," I said to Jamie as I surveyed the buildings slightly uphill from where we stood. The food bowl, as we labeled the orchards and vegetable gardens, was slightly downhill from the accommodation and communal facilities but caught the full afternoon sun. Any water run-off from the daily condensation rain ran down to the gardens. Every roof caught water, which flowed to its own tank, which was then used for showers and small-scale washing of clothes and dishes.

Jacinda's biodegradable products would be essential in ensuring that our crops were not poisoned. With no rain or flash flooding, street drains and stormwater weren't necessary, but every drop that could be caught was used and reused.

Working long, arduous hours the first few months was essential for the establishment of our new community, and no one complained about the hard work. When we were established, there would be more time for leisure. We had one day off per week, and I relished the opportunity to rest and explore the island. A sleep-in was nearly always on the list, although with my body so used to waking at dawn, it was a hard habit to break. The best part was that there was no rush to get out of bed. A leisurely meal followed, not stuffing in breakfast and rushing off to work, drinking coffee on the way, and needing to remember to bring back my used mug. Guilt plagued me whenever I considered all the disposable cups, plastic lids, and bottles I had thrown away during my life. It was a joy, once a week, to sit down and savor a meal. I wished I had a newspaper to enjoy, but even just sitting, eating slowly, and relishing my meal while reading one of the many books here was a delight. I went for long walks in the hills or around the coastline, collecting samples of native plants and flowers. Sometimes I shared these with Jacinda, hoping that they may have medicinal properties.

Diana and Jamie teased me mercilessly, thinking I was mad to want to walk and exercise on my rest day, but I found it peaceful alone, walking in the hills along sandy beaches, looking through the dome out to sea. I noted locations where there was flat green land near fresh water. Some might make appropriate settlement locations at some point. One day a week of no deadlines, no bending, digging, plowing, pruning. Just walking at my own pace, enjoying the view and the serenity. The part I didn't discuss was that exercise was essential to keep my anxiety in check. Hard physical labor was good, but a long walk in nature was the best medication available.

Sometimes I visited different areas of the community, spread out as it was. I found the diversity of skill here quite incredible and realized that a lot of consideration had gone into selecting the three hundred people chosen. One of my favorite areas to visit was the aquaponics ponds. Various varieties of fish, all edible, swam in large above-ground pools with crops, mainly rice, growing on the water's surface. Plants took nutrients from the fish waste, and the plants were thriving. Likewise, the fish fed on the roots of the plants, keeping the fish alive and growing. I found this symbiosis fascinating. Kai ran the aquaponics farming, and I enjoyed talking to him and learning about the setup.

Dad would have loved this, I reflected, saddened by the realization that I could never share this with him. Recollections of my family often impacted me when I least expected it. Working outside and an unexpected scent or sight of a flower would bring back long-forgotten memories. Someone would make a comment, and it would remind me of someone I knew for no explicable reason. Several times each day, I wondered how my family was faring. Were they affected yet? There was no point in talking about it. Everyone here had left someone behind. We had received no word that the protozoa had reached Australia, but conversely, we had yet to learn that the immense international effort had managed to slow or stop it. Australia and New Zealand, where all of our residents were from, were surely the last places that the protozoa would reach, given the relative geographical remoteness from the infected areas. I wondered if the Australian government had implemented quarantine on a mass scale? After all, Australia had a lot of food production. As a nation, it could probably halt imports and exports and be self-reliant, at least for a time. That would slow the potential infection of the country. But could it be stopped? Never having been to New Zealand, I had little knowledge about its fauna and flora, aside from what I had learned as part of my science degree.

Flashbacks of Ashton and the overhead slides showing the expected path of disease spread made me shudder. The problem with globalization is that the well-trodden trade routes of old, being the predicted pathways through which infection could spread, were no longer valid. People and goods traveled all over the globe, every single day in no distinct pattern. Combined with no completely accurate knowledge of where rain would fall, the exact routes of ocean currents, or what new infection sites might pop up, this biohazard was completely unpredictable.

CHAPTER 7

HEIDI WAS ONE OF the vets and the primary beekeeper, a tall solid blonde woman of roughly twenty-five, with a faintly clipped accent and an unapproachable air. Finding her quite intimidating, I usually disappeared when I saw her coming. She preferred to engage with Diana and Kelly, so I left them to chat about what pollens the bees were collecting and the impact this may have on the honey we collected. With only a small supply provided at set-up, Jacinda was keen to collect manuka honey for its antibacterial properties. She had asked me if I could plant some manuka trees at our highest points, and I had readily agreed. The many hives of bees were happy and producing brood and honey, so I didn't feel that I needed to interfere. Di told me one morning that Heidi was pleased that there appeared to be no hive beetle or varroa mites here, which threatened bee colonies, and we didn't use chemicals on our crops, so the bees faced little risk to their welfare.

The vet crew raised a large variety of animals for eggs, wool, or milk. We ate a primarily plant-based diet with a protein source usually twice a week, most often fish from the aquaponics tanks, which were doing so well that Kai was expanding them. Kai was certainly vocal about the additional work this popularity had created. Working so close to the animal fields, I secretly named some animals, especially one alpaca who often wandered over to me when I was working near the fences, looking for a treat like a fallen apple. I kept a close eye on those I was fond of. I didn't want to find out that I had eaten one of my favorites without realizing it.

Most evenings, I ate dinner with Phil, the hydro engineer, Diana, Jacinda, and Jamie. Phil was a brilliant, articulate, and somewhat socially forceful man who liked to dominate conversations, and as a result, had already managed to irritate quite a few people. Despite this, he was highly knowledgeable, and I learned a great deal from him, especially about how the engineering here impacted horticulture. Artificial solar-generated wind turbines operated for a few hours each day and could be heard humming away in the distance. Without wind systems, the warm, moist air under the dome wouldn't move around. The water would still evaporate, but it wouldn't travel, meaning any area away from a large body of water would dry up. Wind was also required for pollination, although the bees helped here to a significant extent. It just didn't *feel* like wind, I decided one day as I worked tying up straggling grapevines. The turbines had a consistent feeling, much like standing under a ceiling fan. True wind fluctuated; it took you by surprise. One moment it was completely still. The next, you were nearly on your back with an unexpected gust. Still, I considered, fake wind was better than nothing.

Injuries were not uncommon, especially among the building crews, but it was nearly three months before I needed to visit the clinic myself. Distracted by a cow mooing loudly in the next paddock, I had looked up to see what the commotion was about while continuing to prune an espaliered lemon tree. Watching the vet approach the cow with a needle, I saw the cow, knowing precisely what was about to happen, backing away, making a terrible racket. Watching the by-play and feeling very sorry for the beast, I withdrew my hand and felt the sting. Returning my attention to my task, I realized I had inadvertently cut one of the wire espaliers instead of the branch. The cut wire, in turn, had sliced the palm of my hand. I looked at it for a moment, puzzled.

"Damn it," I muttered as I realized what I had done, taking off my t-shirt and tying it around my hand to staunch the bleeding. After a few minutes, I carefully lifted the makeshift bandage and peeked. Shit. It was a deep cut. I could see the wound gaping, showing a sickening portion of the fleshy part of my hand. It started to throb, alerting me to the fact that it was indeed going to require treatment. Sighing over the work I was unlikely to finish, I went to tell Jamie, then walked the kilometer or so to the clinic, not so conveniently located on the opposite side of the community from where I was working.

Tasked with building additional permanent and private residences, splinters, cuts, and the occasional serious injury occurred among the building crews on a semi-regular basis, so I assumed the clinic was built close to the housing for that reason. No major illnesses had befallen us yet, proving that the quarantine process had likely been successful. I wondered if we, and the communities like us, were successful, could we eradicate transmittable diseases? If no one has a cold or hepatitis, and the population continued to grow, would those diseases die out? It was a fascinating idea, and I meant to ask one of the medical staff when I had the chance. Likely, they had all studied epidemiology as part of their training.

Walking up the hill toward the clinic, I wound my shirt tighter around my throbbing hand but slowed to take in the beauty of my surroundings. At no risk of bleeding out, I was in no rush. The orchard was spectacular in fall, the leaves on the deciduous trees changing color to golds, oranges, deep reds, and yellows. Small piles of leaves lay on the ground, ringing the foot of some trees but not others. I was following the seasons in a way that I had never really done before. The olive trees were evergreen and still bore green olives, just turning purple-black in places. We would need to harvest them soon. We didn't want to lose those. Olives were valuable, both as a food and an oil source. Jacinda wanted some too as the basis for many of her products.

The days had progressively been getting shorter and cooler, and I was learning the signs that harvest was due. Farming at home was based on a calendar and maximizing the crop for the supermarket purchaser, often harvesting well before the crop was actually ripe. Here, food was picked and consumed the same day, the next day at worst. The cooks worked closely with me to plan the menu based on what was in season or what was ripe and available. We watched, tested the fruit and vegetables, and chose our time precisely for each plant or tree. We simply didn't have the storage for lots of fruit to sit around and rot.

When I arrived at the clinic, after they checked that I wasn't in immediate peril, I was asked to wait in a small alcove furnished with a long bench seat with a back. One of the builders had slipped off a roof and was being treated for a suspected leg fracture. It wasn't uncomfortable as the bench seat had cushions, so I was secretly enjoying the rest, watching the community at work out of one of the large windows facing the dining room.

Almost an hour later, I was shown to the consulting room. Nyah, one of the doctors, gestured me toward a chair and asked, "What happened?"

"Fought with a lemon tree. Lost."

She chuckled. "Better show me then."

A thorough clean, six stitches, and some pain relief later, I was back on my way home, wondering what I could do with one hand, especially when the instructions were to keep it clean.

CHAPTER 8

WAKING SOMETIME DEEP IN the night with a cracking migraine, I lay there for a while, trying not to move and jar my head, willing sleep to come and overtake me. I usually left the window open to get fresh air, something my mother had always done, and I felt claustrophobic with a closed door and window. My door needed to be closed for privacy and the sake of noise, but I loved feeling the slight breeze from the turbines which ran part of the night, the rustle of leaves, the occasional squawk from a chicken, but mostly silence. No hum of electricity, drip of a tap, cars driving past somewhere in the distance, no neighbor watching late-night TV, the light flickering from their window. I hadn't realized when I accepted my place here that I would miss the sound of traffic. I had hated traffic before. Now, it was a sound I associated with life.

It was thunderstorms I missed the most. Solid cracking thunder. Fiery streaks of lightning that lit up the night sky in quick flashes, blinding for a split second and illuminating the world around like an x-ray. Huge torrential raindrops that soaked to the skin in seconds. That freezing ice-cold rain that penetrates bone-deep but makes truly invigorates. Alive. The rain here wasn't really rain but condensation, and it dripped annoyingly slowly. The sun permeated the dome, and water evaporated from the lakes, soil, and plants. But as the evaporated water can't escape, it came back as a misty rain, much how I remembered a visit to London in winter—that irritating drizzle that makes hair wet and frizzy. But not true *rain,* piercing droplets that sting the head as they hit and you run, equal parts irritated and laughing to avoid it.

Occasionally, we could see storms, hear them outside the dome, the rain pelting down and making a muffled putt-putt sound as it hit the fabric. It was the strangest sensation, seeing the darkening sky, visible lightning, and hearing the thunder but not being part of it.

Once, when I was young, I got caught in the rain with my mother and sister. There were enormous puddles forming, and Mum just laughed and let me splash in them, soaking me and filling my boots. It was sheer ecstasy, the sounds as I slammed my boot into the puddles, running and watching the water spread up from the impact of my feet. I fell at one point and landed on my butt, soaked in an instant. But Mum said nothing and just let me play until I was done, then took me home and put me in the bath. Such simple things, puddles. Enormous masses of water, smooth to look at, but so easy to disrupt the glossy surface with a foot or a stone. Impossible to tell how deep they are or how long they would last. Water here was too precious to waste just for fun. Splashing, swimming, and long hot showers were things I may never experience again, and it saddened me to realize this. I would never take a refreshing dive from a riverbank into a crystal blue creek or river or have waves break over my head in powerful demand as I swam out to sea, away from land and the golden sand of the Australian beaches where I had grown up. To make it even more torturous, a short walk away, I could see the beautiful, perfect white expanse of beach and beyond, the glittering turquoise ocean, looking so calm and peaceful. Was it already infected? Was the very virus that would destroy every living being already lapping at our doorstep?

I rubbed at my temples as my head continued to throb. Experience had taught me that basic analgesia for migraine was pointless, so I headed into the kitchen and went straight for the potent stuff. Struggling to crack the small white tablets from the blister pack with my one usable hand, I paused—should I really take these? Previously, I wouldn't have given it a second thought. After all, there was a chemist in every shopping center or local shopping strip attached to most medical clinics. But now, I was second-guessing every decision. We had a limited supply of codeine and no way to make or acquire more. I was in pain, but what if I, or someone else, was suffering later and needed them? Should I grow opium poppies to make morphine and codeine?

As I sat there in the living room, glass of water on the table in front of me, staring down at the strip of small innocent looking capsules in my hand, one of my housemates, Freyja, strode in with purpose, looking every bit the tall Norwegian goddess that she was. Despite wearing pajama pants and a faded gray t-shirt, she owned the room. Self-possessed and confident as always, everyone who had mentioned her found her entirely intimidating. Freyja and I had never spoken before. Our paths just... well, hadn't crossed. She was completely stunning with her tall, powerful broad-shouldered frame, lightly tanned skin, piercing green eyes, and blonde hair carelessly cascading in loose waves down her back. She was also highly intelligent, and quite frankly, downright terrifying.

My heart thumped in my chest so loudly that I feared she could hear it.

"What's that?"

Seriously? Could she really hear my heart thumping away? Feeling like a complete fool, my face flamed bright red with embarrassment, and my throat closed over, making me feel like I had swallowed a sock. A rather smelly sock. Sweat started to bead on my face, and I froze like a child caught doing something naughty.

She nodded at my hand, still holding the painkillers, asking with greater insistence, "What's that?"

"Migraine," I managed to mutter, looking at my long misshapen toes and awkward-looking feet. Most people acknowledge all feet are ugly, but my middle toes, like my dad's, are longer than my big toe, making them look like fingers. Shifting my feet under me so that she didn't see them and run away screaming, I tried again a little more clearly, "Migraine."

She looked at me with more sympathy.

"That sucks. Do you want me to get you some lavender oil?"

Without waiting for a reply, she moved silently toward the kitchen. She returned a few minutes later, soundlessly, and handed me a small white handkerchief with a few drops of lavender oil on it.

Feeling the red flush rising up my neck and into my face, I confessed sheepishly, "I have never used lavender oil. What do I do with it?"

Freyja laughed, an utterly charming, low, rumbling sound like water tumbling over rocks. "Inhale it, although I find that lying down with it over my eyes helps, too."

Unable to work out if she was teasing me, I inhaled the aroma and nearly choked.

Doubled up from trying not to laugh at me, she finally managed, "Inhale the scent, not the entire hanky, you fool!"

Seeing my one-handed struggle, wordlessly, she popped two tablets from the blister pack and handed them to me. She sat in the chair opposite and observed me as I swallowed the tablets, sticking in my throat as they went down. I coughed, resulting in her laughing at me again. She laughed naturally and wasn't at all self-conscious about how she sounded.

"You're Cam, aren't you? You work in the gardens. I've seen you there."

I nodded slowly, speechless that this veritable goddess knew *my* name.

Despite never having spoken directly before, everyone knew who *she* was. She was one of those people who commanded attention and interest, but clearly, she was blissfully unaware of it. She walked past, and conversations ceased. She spoke, and people listened. Evidently, she was so used to this response that she failed to notice her impact. Freyja was knowledgeable, self-deprecating, and charming. So very easy to talk to. One of those people who you could talk to about everything or nothing. Conversation flowed more easily after my initial embarrassment.

She was twenty-two and had been in her final year of veterinary science. Her parents were from Bergen, Norway and had migrated to Australia. Her father was a university professor in international development, her mother a psychiatrist. After several hours, I realized I had completely lost track of time, my migraine had eased considerably, and I had genuinely enjoyed talking to her.

As the dawn started to cast pink and purple-colored shadows on the wall, she looked up, startled. The time had taken her by surprise, too. Standing, she stood and said, "I hope you feel better, Cam." She turned and started walking toward her room at the other end of the hall to mine. Then as an afterthought, she turned, looked me directly in the eyes, and said, "I enjoyed talking to you."

As I stood to return to my room for a brief rest before reporting for work, I noticed a suspicious-looking stain on my pajama pants. Likely water, but unfortunately in a difficult location to conceal.

Crap. She is going to think I pissed myself.

CHAPTER 9

THE FOREST FLOOR CAME up to meet me as I adjusted my stride to the long hillwalkers' gait I had been taught as a child on long walks in the alpine national parks with my family. A long stride from the hip covers steep ascents while clearing low bushes and shrubs. Even my tiny mother could climb mountains with ease, proving that size meant nothing. "Put it in four-wheel drive," she used to encourage me when I was a child. As the sparse salt dune bushes thinned behind me, I saw that the inland foliage was more forest-like: tall trees with thick trunks, most varieties I couldn't identify. I couldn't help but feel that we were not as close to Australia as we had suspected since the landscape didn't resemble any part of Australia that I knew. Catching my breath after a particularly steep incline, I paused, turning to survey the valley below.

Recently plowed fields, rows of housing, and several prominent community spaces, all with rows of mirrored solar panels, glinted in the morning sun. The enormous electricity substation loomed in the distance. The silver shed that held the batteries for the electricity produced by the solar panels and micro-hydro systems that created the community's electrical supply was also visible. Phil, the chief engineer, whom I was on my way to meet, had told me the team desperately wanted solar, hydro, and wind turbines to give us the best shot at a fully sustainable system for the long term. But with no natural wind, wind power was out of the equation.

Solar-generated electricity operated essential items like heating and lights and a small fridge in the dorm blocks. With no way to control usage, and no real way to produce excess electricity, we were encouraged to have showers and use power during daylight hours—slightly difficult when work also needed to be completed during those hours. It went against everything we were used to—showering in the middle of the day. But that is when the sun was at its peak and the panels were producing the most power. Batteries, Phil explained, couldn't hold that much power. Although we had quite a few, they were for overnight and overcast days. It was best to use power when it was being produced by the solar panels, so it could continue to generate more.

"Hellooo!" Phil's voice rang out over the clearing near the substation. It was located on the part of the island I had not yet visited, having had few days off and mainly enjoyed exploring the rocky coastline.

"Hello there!" I responded with equal enthusiasm. Phil could be rather demanding, and a significant percentage of people here avoided him. Privately, I found him a little over-enthusiastic and always willing to press his opinion just a little further than strictly necessary. Still, despite this, he was intelligent and fundamentally had the community's best interest at heart.

Lately, I had noticed some tension between Phil and Erika, one of the carpenters. I made a mental note to stay out of any political or ideological disagreements.

The mini-hydro, he explained as we walked, was indeed a modern take on old technology. Australia had used hydropower stations since the 1950s when engineers and construction workers were assisted in migrating to Australia after World War II to build and operate the colossal Snowy Hydro[6] and smaller schemes.

Once, when returning from a school trip, we had visited the power station at Khancoban. Most of my class were bored and ended up kicking a football[7] around the carpark. But I had been fascinated by the deafening roar of the water. The engineering technology involved in using that natural force to produce electricity was quite simply phenomenal. The museum display discussed the tensions between some workers, Germans and Polish in particular, so close to the end of World War II. But they got on with the job, and many remained in Australia after the scheme was finished.

Much like us, I reflected. *We had a choice to be here, but no choice about who we were here with.*

Our mini-hydro system, being consistent, powered the larger electrical items like the lights in the

---

[6] The Snowy Mountains scheme is a hydroelectricity and irrigation complex in south-east Australia. The Scheme consists of sixteen major dams, nine power stations, two pumping stations, and 225 kilometres of tunnels, pipelines, and aqueducts that were constructed between 1949 and 1974.

[7] Football – Australian Rules Football (contact sport similar to American Grid Iron, only slightly less brutal)

kitchen, dining room, community hall, and clinic as well as the refrigerators in the kitchens. Naturally, Phil had expansion plans. He wanted to build additional generators and make the power supply more stable. Even though Phil's enthusiasm was refreshing, I zoned out after a while, unable to keep up with the technical aspects of his description.

After an hour of explanation and showing me every aspect of the plant, amidst a detailed monologue describing the intricacies of how he transmitted the power from here to the village, Phil took a breath, and I took the opportunity to interject.

"Thank you so much for your time," I gushed as genuinely as I could manage. "I really do appreciate it. It is fascinating. I must get back though—jobs to finish."

Smiling broadly, I turned and started to walk away.

"Come back anytime!" Phil called after me with enthusiasm.

Not bloody likely, I thought as I waved over my head. I would never manage to escape so quickly a second time. But at least we had something to discuss over dinner for the next few months.

CHAPTER 10

THE WEEKLY BROADCASTS FROM Melbourne and Auckland were an opportunity for the community to get together, listen in, and stay for a chat afterward. We had a single solar-powered radio, much like those Sorcha had distributed during one of her development projects in the Pacific. Broadcasts were scheduled for a Friday night, and I was often too tired to remain long. I tried to wait for the broadcast. After all, everyone would talk about it the following day, and it made sense to hear it from the source rather than individual interpretations. But I rarely stayed for the social stuff afterward. People would play instruments, sing, play popular music, talk, and dance. Not that I didn't enjoy music; I did. I just found it a little overwhelming with nearly three hundred people in one building, and exhaustion from long, hard labor didn't help. Besides, returning first to our bunkhouse meant I had it alone, at least for a short time. Sharing with nine people meant waiting for showers, toilets, and the constant need to be polite and make small-talk. For the first few weeks, this was fine, but after several months, it was wearing a little thin.

It was early May when we received the broadcast we had feared. Not only had the pandemic not slowed, but it had reached Australia. Only weeks after we had left, the Australian and New Zealand governments, fearing a catastrophe of this magnitude, had closed their borders. Implemented over four weeks, citizens who were overseas studying or working were given a window of opportunity to come home or potentially never return. No one traveled for pleasure anymore; it was simply too dangerous. But citizens and permanent residents were encouraged to choose before airports closed.

Choose where to die, I thought cynically.

Freight had been stopped. No imports or exports were permitted, minimizing the risk of contamination. Urban dwellers had been encouraged to rip out their grassed lawns and nature strips and start growing their own food, heavily subsidized by their local government. After all, this was the disaster that governments held contingency funds for. There was no point in having money and letting people dying of starvation. No one wanted a famine in addition to an outbreak of deadly protozoa. Entire communities across Asia, Africa, and Europe had already been wiped out. Northern America was heavily affected in coastal areas. South America was trying hard to contain the spread.

"It is really happening," Diana whispered to me, tears in her eyes. I put my arm around her protectively. Looking around the room, I could see the many shocked faces—scared, shocked, distraught people. Walking Diana back to her dorm, it occurred to me that despite all the testing, preparation, briefings, and hardship of the past months, not to mention the goodbyes to loved ones, some people truly believed, deep down, that this was a temporary situation. A solution would be found. A vaccination of sorts. Total faith in science. Myself, I wholeheartedly believed in science. After all, I had chosen to make it my career. But I also believed in the power of nature. Nature would always find a way: earthquakes, cyclones, tsunami. Maybe it was simply nature's turn to conquer after years of being restrained.

The following months passed without major incident, partly as we were all shell-shocked that Australia and New Zealand were now affected—our own communities and families. But around nine months after we arrived, factions developed between the residents, divides based on ideology and ongoing disagreements. Mostly this was the odd argument, usually over something petty. But occasionally, the tension would erupt into a physical altercation.

The two ringleaders were Phil, the engineer, and Erika, the carpenter. Like all disputes, no one could remember how it started. Both being strong-willed people, Phil and Erika had butted heads from the start, but now they were constantly bickering. Then it worsened. New people got involved, taking sides. Soon the conflict was all anyone talked about, and it began dividing the community.

The dispute centered on our social model. Phil considered that keeping the population together made sense—from an engineering and social cohesion perspective. He fully believed in the cohesive community model that we had been brought here to follow. Erika advocated we didn't need electricity grids and reticulated water systems to survive. People should be self-sufficient: have solar panels, biogas, and water tanks; grow their crops; and raise their own goats, chickens, and basic livestock. Erika heavily promoted a barter exchange. Phil was adamantly opposed to this. How would we divide up the land? It wasn't all suitable for housing or growing crops. We all had unique talents and skills, he argued. Erika countered that hard work would be rewarded, and the community should set the value for each product or service.

"That is fine for *you,*" Phil responded, hostilely. "We need your skill as a builder. As an engineer, *my* skills are for everyone, not one individual."

This disagreement went on for weeks and was so uncomfortable that many of us did all we could to avoid Phil, Erika, and the other key agitators. Phil took to spending each afternoon and evening in the dining room trying to engage in conversations with people who, like me, sat on the fence and tried not to get involved. Erika similarly set up camp in the community hall, which, for me at least, made her slightly easier to avoid. I could see merit in both arguments and kept thinking it would blow over. As usual, I was wrong.

Walking home one evening after dinner, I passed the door to the community hall to see Erika with a small group of supporters in a yelling match with Phil, also surrounded by advocates.

"Ahhhh shit," I said to Jamie. "Do you think we should do something?"

We stood in the open doorway watching, soon joined by much of the community, attracted by the noise. It had been going on for some time, and like most events in my life, I always seemed to miss the excitement and come in at the end. They were both visibly angry, and I saw no benefit in interrupting. All that may occur is that I end up with a black eye or missing some teeth.

We only had one dentist, so I wasn't keen on either of these outcomes.

"If you don't like it, then just *leave!*" Phil bellowed, his face beetroot with anger.

"I *will!*" roared Erika, who turned and stormed out.

Phil looked around at the spectators, seething, but now mingled with embarrassment when he realized he had a rather sizeable audience.

"Well?" he demanded.

We all trickled out of the room; clearly, the main show was now over. Only it wasn't.

The following day, Erika and roughly twenty men and women packed as much as they could carry, using some of the builder's wheelbarrows and carts. This included food, medical supplies, solar panels, and building supplies. I also noticed, with some annoyance, that Farid and Anneliese were with them and had some of the best gardening tools.

"Hey!" I started to say but felt a touch on my arm from Jamie. He shook his head at me, indicating that I should let it go. We returned our attention to the group, who were clearly taking their time to achieve the greatest antagonistic effect.

The departing group, including Jenny, the chief cook; Kai, who ran the aquaponics ponds; and Nyah, the doctor, took the main path to the opposite end of the island and over to a distinct area accessible via an isthmus. Despite being under the dome and thus protected, it was remote but had its own fresh water source and arable land. Exploration parties had been sent out on arrival, and several alternate settlement sites had been noted. On my days off, I had been there, citing it as the perfect spot for a community. But until now, we hadn't needed to expand. It had only been ten months, and our population hadn't changed. I was sad to see them go, especially Jenny, who was by far the best cook here. For a moment, I contemplated going with them, but that would mean leaving behind all of my work here, my trees, gardens, and projects I had planned for the future. I was invested here. I didn't want to get involved in politics.

Like Jenny, Kai was a tremendous loss to the community. He had known so much about aquaponics that I was desperate to learn when I had time, looking for parallels with mainstream growing. After their departure, I learned from Di that Kai had created the final drama, causing Erika's team to leave. Kai, it was revealed, wanted to charge people for his fish. He considered that payment was appropriate and had planned to set up his own private pond to barter for goods and services. Phil and his supporters of a cohesive community had adamantly opposed this. No one else had this knowledge, and we needed the fish and rice paddies to survive. Kai and Erika had argued vehemently that it was because Kai's knowledge was so valuable that he should receive a more significant benefit. Fortunately, the ponds were too big to transport, so one of the vet staff, along with Kelly from our team, were reassigned to that role. Most of the trees were in, so both teams could cope with reduced staff for a while.

One afternoon, two weeks after the defectors had left, I was working in the vegetable gardens harvesting late crops. Hearing yelling and a woman's screams coming from the aquaponics area, I dropped my tools and ran toward the noise without thinking. First to arrive, I saw that Kai and some of his colleagues had returned with a homemade trailer of sorts, intending to take the fish and plants to transplant to their new township. Kelly's screams alerted me to where she was being held by two of the building crew as Kai fished the specimens he wanted from the tanks. The noise had attracted a lot of attention, and within minutes, several people had arrived to witness the disagreement.

"Let her go," I said quietly but with a determined edge to Colin and Ezra. They looked at me, realizing that I stood at least five inches taller than either of them and quite a bit larger. They looked at each other, unmoving. Taking a step closer and resting my hand heavily on Colin's shoulder, I repeated my request in a more demanding tone.

"You don't need to hold her; she won't cause any trouble."

Recognizing that I spoke the truth, they relinquished her, and she rushed to my side, tears streaming down her reddened cheeks.

As the first person on the scene, and the one who had already intervened, the bystanders looked at me to resolve the situation. I sighed. Negotiation was not my favorite pastime, but after years of watching Mum in action, I had some idea of what a win/win outcome looked like.

"What do you need?" I asked Kai. Kai and I had always been friendly. He had no reason to be hostile.

"I need my fish. We have built new ponds. Now I need the stock."

"We need the stock too," I tried to reason with him, despite loud objections from Kai's friends. "There are far more people here, and we need to eat as well."

"They are mine," he snapped in a hostile tone. "I raised them, and now I am taking them."

Half an hour and much unnecessary bartering later, we agreed Kai would take one-third of the fish and plants. This was reasonable, we decided, as only twenty people had left and two hundred and eighty remained. Kai begrudgingly agreed, realizing that this was a good deal. Although I was sure he chose the healthiest fish, ultimately, the rest of us couldn't tell. Compared with losing everything, this was still a positive outcome.

That evening, I was greeted warmly in the dining room. Everyone wanted to stop and have a chat and congratulate me on a job well done. Seeing me struggle with the attention, Diana steered me by the arm to the table where Kelly was seated.

"Things could have been much worse," I conceded when finally seated in a quiet corner with Di, Kelly, Jacinda, and Jamie, trying to avoid all the people who wanted to rehash the day's entertainment over and over. Conflict was not something I enjoyed.

"Thank you, Cam," Kelly said softly, the gratitude evident in her voice.

"I doubt they would have hurt you," I said truthfully. "You were just in the wrong place at the wrong time."

"Regardless, I am glad you were there. I was scared."

Di put an arm around her, and I saw Kelly was indeed still shaken by the experience. Petite in stature, she had been no competition for the two much larger men.

"Well, let's hope that is the end of it," Jamie stated firmly. "We have had enough conflict for the first year."

CHAPTER 11

IN DECEMBER, TEN MONTHS after we left our homes and families to be here, the weekly radio broadcasts stopped without warning. Sitting in the hall, waiting for a few minutes, it was rare that the broadcast wasn't precisely on time. As it became obvious that the regular Friday night transmission was late, we started looking anxiously around the room at each other, wondering why the broadcast was delayed. It was the same Australian woman who introduced the segment each week. The radio was checked for faults. We usually had fifteen minutes from Melbourne, then a quick handover, and fifteen minutes of news from Auckland. After ten minutes of static, wild looks of panic filled the room. Without words, we knew what this likely meant. Waiting until the twenty-minute mark to see if New Zealand came online took an eternity. Twenty-one minutes, twenty-two. They were never late.

Some people started to cry. Others got up quietly and left the room. Others remained, comforting each other or speaking in hushed tones. Silently, we trickled out of the hall in ones and twos and made our way back to our rooms, to work or a hobby to distract us from the obvious. It was gone. We couldn't go back. Diana, seated next to me as usual, whispered, "Do you think we should go and tell the others?"

I nodded. "I'll go." Even after the situation with Kai, I was still welcomed at the new community and called many of them friends.

It hit some harder than others. Some people had believed that a solution would be found; the spread would be stopped. Several people quietly withdrew from social occasions, turning up for meals only. Interactions were more subdued, mealtimes quieter. We were alone. Completely and utterly alone. The pressure placed on us to allow humanity to survive had suddenly become a lot more real.

Despite the emotional blow, August continued to thrive, although increasingly, people moved to the new community, leaving us depleted in both number and skill. I grumbled when I discovered that yet another of the metalworkers had migrated. I needed a shovel repaired after hitting a large root and snapping the head from the handle. Now I would need to wait until the remaining guy could do it. In the months since our community had split, I had thought long and hard about each perspective, realizing that I liked the idea of being genuinely co-reliant. I grow food, someone else cooks it, and everyone is treated equally. The concept that a higher value is placed on my skill and lower on other proficiencies didn't sit well with me. How do you value a doctor's service? In reality, you only appreciate their training when you need them. But then, when you require it, it is of significant value. In my case, the skills I brought were required by all on a daily basis, but growing food in itself was not life-saving.

That is how our society in Australia had worked, with people prepared to pay a higher price for a service they perceived as being of higher value. People had a choice—premium products and services or more economical ones. Public healthcare or private. State schools or high fee private education. Wasn't that the point of coming here, to learn from the mistakes of the past, and to try to change them?

With all the conflict around ideology, a conscious decision had been made not to encourage religion in our new world. Partnerships were formalized in a civil sense—two people professed their love, and a celebration was held in their honor. Couples who declared a relationship were afforded a small private home, a two-bedroom cabin with its own basic bathroom, kitchen, and living space. The natural consequence, of course, was several expecting couples. The building team, with foresight, had been steadily building new cabins since our arrival, anticipating that eventually most people would partner up and move out of the dormitories, which would be turned into child care, schools, hospitals, and other community facilities. Built to a standard blueprint, each home was suitable for a small family, at least for the first few years.

With immense gratitude, I accepted the generous offer of one of the new cabins earlier than most singles because of my long hours working in the gardens. As much as I agreed with the principles of cohesive communities, communal living was not my thing. Eleven months of living with nine other people had been quite enough. Listening to people shower, toilet, have intimate conversations, and hearing events that should remain private was ten months too long.

Timber clad and timber-lined with wool insulation, courtesy of the island's sheep and alpaca population, my cabin was rustic, warm, and cozy with two bedrooms, one big enough for the handmade carved wooden double bed it contained, a small wardrobe, and bedside tables. The second room was empty but designed to be big enough for a cot, single bed, or possibly bunk beds. A small kitchen/dining room took up a quarter of the plan, including a fridge powered by the solar panels which also ran the lighting, aligned to maximize exposure to the sun. My kitchen had a cooktop fired by my biogas unit, which still lay flat behind the house, awaiting expansion with gas as I fed it waste.

The living room had a couch, and as a lovely touch, a bookcase—currently empty. I wasn't sure why a bookcase had been included when the only books here were in the library, but I enjoyed displaying the photographs I had brought from home. The last room was a combined bathroom/laundry. There was even a small, fenced courtyard I was dying to plant out, using the water tank that caught the condensation from the pitched roof, cleverly designed so that it all ran into the tank for re-use, a filter installed to keep the water clean.

The day I moved into my own home was one of the happiest of my life. There are no words to describe the feeling of knowing that something is *yours*. My family had owned our home, so I had always felt safe, but it wasn't mine in the same way that this was. I wondered if renters ever truly experienced the same feeling about a place—that complete sense of comfort knowing that it was your own. Placing my few possessions away in the kitchen cupboards and wardrobes, I realized that my entire life had been about collecting *stuff*: pictures on walls, displaying collectibles. None of it had been necessary, though. It had taken something catastrophic, my entire family being wiped out, for me to realize that stuff just wasn't important. What was important was *people*. But the people I wanted to be with... weren't here.

Sitting on one of the two chairs at my kitchen table, I could visualize my own childhood home on a weekend morning, Dad cooking breakfast, the radio on in the background, singing away to some dorky 1980s power ballad. Mum, Sorcha, and I at the table, eating breakfast and reading the paper. The dog or cat lurking at our feet, hoping for scraps. The picture of normality. But here, in this place, it was no longer my normal. There was no such thing here as a newspaper. Simple things that I had taken for granted. It wasn't the objects I missed; it was the *people*. Why hadn't I valued them when I had the chance?

I didn't feel the need to decorate this house, yet it still felt like my home. Looking out the kitchen window, I mentally made a note to make a planter box to grow herbs, close enough to use them fresh. Plant a lemon tree in a sunny spot in my garden.

I valued alone time, but I was not isolated. I was part of a thriving community. People knew my name and what I did and always stopped for a chat when I passed. I always had someone to sit with when in the dining room for meals or at the hall on a Saturday night when we screened movies. Despite living alone, I was never lonely.

Jamie and Jacinda were now officially partnered to the point where Diana and I were often left alone together instead of the foursome we once were. A more unusual couple I couldn't imagine, yet they seemed to balance each other out. He was quiet, reserved, and gentle while she was a free spirit, happy and outgoing. But they both loved the earth. He grew things; she made things from what he produced. They had moved into their own tiny cabin a few down from my own, leaving Di and me spending much time together, enjoying each other's company. The town gossip about us was constant: "Are they or aren't they?" I contemplated a relationship with Di at length, but Diana was like a sister. She was my best friend, and I was completely comfortable with her, but not in a relationship kind of way. I hoped she felt the same way but didn't have the courage to ask.

Despite the sadness of knowing that we were now alone, or perhaps because of it, the collective decision was made to celebrate our New Year's Day. A public holiday, our first, was declared for 20 February, August Day. One year since the dome had been placed to protect us, and we had become Augustinians rather than Australians and New Zealanders. More than once, the idea of having an August Day in February struck me as absurd, but I said nothing. It was just a name, after all, and still better than some suggestions that had been made that night. *Utopia,* this most certainly was not.

Completing my urgent tasks, I headed toward the party around midday. The celebration was in full swing, music pumping through the speakers temporarily set up outside the community hall as people stood talking in small groups. Long tables lined up outside the hall with more food than I had seen in a month. A large biogas barbeque had begun early, the smell of roasting meat filling the air from platters of beef, lamb, chicken, and pork. There was a table filled with salads, fresh bread, cheeses, beer, and wine. I noted the extensive selection of alcohol, and knowing that we had only just started making our own, was surprised to see so much laid out. Clearly, the catering team planned for this to be a memorable event.

Everyone rushed to finish essential tasks to join in the celebrations. The catering staff took turns to serve, although it looked like most of the food had been prepared well in advance. The clean-up would take place tomorrow. Today was for celebrating.

As I was friendly with most people, I had been tasked with the role of intermediary between our community and the new one; thus, I had delivered the message a week ago inviting all to the celebrations. They had named the new settlement Green Island, representing the green pastures and a fresh start. They were surrounded by people happy to see them, including me. I had missed Jenny, in particular, who had thrown her arms around me in a warm embrace when she saw me. She was happy, pregnant, and glowing with health. Hoping that there would be no nastiness between Erika and Phil, I kept a close watch as I spoke to people, but so far, everyone was in a jovial mood, aided by music and copious amounts of food and drink.

By mid-afternoon, the several hours of festivities were wearing me down. The constant thrum of noise was buzzing like a swarm of bees around my head. Unable to pick one conversation out of the din, my vision struggling to focus, I could feel my senses shutting down and that desperate need to retreat into myself. Taking advantage of the whole community gathering today, couples had chosen this as their day of celebration. As a result, there had been partnership celebrations. We were a young community. Naturally, people were pairing up and having children. I wanted to be social. I just needed some time alone, away from all this noise.

During the last ceremony, I fidgeted through the formalities of couples pledging themselves to each other, making several people turn and glare at me. Standing at the back with Diana, Jamie, and Jacinda, Diana placed her hand on my arm to calm me. Waiting for my turn in line as Amelinda, one of the vets, and Helena, the potter, walked through the guard of honor, I smiled, nodded, and wished the couple all the best as they passed.

Cautiously, I made my way to the edge of the central grassy clearing where people were still coming and going, eating, and laughing near the tables. The tables with crisp white tablecloths, only used for special occasions, were now spread with all kinds of cakes, pies, fruit, and sandwiches. It was still early and broad daylight. Six hours down, and there were six or more hours of celebrations ahead, but I couldn't stay any longer. Lingering near the furthermost table, I waited for an opportunity to make my escape, trying to make it look like I was perusing the food selection.

When the music started, Felipe, one of the doctors, who was also a talented violinist, began playing an Irish jig. People started moving toward the space allocated as a dancefloor which had been cleared for the occasion. I saw my opportunity, turned, and bolted.

A gut-deep urge to run gripped me, to get away, but I knew that flight would just attract attention. Plastering a fake smile on my face, I greeted the people I passed on the path, stopping for a few words when needed. Yes, they did look so happy. How excellent the food was, the music. Yes, the weather was lovely. After hours of celebrations, my stomach was clenched so tightly that I couldn't eat. There was too much noise, chatter, light, and sound.

Nothing annoys me more than when people jokingly say they were anxious in a way that makes it apparent that, in reality, they were nothing more than a little scared. Anxiety isn't being scared any more than a caterpillar is a python. Genuine anxiety overrides everything: unable to move for fear of dying—a bone-deep, paralyzing fear. My stomach cramps so hard with spasms wracking my body that I can't stand up straight. I can't even smell food without wanting to throw up.

Anxiety is every molecule in my body, screaming at me to *Stop! Stay safe! Don't do it! Find a hole, and hide, alone in the dark. Go to bed and block out the world. Stay in your protected place.* Everything shuts down—thoughts, senses, the ability to form complex sentences.

My palms go sweaty, my heart races, and my body just feels numb. I know I can't hear properly, so there is no point in talking *at* me. I just can't absorb it. I don't need to look in the mirror to know that I look terrible. The blood drains from my face, and black circles appear under my eyes, my cheeks sunken like a zombie. But unlike someone scared momentarily by a snake, often the paralysis doesn't pass for days.

Changing schools was like that. I had kept busy with sports and activities over the holidays: nothing momentous, just one thing a day to focus on. But the last night of the holidays, it struck me like a hammer blow to the stomach. Despite all the preparation, buying uniforms, planning routes to get there—it hit me. Change. Immense, looming change. It was like Godzilla crushing skyscrapers, moving closer and closer toward me but being trapped and unable to escape. One minute, I was playing games on my computer, the next I was unable to think, move, or breathe. Panic set in. I had made a mistake. I was better off at the school I knew, even if I had been bullied.

But new people. Strange buildings. The unknown.

The warning signs had been there for a few days. Being grumpy, snapping at people. Emotional withdrawal had been my way of dealing with anxiety when I was younger and couldn't process the feeling. As the stress increased, I withdrew into my room, my safe place. I didn't want to join in for meals and activities. I just wanted to stay *safe*.

If you had asked me any other time if I considered myself unsafe with my family, I would say, "well, of course not!" but that is the nature of anxiety—the overriding irrational fear of ordinary, everyday things. So, we withdraw. We pull into ourselves, like a snail into its shell, blocking out the world. I didn't sleep—couldn't. I was exhausted, yet my body was tensed, like I was going into battle. The night before starting school, I must have drifted off at some point but woke even more fearful. There is a weird phenomenon with anxiety. People think you can sleep it off, but the reality is that you wake even more unsettled than when you went to sleep.

The sounds of the party, laughter, and music echoed behind me as I sped up toward my home, the same fake smile plastered on my face. As I approached the last corner to freedom, I dropped my head and ran full pelt into Freyja, who was hurrying toward the party. Being larger and moving quickly, I knocked her flying, and she landed painfully on her hip as she crashed onto the path in front of me. Stunned and unable to move, it took a few seconds to jolt out of my stupor and process what had happened. Apologizing profusely, I crouched to help her up.

Dressed in a khaki skirt and white top with her long, wet blonde hair now fallen into her face, she was evidently running late for the celebrations. Time had a way of slipping by here with limited clocks and no smartphones. Freyja bent to brush the dirt off her skirt, flicking her hair contemptuously, and started to say something, her face as black as thunder. Then she looked into my face, and instead of bellowing at me as I had deserved, she cut off the insult that had been forming on her lips. She saw straight through the façade. Standing with dignity and purpose, she firmly gripped me by the upper arm, steering me down the path and into my house. Mine was the farthest away, but the closest to the vet clinic and paddocks. I needed to get to it: my sanctuary, my refuge. Relief oozed from my muscles as she closed the door firmly behind me, and I sighed with relief.

"Are you alright?" I tried to ask again, genuinely concerned. I had knocked her flying, and she had hit the ground with a sickening thud. The mud still stained her skirt. She ignored me completely. Gripping my arm, she walked me across the room and pushed me onto the couch. Freyja sat next to me, holding me by the shoulders, staring at me.

"Migraine?" she interrogated.

I shook my head, though I winced from the movement. I could feel the tingling warning signs behind my eyes of one about to start.

She pushed. "What then?"

"I'm.... I'm okay."

She gave such a manly snort of derision that I laughed. Never had I heard such a tall, graceful goddess of a woman snort like that! Realizing I had no escape, and that she would not tolerate any lies, I told her—all of it. Starting with a few words, it became a torrent unleashed of emotion, stress, and worry.

She listened calmly and without comment until I was done. I sighed and wilted. *Well, that was that then. Soon the entire village would know.*

"So, how do you deal with it?"

I shrugged, still looking down, unable to make eye contact. I picked up a pen that sat on the small table beside me and fiddled with it.

"I don't really know. You develop little coping strategies. For me, I just focus on one little thing."

"Like what?"

"Something tiny, like... getting out of bed. When I have accomplished that, I tackle getting dressed. Small steps. Set a goal, no matter how small, and achieve it."

The part I didn't mention was that there had been days of my life when even simple things like brushing my hair was a challenge I just didn't feel up to. The warm, encouraging look from her sparkling green eyes motivated me to continue, even though I had never exposed this part of myself to anyone before, not even the many psychologists my parents had engaged over the years. As the words flowed naturally, it astonished me I was doing it now.

"For some people, a hot shower is calming. For me, I hate stripping off. I hate being naked and feeling vulnerable. It is that space *between* being clothed and being immersed in warm water that I struggle with. Of course," I smiled, and genuinely this time, "once I am actually *in* the shower, I feel safe and then don't want to get out. I could live there. How I miss long hot showers," I said, drifting off, remembering the sensation of a long hot shower with fabulous water pressure. Here the showers were gravity-fed and barely lukewarm. Basically, tolerable water dripping onto you. There was no desire to linger in a shower.

Freyja studied me with that direct stare of hers, then reached a conclusion.

"Come with me."

It was a tone that brooked no disagreement. She would have been the perfect military commander. Putting down the pen I was fidgeting with, I obediently followed her. She pointed to my solid walking boots, muddy but waterproof and with good grip, and I changed into them, a puzzled look on my face. But she didn't speak. I didn't ask. We stopped at my old dormitory, the one where she still lived, for her to change into jeans and a t-shirt before putting on walking shoes. As I skulked outside, unable to deal with meeting anyone else, she returned from her room carrying a small backpack. With no time for me to ponder why, she set a cracking pace, choosing a path up into the hillside behind the medical center, a small, lightly worn path, clearly not one well-traveled by people, and a path I had not previously explored.

I walked the first part in silence, still embarrassed about my earlier revelations about my anxiety.

She chatted about the weather, the goings-on of the shared house since I had left, and the animals she was raising. She had been late to the party as a hembra, a female alpaca, had given birth to twins and needed some help. Recognizing that I couldn't allow her to continue running a monologue, I finally let my guard down and joined the conversation, telling her about the crops, my plans for a vineyard. Neutral things. When we reached the steeper parts, we stopped talking altogether. Despite being only a few inches off my own height, she had legs that were built for walking: long, lean, and lightly muscled. I struggled slightly to keep up, trying not to puff audibly and have her judge me unfit. Within half an hour, we had reached a plateau at the top. From this vantage point, we could see through the transparent dome and out to sea, crystal blue ocean as far as the eye could see. Thoughts drifted to my family across that sea, wondering whether they were still alive or suffering a slow, agonizing death. Clearly, my face showed what I was thinking as Freyja put an end to my musings by abruptly barking, "Come on. Not far now," and taking off up the slope like a mountain goat.

Sighing heavily, I followed, wondering why on earth I was following this bossy woman—with whom I had spoken a grand total of once—up a hillside on what felt like a nature walk when I really just wanted to be alone, curled up in my bed in the dark. Safe and at peace.

Abruptly, she stopped at a rocky outcrop with a cleared level patch of dirt in front. There was nothing special about it, except that a large and established bush, bent in an unusual shape, grew almost horizontally out of the earth. The plant had long, thin branches with needle-shaped leaves, green at the roots and almost orange at the tips. From my time working in the nursery, I was reasonably sure it was called an inaka. It was several meters in diameter but grew in a straggled aspect.

Another plant not native to Australia, I considered abstractedly. There had been a sample at the nursery back in Melbourne. Memory told me they grew in the southern parts of New Zealand, though. Freyja pushed it aside and disappeared.

Following her, I realized with a jolt that the huge bush was concealing a tunnel, narrow at the entrance, less than a meter across, and more than a meter high. I squeezed in behind her, a little worried about getting stuck in the tiny space. To my astonishment, within a few paces, I could stand upright. Filtered light came through the camouflaged entrance, just bright enough to make out the rocky floor and walls. The cave we stood in was about three meters wide by six or seven meters deep and barely high enough for my six-foot frame to stand upright, although it took a few minutes for me to feel safe about walking around without cracking my skull on the rocky ceiling.

I could feel the roof brush the top of my scalp in places, so I moved slowly and with care. Rounded walls displayed shades of sandstone, gold, and yellow. Stalactites dripped from the roof near the edges, almost to the floor in places, thousands of years old. The rocks looked wet; I touched the wall. They *were* wet; it was undoubtedly warm in here and humid from the stale, moist air. Freyja smiled at my astonishment and switched on a torch pulled from her backpack.

Watching Freyja in the gloom, I took several paces, following her to the back of the cave. There was a rocky shelf midway along the back wall, and in the dim light, I just spotted her doubled over to fit through a narrow crevice, almost like a tunnel. Not really liking enclosed spaces and being significantly larger, I hesitated. She sensed my resistance as she looked over her shoulder and called back, "It isn't far. But I promise it is worth it."

Feeling panic rising, my heart rate increasing, and my palms sweating, I knew I needed to get back out into the fresh air outside. But humiliation is a fantastic motivator. Not wanting to look like a coward in front of this gorgeous self-possessed woman—who knew my name no less—I took a deep breath, exhaled heavily, and crouched into a position where I could maneuver myself down the narrow passageway. Taking a step, then another, I squeezed myself along the underground passageway. Unable to close my eyes for fear of tripping on the uneven, rocky floor, I focused instead on counting my footsteps on each exhalation. Six, seven, eight. On my ninth step, I stepped out into the opening of an enormous cavern.

The ceiling rose abruptly and was suddenly much higher than me. Straining my eyes to see the top, I could make out cracks where flashes of sunlight trickled through. Straightening up slowly, I took it all in as my eyes adjusted to the dim light. The cave sloped down slightly toward a crystal clear, pale jade pool that took up the lower half of the cavern. The pool lapped against the far wall of the grotto, like it was built to contain it. Directly in front of me, several roughly hewn steps of rock led into the pool edge nearest us. Freyja turned her torch off and stepped to the side to aid my first view of the spectacular space. The light filtering from the passageway and natural cracks in the ceiling above was just bright enough to illuminate the space, the water glowing a beautiful aquamarine. As my eyes adjusted, I gasped when I saw it. The naturally dirty brown and black-colored walls were glinting with veins of silver, wet glossy black, and shades of metallic luster. Freyja turned to me with more enthusiasm than I had ever seen in her usually calm demeanor.

"Do you like it? Isn't it *wonderful!*" She was positively reverberating with excitement.

She took the three steps down to the water's edge, and to my absolute astonishment, stopped at the steps, stripped off, dropping her clothes on a nearby rock, and waded into the pristine pool completely naked.

"Come *on!*" She repeated in a tone that strongly suggested that I was not to argue.

I didn't. Following her down to the steps and not wanting to feel like a prude, I also stripped off, realizing as I did so that a year of hard labor had left me trim and somewhat defined. As the water touched my foot, I sucked in my breath audibly. It was hot! Not just lukewarm, but seriously hot, much like the Japanese onsens I had visited with my father.

"Wow!" was all I could say, knowing that it was woefully inadequate.

A low chuckle filled the cavernous space. "Do you like it?"

I blinked and took a few steps, the water now up to my waist. She was floating on her back, and I registered the distinct mineral scent. Natural mineral springs. A few more steps, and the bottom fell away entirely. It was far deeper than it first appeared. For a pool roughly fifteen meters by ten meters in size, it was deceptively deep in the center. Keeping my head above water, I took the few strokes to the far wall of the cave, discovering a ledge several meters wide. It was warm to the touch and strangely charged.

"It is glorious," I breathed as I let my entire body relax. My legs floated out from under me, buoyed by the natural minerals, feeling weightless. The stress evaporated from my body as I lay there, floating with my eyes closed, absorbing the sheer blissfulness of the warmth, the water, and the room. I hadn't had a bath since I left home, and never had I considered it something I would miss. Usually, I had a quick shower at home. I rarely lingered in a bath, risking my parents or sister barging in. But the option had always been there. But now, with the limited water available, every drop was precious. Four-minute showers and even that water was captured, recycled, and reused.

There were hot mineral springs about an hour's drive from my home in Melbourne. My parents had been and loved it. I couldn't imagine anything worse than taking a hot bath with a group of strangers. But here... this was different. Closing my eyes, I relinquished my last scrap of control. It was simply divine to float, drifting effortlessly in a hot mineral bath. The serenity and total relaxation engulfed me with no judgment, no interruption.

The slow, deliberate, but decidedly passionate kiss startled me so much that I jerked and sank, torso first, feet and arms flailing. Instinctively, I opened my mouth, gulping a large volume of water as I submerged, choked, and started coughing. This coughing spasm made me go under again in the deepest part of the pool. Hot, heavily mineralized water is not pleasant to swallow, and it took me some minutes to regain control of myself. Freyja pulled herself up to sit on the wide ledge as I was clutching onto it, trying not to die, looks of amusement and concern competing on her face. When she realized I was fine, hilarity won out. She laughed so hard that she doubled over, clutching her stomach, trying to control herself.

Annoyed that she was laughing at me, I grabbed her by the waist and pulled her off the shelf. As she slid off, her legs wrapped around my waist, she cupped her arms behind my head and kissed me again, but this time I was ready. Kissing her thoroughly, I simultaneously ran my hands down her athletic body, making her shiver with delight. My hands learned what her body already knew; we were better together than apart. Unable to keep myself from caressing her warm, velvety skin as I lifted her back onto the pro-truding ledge, she responded to my touch in a manner that suggested I better not stop.

Several hours later, we left the hot springs in the dark of the night, together and inseparable, ready to face the new year. The return trip took far longer as we stopped every few hundred meters, unable to keep our hands from each other. I was tingling all over; she had made her desire evident, and I had no say in the matter. Not that I cared. She was a goddess. Charming, stunning, intelligent.

And she had chosen *me.*

CHAPTER 12

WE SAT APART AT mealtimes and were careful not to be seen together, not wanting to draw attention to our fledgling clandestine relationship. It was ours, private, not to be shared.

Di and I continued to spend much public time together, and people assumed we were, or would become, a couple.

The springs were our private place, and I was grateful that, of all people here, she had chosen me to share her secret. We met surreptitiously whenever our schedules would allow, always being careful not to be followed. Gossip ran rampant in a close community like this, and everyone knew everyone else's business. While this could be a positive thing, people knew if you were sick or injured, and everyone helped; keeping a secret was exceedingly difficult and required a great deal of foresight and planning.

"Goodness, can you imagine the gossip if Ilana saw us together?" I whispered once to Freyja, furtively looking around before gathering her in and kissing her passionately as I delivered a box of early apples that had fallen from a tree.

"Well, the world would know in roughly six minutes," she whispered tantalizingly into my ear while running her hands up the inside of my shirt and raking her fingers down my chest. "And I enjoy having something that is just *mine*." She kissed me with such intensity that it took my breath away before pulling back slightly and whispered, "Though I do miss mobile phones. It was so much easier when you could just message someone."

Knowing that we could be seen at any moment where we stood in the open outside the vet sheds, I reluctantly inhaled, breathing in her sweet scent, and stepped back. "Do you miss social media?"

To my surprise, Freyja blushed. "I missed social media when we first arrived," she confessed. "It was just what we *did,* you know? You saw something, snapped a photo, and uploaded it for your friends to see. Not that all of them were friends in the genuine sense of the word. I didn't really have many real friends," she confessed shyly. "Women tend not to like me very much."

Not wanting to pursue that observation, I admitted, "What I never realized until I came here was that for me, social media replaced the need for actual interactions. Some people used it to show off their real-life social connections: who had been to a particular restaurant, watched a movie, checked in at a holiday resort. For me, that was a relief. If I knew who was dating, who had broken up, I didn't need to engage with them *in person* and talk about it. I already knew, and they assumed I knew as they had made that news public. But sometimes, it became a problem that fed my anxiety. Why were my friends at a party and I wasn't invited? Had I offended someone? Then there were the people who broke big news like an engagement or break-up via social media with the rationalization that they had told the news once, and that was all they needed to do. Then if you missed it, the next in-real-life meeting was awkward. The problem was that there is absolutely no empathy when you are engaging with a screen. I wonder now if that lack of empathy is partially responsible for the situation we all got into. Placing such a high value on buying the newest phone or gadget, being seen to check in to the coolest club, but not focusing on what really mattered."

"What really matters to you, Cam?" she asked coyly.

"You," I said simply, before kissing her again, not caring if I was seen.

Several glorious weeks passed where we tried to meet most days, sharing furtive kisses, clandestine visits to the springs, late-night visits to my house with Freyja leaving before dawn to avoid being seen. On one visit to the grotto, as we pushed past the inaka bush concealing the cave entrance, it occurred to me to ask, "Honey, how did you even find this place? It isn't exactly signposted."

A low-pitched, utterly charming laugh resonated back down the tunnel. "Fred!" she called back.

"Fred?"

"You know that noisy white cashmere goat with the black face that is always busting out and exploring? Well, I named him Fred after Fred Flintstone. He is gorgeous, but not that bright, even for a goat, who are notoriously not blessed with intelligence as a species.

One day he went missing, again, and I was tracking him. He leaves such a mess behind him, so he isn't hard to follow. I found some of his droppings outside on the ledge. I would never have found this place otherwise. He was standing in the outer cave, waiting for me. He wouldn't follow me but kept nudging me to the back of the cave. I didn't have a torch at the time, so I was a little apprehensive, but he was nudging me really insistently. Purposefully. So, I took a chance, hoped like hell he didn't have a murderous streak and wasn't planning to entrap me, and I found... this. When I was inside the inner cave, I realized my compass didn't work, so I have always thought that there must be something magnetized somewhere. But it works fine from the outside, so it can't be very strong. So," she corrected, "technically, *I* didn't find it. Fred showed me."

"Remind me to thank him," I murmured as I leaned in to kiss her as she undressed.

"You should," she said pointedly as she playfully dodged my kiss. "Heidi hates him and wants him gone. Never met a vet that disliked a simple creature like a goat," she mused as we entered the sea-green pool.

Floating on my back and staring up at the stalactites hanging from the ceiling, I murmured, "Thank you, Fred. And thank *you* for sharing this place with me."

The events that followed were thanks enough.

Before my flesh cooked and fell off my bones, I reluctantly pulled myself from the steaming water that changed from jade to olive to emerald and turquoise, depending on the time of day and the light that filled the cavern. To avoid unwanted attention, we brought no towels or items that may look like we were going somewhere together or leaving the community with a purpose. Standing in the cavern, the rising steam that filled the room air-dried me, and I spent some time poking around the dirty brown and black walls of the cave. As the light from the entrance hit the side wall, I noticed a distinct silver thread running through the stone.

"Hun—did you bring a torch?" Freyja had a higher tolerance for the heat than I, possibly her Norwegian heritage and all those saunas her ancestors had enjoyed. For me, sustained heat was a trigger for migraines, so I was mindful of my tolerance limit. Turning to watch Freyja reluctantly extracting her tall, graceful form from the water, her hair dripping down her back, I mentally pinched myself for the millionth time that I could be so damned lucky. The heat was too much for me after half an hour, but almost as soon as I had cooled back to normal body temperature, there was a hunger to immerse myself in the healing waters again.

Freyja bent to pull a small torch from her pants pocket, which she had left on a small rocky shelf that jutted slightly over the edge of the pool, adjacent to the natural rock steps. She took several strides across the cavern and handed it to me with a kiss so purposeful that I nearly forgot what I was looking for.

Smiling with the complete satisfaction of one who had accomplished their mission, Freyja sprawled on a step, drying herself, as I turned back to the far wall. Moist with the heat, dark and strangely static, I shined the torch at the wall. Feeling the strange vibrations, I ran my finger down the silvery spiderweb of thread and felt an energy that drew me closer. Closing my eyes, I could sense the cave gently vibrating all around me, dark, shadowy, and mysterious.

I must ask one of the engineers what type of rock this is, I thought absently as my thoughts returned. *At least one of them must have studied geology.*

Reluctantly turning to go, I nearly missed it. As I turned, torch held at chest height, my foot caught the edge of an enormous stone on the ground.

"Oww!" I exclaimed, bending to rub my skinned little toe. Standing, I turned the torch to point down, and the beam of light illuminated what had previously been in shadow. It was pure luck that I saw it. A set of strange carvings on the back of the large stone on the side facing the outer cave wall, living in the darkness. An enormous menhir[8] was lying flat along the side of the cave. Peering closely in the low light, I realized it hadn't naturally formed there. This monolith had been intentionally placed and had fallen at some point. Scanning the torch around the stone floor, I could just make out the indentation in the ground where it had originally stood. Studying the carvings, I ran my fingers down the patterns, feeling guilty but strangely electric as I did so. My finger traced the large spirals, joined in patterns of two or three. A memory stirred. *They had a name. Triskeles? Triquetra? At the edge of the spirals was a circle, and a chevron. I had seen something like this before—but where? A museum? One of mum's books?*

Sensing Freyja standing close behind me to see what had caught my attention, I realized I must have been staring at it, oblivious to her presence.

"Wow. That is beautiful." She gently traced her finger around one of the spirals. "I think this is quite old."

---

[8] A standing stone, usually prehistoric, can be single or part of a series of standing stones

"It is," I responded, touching it tentatively, feeling like I was in a museum and shouldn't be touching the display. "We certainly aren't the first people here."

As soon as the words were out, we looked at each other in shock. There was no evidence on the island that people had been here before us. We returned our attention to the lying menhir and looked at the rock with greater interest.

"It looks so... familiar." I was struggling to recall where I had seen such a design before. Freyja could sense my irritation.

"What is wrong?"

"I have seen this before. This design."

"I gather you are a little distracted and can't remember where," she teased, gently nibbling my earlobe from behind me and started kissing the side of my neck. She knew that was my sensitive spot and loved exploiting any weakness.

Taking the torch from my hand, she started exploring further afield while I crouched, unable to remove my fingers from the spirals carved into its surface, wracking my brain to remember where I had seen it. Somewhere I had visited? I had physically seen this pattern, I knew.

A few minutes later, Freyja called out, "Cam! Over here!"

With immense reluctance, I left the monolith bearing the strange design and carefully made my way to where she was standing at almost the exact place on the opposite wall. A second large menhir, almost identical in size, but this one still stood, the carved side facing the pool. This one had only one spiral, various small circles, and a series of diamonds.

"This is very Celtic," I muttered. "I can't believe we haven't noticed this before."

"Celtic? Here?" Freyja looked at me in surprise. "We traveled a fair bit in South America, Africa, Asia, and the Pacific. My parents wanted us to experience different cultures, especially developing ones where my father did his work. After they migrated to Australia, we returned to Europe every second year to Norway to visit my grandparents, although we did a stopover in London or other parts of Europe."

Nodding, I said, "I have told you before that my mother is Scots. We traveled quite a bit across Scotland and Ireland. This looks very much like Celtic designs I have seen before at ancient sites. Possibly older. Pict maybe, not Celt. I'm no expert. What I can't work out is how they ended up *here*. On an island off the southern coast of Australia. Literally in the middle of nowhere."

Searching the cave and inner tunnel thoroughly, we turned up nothing else of interest.

Reluctantly, we dressed, checked that we had left nothing behind, and made the slow descent back into town. Our routine was to avoid being seen together and sparking unwanted gossip. Freyja went via the animal pens, and I went directly home. We paused behind the enormous kauri tree, our regular last-goodbye place, before we left each other. The farewells were getting harder and harder as was keeping our secret. But it was important to us that we kept this strictly private. I pulled her close, and we held each other for the longest time.

"I love you, Freyja Jorgensen," I murmured in her ear.

"And I *you,* Campbell Mackintosh."

At that moment, I could have sworn that I felt my heart burst.

CHAPTER 13

"I MISS SUNDAYS," I murmured.

"Hmm?" asked Freyja, lying naked next to me, her arm leisurely resting on my stomach. She was dozing but not asleep. We had long since given up any pretense of not being a couple. As my closest friends here, Diana, Jamie, and Jacinda had been let in on the secret early, knowing that they would both support us and not betray our confidence. Freyja had moved into my place seven weeks after our first visit to the hot springs with no public fanfare. The longer nights and shorter days of winter meant we now had greater periods at home—alone.

"I haven't thought about it in years. Sundays. It was the day we spent as a family. Mum always cooked a roast; the smell of roasting meat used to fill the house. Each weeknight had been filled with sport or activities, Mum attending meetings, Dad often working, so we had rushed meals, often reheated in the microwave. But Sundays were always family night. Mum had insisted on it. One night a week where we sat as a family and talked. Teased each other, really caught up, and connected. After we cleaned up, we played games—poker, Monopoly, Scrabble. As we got older, Cards against Humanity. Basic stuff, but it wasn't about the game. I didn't know it at the time, but it was only about spending time together. The simple things you do as a family that you kind of fit in around the busyness of life."

"The business of life or the busy-ness of life?" Freyja asked.

"Both, I guess. Life is going to work, school, paying bills, following rules, isn't it? But family time, however you get it, is so important. You realize how hard families have to work to actually be a family. When I was younger, I thought you chose a partner. You had kids, and wham! Instant family. But what I know now is that isn't what makes a family. Family has nothing at all to do with blood. A family is the people you know will always support and nurture you. The people who truly know you, look out for you. Knowing someone else has your back, will always *be* there if you need them. Mum once described it as knowing that there was someone in the world you trusted so much that you knew, without even asking, that they would help you hide a body."

"I would, you know."

"I know. As I would, for you," I murmured as I ran my hand down the length of Freyja's spine, making her shiver with delight.

A surge of regret struck me as I thought of Sorcha and Sam. She had loved him so deeply. Had chosen him to be her family, her husband. Following hours of unanswered calls, I had gone with her. Her blood-curdling screams echoing through the tiny apartment is a sound I will remember until the day I die—until then, I hadn't realized that there was a sound of grief. The look on her face at that moment when she saw him, lying there in his bathtub, wrists opened to the elbows, drenched in a pool of his own blood–the expression of love and hope transitioning to disbelief and despair in a split second. Shoes lined up neatly next to the tub, clothing carefully folded on a nearby chair. His eyes, wide open in shock. Hers in betrayal. I will never forget picking her up after she hit the floor, carrying her to the couch, and calling an ambulance. The rest was a blur. Closing my eyes, I tried to focus on the sequence of events after that, illuminated with flashing lights of red and blue.

"My family used to take holidays," Freyja said suddenly, rolling onto her side to face me, pulling me from my melancholy. "Not often. Sometimes only once a year. We weren't a normal family. In that we weren't close, I mean. We only spent time together whenever my parents could align their schedules. I didn't appreciate how busy, how important they were back then. They both did vital jobs and helped people. But I hated them for it. I resented the fact that they weren't there every evening like my friends' parents. Most of my school friends had a father who worked, but mums who generally didn't. A mum who picked them up from school in their flashy cars and took them to sports, parties, or clothes shopping. Mine did not." Freyja closed her eyes. "I yelled at my mother at least a dozen times, trying to make her feel guilty that she worked and all of my friends' mums didn't. But she never berated me for it. I know they paid for the best private schools and opportunities they could afford, but what I wanted was *them*. We never had a regular Sunday dinner. I had a nanny when I was young, then childcare, and after-school care in primary school. By upper primary school, I was getting myself there and home and often cooking meals for Katrin and myself. I went to sport, I played hockey, and I swam competitively. They would leave me money and let me buy my gear. Anything I wanted, really. It made me independent from a young age, I guess. I never really recognized how much effort they put into taking us on a family holiday. We went skiing or sailing most years and did it as a family most days, once Katrin and I knew how. As I got older, it was trips to developing countries where my father was overseeing aid projects. Africa, Asia, the Pacific. Even Papua New Guinea and East Timor. But sometimes, not always, we stopped somewhere on the way home, just for a few days. Hawaii, Disneyland, Sea World. On those holidays, they never put us into a kid's program or got a babysitter. Not even for a single dinner. They spent all day, every day, with Kat and me."

She paused, recalling something that made her smile.

Touching her arm gently, I prompted her to continue.

"Every holiday, Mum had a ritual of getting a family photo with all of us in it. She said that someone always missed out otherwise as they were taking the photo." Freyja rolled her eyes. "I used to hate posing for professional photos and couldn't wait until the serious one was done so I could pelt a snowball or flick water into my sister's face. I never thought about it at the time, but... I loved those holidays. I felt so... connected for that short time. Then we would come home and... well, things went back to normal." Freyja trailed off, and her eyes gazed off into the distance, clearly remembering holidays with her family. She didn't mention her family often, and I wondered if I should ask. I didn't want to invade her private memories. I could tell by her tense posture and shadowed eyes it had clearly taken her to a less than pleasant place.

"It will be different here, honey," I murmured, trying to lighten the mood. "There are no schools yet, especially not elite private schools with ties and blazers. No nannies. Certainly no capacity for holidays with babysitters or kids' clubs."

"Oh, I intend to take our children to work with us," Freyja answered like it was the most natural thing in the world.

I rolled on my side to look at her, wondering if I dare draw attention to those powerful, beautiful words just in case she took them back. I held my breath, waiting.

Anticipating.

"Yes," she said, her voice dripping with sarcasm and exaggeratedly rolling her eyes as she looked at me. "I said our children." She smiled. "I would never outsource the raising of our child, not like happened to Katrin and me. We will co-parent," she announced with absolute conviction. She had made her decision.

Rolling toward her, my body leaning against hers, I reached over and cupped her smooth, tanned cheek lightly with my large, calloused hand. "I would like that very much."

CHAPTER 14

ONE GLORIOUS SPRING DAY in October, after harvesting a particularly delicious crop of sun-ripened tomatoes and salad vegetables, I took a small basket up to Freyja. Spring was a busy time for her, and she rarely stopped for lunch, births and animal maintenance keeping her busy from dawn to dusk.

Freyja was in the paddock of Dorper sheep, a pretty breed with black faces and necks, but white bodies and wool, looking very much like someone had stuck the wrong black head on a white sheep body. A hardy breed, they coped well in the temperature extremes, but equally significantly, they dropped their wool, meaning one less job for the staff. Scratching one of the sweet Dorper sheep behind the ears evoked memories of our family dogs and that time in my life when I had contemplated becoming a vet myself. That triggered me to ask, "Frey, what made you want to become a vet?"

The sheep she held was having its hooves trimmed. She bleated in protest, but Freyja ignored it. "Well,

I was good at science, and I didn't want to work with people."

"So, not memories of your own pets then?" My entire life, we had shared with pets, evoking joyful memories: the two enormous loyal St. Bernard dogs we had as young children. I recalled waking unable to feel my legs and finding one of them sleeping on me— Khan, the enormous fawn Great Dane my parents had adopted when I was about ten. Mum had been told that he was a "puppy" who needed re-homing. When she arrived to adopt him, she discovered that he was huge, and Mum needed to fold him in half to cram him onto the back seat of her little hatchback. Devoted to us but fundamentally a coward, Khan had a head like a football, was big enough to take down a wildebeest, but was petrified of water. He would panic and run along the bank of a river, barking madly if we went in a canoe or boat. Later, we had Odin, the schnauzer.

Then there was the collection of cats who had owned us over the years who also held a special place in my heart. Merlin most recently, but also tubby Wookiee, a glossy black boy who had kitty psych issues and stole the dog's food. Oscar, the opinionated gray tabby who liked to climb on the roof, then meow at us when we walked outside. Oscar had been my constant companion when I had glandular fever[9] at seventeen. Always asleep beside me, he would accompany me everywhere. He had appointed himself my protector and didn't sleep elsewhere until I was well and returned to school. Smiling, I remembered them all, their personalities, and the unconditional love of what mum had called her fur children.

---

[9] Mononucleois (mono)

"We never had a pet," Freyja responded to my question without rancor. "My parents were simply too busy. I begged them when I was young, but it never happened. A cat, dog, horse, even a rabbit, but they wouldn't allow it. Once I found a sweet ginger kitten on my way home from school. He had the most gorgeous face. I took him home, made a bed for him, and fed him. I named him Pierre. By the time my parents arrived home, I was already besotted. I cried, begged to keep him. He was homeless. No one wanted him. But they insisted no, we must find the kitten's owner, and took him from me. I never saw him again. Every birthday or Christmas, I secretly hoped this is the year—but it never was. So eventually, I stopped hoping and stopped asking."

My heart shattered for her in that moment. Sharing life with a pet was one of the joys of living. They trusted you, and you worshipped them, spoiling them for the comparatively short time they had to share with you.

"Is that why you wanted to be a vet?" I asked kindly.

Freyja shrugged. "It took me a long time to realize that I resented all the unknown people that needed my parents during my childhood. I was bitter at them for never being around. You wouldn't think it, but a lot of science is dealing with people. I just couldn't see myself doing a research job in a laboratory. So, I chose veterinary science. I get a lot of diversity, a variety of different animals with different pathology and medical issues, which I find really interesting. They can't tell you what is wrong, so diagnostically, I enjoy that. It is kind of cool to investigate something when the patient is clearly unwell but can't tell you what they are feeling. They also can't complain like people."

She stood, slapped the sheep gently on the rump, and the indignant sheep ran off to re-join the flock, protesting loudly at her perceived mistreatment.

Casting my eye around the green grassy field with timber fencing separating some of the animals, I noted, "Well, you certainly have a lot of animals now. "

"I do," she admitted. "But none of them are pets. It is different."

"I guess it is." There was no such thing as a pet here. We couldn't afford to become attached to animals that may one day end up on our plates. Silently, I wondered at what point a society started to have such luxuries as pets, animals who served little purpose aside from companionship and love, a devotion that I had always known. A dog who excitedly greeted you at the door and made it obvious that they missed you. A cat who sensed your mood and came and slept on your lap or curled up next to you in bed.

Fred bleated from his adjacent field. He could see Freyja, whom he adored and would follow around everywhere if he had the chance. We started walking over to him, Freyja carrying her black leather bag of equipment. All the animals knew what that bag meant. Fred was unusual in that he just didn't care. Bad attention was better than no attention, as far as he was concerned.

"Except Fred," she murmured as an afterthought. "He is special."

Fred was special. Fred had found our special place, had been responsible for bringing us together. Fred was bouncing up and down in his excitement, ecstatic that Freyja, with whom he was enamored, was coming over to him. Without warning, he let out a high-pitched squeal followed by a series of shrill cries. Freyja dropped her bag and sprinted. Picking up the bag, I followed.

By the time I reached her, she had leaped the fence and was on the ground holding him in her lap. A large white cashmere goat with a dark face and large somber eyes that made him look more intelligent than he actually was, he looked soulfully into hers. Two small horns indicated his relative youth. His winter coat was coming off in handfuls. Freyja gently pulled the wool away as she examined him and collected it abstractedly into a pile. Goat cashmere was valuable and highly useful. We only had a small flock, mainly fathered by Fred. Since living here, I had learned that our breeds of sheep and goats molted their coats if not shorn, and I found the process fascinating. Aside from some small clumps, it came off like a blanket.

"Is he ok?" I asked, concerned, as I hurdled the fence carrying her bag.

She was stroking his neck with one hand and crooning to him like a baby. This was the first inkling I had ever had of her maternal instinct, deeply hidden as it may be, and I tried to suppress a smile.

"He is fine," she said to me as she continued to palpate his legs. "He has pulled a ligament, I think. It isn't a break." She addressed Fred in a reassuring, motherly tone.

"You are a lucky boy. Nothing is broken this time. This is what you get for being a fool, though." He butted her affectionately with his head.

She looked up at me. "Cam, do you think you could carry him?"

I considered for a moment. Fred was a big goat, but he couldn't be heavier than forty kilograms.

"Sure. Where do you want me to take him? One of the sheds?"

"Our place."

Opening my mouth to protest, I thought better of my objections and promptly closed it. Who was I to say that Freyja couldn't have a pet goat? Me, who had been surrounded by animals all my life. If I could share this joy with her, I should. Fortunately, it was mostly flat from the goat paddock to our place. Our home being at the end of the row, deliberately chosen so that I didn't feel surrounded by people. I had dreams of building a cottage further up the hills, the two of us alone in an isolated green valley with views of the mountains and ocean. For now, that would have to wait.

Freyja continued berating Fred all the way to our house. Oblivious to the actual words Freyja was using, Fred continued to baa lovingly at her in reply, intermittently chewing on my hair, which was quite long by now. Lifting one shoulder to dissuade him from chewing on my hair, Freyja laughed, pushing his nose away. That just made him more determined, so I adjusted my grip so his front legs were over my shoulders and he was facing behind me. Freyja slipped behind me so she could continue to talk to him, and Fred enjoyed this immensely. Being carried and simultaneously being spoken to like a naughty toddler gave him the attention he so clearly desired.

"Where are we going to put him?" I asked as we neared the houses.

This took quite a bit of negotiation. I had only recently designed and planted a small herb and vegetable garden, which would last precisely three minutes if Fred was allowed access to it. Our tiny spare bedroom held our coats and boots, so that was also out, unless I wanted randomly nibbled clothing. So, it came about that Fred temporarily moved into our tiny bathroom. Having an active observer each time I needed to use the toilet or shower and continually cleaning up goat pellets hurriedly made me prioritize enclosing part of the garden away from the vegetable patch. I also began immediate plans for the shed that I had been putting off building for months.

After his relocation, Fred greeted me each morning at the kitchen window, seeking toast crusts or scraps of food instead of chewing on my towel as I showered. He loved being scratched along his neck and was better than any watchdog I had ever owned, bleating loudly when anyone walked past and butting them indignantly if they dared walk toward our door.

Secretly, I was thrilled. Unannounced visitors I didn't appreciate, although I was always happy to have planned guests. Friendly, not social, is how Mum had described me. Happy to chat, share a meal, and make plans. Not good in a large group or party. Fred became our protector, a dopey, loving creature with a fixation on Freyja and now, by association, me.

CHAPTER 15

"**DO YOU EVER FEEL** guilty for being chosen?" I asked Freyja one afternoon as I wrote in the logbook about the crops we had planted: what was thriving, what wasn't. It was nearly harvest time, and it was essential to keep track of our successes for future years.

Freyja looked up from her battle, trying to mend the hole in her sock in surprise.

"Chosen? To come here?"

I nodded and repeated my question. "Do you feel guilty? That you were chosen, I mean."

"Guilt? No." She sounded a little incredulous.

Perhaps I wasn't explaining myself very well. I tried again. "Really? You don't wonder... why me? Why was *I* chosen?"

"No. I know why I was chosen. We all went through the same testing."

I sighed, and she sensed my frustration.

"But you do?" she asked, rather tersely.

"All the time. There are no children here, no one under twenty, no one over thirty either. No one with medical conditions. Don't you feel like, well, like it was a little bit... discriminatory?"

"Discriminatory? No." The look of incredulousness was turning into annoyance. I knew that look well. Sorcha had often sported that look right before she called me an idiot or a moron.

"Why on earth would you feel that? There is a wide mix of races and cultures here. In fact, I think they did a great job in ensuring a representative sample of cultures were included."

"Maybe not discriminatory then. Maybe, well, unfair."

An exasperated sigh erupted from her chest. "The word you are looking for is Darwinism," she announced, a touch harsher than was absolutely necessary.

I cringed at the word. "Natural selection, you mean? Survival of the fittest? But it *wasn't* natural selection, was it? It was a very calculated process to choose some people over others. We all sat a battery of tests and medical assessments. Then a group of nameless people in lab coats made a choice—you, me, but not thousands, actually, millions of others."

"What's your point?" she asked, rather hotly, slamming down her sock.

I faltered there. I wasn't sure I had one. How could I explain the guilt I felt every single day that I had been chosen and millions had likely died?

"I know we need to survive as a species, but don't you ever feel, well... why you?"

My gut sank as I saw the Sorcha look of superiority had returned.

"Honestly, no. I was chosen because I was the best candidate. It was like applying for a job. They review the field of potential candidates and choose the best person for the position. Besides," she pointed out, "children couldn't have come without parents. Emotional bonds would impact people's capacity to work, and children couldn't be put to work, so they would be a burden. We can't deal with burdens yet. What if the parent had a medical condition? Older people, typically, have medical issues. We simply couldn't cope with that here. So, they made the best decision they could: young, fit, healthy, well-educated men and women who were best placed to build a new society."

"It all sounds so logical the way you describe it."

"Because it is logical. Well, except for choosing Ilana. That wasn't logical, but everyone is entitled to one mistake."

With a chuckle, I had to admit she was right. Ilana was a downright pain in the ass. Technically here to be a cook, she had quickly been moved to looking after the chickens as no one could stand working with her as she didn't pull her weight, and couldn't, or wouldn't, work as part of a team. She disliked Freyja intensely, and the feeling was mutual. Freyja had no tolerance for time wasters and usually let them know it. The problem was that Freyja now needed to oversee Ilana over the care of the chickens. No one on August was immune from Ilana's malicious gossip. The worst part was, she was one of those people who was so clueless that she genuinely believed that people liked her when, in fact, people did their utmost to avoid her, her gossip, and thorough nastiness.

"There is a word for people like Ilana," Freyja said suddenly. "Pronoid. It is a psychological condition, the opposite of paranoia. To be pronoid means that you think everyone likes you, even when there is evidence to the contrary."

Grinning, I recognized Freyja was doing her best to make light of the conversation and move it on.

"I can't help it. I still feel guilty," I whispered.

"Surviving doesn't change anything," Freyja said with her characteristic matter-of-factness. "You are here. Make the most of it."

The fate of my parents and sister weighed on my mind. I could see them every time I closed my eyes. Suffering, starving. My next words slipped out without really meaning to.

"You don't think that is a little... cold?"

"Cold." Freyja spat back as she visibly bristled. "*Cold*. Just because I am logical and not emotional, you think I am an unfeeling *bitch*?"

The volume and pitch of her voice wavered and was getting dangerously high, and I knew I was on unsafe ground. But I couldn't help it. Perhaps I was emotional, but it was an emotive subject.

"Honey, I didn't say that. But don't you feel at all guilty that entire families died? Children, babies, and yet we live?"

"Guilty? Why would I feel guilty? I didn't make the decisions about who would stay and who would go. I have nothing to be guilty about."

"So, it is the government officials' fault then because they chose?"

"That isn't what I am saying!"

"Then what *are* you saying, Freyja? That it is okay that some people were chosen?"

The piercing glare cut me to the bone as she growled, "That's *life*, Campbell. Get over it. People live; people die. There is always a set of criteria. For a job, a scholarship, and yes, to come here. You either meet the criteria, or you don't. I didn't say it was fair. I just said that it is real life. Honestly, you and your bloody ethics."

I paused, seeing the merit in her argument despite it not being a position I shared. The problem for me was that people I loved deeply hadn't been chosen and had most likely died as a result. Died too young and too soon. Quite simply, I had survivor's guilt, and I knew it. I tried to soften my tone. "I just... well, I feel guilty, that's all."

"Argh! I can't deal with you when you are like this! You are so fucking emotional, so *weak*!" Throwing down her sewing, she grabbed her jacket, took two strides across the room, and slammed the front door so hard the windows rattled, as did the few items of china we kept in the cupboard above the cooktop.

Unsure of what to do next, I did nothing. It wasn't like we hadn't disagreed before. All couples did. Anyone who said otherwise was a liar. If there was an Olympic category for door slamming, Freyja would undoubtedly be a worthy medal contender. But this was the first time she had accused me of being weak and that stung more than I would have thought possible. Freyja had always told me she loved my nurturing side, saying my compassion made her a better person. "I am your logic, and you are my conscience," she had said. "Two halves of one whole," was how she often described us. She had never called me weak before, and it made me wonder—was that truly how she saw me? Weak? Illogical and emotional?

Pondering going after her, I decided against it. When Freyja was in a temper, the best course of action was to leave her alone for a few hours. She would calm down on her own. We had never gone to bed angry with each other. Sitting here replaying the argument was pointless, stewing over her hurtful words. I may as well finish training the grapevines.

CHAPTER 16

STANDING ON THE BRINK of the abyss, I could see the void with perfect clarity. A chasm of flawless black that dropped away under my toes into perfect nothingness. Poised on the precipice, I was afraid to move. Too scared to move forward lest I fall and hasten my inevitable demise, but equally too fearful of moving backward, back into the unknown. Deep in my soul, I knew I was ultimately utterly alone—that sense of aloneness that physically hurts. As I looked across the chasm, I could see the thick smoky gray fog moving closer, reaching out unnervingly toward me. The fog cast a dark shadow that felt alive, possessed. As the haze's fingers reached me, its terror gripped me, and I shivered from the cold, the bleakness that was threatening to engulf me. The sinister dark shadows that followed the fog reached for me and swirled around my feet, rising from my calves, past my knees, and paralyzing me. I stood there, frozen, as I watched my stomach disappeared from view, knowing I would soon be wholly consumed by the dark.

I could hear the echo from a great distance. Someone was calling my name, but it was too hard to focus, too faint. Unable to respond, I was falling, drifting, being pulled down and under. The dark, swirling mist had taken me now. Its weight was dragging me down, down into its empty oblivion. The voice came again. Louder, more insistent. I strained, forcing myself to hear it.

"Caaaammmmmmpbell..... *Cam*! Can you hear me? Listen to me! *Focus—goddamn you!*"

I couldn't open my eyes. They were stuck down with glue, heavy, wet, weighted down from the fog that engulfed me with its cold dark fingers of terror. The voice came again. Straining against the dark, I knew that voice. With all my strength, I strained against it and forced myself to open my eyes. Everything hazily swam in front of me as I struggled to maintain consciousness. Unable to maintain my strength, I closed my eyes again.

"Oh no, you don't!" said the voice with certainty. It was Freyja and someone else. Someone was gripping my arms tightly and shaking me like a recalcitrant teddy bear. I tried to force my eyes open but couldn't. Too heavy, too... An almighty shake roused me enough to open my eyes, slowly, struggling to adjust to the bright invasive light. My eyes were watering and hurt. Gradually, things began to take their regular shape. I could see a hazy window, a door, a chair, wooden with a ladder back. I recognized that chair. Why did I know that chair? Then it came back to me, sluggishly, my brain fogged and confused. I was in the room in the medical clinic where my hand had been stitched a year ago.

With such a small community on August, the clinic was a single building with two identical rooms. Both were largish, clean, and white. Cupboards containing a vast array of medical equipment and supplies lined the walls. Three single beds, one beside me and two opposite, were all empty but freshly made in the room with me. Sensing I was lying down, the thought struck me. *Am I in a bed, too?*

As I slowly focused my eyes, I could see the look of concern in Freyja's face as she looked down from above.

"Thank goodness. We thought we had lost you."

"Lost?" I managed to croak, my voice surprising even me with its rustiness.

"You have been unconscious for three days," Freyja said with more tenderness in her voice than I had ever heard as I sipped the water she held out for me. That alone scared me. Freyja was not an emotional mushy person.

"Jamie found you passed out cold. What were you doing?"

I tried to think, but my head was too woolly to focus.

"I remember training grapevines along a trellis," I said slowly. "I needed to get some wire from the shed."

"Then?"

"Nothing. I can't remember anything."

Freyja turned and spoke in a low tone to Nalini, one of the doctors. She was nodding in agreement to whatever Freyja said. Freyja turned back to me and spoke cautiously. "We think you might have been poisoned. Do you remember eating or drinking anything?"

I shook my head, instantly realizing that it was a mistake. Groaning aloud, I reached for my aching head and held it in my dry, cracked, and calloused hands.

"Poison?" I croaked.

"Well, you had been vomiting. Likely before you were found unconscious, and several times you stopped breathing." She looked over at Nalini with immense gratitude. "Nalini saved your life. Three times."

I looked at Nalini. "Thank you," I managed, although my voice was raspy.

"My pleasure." Nalini handed me another glass of water. "Sip. Don't gulp," she advised.

"Poison?" I repeated, utterly perplexed. "Who on earth would poison *me*? Are you sure?"

"Fairly sure. You have a decent wound on the back of your head, indicating you were hit. Jamie found you out in the open, but there was evidence that you had been dragged, most likely by your feet, if the mud caked in your hair is any indication. There were signs of a struggle in the shed, but your vomiting started in the fields. There is none in the shed. As for who would do it... I have no idea. But I fully intend to find out."

This last sentence was delivered with such conviction that I was concerned for the person responsible for a moment. Then it occurred to me it was me they had poisoned and belted across the head, and my concern for my assailant lessened somewhat.

Five days later, I returned home, weak, pale, but happy to be out of that white sterile environment where I had been bored witless. Fed regularly, cared for, and even bathed and shaved, I should have enjoyed the attention. I didn't. Unable to focus my eyes to read, I just lay there, desperately wanting my home, my own bed. Privacy. Like all the men here, I hadn't shaved since I arrived. Shaving was just one more thing that just didn't seem important when facing a global crisis and struggling to survive. I had been shaved so they could see the extent of the poison and damage to my head. Freyja had done a double-take when she first saw me without bandages around my skull.

"What's wrong?" I croaked.

"It... it just isn't *you,*" she finally responded. "You aren't my warrior without that long hair and fierce black beard!"

I laughed out loud, despite the shuddering pain shooting through my skull.

Freyja visited the clinic several times a day, bringing food and stories of what had happened. She had sworn Nalini to secrecy, and they kept their suspicions of poisoning to themselves. After all, there was no definitive proof. It may just have been an allergic reaction, the story Freyja spread to anyone who asked. Nalini and Freyja considered the options. A bite or sting was unlikely to cause alarm, unlike a raving murderer. Better to go with something innocuous, like an unknown allergy. For my safety, I was not permitted visitors until I got home, just in case my assailant tried again.

"I am so sorry I left you," Freyja said, her face crestfallen, as she sat beside me. "If we hadn't argued, you wouldn't have been there, and this would never have happened."

"That isn't your fault," I soothed. "We both had a hand in it. Besides, who would have thought that someone hated me enough to do this?"

"That is the part I simply cannot fathom," Freyja said. "Everyone likes you. You are gentle and take care of everyone before yourself. When someone is in need, you are there. You ask everyone else what they want and do your best to provide it, even if it means working yourself into the ground. I don't think anyone has moved into their own cabin without you offering to assist. You were asked to be the liaison between the two communities as you get along with everyone, Kai, Erika, even painful Phil. Few of us can say that. So I am wondering...." she trailed off.

"Wondering what?"

"Well, I am wondering if it was it someone who hated *me*?"

"You?" I asked, completely dumbstruck. "Why would anyone hate you?"

Rolling her eyes, Freyja slumped, her head resting on the mattress beside me. "I rub people up the wrong way. Unlike you, who shows everyone kindness, I can be sharp and a little blunt?"

"A little blunt?" I gently teased.

"Okay, I call a spade a spade," she retorted in mock outrage. "Sometimes, I am not very subtle. People like Ilana, Phil, Amelinda... they don't like me."

"Surely not enough to hurt you, though."

"Possibly. Maybe. I... I just don't know."

Once home, I was inundated with callers. Diana brought me a selection of delicious fruit, making me feel guilty about all the time I had taken off work. Jamie and Jacinda, after being thanked profusely for raising the alarm and possibly saving my life, announced proudly that they were expecting their first child. Jenny, who had returned to our community with her partner and child after a disagreement over the value of her cooking on Green Island.

Jenny brought me a delicious hearty stew with crusty bread and butter followed by hot pancakes and maple syrup.

"How did you *know*!" I gushed as the maple syrup dripped down my freshly shaven chin, and I licked my lips in ecstasy. "How did you get maple syrup?" We weren't growing a maple tree, though I quickly made plans to redress this situation. Surely there were seeds in the seed vault.

Jenny beamed. "Freyja told me it was what your mum made you."

"She did." I sighed in complete ecstasy. "Who would have known that maple syrup would taste *so damned good*?"

Jenny looked like she was going to burst with pride. Freyja came in and saw my face.

"I don't think I have ever seen him so happy. What a wonderful Christmas present."

I looked at her in amazement and a touch of sorrow. "Christmas? Did I miss it?"

Freyja smiled a little sadly, knowing how much I loved Christmas. "You did. You were in the clinic and in no state to feast or celebrate. We thought it best just not to tell you."

I looked at her despondently. I had adored Christmas growing up. Not just the presents, but the magic of it all: decorating the tree, hanging lights on the house, driving around the neighborhood to see all the decorated houses, visiting family and friends, sending cards, listening to cheesy carols, visiting the Christmas windows in the city, and having a meal in Chinatown afterward. Eating so much, I knew I would burst.

One year, I convinced Mum to buy us a real tree instead of putting up the fake plastic one we had. The tree sales were a fundraiser for needy children—I researched and played this card well, knowing she couldn't resist a child in need. She succumbed. But it made such a mess, dropping pine needles everywhere. The cat climbed it and knocked it over twice, smashing decorations. Finally, the dog spewed on the lounge room rug after insisting on drinking the water in the bucket that the tree sat in. None of us argued when Mum declared she would never buy a live tree again. Our first Christmas here had been wonderful, but I badly wanted to share my first Christmas with Freyja.

"We will have plenty of Christmases together," she said kindly, seeing my disappointment. "I'm not going anywhere."

Checking the plate, I took the last bite of Jenny's delectable gooey goodness. I ran my finger around the plate, mopping up the remaining sweetness. Jenny waited patiently until I sank back onto my pillows and took the dishes from me, returning them to the tray.

"I've missed you, Jenny," I declared with complete sincerity. "I'm so glad you are back."

Jenny beamed. "I've popped a pie and some goodies in the fridge for your dinner. For both of you," she said, looking directly at Freyja. Freyja wasn't ter- ribly popular among some of the women here. She was loyal to those she trusted, like Di and Jacinda, but didn't tolerate gossip or time-wasting. Freyja knew women were intimidated by her but simply didn't care. She had few reservations about how others saw her. After my recent experience, I had enough concerns for both of us.

Freyja nodded her thanks to Jenny, recognizing this for what it was: a kind gesture and one meant to convey respect to us both. Me, for my part in establishing a thriving food supply which kept us all not only alive, but able to enjoy a wide range of foods daily. To Freyja, this was thanks from a friend for nursing me back to health.

After Jenny's departure, Freyja sat next to me on the bed. "Honestly, I think that maple syrup has healed you faster than an entire week in the clinic! You have color in your face and look far healthier than you have looked since...." she trailed off, clearly not wanting to use the word poisoned.

"I feel better," I announced, swinging my legs to the edge of the bed. "I think..."

"*No!*"

"Huh? I didn't tell you..."

"*No*. I know exactly what you were going to say, Cam Mack, and the answer is no. You are not going back to work just yet, even just for a check-in. Jamie, Diana, and Kelly have it all under control. They have roped in some help for the planting. You can stay here and rest."

"Planting..." I protested. "All winter, I have been planning..." but was cut off. There was to be no further discussion.

Unable to rest entirely, the next day, feeling completely useless, which I decided was a highly overrated feeling, I wandered about the cabin. The other goodies Jenny had left us comprised a weeks' supply of meals: pies, casseroles, lasagna, even sausage rolls. I stared in amazement at the fridge, neatly stacked with dishes and trays. Fred, who had kept Freyja company during my hospital stay, bleated mournfully from outside. Closing the fridge, I opened the door to find Fred on the doorstep, baaing happily at my appearance. Scratching him behind the ears, I blinked at the sudden onslaught of light coming through the door. I looked at the garden and made a decision.

That afternoon when Freyja returned home, she found me collapsed on the step, exhausted, dirty, but deliriously happy about the new garden beds I had dug, mentally planning out the fruit trees, herbs, and the summer vegetables for our home garden.

"I could use a soak," I whispered when she had helped me inside. The hot springs were still our private place, but with work commitments and then my recuperation, we hadn't been there in weeks.

"Soon," Freyja promised. "When you are strong enough to make the journey."

CHAPTER 17

OUR SECOND AUGUST DAY celebration arrived. I made my excuses and didn't attend the large community function. While Freyja and I could have attended, we would rather be alone. Despite being far more social than I, Freyja recognized I was loyal to my friends and loved small gatherings, but I struggled in large, loud groups. Di came for dinner several times a week, and the three of us got along fabulously, often staying up late talking with Di staying over in our spare room. Jamie and Jacinda also came for dinner every Friday night, often with Diana as well.

On the afternoon of August Day, when we knew everyone would likely be at the village green, we unhurriedly made our way to the hot springs to celebrate in private. Freyja brought a backpack filled with delicious treats: cheese, grapes, wine, crusty bread. Noting that she had brought some chocolate, I vowed to leave it for her alone. Chocolate was a rare treat. The supplies were low now that we were entering our third year here, and no one had quite perfected the art of making it. It still tasted much like cooking chocolate, close, but not quite right.

Bathing first, we spread a towel on the rocks and lay eating, languorously, towels wrapped lazily around us. We had nowhere to be, no one looking for us. No jobs to get to, no fear that we would be missed. We could take our time and enjoy the sensation of being completely and utterly alone.

Freyja plucked a grape from its stem and fed it to me, saying, "I think it is time."

"Time for what?" I asked abstractedly.

"Commitment."

I did react to that. Shocked, I looked at her, trying not to choke on the grape, which was now stuck halfway down my gullet.

"Really? Are you sure? You always said...."

"I know," she said. "I always said I didn't care what people thought. Our business is our business. It isn't for public consumption. I do still think that. But I also think..." she blushed, making me intrigued.

"What?"

"I want to make a pledge to you. But just us. Not public. If... if *you* want to, that is."

Freyja looked away, for once embarrassed at her forthrightness.

"Want to?" I echoed. "Are you kidding me? From the day I met you, I have never wanted anything so much in all my life. Have I not spent the past year telling you how much I worship you, how amazing and wonderful you are? How my heart is now full because you filled it? You are, without doubt, the single best thing that ever happened to me. The past year I have felt lighter than I have ever felt in my life. Finally, I feel like I have a purpose. What on earth would make you think I didn't want *you*?"

"People who have told me they loved me before have left me," she whispered.

"Well, I won't," I said with utter conviction. "I love you. I always will. Your direction, logic, focus—all the things that complete me, make me whole. There, is that what you need?"

"It is." Throwing herself into my arms, she asked, "Can we do it now?"

"Ahh... wha... what? Right now?"

"Why not?"

There was no adequate answer to that. Looking down at my complete state of undress, I checked with her for confirmation.

She shrugged. Evidently, she didn't care. Since there was no reason to refuse, I nodded consent.

Taking a moment to compose myself, I had a twinge of guilt that my parents wouldn't be here to share this moment. They had missed Sorcha's wedding after Sam's death, and now they would miss mine, although perhaps clothed would have been ever so slightly more appropriate had there been guests. Blinking hard to dispel the image of my parents from my mind, I stood up and took a few deep breaths to prepare for what was the most incredible moment of my life.

Freyja was smoothing and laying out the towel, an altar of sorts in the center of the room, and beckoned me over. Kneeling on the towel, facing each other, adjacent to the water's edge, and with our backs to the monoliths, we clasped hands and gazed into each other's eyes. This was private, for us. Not a spectacle for everyone else. Our commitment to each other. And for us, this was the perfect way for this to occur.

Freyja began:

"Campbell Edward William Mackintosh. I love you.
You cannot possess me, for I belong to myself.
But I give you love, which is mine to give.
You cannot command me, for I am a free person.
But I choose to serve you, in order to aid you.
I pledge that yours are the eyes that I will smile into every morning,
I shall be a shield for your back, and you for mine.
I shall not slander you, nor you, me,
I will honor you above all others.
When we disagree, we will do so in private,
And tell no others our grievances.
This is my pledge to you,
For this is a marriage of equals."

Unable to resist beaming at her, I recognized part of the Celtic handfasting vow. She had planned this, researched this, but made it her own, acknowledged my cultural heritage and, in some strange way, the heritage of this place. It was perfect.

"Freyja Jorgensen. I love you." Pausing, I asked. "I loved your vows. Can you teach me?"

Repeating solemnly after Freyja, I echoed her vows and made them my own. At the end, I added the traditional Celtic handfasting commitment, "I commit to you as long as love lasts between us."

"As long as love lasts," she repeated.

The kiss that followed was long, slow, and ardent, with no witnesses to judge. I was complete. We lay on the towel and slowly, passionately made love like it was the first time, kissing, caressing and exploring each other, centimeter by centimeter, like we were strangers. The feeling of newness struck me, although we had already been together for a year. Her skin molded to my hands as we found pleasure in each other. As we lay together in the hot steamy space, we became one, husband and wife, and my life had never held so much meaning, felt so much joy.

Begrudgingly, we left the cave and began the slow walk back to our cabin just before sunrise the following morning. Neither of us wanted to abandon this state of euphoria, but knew that if we were missing, people would look for us. In no way did we want anyone to find this place—our place. Reaching a section of the already tight path where it narrowed to a single foot width, I slowed, cautiously watching where I put my feet. Much of the route was single file. Some we could walk side by side. Blissfully happy, we had taken every opportunity to stop every few steps to kiss, hold hands, or embrace. It was slow going. But here, I was slightly in front of Freyja as we navigated the barely perceptible path. I still hadn't returned to full strength after the poisoning and was more vigilant than usual.

My ears pricked up as I heard Freyja speak softly behind me, "Can we have a baby in the winter?"

I stopped so suddenly she crashed into me, and we both subsided in giggles.

Turning to hold her, I said, "Whenever you want. But... why winter?"

"Well, winter is a quiet time for both of us," she pointed out logically. "It is mostly just caring for the animals. The spring babies are independent. None are lactating or pregnant. Most of your work is inside. It is a good time to spend time at home caring for a new child, don't you think?"

This logic took me by such surprise that I laughed out loud. "Seriously. You are the most ridiculously practical person I have ever met. Only *you* would plan a baby around work. What happened to the miracle of life?"

"I like to plan things," she muttered, a little perturbed by my teasing. "It is a big step. Besides, we are both needed in the community."

"Oh, honey, I didn't mean that. I just meant... well, that when we become parents, we will be the most important people in this child's life. We will love him or her with all our hearts, and nothing else will come close. Children need their parents so much in the early years. There are enough people to look after the animals and crops. When we become parents, we will need to focus on our child to the exclusion of all others."

As the dawn light filtered through the trees, Freyja looked at me, a little perplexed.

I tried to clarify. "My parents told me once that they made a vow to each other. When they married, that *their* family, the two of them, then Sorcha and I, would take priority over their respective parents and siblings. The family they made was the most important thing. Do you know what I mean?"

Freyja nodded slowly, understanding.

"I want it to be that way for us."

Freyja looked at me, tears filling her eyes. "I wasn't a priority for my parents. In fact, I don't think I know *how* to be a mother." A single tear escaped her eye and rolled down her cheek.

I blotted the tear with a kiss. "You will be the most amazing mother," I said with complete confidence. "I've seen you with that goat. Besides, our children will be told every single day how much they are loved," I promised. "For our family, it will be different."

Finally, I truly understood what that word meant. Family.

CHAPTER 18

WEEKS TURNED INTO MONTHS. It took some convincing for Freyja to not plan for *when* a baby would join us and just relish the fact that one *would*, in time. We visited the hot springs whenever time allowed; it was still our secret place. We pondered endlessly about the stones in the cave. Both of us tried to research using the library, trying to avoid drawing attention to what we were doing. But not knowing where we actually *were* made it exceedingly difficult. My focus switched to researching our location, and I believed we were off the southern coast of New Zealand more than ever. The flora matched as did the climate. But with thousands of square kilometers of ocean to search, plus more groups of islands than I thought possible, I couldn't narrow it down much more than that.

"You know," I said one morning as I was eating breakfast and Freyja was singing behind me, washing dishes in the kitchen, "I can't think of a time when I was ever this happy."

Freyja wrapped her arms around me as I sat in my chair, pressing her head into my shoulder. "Me too. I finally feel like this is home."

Reaching around, I pulled her across my lap and kissed her, taking my time. The chair creaked ominously with the weight of two of us on it, making us both look up in alarm, but it didn't break. But it destroyed the moment, and Freyja returned to her task.

I had always thought of the house in Melbourne, where I lived with my parents, as home. But this... this was different. Here I was an equal, not a child. I handled everything—the maintenance, the cleaning. It made me more attached to the building; I cared more about the life I lived in it. Freyja and I shared all domestic duties: washing dishes, preparing food, taking scraps to the biogas unit. I was becoming quite adept at making beds and cooking meals for two. Freyja had faced a steeper learning curve, having been raised with a cleaner. I knew we would learn to change nappies and look after a baby together as well, although I regularly teased her that I didn't have the equipment to assist with the feeding in the early months.

Di still visited us often, although Jamie and Jacinda were nesting with the pregnancy progressing well. We still saw them weekly for dinner, but we more often visited them rather than them visiting us. Jamie regaled me with tales of life with a pregnant woman, the cravings, odd demands, and despite the hilarity, I felt the occasional pang of jealousy. Freyja, not a jealous woman by nature, was saddened as each month passed with no imminent child of our own, but she never let it show publicly.

"What did you do in those days between knowing you had been chosen and coming here?" I asked one evening, sitting on the couch, working on my planting records. It was nearly late fall, and the harvest was looming. I was planning how many garden beds I would need for pumpkins the following year to accommodate the expanding population. There were eight new babies now and several on the way. That was a lot of vegetable puree to plan for.

Freyja sighed, looking up from the book she was reading beside me.

"I sat in my flat, wondering what to take and mainly just checking out Pinterest and Instagram."

"What? Alone? Didn't you just spend time with your parents?"

"They weren't there," she replied simply. "As soon as I got home from the testing and knew I had been offered a place, I kept calling them, but there was no answer. I knew Dad was at an international conference in Brisbane. I had no idea where Mum was."

"Seriously? I know you said that you weren't close, but you didn't actually come here without speaking to them about it, did you? They must have been worried sick!"

"Of course not. I spoke to them, eventually. I had five days between being told I had been selected and the time I needed to present myself at the facility in Melbourne. Dad was the keynote speaker, and couldn't, *wouldn't* come home to say... to say... goodbye." She choked on the last word. "Too concerned for his professional reputation, I guess."

My stunned silence and look of disbelief spoke volumes about what I thought about *that*. Placing both books on the floor, I held Freyja in my arms as she dissolved into a flood of uncontrollable tears. Years of pent-up distress flooded out in a torrent. I knew better than to interrupt. I just sat there, smoothing her hair and waiting, knowing she would cry herself out eventually.

Finally, she managed to form words between her tears, "Mum... Mum came home, came over to my place, and told me it was my *duty* to go." The sarcasm was dripping.

"Your duty?" Even I was incredulous now. The time for silence was long past.

"Are you serious?" I was getting a better picture of the type of people Freyja's parents were, and I wasn't impressed.

"That was her exact word. It was stressed upon me that I was all they had left, and it was my duty."

She veritably spat the last word, and I was almost fearful of asking my next question, but I had to know. Tentatively I asked in a low voice, "What about Katrin, your sister?"

Big fat tears rolled down her already tear-streaked face, red with anger and now flushing white with awful memories. I barely heard the words as she whispered, "Katrin took a drug overdose when she was eighteen. I was nineteen."

I gulped, unsure of what to say. "Oh, Frey, honey, I am so sorry."

"Crying out for attention, Mum called it. Oh, and selfish too."

"Oh honey, I had no idea you had lost—" I started.

"She didn't die," Freyja interrupted, seeing where my processing had taken me. "But her brain was so damaged from the massive hit that doctors said she would never recover, never lead a normal life. She never came home from the ED where she was taken by ambulance. She overdosed at home. The doctors thought it was likely an accident. Experimenting and took too much. She was moved to a permanent care facility—a nursing home, truth be told. My parents... my parents said that she would be better off there. Maybe she was. I don't know. But they didn't even *try*. They just paid for the best care available and made her someone else's problem. Treated her like she *had* died, only she hadn't. She was still alive. But... I was left all alone. She left me..." Freyja's voice trailed off before she found new courage and spoke in a firmer tone, clearly for the first time on the subject.

"I found her there. Lying on the bathroom floor, unconscious, lying in her own filth. I had been away for the weekend, so she had been alone. The doctors thought she had taken the overdose sometime on the Friday, and I didn't find her until Sunday evening. If only I hadn't gone away that weekend, I would have been there."

"You can't blame yourself. You couldn't have known."

"I moved out not long after that. I couldn't bear being in that enormous house, seeing that bathroom every day. It was no longer my home. It was just the place where she had been taken from me. So... I left."

Stunned into silence, I just held her as the large tears dripped from her nose and chin, soaking my shirt.

"I'm so sorry. I had no idea."

I scooped Freyja into my lap, curled up like a child, crying in my arms in a way I had never seen her do in the year we had been together, sobbing, hiccupping, unable to stop. I stroked her hair and murmured meaningless endearments, like I remember my mother doing for me when I was a child. I wondered if she had grieved at the time, but it didn't appear that she had. Strangely enough, I realized that this made me love her more than ever, something I didn't think possible. She had trusted me enough to tell me, to share this with me, her deepest pain. Maybe that is what family is? The people who share your greatest joys and your greatest pain and still love you.

After what felt like a very long time, the crying slowed. She sniffed and turned bloodshot eyes to look at me, the redness making the crystal green more prominent. She looked utterly exhausted. When she spoke, her voice was harsh and rusty.

"I went and said goodbye to her, not that she could process what I was saying. I just sat there for hours, talking to her, holding her hand. At one point, she squeezed it. I screamed and called for a doctor. When they finally responded, she was still. They told me it was electrical impulses in her body, that she hadn't reacted to what I had been saying. I looked at her, really looked at her, and at that moment, I realized she had gone. What was left was a shell, a mockery of what she had been—alive, vibrant, beautiful. I had nothing left... there. So, I walked out, packed my bag, and arrived at the facility a day early."

"Wow, you arrived early?"

"I had nothing else to do," she admitted. "No family, no real friends, although lots of acquaintances. The one person I wanted to say goodbye to had already left me." She adjusted herself on my lap. "What about you? What did you do? You know, before you left?"

"Most of it was like wandering around in a daze," I admitted, settling her so that we were both more comfortable. "Second-guessing my decision, wanting to call a million times and say 'Hey! I've made a mistake. Changed my mind!' I didn't, obviously." I grinned sheepishly. "Spending time with my family—they knew, of course. Where I was going, and despite them being upset, they fully supported me coming here. Trying to see friends but not letting them know. That was difficult. Choosing what to bring, what to leave. Wondering if I would ever see familiar places again." I paused, trying to think what else I had done in those last days. Memories came flooding back, and I smiled. "Eating. A lot of eating. Meeting people for meals, pretending it was just a catch-up, but secretly knowing it would be the last time I saw them. Trying to make... well... memories, I guess."

"I never second-guessed my decision to come here. I was always going to accept."

"I am so glad you did. It wouldn't have been the same if I hadn't met you." A thought occurred to me. "Do you have a photo? Of Katrin? I can't believe I never thought to ask before."

"I do." Freyja stood and walked into our spare room. I could hear her fumbling around in the wardrobe. Walking into our bedroom, I pulled my backpack from under the bed, retrieving the other photos of my family. I had a few on display on the bookcase but had many more. It had been a long time since I had been able to look at them. It caused me immense sadness to remember them that way and know that they were likely all dead now. Perhaps in time, I could display them...

Returning to the living room, photos in hand, I sat next to Freyja on the couch. She was holding a picture, mesmerized, and barely registered my return.

Tentative for a moment, I looked over her shoulder and smiled at the photo of Freyja, dressed in a purple bikini, standing on the deck of a boat, her arm around a smaller, younger version of herself.

"Look at you!" I gushed. "What were you there, about fifteen?"

"Sixteen," she admitted.

"Oh my goodness, how much does Katrin look like you!" I exclaimed.

"People often mistook us for twins," she admitted. "We looked very alike."

"Where was this taken?" I asked in an effort to channel our conversation on the good times behind the photo and not the sadness.

The autumn harvest kept me busy for weeks. The olive grove I planted had been expanded, partly for Jacinda's products. It was thriving, and collecting and sorting the glossy black fruit took me days. Thank goodness the job of preserving them for eating wasn't mine. One year in high school, I had been invited to help a Greek friend and his family process olives. It had been their family tradition with each person sitting around the kitchen table and taking an olive from the enormous basket in the center. Checking it for perfection, they sliced each individual olive before transferring it to the colossal vat where they would be soaked in salted water, which was changed every few days to pull the bitterness from the fruit. They had laughed, joked, and told stories. It was valued family time with several generations present. My hands had been stained purple from the juice for days afterward. I never looked at an olive in the same way after that.

But I knew these olives were useful: for eating, oil, as a base for shampoo and soap. *The ancient Greeks got countless things right,* I contemplated as I continued picking the fruit: horticulture, plumbing, mathematics, astrology. But also inventions like the clock, the screw, and cranes were all attributed to the Greeks. Was our life here so fundamentally different from what it was like then? Growing crops, living in communities, caring for family and friends, and creating new life. Even with new technologies, had life changed so much, really?

Despite the underlying ripple of sadness at not expanding our family when we were surrounded by the abundance of new life, Freyja and I were blissfully happy. Everyone knew that we were official, not that we cared. We didn't need validation. We worked, spent time in the garden pottering, cooked meals, and ate them together. We made time to visit Fred, who was now back in the paddock with his several pregnant female friends, proving that he was a more than adequate father. Sometimes, I felt a pang watching his evident virility—was it *me*? Maybe I couldn't father children? Fred always came dashing over to greet us. He loved being scratched behind his long floppy ears, bleating with pleasure. I didn't realize how much I had missed him, how fond of him I was. Evenings were always spent together, often with Diana, with whom we were very close, except for the rare occasion when a medical emergency pulled Freyja away. Freyja and I talked long into the night about our childhood, schools, places we had visited, our fears. We fell more in love each day, and as the cooler months set in, we relished the longer dark evenings together. Some days I wondered if we could fit an additional person into this partnership. Echoes of a friend with two children rang in my ears, "Your heart has the amazing capacity to expand as many times as it needs to." Not that I didn't want a family with Freyja—I did. But sometimes, I worried about sharing her. My ability to love another person. What if they were like me? Could I cope with someone else's problems?

Thinking of my parents, I smiled. They had been young when they married, younger than Freyja and I were now. Yet Sorcha and I knew we were loved. They were always there, no matter what, my champions prepared to fight any battle alongside me. Even so, the doubts niggled at me. What if I was no good at parenting? What if I failed my own children?

CHAPTER 19

MY BACK HURT. DIGGING new vegetable beds over the winter, getting them ready for the spring planting was therapeutic, allowing me to focus on something purely physical. It was strangely satisfying the way the shovel tip pierced the earth, slid in when I applied pressure to lift the rich brown earth from the ground— the color of chocolate. I missed chocolate. I had never been a huge chocolate eater, so it was strange that I missed it so much now. We tried to grow cocoa beans in the first two years, but now, as we were in the midst of our third winter, we had to admit that this crop had been an epic failure. The climate wasn't right, Jamie and I agreed, and we passed on cacao rather than trying again. We also stopped growing brussel sprouts when nearly ninety percent of the population told us they detested them, and they ended up in the biogas. No point wasting our time with that, although part of me hoped that the plant wouldn't become extinct.

We had a growing population with five new babies arriving in the past month, so we focused our energies on growing crops with a higher yield like potatoes, tomatoes, and beans. We also grew seasonal fruit and vegetables that kept well over winter, like pumpkins and apples. Since it was winter, most of our growing was in greenhouses, where Jamie was today. At this rate, the population was expanding faster than we could plow new ground. Looking at the rich earth I had tilled, I felt guilty at depriving everyone else of cocoa and chocolate. I sighed. Freyja loved chocolate. You wouldn't think it with that tall, strong athletic frame, but she had a secret sweet tooth. I relished the few memories of walking into the tiny cottage we shared and finding her in ecstatic bliss, devouring something sugary. It was June now, not quite four months since our commitment on August Day, and sixteen months of being together, yet I still couldn't work out what she saw in me, why she had chosen me over everyone else. Occasionally I saw men, and sometimes women, look longingly at her, her imposing upright carriage, her long slender legs that went on for days. She never noticed and was oblivious to the drooling ogling. More than once, I had caught the lingering stares at her, then at me. The "how did you catch *that,* mate? You are clearly punching above your weight." I would smile coyly. Let them think she knew something that they didn't. Then I stopped, remembering the painful time I had spent in the clinic after being poisoned, and the months it had taken to get back to full strength. Maybe I shouldn't be so relaxed about the competition here.

After three hours of bed digging, I was ready for lunch. It would be a quick lunch as the daylight hours were limited in winter. Amelinda was chatting excitedly about the goat kid that had been born the night before, even though it was winter. Even after all this time, we still celebrated the wins—the births, the partnerships. Strange that Freyja or Heidi weren't with them as they usually were. Obviously, they were busy taking care of the new arrival.

Returning to work after lunch, I sought a more upright task to spare my aching back, selecting the dormant fruit trees to prune to promote the new season's growth. I always suspected I was hacking off too much. Still, when they sprouted in spring, I released an enormous sigh of relief, knowing that they had benefited from the attention I had given them over winter. Working my way through the orchard, marking out the trees for tomorrow, I took the cut branches to the compost heap, then cut the thinner ones into smaller pieces and fed them to the biogas.

Exhausted, I contemplated going straight to bed, but the motivation of a hot dinner was enticing. A quick wash at the tap outside, and I ambled into the communal dining room. We had little food at home this time of year. During winter, we ate a wide variety of stews, soups, curries, and casseroles, mostly made with the vegetables in the root cellar combined with rice from the aquaponics pond, pasta, or bread made from the large silos of wheat. Once again, I was relieved that the wheat, oats, barley, sugar beets, and rice paddocks were not my responsibility. I liked the diversity of growing fruits and vegetables, each day focusing on something different.

"Cam!" Phil called me over, keen to chat about the new solar installation. Soon I was caught up with a small group, discussing plans for building new cabins and village facilities. After a while, this turned to who was dating, pregnant, arguing. Personally, I found all this gossip overwhelming, not to mention highly invasive. Thank goodness Freyja did too.

When dessert was finished, one of Jenny's specialties, a delicious apple cake, I murmured my excuses and went home. To my surprise, the cabin was dark and empty. I contemplated putting my boots back on and walking up to the vet clinic. She couldn't be far away. Looking out the window, I could see the light on in the vet clinic in the distance. I wanted to lend a hand, but exhaustion from the day won out. I removed my boots, sank into one of our armchairs, and waited for her.

I woke to the sound of banging on the door. As my eyelids burst open, I immediately closed them again as the daylight pierced my eyeballs like a red-hot poker.

"Crap," I muttered and staggered to the door, struggling to focus. Heidi was there, looking annoyed.

"Is Freyja sick?" she demanded.

"Um, uh... I don't know," I managed, barely awake.

"Well, where is she?" Heidi queried.

Leaving the door open, I took the few steps to the bedroom. Cold, dark, and quiet.

"She didn't turn up to work this morning." Heidi's tone was accusing. She wasn't exactly known for her tolerance. I had always found Heidi harsh and prickly. My addled brain tried to form a linear sequence.

"She left for work yesterday, Monday, I mean. She was on the afternoon shift, but I was on early, and I left before daylight. But she spoke to me as she went past to the clinic."

Looking around confirmed my suspicions. She hadn't come home last night. "I came home after dinner and sat down to wait for her. I must have fallen asleep," I admitted sheepishly. "When did you last see her?"

Heidi wrinkled her nose, thinking. "Early evening yesterday?" Her tone indicated that she was unsure, but then she nodded as she made up her mind. "Yes. She was there when I started the night shift, but she left soon after I started. She went to find that stupid goat. He escaped during the afternoon. She was supposed to relieve me at 7am but didn't show up."

"Fred?" I ventured a little cautiously.

"That one," she growled, the anger bubbling to the surface. Heidi didn't like Fred. Since his sojourn at our place, he had escaped regularly, and they struggled to work out how he managed to get out of a well-fenced paddock that no other livestock escaped from. After a few months of living with us, he returned to the paddock, where he was needed to take up his masculine duties, but clearly, he preferred life at our place with food and affection on tap. He would go missing and turn up at our house or at the orchards looking for me. Several times Heidi suggested that they use Fred for Sunday curry, but Freyja steadfastly defended him. As he was virile, she had so far managed to stay his execution on that basis.

"So, Freyja went off after Fred. At what time?" I was fully alert now and worried.

"About 7:00, I guess, maybe 7:30," Heidi responded. "I started at 7:00 pm, and she left not long after. It was well dark."

I looked at the sky through the open door. "So, you mean she has been missing for more than twelve hours, and no one bothered to *check*?"

"We were busy," she sniped caustically. "I had a sick cow, newborn goat kid, and a birthing ewe. She was supposed to be finished, anyway. We all knew she was off finding the grumpy old bugger, and no one thought anything of it until she didn't turn up to work this morning."

I found that odd and wrinkled my nose, thinking. Freyja had always said that aside from bees, Heidi had shown little interest in any of the animals, especially those in labor, always letting the rest of the team do that work. Still, now obviously wasn't the time. Freyja had been gone all night.

I hastily threw on my coat and boots and started out the door. "Which way did she go?"

"She suspected he had gone up the hill." Heidi gestured. "Do you want me to come?"

"I'll go," I assured her, not wanting to spend more time with Heidi than absolutely necessary.

Checking around our place to ensure he hadn't tried to visit yesterday, I found no evidence of recent goat visitation. *Where to next?* I headed to the vet sheds. He adored Freyja and would often try to intervene when she was working with other animals. Thoroughly searching all the paddocks and sheds left me hot, tired, and dirty, but no sign of Freyja or Fred. Two choices then: into the township or up into the hills. Assuming that the word was out by now that Freyja was missing, the best bet was to explore the forest that grew down to the upper slopes of the fields. It wasn't the first time Fred had gone exploring in the forest. Although there were paths, most were barely wider than a goat track. It was tough going, steep, and I constantly pushed my way through the thick forest, pausing every few meters to check for footprints, broken branches, or evidence that someone had been here recently.

"Frey-jaaa," I called, again and again, until I was hoarse. Waiting for a reply, a noise, evidence that she was hurt and unable to call back. Stopping and listening every few steps but hearing nothing but the sound of my breathing. Occasionally, I could hear people calling far off in the distance. Heidi had sent out other people. This was good. More people meant we had a greater chance of finding her soon, especially if she was hurt. Not being a goat-tracker, I didn't know where to start. Making my way slowly through the forest and around the coastal path, I found nothing. I wound my way back inland to the path that led to the cave, our cave. After all, Fred had been here before.

Pushing my way past the inaka, it was quiet, dark, and still. Calling her name over and over, the reverberation came back to me immediately, making me recoil. Taking a torch from my belt, I shined it around the outer cave, but the damp stone floors made it impossible to tell if anyone had been here. Pushing my way down the tunnel into the cavern beyond, I half expected to find her basking in the hot springs. But when I moved the torch around, the cave was dark and deserted, but still held a strange static charge. It felt more electric right now, but it was likely just my heightened anxiety. Where *was* she? Despondent, I turned to leave. My foot kicked something hard, and I heard it bouncing across the cave's rocky floor. Shining my torch down on the floor, I searched until I found a torch. Freyja's torch. I tried to remember the last time we had been here, three or four days ago? Did she have it then? Had she left it behind? Or had she been here yesterday while searching for Fred and dropped it?

Panic flashed, and I had an image of her, drowned. Freyja was a strong swimmer; she had competed for Victoria during her school years. But accidents happened. Had the heat overwhelmed her, and she had fainted and drowned? Did bodies float or sink? That awful idea uppermost in my mind, I started stripping off my boots.

Logic, Cam, logic, I told myself sternly. If she were here, there would have been evidence. Clothes, boots. Calming down slightly, I recognized the sense in this. If she had come for a swim and drowned, there would be clothes. Her torch could easily have been dropped last time we were here. She had been tickling me as we left, I remembered faintly. She loved the fact that I was so ticklish and enjoyed making me squirm. Freyja regularly teased me that it was implausible that a six-foot man could be so ticklish. It was possible, likely even, that the torch had been dropped then. Deciding not to tell anyone about it, I re-tied my boots and left the cave, taking Freyja's torch with me.

CHAPTER 20

WALKING, CALLING, SEARCHING. THE condensing raindrops began dripping from the canopy of the tall rata trees overhead, some over ten meters tall. All I knew was that I couldn't go back, not yet. I found myself on the path to the river. The rain continued to fall, landing on my head, my face, my nose. I didn't really care. With no energy to wipe the moisture away, I kept walking. I found a sheltered spot under an overhanging tree and sat still, my back against the enormous trunk, knees drawn up, arms wrapped around my legs.

Where is she?

Subterranean rumblings, not quite strong enough to be called doubts, pricked the surface of my thoughts. I found it increasingly difficult to keep them suppressed. *What if she ran away? What if there was someone else?*

No. I scoffed at my self-doubt. *No. I know she didn't. She is happy. We are happy. She told me so, a hundred times, in a million different ways. We are a team, a partnership.*

But the tiny needle continued to prick at me despite my affirmations.

"No!" I said aloud, loud enough to surprise even myself. There wasn't anyone else. I would have known. August isn't that big a place. There would have been gossip, rumors.

But, said that small niggling voice inside my head, *you and Freyja managed to keep it a secret for weeks. If she kept a secret once, she could do it again. She wanted a baby. You couldn't give her one. Maybe she did find someone else?*

I closed my eyes and swallowed down the rising sense of nausea.

"No," I said again, trying to convince myself. "No." It was like I had swallowed a clod of earth, and it stuck in my throat. She hadn't. She wouldn't. Beyond all things, Freyja was honest, honorable. She would never betray me. Kick me out into the dirt and slam the door. Yes. But cheat? No.

I was safe from the rain but not from my own thoughts. It wasn't far from here that she had kissed me for the first time. We had met here so many times, in secret, on our way to the springs. I began to realize why this place had called me, why I had needed to come here.

It was nearly dark when Jamie came. I didn't hear him arrive. He was just suddenly... there. He sat next to me. He had been out for some time; he was dripping wet. He was holding Fred, a loose rope tied about his neck.

Fred didn't look injured, just bent to chew on some grass growing at the side of the path.

"It will be alright," he said calmly.

"How? How will it be alright?" I asked despondently.

"It will be alright, man. She will turn up. You'll see."

Half leading me, Jamie walked me back to the village and home. Diana was there. She brought me a meal she had made, sat with me.

"Thank you," I said, meaning it, but unable to taste anything.

"Did I ever tell you about my family?" I knew she was trying to distract me, and I appreciated the effort.

Shaking my head, I asked, "Were you born in China?"

Diana laughed deeply. But in her, it was a delicate tinkling sound, like a glass bell. "Goodness, no. My family originally came over for the gold rush in the 1800s. I am an eighth-generation Australian."

"You are more Australian than me."

"I know. It is funny. Back home, people saw my coloring, my features and assumed I was fresh off the boat. But the truth is I can date my ancestry in Australia back over a hundred and fifty years. Not all of them, some were new migrants, but there has been a Li family in Australia since 1860."

"That is impressive," I admitted. "I am first generation Australian, yet I felt nothing but Aussie."

"You know," she said introspectively, "despite being born in Sydney, raised near the Blue Mountains, my entire life in Australia, I felt like an immigrant. My family spoke Mandarin at home. It was my first language. But here I feel, well, I feel like a local. No one judges me by the way I look. Everyone here is an immigrant, and we treat each other like Augustinians."

"The way it should be," I agreed. "Everyone treated as equal. But you know, when I look at you, I don't see your Chinese features," I admitted. "I just see *you*. The gentle, kind, and loyal friend you are. That you have always been. Thank you, Di. It means a lot."

Diana closed her hand over mine. "You will get through this, Cam. I know you will. I am here for you. I'm not going anywhere."

CHAPTER 21

WORDS WHISPERED IN THE distance, not quite loud enough to catch, but with an unambiguous edge. Accusing. People I had considered friends looking away a fraction too quickly, a touch faster than necessary or polite. Awkward half-smiles, then looking at their feet when I happened to glance in their direction. A lack of conversation beyond a stilted hello. That gut-deep feeling that people didn't want to be near me. Not being trusted. Being suspected.

The first few weeks after Freyja went missing, I wandered around in a daze, still expecting her to come back with a broken leg, amnesia. Friends from all over the community, including the new township on Green Island, came to see me, check I was okay, bring me meals. Jacinda, Jamie, and Diana regularly took turns to stay with me overnight, just to confirm I was eating and sleeping. I wasn't. I was sleepwalking through a constant state of nightmare.

After a month, the rumors started. Never directly to my face, but a quickly hushed conversation when I walked into a room. Groups of people breaking up as

I came near, a touch too hurriedly. Once, as I walked toward the kitchens, I heard the cooks standing outside gossiping and taking a break. They didn't see me as I approached from the garden, basket in hand, and walked along the side of the building. Before I reached the corner, I stopped short as I realized what they were saying.

"I heard they were having problems conceiving," Floss announced with an air of glee. "Freyja told Heidi that she wanted a baby, and he couldn't give her one." A unison of affirming ahh-ing noises from the group followed.

"I heard she had second thoughts about their relationship," Sophia chimed in a snarky, malicious tone. "She is so confident; he is so quiet. They are an odd couple, don't you think? My mum always said that it was the quiet ones you needed to watch out for."

Murmurs of accord agreed with this sentiment.

I had heard enough. Placing the basket of winter vegetables brought fresh from the greenhouse on the ground, I quietly turned and walked away before I heard more.

The tide turned against me. I realized this when the isolation became blatant. Not being invited to sit at a table when I walked into the dining room, being ignored when I walked into a room. Being made to feel invisible. I took to cooking and eating at home when it got so bad that I couldn't walk anywhere without feeling the knives in my back and the lack of eye contact from a hundred people. Most days, I just didn't bother eating at all. The weight of suspicion wore me down. I could hear the unspoken questions.

Did he kill her? What did he do with the body?

Then the meetings started, carefully timed so that I was excluded. There were no laws here yet, no police or detectives, so it was evident that people were unsure what to do. Conversations fueled the gossip, the rumors. Proof. They needed to hunt for the body. I watched them form small teams and head out with backpacks, clearly looking for something.

Someone. She has a name. Freyja. And I love her. I know her in a way that none of you could possibly understand. I miss her terribly.

The grief was hard enough to deal with. Not knowing what had happened. Had she found a way out of the dome? Did she have an accident and was still lying in a ravine with a broken leg?

Each day I rose before sunrise, in part to avoid people, and did my urgent tasks, still feeling a responsibility for the collective, although I knew the community no longer felt a responsibility toward me. Most daylight hours I spent roaming the hillside, the beaches, searching for her, looking for a clue. Anything. No matter how tiny. Searching. A scrap of fabric. A footprint. Nothing. Sometimes I passed another team of searchers, looking. Looking for a body. For clues of what I had done. They carefully avoided me, and I them. I walked. Walked for hours. Every day I walked and walked, calling until I was hoarse and unable to speak anymore. My clothes hung on me, and I knew I looked haggard from not eating and not sleeping.

If it hadn't been for my few loyal friends, I know I would not have survived. There was no doubt about that. Diana, Jamie, Jacinda, Jenny. These people alone stood up for me, brought me meals, checked in. But time is a funny thing. People eventually need to return to their own lives; they can't continue to wallow in *your* pain. The overnight visits and dropped off meals slowed, then became sporadic, and finally stopped. Jamie and Jacinda's daughter arrived. I visited when baby Aroha was a few days old, genuinely happy for them. But it was impossibly hard to be around people in a constant state of joy while struggling with your own loss. Jenny had two children of her own and a kitchen to run. She dropped by twice a week in the early months and left food in my fridge. I knew it was her. I would know her cooking anywhere. It was kind of her, and I knew it was difficult for her. But this too slowed and finally stopped.

Spring came and went. I knew I should have assisted with the planting; it was a critical time for food production. I had planned another greenhouse, over winter, before... I wanted to focus on my job, but I couldn't. I was far too distracted. In the first months, I went to work early, trying to avoid my colleagues, although I knew Jamie and Diana were worried about me, but as time passed, I was too frantic. Every waking minute was spent searching—for her. October passed, then November. Nothing. Five months and not a trace of Freyja. I had never really considered what that phrase meant until it applied to me: without a trace. Not a single shred of information left, no leads, no clues. She was gone, and it was like she had never been. It was apparent to all by now that she had died, but how? Where was she? It wasn't like there was infinite space here. There were no ports, no airports, no way off this goddamned island. She hadn't left, so where *was* she?

Sleeplessness consumed me. Unable to tell day from night, I drifted through life, no longer caring if I ate or slept. I stopped washing my clothes and rarely went to the house we had shared. It pained me to see the bed we shared, the sheets we had last slept on still on it, dusty, but still with the slightest scent of her. The table where we had eaten our meals, now covered in a light layer of dust, evoking memories of her. My hair and beard grew long and ragged. I didn't care. As the days got longer, I slept for a few hours each night, eventually questioning my sanity. *Was she real? Is this a dream? Am I still in Australia, lost somewhere?* I couldn't sleep without seeing her face and would wake, drenched in sweat, thinking I had heard her speak to me. Call my name. Each time I called out, desperately, but she wasn't there.

I roamed night after night, too scared to fall asleep. *I miss her. I need her.* Utterly alone. Lonely. I had never really considered how those two words were so alike, yet so different. To be alone is fine if one is comfortable with their own company. To be alone can be a blessing. To be lonely is agonizing. No contact. No smiles or pointless conversation. To feel so completely isolated. Mistrusted. Ostracized. Alienated.

Di still cared. She left food out for me, but I carefully timed my visits home to avoid her. I didn't want to drag her down, have her tainted by my poison.

Murderer, I could hear them think. The looks gave that away. *He killed her; I wonder what he did with the body? Why?*

By late November, I couldn't bear the isolation anymore. To be so close to so many people yet to be so isolated. I couldn't stay in that house, a house that reminded me of her. Of us. Loading up my pack, I walked up into the hills. Wandering. Searching. I never stopped searching for her.

Looking down, I saw my boots caked in mud. On the odd occasion, I caught sight of myself in a still pool or stream and jerked back, shocked. Sometimes I scared myself. I looked wild, half out of my mind with grief. I laughed aloud. Half? Fully. I could never be the same again.

Desolate. *Grief-stricken*, people would have said at home. But it was so much more. It was a combination of soul-destroying grief, combined with not knowing what had happened and facing the blame. Blame was the worst part. To think I could hurt her? She had known that I would never harm her. Foolishly, I believed that these people, my friends, my community, would also think I couldn't hurt her. But they didn't. Social isolation when living in close proximity is akin to living in constant fear. Being alive, but constantly smothered. Scared to make eye contact. Initially, I tried to speak to people about inane things, the weather, the animals, and crops. But after too many forced excuses to get away, or monosyllabic replies, I stopped trying. There are only so many conversations you can try to start when people don't speak back *to* you. So, you stop talking. You turn into a shadow of your former self as you drift through your daily routine.

Get up. Get dressed. Eat. But none of it has any meaning. Shadows appear everywhere. The world seems darker, somehow. Grim. It feels like the sun will never shine again.

I rise when the sun wakes me and wander aimlessly until I am exhausted, find a tree or bush, and lay down to sleep. Occasionally, at night, I find myself near the community and take some food, never much, just enough. They don't care. They don't have to see me anymore. Perhaps it would just be easier if I just went too. Then they could wrap it all up neatly with a bow. The murdered and the murderer, both neatly dispatched.

It is December now, I think. Midsummer. I can tell by the long days and short nights, only a few hours of darkness. Roaming, I find myself climbing the steep mountain path behind the town. I look up in my fogged state to realize that I am near the hot springs cave with no idea how I got here. It is close to midday; I can see the sun high in the sky at its zenith. A strange word, *zenith*. *I wonder where it came from?*

I know where I am. I could find my way here in the dark. I have been here so many times with her. I wander toward the cave, feeling inexplicably drawn to it—a sense of being pulled. A single word floats into my head. *Trust*. It is just a word. A simple, innocent word. But now, it is loaded with meaning. *Trust. Mistrust.* Freyja had trusted me. I let her down. I can't find her. I trusted her. She left me alone. I was hated. I was not trustworthy, not worthy of being trusted. I was alone, truly totally alone. Was this the last place where we had been truly happy? Perhaps then it was appropriate that it was my last. I trusted in that.

Staggering toward the cave opening, not caring about anything, I banged my booted feet against the rocks, my head against the tunnel, heading into the inner grotto. Numbness overwhelmed me. I couldn't feel anything, but my head was spinning. Soon it would be over. The agony and the torment would be gone. I was not religious, and I didn't think we would be reunited in an afterlife. I didn't believe in heaven or hell. I just wanted *this* hell to stop. I just couldn't do this anymore. Dropping my backpack, and with no conscious effort, I half staggered, half fell chest first into the swirling water. I didn't even put my hands out to break my fall. *I just... let... go.*

My face goes under first. Hot, wet, dark, but strangely charged, alive. My head started to spin like I was drunk, like a bad case of vertigo. The suction pulled me down. The swirling vortex swallowed me whole. The pain was gone.

PART THREE

CHAPTER 22

"CAN I ASK YOU something?"

Opening my eyes, I tried to mumble something that I hoped sounded affirmative and attempted to focus on the speaker. His face, close to mine, was spinning out of control, surrounded by blackness. Reflexively, I closed my eyes to make the spinning slow.

"What... uh, what did it feel like?"

Cracking open one eye, I promptly closed it again. He was still there. *Do I know him?* It is hard to tell with all the movement.

He is still talking. "You look a bit peely wally, so I'm guessing it was quite a ride?"

Hearing the expression *peely wally*, something my mother used to say when I was pale and sick, made a fresh wave of nausea rush over me. Gradually, I was becoming aware of my body, immensely uncomfortable. I felt like I had received an enormous electric shock and was now paralyzed with aching pain and queasiness, the world spinning out of control. There was a slab of rock under me, pressing harshly into my spine. I was on my back, and the insane notion crosses my mind that I should roll onto my side in case I do vomit.

Lateral recovery position, I could hear my dad say. I just couldn't get my brain to send the message to my arms and legs to actually *move*. I could feel them, attached and wildly flung about, but numb, and I was unsure if they were broken or bleeding. *It is like having a high fever*, I contemplated abstractedly—that surreal out-of-body experience when you aren't sure if something is real or not.

Another wave of nausea swept through my aching form, making me groan audibly. No, this was definitely real. As I lay there, I could hear the guy still yammering away. Focusing hard on what he was saying, I tried to listen to the words through my brain fog. It had been so long since someone had spoken to me that it took me a moment to process the sound and formulate a response. It was like he was speaking to me in a foreign language, one that I had known at some point, but had long since forgotten.

He was asking me again about the journey. The voice seemed miles away, like he was speaking to someone else. A toe nudged my ribs. "Are you alive, man? The way you came flying out was something else. Wow, that must have been some ride."

What the bloody hell is this twit yapping about? I thought crankily. *Why can't he just leave me alone?*

Everything hurt. I tried to think about what had happened. Where I was. The last thing I remembered was feeling drawn into the cave, our grotto. Then staggering into the water, being sucked down. A strong, magnetic pull I couldn't escape, then a deafening roaring in my ears as a swirling vortex of darkness spun me into nothingness. I shuddered, remembering that feeling. There were no words adequate for describing that churning, spinning, powerful vortex of death, extracting the life from me. Just when I truly knew beyond any shadow of a doubt that I was going to die, it had stopped.

"A washing machine," I murmured without opening my eyes. "It felt like being trapped in the spin cycle of a deafening washing machine."

He snorted and peered at me closely. "Are you serious?"

Nodding in reply, then realizing that moving my head was a mistake, I groaned and tried not to move, the bile rising in my stomach.

After a few minutes, I tried again, cracking my eyes open to see my rescuer. The sense of vertigo hadn't yet left me. The man was spinning rather hazily in a counter-clockwise way with soft black clouds all around him.

I don't know him, I thought as I closed my eyes. He spoke again, and this time I heard the accent as well as the words. There certainly wasn't anyone on August with an accent like that.

Attempting to roll onto one elbow, I succeeded, albeit clumsily.

Forcing myself to open my eyes, I saw he was looking at me in a perplexed kind of way, illuminated by torchlight. I tried to speak, my mouth claggy with lack of moisture despite my clothes being sopping wet. I licked my lips, trying to moisturize my mouth. He noticed my struggle and handed me a metal drink bottle. I accepted with alacrity, struggling to partially sit up but managing to take a sip, although much more splashed down my chin as I misjudged the movement from hand to mouth. It was cold, fresh, and soothed my sore mouth, making me desperate for more. Taking a larger swig loosened my vocal cords. I spoke slowly, trying to put the sensation into words.

"Each year where I am from, there is a big show: animals, huge rides, a sideshow alley. One of the rides is a round thing called the Gravitron. It looks like a spaceship. Basically, people get inside and line up around the edge, and they lock you in. Then it spins and spins at high speed, and you stick to the edges. You can lie in any position, even upside down. It makes you feel weightless, but also," I grimaced, "really, really sick. As it slows down, you kind of regain control of your body and can move your limbs again."

A light of recognition crossed his face. "Ohh, aye! I've been on one of those once, but I think it was called the Spaceship. I bloody hated it."

"That's it. Well, imagine that, but about a thousand times faster, in total darkness, and completely out of control. Add the most deafening roar that makes your head feel like it is being smashed with a sledgehammer while listening to death metal. That is not a fraction of what it felt like. I have had vertigo before, but it is nothing like this. It is like feeling drunk, seasick, and dizzy while being spun at high speed. It is impossible to hold your eyes open. And your body. It feels like your body is being pulled apart, the skin being sucked off in all different directions at the same time. Then... then I guess I lost consciousness."

Silently, I vowed never to go on an amusement park ride ever again. In the next second, when I remembered that the likelihood of me ever being able to go on such a ride again was pretty much zero, I smiled as I recognized the ludicrous thought. Thank goodness

I had thought it and not said it. This guy, whoever he was, would think I was a right moron.

Able to open my eyes fully now, I focused on his face, although it was dim in the poor light of the torch and challenging to make out his features. Even from my position on the ground, I could tell that he was tall and lean but in a broad-shouldered kind of way. Longish dark hair hung around his face. I shivered; it was freezing. Being wet didn't help.

He shuddered. "Well then, I can see why your friend didn't want to do that again."

Grimacing, I responded, "No one would do *that* twice, not on purpose. The darkness sucking at you, swallowing you alive and then the spinning, throwing you around until you passed out." I had to try hard not to vomit, just remembering it. It took me a moment for comprehension to kick in.

"Hang on. You said friend?"

"Yeah, a woman. Tall, pretty, blonde. Not overly chatty. Freyja."

At the mention of Freyja, I sat all the way up, wobbled, but maintained my balance this time. Trying to control the tremble in my voice, I could only think of one word..."When?"

He looked at me closely. "Oh, six months ago, on the summer solstice."

"I'm sorry. What? It's summer now." Bloody cold tonight, though.

He looked at me sympathetically. "You didn't mean to come here, did you? Today is the winter solstice, Yule, you know. The mid-point of the year."

I knew what Yule was, the longest night and the shortest day. Mum loved having a Yule dinner. But Yule, the winter solstice, was in June, and it was

December now. And I still couldn't work out what it had to do with Freyja. My head was spinning off my shoulders. None of this made any sense.

I ventured a simpler question: "Where is here?"

He smiled. "Sorry, man. I thought you knew. You are on Lewis."

My brain struggled to process this. *Lewis? Lewis. Where the hell was Lewis?* "You mean Lewis, like, *Scotland*?" I was already sitting, but this made me jolt bolt upright. The spinning was slowing now.

The guy laughed, a deep guttural sound. "Like the accent didn't give it away!"

I couldn't help but smile. "My Mum was from a crofting family near Achmore."

His grin widened. "Seriously? My family is from near Leurbost."

In that peculiarly Scottish way, he started drilling me with questions like a teacher interrogating a student. He managed to link our family history within a few brief minutes. Our mothers had gone to high school together at the Nicolson Institute, albeit a few years apart. At that point, I realized I didn't even know his name despite now feeling like I had known him for ages. "I'm Cam," I ventured. "Campbell. Mackintosh."

"Fraser," he replied with a grin. "So, you are one of us returned home?" He closed one eye in mock suspicion.

"Well, yes. And no. I was looking for my partner, Freyja. She came here too?"

He nodded. "Of course! She came through much like you, dazed and confused. Only you are far luckier, being thrown clear of the rocks. She ended up with a ripper head wound."

"Came through? Through what?"

"The portal."

"Portal? What bloody portal? Why am I here? What the bloody hell is going on?" I could feel my agitation rise.

He saw the wild look in my eyes. "You are wondering why the link between Australia and Lewis? Freyja spent some time here pondering that one, too. She spent a lot of time talking with Angus. He was some kind of scientist for the government, you know, those who brought us here. Before."

On August, we too talked about before. Before our lives changed, the world changed. I had a million questions, but each one just triggered more. Fraser could see I was bursting and put up a hand to stop me. "All in good time. Can you walk? Let's go. It is bloody freezing out here, and it is a fair walk back. I was only here to see if someone was crazy enough to come through tonight."

"Only me," I muttered. I could stand and did. He helped me to my feet and continued to chat away to me as I walked. Occasionally, I managed to interject a question.

Fraser was a logical and natural storyteller and started from the start. That much I appreciated. Freyja had come through at midday on the summer solstice six months ago. Dazed and confused, they had originally suspected that she was an outsider who had hit her head, evidenced by the wound and blood in her hair.

"She was making no sense," he admitted. "At first, we thought she was loony. Had somehow made it in from the dead side. But then, well, she had a way of making us listen."

I snorted. "Yes, she is a rather forceful woman! So that is what you meant by solstice? Winter solstice is December here, but it is summer solstice at home."

"Aye. We think that the passage is only open at the mid-points of the year. Something to do with antipodes, magnets, and sun/moon alignment."

"An-tip-oh-dees? Antipodes? You mean like the Southern Hemisphere?"

"Yes and no. I know the English like to call Australians and New Zealanders antipodean, but the idea is far older. It originates from a historical, or perhaps geographical, concept. Basically, the theory is that if you tunneled through the earth, the place on the other side is called an antipode. The point that is diametrically opposite if you ran a line through the center of the earth. When you were a kid, that idea of digging to another country? Well, it had a historical basis. Who knew!"

"Ahh yes, An-tip-oh-dees? I vaguely recall hearing about that in high school. Not sure that I paid much attention."

"Aye then, well, most of us here hadn't. But Angus said that the theory has been around for thousands of years. I am fairly sure he said Middle Ages, ancient Greeks, Plato, and that lot. You should have seen him." Fraser smiled at the memory. "He was incredibly frustrated that he couldn't access all of his books, the internet! Kept raving about it. We have quite a library here, but not everything. Relying on memory for something a little obscure was a wee bit difficult."

"We had quite a reference collection on August too. Mostly housed on a few iPads. But lots of paper copies too as they knew that the technology wouldn't last forever, so paper books were better in the long term.

Kind of like going full circle. Remember when you could just Google something?"

Fraser sighed heavily. "Aye, I do. I miss that. Anyway, Freyja and Angus would talk long into the night, every night. Sometimes people would listen in, ask questions, sometimes not. New Zealand itself has various antipodes in Spain, which geographically is just not that far, well... not by Australian standards. And if I understand correctly, you aren't exactly sure where your island lies, but there is a decent chance that it is well south of New Zealand, which makes it a lot closer to Scotland. Your island, August, and Lewis, where you are now, while not precisely antipodal, are fairly close. If you tunneled directly through the earth, you would be in the rough vicinity. Then they started theorizing about how or why there was a variation. This went on for days, and to be honest, most of it went over my head. In the end, they decided that the slight difference was because of magnetic force."

"Magnets?"

"Well, not really. I don't understand it fully myself. The way I heard it, the earth is round, and there are constant forces—the moon, tides, rotating around the sun in orbit. The bit I did catch was that the earth's main magnetic field is believed to be generated deep down in the Earth's core, which is the result of the Earth's spin. I remember Angus saying that this is what causes swirling whirlpools and water to flow down a drain in a particular direction. As the Hebrides are near the north pole, and the southern parts of New Zealand are near the south pole, where the magnetic fields are stronger, this causes forces that pull things slightly off-center. Also, they suspected that there were lodestones, a type of natural magnet at each end. Freyja said your cave was made of a special kind of rock, but that it was magnetized?"

"That's right."

"So, the idea of a straight line, an antipode as a direct line, is a little skewed. Then, they started talking about why these two points—your island and Lewis, I mean."

"And?"

"Well, they didn't really know. But the only answer they could come up with was the standing stones."

"Callanish, you mean?"

"Aye. You know them?"

I nodded; I had been there several times. It was one of my mother's favorite places in the world. She had been drawn to them, fascinated by their history and mysterious purpose.

"Well, where I found you, back there, is in the middle of Callanish I[10], you know, the largest circle."

In the darkness, I couldn't actually see where I was. I could be in the middle of a shopping center car park, and I wouldn't know. But now that he mentioned it, as my eyes tried to focus in the darkness, I could see enormous looming figures and feel a strange vibration that I had put down to my passage.

He saw my flicker of recognition. "That's right. The stones here are over 5000 years old, but as the climate changed in the Hebrides, the peat developed and took over the sites. There was more than six feet of peat in places. The stones were buried for thousands of years, with the peat not cleared until the 1850s. Historians believe that there were many more stones, but local

---

[10] Callanish or Calanais Standing Stones, a Neolithic stone circle on Lewis.

farmers likely used the stone for building barns, byres, and fences over the years. It happened." He shrugged. "There are actually three stone circles within a short walk of the main Callanish stones, part of five still obvious. But archaeologists have long believed that there were once more, up to eight separate stone circles. But even now, there are over twenty archaeological sites within a few kilometers. They must have been here for some reason. Marking something."

I nodded again, feeling much better now that the world had stopped spinning. I vaguely remembered that. Mum driving me around to see stone circles, monoliths, and cairns. She was fascinated by them, regretting not spending more time visiting them when she was a girl living here. At twelve, I was not enamored of spending so much time in a car with my parents and sister. Online games were what I wanted to do. But the last time I was here, attending my grandmother's funeral and clearing out her croft ready to sell, I paid more attention to the history of this place. I remembered stone fences marking boundaries and seeing cottages built of ancient stones with burned-out roof frames and thatched or shingled rooftops. One of my memories was the sheer number of ruined crofts, homes, and barns—unique stone buildings, ruined, with no roof. Australia being a relatively modern country, I had never seen so many old, ruined buildings as I had in the Hebrides.

"The site where you came through is the chambered tomb, specifically in between the central monolith and the eastern stones. Unlike you, though, Freyja wasn't thrown clear. You came out face first. From what we can tell, she didn't. She suffered a nasty knock to the head on one of the stones and passed out. We think she could have been out here for days by the time she was found, sopping wet, barely able to speak, and with a bruise the size of an asteroid. But she described the stones well enough. She came through in the day, you see, but she said it was night when she accidentally stepped into the portal back on August. I was here tonight, trying to find the portal, to prove the theory in reverse. Then you appeared. Freyja said that the... gate, portal, whatever you want to call it, was in a cave where you came through?"

I nodded in agreement. "A hidden underground cave with hot springs. It was strangely magnetic. None of our compasses or equipment would work there."

"Aye, that's what she said. Angus and Freyja theorized that there were poles, if you like, antipodes between two points on the earth. The other part they theorized is that the portals were only open twice a year, at midday your time on the summer solstice, and midnight our time on our winter solstice—the midpoints of the year. When the portals are aligned—the longest day and shortest night, and vice versa. What they didn't know was how long they are open *for*."

A sudden thought struck me. I gripped his arm. "Did she? Did she go back?" *Had I missed her, passed her in that swirling vortex of terror?*

Fraser looked at his feet, stammering a little. "Ah, well, no. Freyja said no power on earth would make her repeat that journey. It took her weeks to recover from her injuries. She also knew that the chances of someone else from your place finding that portal were minimal as no one else knew it was even there. Other than you, I guess. So, she, Angus, and three others started the journey overland."

Again, the questions formed in my mind faster than I could get them out. So many things I needed to know. One question bubbled to the top. "When?"

"About four months ago, late August. They wanted to go while the weather was good."

Recognizing this logic, I nodded, but my heart sank into my boots. *She was gone. Again.* All I could manage was my next question. "How?"

Fraser didn't seem perturbed by my monosyllabic questions. Despite the swarms of questions churning through my brain fighting for supremacy, all I could manage right now were simple queries.

Fraser looked at the dark sky, then at me, assessing something. Seeing me shiver in the frosty night air, he shrugged out of his coat. While I was wearing pants and a shirt, I was wet from the portal and shivering so hard my teeth were chattering. I wanted to decline but was so cold I just nodded my thanks as I clumsily put on his thick, warm coat. Still shivering inside it, I slowly warmed and felt slightly more human.

"She mentioned you had no way off your island. Well, it is slightly different here. We also have a geodesic dome." Fraser walked swiftly down the hillside, not appearing to need the torch to see by. My boots were uncomfortably sopping wet, squelching as I walked. I struggled to keep up and listen to him as he strode along the uneven ground, covered in heather, bracken, and rocks. The little light from the stars was making visibility difficult.

"The way I understand it, all settlements were built under a geodesic dome. We were told that a normal, round dome is not all that strong and collapses under its own weight. A geodesic dome is made up of lots of triangles, basically a polyhedron. Pair domes with triangles, and you have one extremely durable structure. Triangles are the strongest shape because they have fixed angles, are structurally rigid, and disperse the stress throughout the structure. So, they can withstand weighty loads. There are some really famous ones."

I nodded. I knew what he was talking about.

"Ours is just a huge one. I guess yours was too."

I knew this part. "We were shown the fabric, based on Gore-Tex. Breathable but waterproof. I just didn't know we could open it."

"Nor did we. It wasn't until after Freyja arrived that Angus admitted that there *are* doors, access hatches he called them, built-in at various points."

I stopped walking, and Fraser, sensing my hesitation, stopped and turned to face me.

"A door? So, all this time we could have left if only we knew how?"

It made more sense to know there were escape hatches than to think we were permanently trapped. I was just surprised no one thought of it before and went looking. Fraser was watching the emotion and thoughts play across my face. No simple task in the dark. He was waiting for me to speak.

"We knew about the dome structure," I told him, "but we were never told about the escape hatches."

"Angus, he was part of the government team. He talked his way into the settlement as even though he was older than the rest of us, he was brilliant, and had immense scientific knowledge. Also, originally, he was from Harris. So, he knew the landscape, how to be self-sufficient, and work the land. Personally, I think he was such a royal pain in the ass that they wanted him far away!"

I pondered this. "Not that way for us. None of the scientific team came with us. We were... well, abandoned."

Abandoned was perhaps the wrong word. They had set us up with equipment, resources, and food. We had been chosen to ensure the survival of the human race. Fearful of what would happen to us if we remained in Australia, we had gone willingly, never questioning the structure and design. We had been provided with resources to start a new life, but knowledge, no. We had no idea. This community had a person who understood it all, the how's and why's. Perhaps abandoned wasn't the wrong word after all. How much easier would things have been for us if we had understood the science? Known that we could leave if we needed to?

Another question occurred to me. "Did Angus know about the portals?"

"No, he appeared to be as surprised as the rest of us about that. But he and Freyja came to agree that someone must have known; otherwise, why would these places have been chosen? He even said that he had recommended Harris, the south part of the island, as the settlement site as it is less rocky and has a greater quantity of freshwater but that he was told no. This was the chosen site. He never knew why."

I took this in. "We were told that there were twelve settlements in total."

Fraser nodded in agreement. "Yes, we were told the same, eventually, although we didn't know it at the time. Lewis plus eleven others. So," he looked at me, "now that we have proven the theory, ten others."

"Freyja? Where is she now?"

"I don't rightly know. Angus knew which of the triangles in the dome was the access hatch. He never told us, but one of our people followed as they left, so now we know too. Took us a bit to work out how to open it, though, but we have our ways." Fraser grinned. "He, Freyja, and three other men from here left back in late August."

"What do you mean? You mean she went out.... there?"

Sighing deeply, Fraser halted his long stride and looked at me. "It has been nearly three years. But truthfully, we don't know if it is safe out there either. They were the first to leave. Like you, we didn't even know we could until Freyja arrived, and Angus admitted it."

I stopped walking too, although as much to catch my breath as continue the conversation. I was reasonably fit after a few years on August, but lack of food over the past months, combined with the heather and peat on Lewis making the ground boggy and uneven, made it tougher going here.

"Freyja refused to stay here or go back through the portal. Angus was champing to get going, too. So, they took a chance, took a boat from the harbor in Stornoway, and left."

"A boat?"

Fraser grinned again. "Well, we are on an island, you know! There is a small airport at Stornoway, and although they had access to small aircraft, they didn't know if they could find fuel on the way. Also, a little tricky to use a plane when no one knows how to fly it."

"Where did they go?"

"Well, the plan was to get back to you, Australia, I mean. Though, to be honest, they were both fairly sure by then that you were actually on an island south of New Zealand, and you had been given misinformation to stop people from trying to find you. Family members and such. But they also planned to see if they could discover any other communities on the way. Prove the theory of the twelve communities and portals. Make contact."

Something occurred to me. "You have to wonder how people have not been popping through these portals for years, don't you? I mean, Callanish is a popular tourist attraction. Midday on the summer solstice is a prime time for visitors. Surely they don't just snap a photo and pop off to an island off the coast of New Zealand for six months. Fairly sure the media and the Government would get wind of that fairly quickly."

"Agreed. It doesn't look like anyone has traveled for a long time. Yet there are certainly records dating back thousands of years about the antipodal points, so someone must have known precisely where they were, and how to open them."

We continued walking in silence, the bone-deep weariness of fatigue making moving forward difficult. Sometime later, shadows of low-rise buildings came into view.

"Where are we going?"

Fraser didn't slow his stride. "To the village. You'd be hungry, no? Besides, you need some dry clothes, and I need my bed. It is the wee small hours of the morning, man!"

"Village?" I enquired tentatively. The last time I was near people, I hadn't fared so well.

"Well, village is a loose term," he admitted. "We were granted an estate with freshwater rivers and lochs, good hunting grounds. But also a mill, stables, and dairy. So, the basics were here already. Freyja told us you had to start from scratch?"

"We did," I admitted. "It was tough."

"I doubt it was as tough as here," Fraser said with a harsh note in his voice. I started to ask what he meant but saw that he had bounded off ahead and was announcing our arrival with a loud "hellooooo!"

People in various stages of undress appeared bleary-eyed in doorways, staring at me with amazement. Despite the unearthly hour and disheveled appearance, I was welcomed with typical Scots hospitality. A small, delicious-smelling hot pasty filled with meat and vegetables was thrust into my hand, and a dram of whisky into the other. I closed my eyes and tried not to drool. I was starving! I couldn't remember the last time I ate. Who on earth had hot food at well past midnight? I didn't argue as I devoured it in three large bites and washed it down with the glass of whisky.

Villagers kept introducing themselves in a range of English and Scots accents, the occasional Welsh or Irish one. But the faces swam in and out of view, and I struggled to focus on faces and voices. I felt like I might faint. *That would be a great look,* I thought, forcing myself to stiffen my spine and remain upright.

A sweet-looking woman of about twenty-five, clad in a winter coat over striped flannel pajamas and long thick dark hair neatly plaited down her back, finished talking to Fraser, glanced over at me, nodding in agreement with something he had said. Seeing the fatigue on my face, she beckoned for me to go with her and shooed everyone back to bed.

Too weary to resist, I followed her to a small cabin, clearly prefabricated and transported here, and despite the pitched roof and thicker walls, not so different from our own. Inside was a small but functional kitchen with a small round table and three chairs, a lounge room with a couch and a bookcase, and two bedrooms at the end of a short hallway. She steered me silently toward the smaller of the two rooms, furnished plainly with a large comfortable looking bed, a bedside table, and a single chair. I sat in the chair as she helped me to unlace my boots, my hands frozen and unable to manage the cold, wet laces frozen into muddy knots. She helped me remove my boots. As I shrugged out of my clothes, she gestured me toward the bed, taking my wet clothes. Comfortable looking, it turned out to be blissful as soon as I lay down. I was grateful that she didn't want to talk. I lay on the deep mattress, the woman engulfing me with heavy blankets that made me relax almost instantly. The weight of blankets always helped me sleep. Hearing the door gently close, I lay and listened to the muffled sound of the wind howling outside the dome. It was wild out there. I tried not to think of Freyja on a boat in the ocean. She was smart. She would know to make landfall if a storm was brewing. But then, hadn't Fraser said that she left months ago? She would be well away by now, possibly nearly as far as August? *Oh, Frey, where are you?*

Despite desperate exhaustion, my head was spinning from the events of the past few hours. The journey to the cave, and the passage through the vortex still made me feel nauseated. The sense of vertigo hadn't completely passed, and I put my hand on the icy wall to steady myself, even though I was already lying down. Here. Scotland. Mum's home. How on earth had that happened? If nothing else, I had some fantastic news: Freyja was alive! She had arrived here by accident. Now, so had I. Only to learn that she had left. How I missed mobile phones! In the old days, I just would have picked up the phone and called. Now, I faced a decision. Stay. Return. Go after her. None of these options were attractive at the moment.

Falling into a fitful sleep, I dreamed my limbs were slowly being plucked off by a giant spider who spun me at the end of a thread for entertainment. He grinned at me, the light glinting maniacally from his hundreds of black beady eyes.

CHAPTER 23

A DIM LIGHT CREEPING UNDER the door and around the curtains woke me, lighting the basic but pleasant room. Looking around, I took in the décor. Simple but cozy. The walls were plastered and painted an off-white, but judging by the frost on the outside of the windows when I opened the curtains, the insulation was good. Simple dark-colored curtains hung on the single window. No prints or decoration, and cold timber floors, I discovered as I swung my legs out of bed. Opening the single wardrobe, I found it was empty except for a few hangers dangling silently, waiting to be useful. Clearly, no one lived here with her. It was a guest room, maybe? I snorted as I dismissed that idea. How many guests did you get wandering into a protected village? Well, aside from me, that is. And Freyja. Okay, so maybe they did get the odd guest.

There was a clean t-shirt hanging on the chair, presumably for me, so I put it on and went looking for my clothes and boots as well as a toilet, desperate for a piss. Surreptitiously, I looked in each of the four rooms as I passed. Damn. No toilet. This was becoming awkward. No plant pots either. Do I just make a run for the front door?

The cottage being quite small, I almost immediately found the pretty dark-haired woman I had met the night before in the kitchen, making something that smelled delicious. My stomach churned with hunger pangs. With a sinking feeling, I realized I couldn't remember her name. Shit. How rude. I knew she had introduced herself the night before, along with everyone else. Here I was, a stranger in her home. She was making me breakfast, and I couldn't even remember her name. Hoping she wouldn't kick me out, I smiled at her, taking a direct approach.

"Hi, I'm Cam," I declared cheerfully, trying to look dignified, despite the fact that I was wearing a t-shirt and not much else.

"Aye, I know," she said, not looking up from her cooking. "We met last night."

Gulping, I realized she wasn't going to make this easy.

"Or do you not remember?" She turned back to face me, a glint of good-natured teasing in her exotic almond-shaped brown eyes.

I flushed. Sometimes honesty really is the best approach.

"The truth is, I don't remember much about yesterday at all. That trip was… well, let's just say it isn't something I ever want to repeat."

Her grin turned to a look of sympathy. "I'm sorry. I shouldn't tease you then. I'm Laetitia, but most people call me Lae. Don't be calling me Tish mind!" she warned in mock sternness.

Relief must have flooded my face as she laughed. "Come. I've made breakfast. You must be half-starved." She gestured toward one of the seats at the table.

I stood and fidgeted, unsure what to do or say. Fortunately, Lae guessed my plight.

"Do you need the cludgie, then?"

Silently blessing my mother for using such words, I nodded with relief. Gesturing toward the external door, she said, "Outside and to the left."

It wasn't difficult to locate. The actual toilets were very similar to August, deep pits with a toilet seat and lid, but here it was a small, enclosed room between houses, not one per house. Looking curiously around the small space, and picking up the leaves on the bench to the right of the seat, I learned toilet paper here was a different plant to August. Feeling it between my fingers, I recognized it as a plant called lamb's ear. From my days working in the nursery at home, I knew it wasn't native. Soft gray woolly leaves. It did the job and was surprisingly comfortable as well. As I left the small room, I saw it grew in large tracts throughout the village, so it had naturalized. People evidently just grabbed a few leaves on their way. I was most fortunate this morning to find that some kind soul had left me some. On August, we had used a native plant called rangiora that grew in the coastal areas and forests. A flowering shrub that looked like a daisy, the underside was soft with light hairs. Jacinda had told me once that it was called bushman's friend in New Zealand, as the first white settlers had used it for the same purpose. *Funny how things go in cycles*, I contemplated. Toilet paper was such a modern invention, yet for thousands of years, people had used natural products. We were so accustomed to sterile bathrooms and white toilets, yet it had not been that way for a long time in the overall scheme of things, so it wasn't hard to adapt. A memory of Sorcha as a young teenager wanting to take toilet paper on a family bushwalk in the mountains flashed into my mind. Dad had declined, resulting in her refusing to go. She would be horrified here. Then again, maybe like all of us, the will to survive, to thrive, would over-come all of our personal eccentricities.

Returning to the house, much relieved, I found my cleaned and dried clothing on the back of one of the wooden kitchen chairs. Hurriedly I put them on, but Lae respectfully kept her back turned, focused on cooking breakfast and chatting to me. Laetitia was a happy, friendly woman and kept up a steady stream of chatter which slowly broke down my reserve. Tiny in stature, her head would easily fit under my chin, she was also humble and quite prepared to make fun of herself, a trait that Scots and Aussies seemed to have in common. Her long dark hair regularly fell in her face, and she pushed it back unconsciously as she cooked. Golden highlights glinted in the light as she floated about the kitchen, light on her feet. Noticing that there were three places set, I asked, "Is someone else coming?"

"Fraser. He lives next door."

"Your boyfriend?" I asked without thinking. She looked up, startled at the boldness of my question, and I flamed red, embarrassed that I had overstepped the boundary of social etiquette.

"Goodness, no!" She laughed, a lovely bubbling sound. "He has a partner. But she works nights, a vet, you know. So, he comes for breakfast, so Isla can sleep.

He wanted to keep an eye on you, so he asked if I would take you in."

My face must have shown alarm at the reference to a vet, as she looked distressed.

"Are you alright then? Do you need me to fetch the medic?"

Shaking my head in negation, I tried to cover my embarrassment in the cup of coffee now in front of me. I took a large gulp, coughed at the extreme heat, and nearly choked as I tried not to spit the retained coffee all over my host's dining table.

You bloody fool Mackintosh! I berated myself. *Now she will think you rude and with no manners.*

Lae came and wrestled the cup from my death grip as I continued to cough and splutter. Probably just as well before I snapped the handle off in my attempt to recover myself. My hands freed, I managed to cover my mouth, swallow the steaming hot coffee, and stop coughing. Tears streamed down my face, and I wiped at them with my sleeve.

Lae handed me a clean tea towel and sat down next to me, concern wrinkling her sweet face, gazing at me with the most enticing pair of honey-brown eyes I had ever seen. Warm and alive with intelligence, with the slightest flecks of gold.

"Was the coffee that bad then?"

Fraser arrived soon after, bringing me a change of clothes and a backpack for my use.

After thanking him profusely for helping me the previous night, we talked about life on August compared with life here.

"Do you not know where this island of yours is?"

"I really don't. There is a forest of rata trees, inaka, and even rangiora, and you don't find any of those in Australia."

"What's a rata tree?" he asked.

"Well, it is a tree native to New Zealand. Some of them were ten or twelve meters tall with a trunk up to a meter in diameter. It produces these masses of red flowers between December and February, our summer, and is quite stunning. The timber is strong with rough, flaky bark. There is nothing like it in Australia, I am fairly sure, so I have a fairly strong suspicion we are actually off the coast of New Zealand."

"Angus and Freyja came to that conclusion, too. There is a greater chance of an antipodal point near New Zealand than Australia. They calculated that most of Australia's antipodes were in the ocean, unlike New Zealand. They pretty much narrowed it down to Auckland Islands, Macquarie Island, or Ruapuke Island. Those are the closest to here in terms of antipodes. But Macquarie Island didn't have the fresh water supply that Auckland did, and when Freya described the terrain as two prominent hills, they were both fairly sure that it was the Ruapuke Islands you were on. Angus swears he remembers reading an article about a magnetic anomaly in that region that included those islands. Being volcanic, with a magnetic anomaly and not inhabited—swell, they think they had narrowed it down. They were just going to head in that direction and, well... explore, I guess."

"I have never heard of those islands. Where are they?"

"South of New Zealand, closer to Antarctica but New Zealand territories."

"That makes sense," I considered. "Long summer days and very few daylight hours in winter. But cool year-round. What I still can't work out is how people weren't disappearing all over the place on the solstice. If antipodes are real, and I now have reason to believe that they aren't, then why have they not been active until now?"

"Angus was obsessed with that, too," Laetitia interjected. "He said he found written references to antipodes dating back thousands of years, to at least the seventh century. Some Spanish scholar wrote about them, but there are Greek references that are even older."

"But the stones here are much older than that. They are something like 3000 BC, aren't they?" I asked.

"They are. So, it means that people throughout history knew about the antipodean portals, but someone, at some point, has worked out how to close them," Lae responded.

"Who, and why?"

"Both excellent questions. But sadly, ones we do not have the answer to." Fraser shrugged.

Conversation ceased as we tucked into Lae's breakfast of bacon, eggs, toast, haggis, and the most fantastic tattie scone I had ever tasted. I poked at the haggis dubiously, despite being ravenous.

"Don't tell me you have never eaten haggis?" His accent was deliberately stronger than usual, taunting me.

"No, I have. Just not... often."

"Not a fan?" Lae teased.

"It isn't that," I responded quickly, lest she thought I was offending her and her cooking. I had been in this place for less than five minutes. I didn't want people to think I was insulting them at my first meal. I might find myself homeless immediately after breakfast. My grandmother had made haggis. My mother was quite fond of it, although she always complained that she couldn't get a proper haggis in Australia. It was close, but not the same as home, she said. Once when I was about eight, I had watched my granny making it in a large wooden barrel outside. She had added oats, herbs, and salt and pepper. Using her arm, she had mixed the ingredients well. It had turned my stomach as I had watched her mix the warm blood, heart, lungs, and liver with the grains. Quietly, I had disappeared into the bushes behind the shed and promptly thrown up.

"You know how it is made?" Lae asked gently.

I nodded. I knew exactly how—blood and all the offal and bits of the animal that no one would eat.

"You know, personally, I think it is an honor to the animal," she said quietly.

That surprised me, and I said so.

"Well, we eat the meat." She lifted a piece of perfectly pan-fried bacon on her fork in illustration. "We tan the skin to make leather. The bones are boiled up to make gelatin, for glue and such. The blood is used to make haggis or sausage. All of the animal is used in some way. I think it would be far more disrespectful to the wee beastie if we just wasted most of it."

She had a point. Swallowing the memory of my grandmother pouring warm blood into the barrel and it streaking her forearms as she mixed, I forked a piece of haggis into my mouth and chewed industriously. Fraser just sat there, grinning.

"Well, at least you don't eat your national animal," I pointed out. "Australians eat kangaroo."

It was Laetitia's turn to look horrified. "Really?" she gasped.

"Well, rarely. But you could. Then."

I learned that the village here was centered near Garynahine, a place I didn't recall, at the crossroads where the roads that led to Uig in the south, Stornoway in the northeast, and the west coast of Lewis all met.

"Basically in the middle of nothing at all," Fraser announced with some sourness.

The village wasn't in the center of the dome, but unlike us, not on the coast. Lae confirmed what Fraser had told me the night before. When the site had first been chosen, there was a large hunting lodge here, and that now formed the common areas, the central kitchen, and storage cellars. Portable buildings had been brought in to create village housing for families or couples. People who worked in the kitchens usually still lived in the main house to access the larders and communal facilities. I didn't dare ask why she had a two-bedroom home to herself, although there were no dormitories here. Part of the site adjoined Loch Beag, a freshwater loch, and at the opposite end Loch Roag, a saltwater lake that ran out to the Atlantic Ocean originally, but it had been dammed and formed an enclosed loch. There were also forty smaller freshwater lochs on the estate, all of which offered good trout fishing.

"Do you like to fish?" Laetitia asked, somewhat hopefully. "We are always short of fisherman.

Although, they are progressing well in building the salmon farm."

I confessed that I didn't. I always struggled to kill fish as they thrashed, dying on the hook.

"So, what is your thing?" Fraser asked. "Hunting?"

I grimaced. "Australians are not big gun owners."

"Aye, I remember that. My brother and I visited Australia for the summer of my first year at university. Beautiful place. I didn't get to see much of it. I had no idea how big it really was. I thought I could see most of it in a few weeks. How wrong I was!"

I laughed. "We hear that a lot. People don't seem to realize that Australia is bigger than all of Europe. No, I'm much better at growing things than killing them. I worked in the gardens and orchards on August," I said, noticing even as I called it that, I didn't say home.

"Ahh, that's my job, too. Well then. If you like, you can come to work with me. I'd love the company," Fraser declared. "But tomorrow, though. You will want to explore the village and rest a bit today, no?"

Fraser left for work, and Lae suggested a shower, to which I enthusiastically agreed.

"Would you like a haircut?" she asked cautiously, clearly not wanting to offend me.

"Do a look a little wild?"

She laughed. "Let's just say that you might get a better reception if you are groomed a bit."

Finding the main house they mentioned wasn't hard. A multiple story, and rather imposing nineteenth-century manor house at the top end of the village, it was unmistakably the only older building here and one that had been cared for. Lovely rendered white walls with a charcoal slate roof and multiple chimneys were topped with chimney pots, now in disuse. I smiled, looking at them. I hadn't seen chimney pots in years. Enormous windows let the light in on the lower floors, gabled on the upper floors, built to give a glorious view of the surrounding countryside. It was the perfect place for a hunting and fishing lodge as it had been in its former life.

Feeling it was rude to wander through the house uninvited, I took to exploring the extensive grounds. There were a lot of outbuildings, many quite some distance from the house. Heading west so the sun wasn't in my eyes as I walked, I spotted a timber building with double barn doors, an old slate roof and hay scattered around as well as long paddocks for exercising horses and saddles hanging over rails. A man was resting outside, clearly taking a break from rubbing down horses. He smiled in a friendly manner and invited me to sit with him.

Striking up a conversation, we spoke about Australia, August, and life there. He seemed genuinely interested and was surprised when I told him we had no horses. I guessed Freyja hadn't engaged in chitchat with many people. She could be a bit standoffish with strangers. I soon learned that Mike had been studying agricultural science at Nottingham and was from an affluent, multi-generation farming family from Norfolk. I cringed a little when an off-the-cuff comment implied that Freyja had treated him as nothing more than a stable boy, preferring the company of her people. Angus by the sounds of it.

I was delighted to see horses had survived and said so. There weren't any on August. Sorcha had owned a horse and was a talented equestrienne. Personally, I wasn't great with horses. Sorcha's horse had detested me, but I always loved seeing them in their paddocks on our way to our place in the country with their beautiful, intelligent eyes.

"The terrain here can be rough going. The decision was made to keep horses to help with the heavy work," Mike advised.

There were quite a few horses in the yard in front of me: several large chestnuts, bays, and a beautiful black stallion with a demonic glint in his eye. Mike saw me watching cautiously. "Aye, I'd steer well clear of that one. Foul temper he has. Would sooner bite you than the food you are feeding him."

That reminded me much of Dougal, Sorcha's evil beast.

"Why do you keep him them? Surely when there is room for only a few, you would only keep the good-natured ones."

Mike sighed. "He is a decent breeder and has fantastic bloodlines. We just hope we can train any cantankerousness out of the foals. So far, so good," he acknowledged.

"How many horses do you have?"

"We started at twenty. Lost two but gained six. So, we are doing well. If we get another stallion with good bloodlines though and a better temper, Hades over there had better watch out."

"Twenty-four horses. That is quite a lot for a small community. How many people are on the island?" I asked curiously. It seemed much more extensive than August.

"There were 350... well, inside the dome."

I raised my eyebrows. This raised several questions, and I was unsure what to ask first. "Inside?" I asked tentatively.

He sighed, looked down at the ground, and explained. I soon realized that this was what Fraser had meant with his cryptic comments on the way from the stones at Callanish the night before.

Twisting a piece of hay between his fingers, Mike explained that when most of Lewis and Harris had been forcibly cleared, some residents had simply refused to go. This was all they knew. They had lived here for generations, farming this land. Many of the older folk had never left the island.

"They knew it was the end, and they wanted to die here in their homes. It appears that the authorities had better things to do than force it." He grimaced. "Probably getting home to their own families. But," he continued, "most of the locals had seen the trucks, helicopters, and large freighters come and go, so they knew that something was afoot. About two weeks after we were in place and the dome was sealed, they started coming," he said, choking back emotion. He flicked the piece of hay to the ground.

"Coming?" I asked tentatively, but I knew what he meant.

"We could see them perfectly—through the dome, you know. They could see us as well. But they couldn't get in, and we couldn't help them. They banged, and they cried. Tried to cut the fabric, burn it, even ran a car into it. But it held. Stood there for hours in the pouring rain, knowing it would likely kill them. Brought their children, their babies." Mike looked down, ashamed. "We could hear them, and they us.

Muffled, but you never forget a mother asking you to take her baby. To save her life. It was singularly the most horrific thing I have ever seen in my life." He slammed his hand down on the dirt, clouds of dust rising around us.

Mike looked up at me. "Have you ever seen someone die in front of you?"

I shook my head, speechless.

Mike stood up and looked down at me. "It wasn't until Freyja arrived that we realized Angus *had* known the way to open the dome. Let's just say that it didn't make him very popular around here."

Silently, I questioned the ethics of this man who was now with my beloved Freyja.

"I can't imagine it did. What would you have done?" I asked curiously, knowing what I would do. Survivor guilt had always eaten away at me, even when it wasn't in my face.

"We would have let them in, of course. We all wanted to. They were people the same as us; they were innocents in all of this. This was their home. They lived here and probably had more right to be here than all of us. Who were we to let them die? But we didn't know how to help them, and they died. Slowly and in pain. Literally in front of us. They never gave up, and we never forgave ourselves. I can't really describe what it feels like to see innocent people, children, die in front of you and feel helpless to save them. It caused a lot of grief here in our first year."

Mike paused, clearly remembering the events of that time. "Several here wanted to go out, die with the rest. Others said that was stupid. We were chosen, and we had a responsibility to ensure we survived as a species. The arguing didn't end until... well... when we realized…. that we *were* all alone. We assumed that there was no one was left in the world. So, you can imagine our shock when your friend Freyja turned up, soaking wet and raving like a lunatic about another sustainable village off the coast of Australia. That she had come through a portal at Callanish. Initially, we believed she was mad."

"I can imagine that it was a little difficult to swallow."

"After Freyja arrived, Angus told us about the other communities around the world. Twelve of them, he said. Before that, we assumed we were all alone. We had certainly been led to believe that was the case. The part that people here took issue with was the fact that Angus *knew* most of it but had kept it from us for more than *two years*."

"How much did he know?"

"Most of it, I think. When Freyja came, and we learned Angus *knew* that there was a way to help those poor people, he was *detested*. Loathed. Despised. I don't think there is a word powerful enough to sum up the sheer venom people felt toward him. But Freyja, she seemed to like him. She certainly spent a lot of time with him, listening to him, and as a result, people stayed clear of her. People here think that is why he left with her. He knew no one here would ever trust him again. The strange thing is, with Angus gone, the community is… well… happier."

My stomach clenched. *Just who was this man Freyja was traveling with? If he had no morals about his fellow man, did that extend to her?* In an attempt to quell my rising temper, I asked, "How big is this site?"

"About 400 square kilometers. About as far as Arnol in the north. One part accesses the sea at Carloway, not the water mind, just to the cliff edge in the west.

Not quite as far as Stornoway in the east. Otherwise, lots of grazing and hunting land, lots of freshwater lochs and rivers. We have a salmon farm doing well. Even a large saltwater loch where we are building a herring farm. Enough to keep our small community alive."

"Down as far as Harris?" I asked, not sure where the border was.

"They aren't two islands, you know, though they are referred to as if they are. The island narrows between two lochs, Loch Resort and Loch Seaforth, which is considered the border. But no, back to your question, the dome falls farther north than that, near Balallan."

"You said before that there were 350 people here? That is more than August. We only had 300. Well 298," I corrected. "But then there were the children born there."

"We started with 350 people, but we lost five in the first year or two. Accidents, mostly. But we soon made up for that. Now we have 385," he said proudly.

"Forty babies in three years!" I exclaimed.

"Aye," he said as proudly as if they were his own. As it turned out, two were. Twin boys, born eighteen months ago with another on the way. "Little horrors they are too! Into everything. Good thing Laetitia keeps them in order. She takes no nonsense from any of them."

"Laetitia?"

"Aye, she is the teacher, you know. Damned fine one too."

I found this hard to believe. Soft, kind Laetitia, managing a group of rowdy children?

Something occurred to me.

"When did you come here? When did they install the dome, I mean?"

"13 April, coming up for three years ago now."

"In April? Really. So after us then. It was on 20 February for us." *Freyja and my anniversary,* I thought sadly.

Hesitantly, I asked, "Can I ask when you saw the last people... outside?"

"July 24. That was the... last."

July. Not long after we learned the pandemic had reached Australia. But six months before we lost contact.

We sat in silence for a long time. Mike finally got up, excused himself, and went back to the horses. I continued to explore, troubled by what this community had endured. Maybe it had been less traumatic for us, being relocated to an uninhabited island. As hard as it had been to start from scratch, we didn't feel that we were taking anyone's homes, their land. To see people dying must have been gut-wrenching. Who was this Angus who was now with Freyja? Steeling myself, I resolved to find her, and him.

CHAPTER 24

BEING TREATED WITH SUSPICION is different from being treated with outright hostility. As a stranger in a new place, there is an element of interest in the shiny new thing. Upon first meeting, I was treated with polite caution, friendly but just a little distant. Now that I knew the history, I understood. They had come closer as a community because of the trauma they had witnessed. Freyja had not been engaging and had most unfortunately aligned herself with the most hated person here. But I was included in meetings from the start, asked for my advice and my horticultural experience. People were genuinely interested in our community on August. Fraser first, but later, others in the community consulted with me about expanding the gardens, and this advice was acted upon without question. I felt valued and trusted. Not like August. By the time I left, I had felt untrustworthy, and by association, I felt guilty. As stupid as it sounds, I *felt* guilty, despite knowing that I was completely innocent of what I was accused of. The problem with innocence is that often you still feel guilty as you didn't stop the event from occurring. After Freyja's disappearance, I had barely existed. On Lewis, I may have been a stranger, but after the first week, I wasn't treated as *strange*. I realized I was sleeping better, and I hadn't had a migraine since I had arrived.

Early in our second year on August, Ilana had died after falling down a cliff. Some of the community had rallied together afterward. She wasn't liked, being a nosy interfering person with a blatant disregard for people's privacy and no knowledge of acceptable social boundaries. But we had talked and generally supported each other after the first death of our new world. Freyja hadn't liked Ilana, but I had convinced her it was necessary to mark her life. We had agreed on a ceremony, burial in the new cemetery—cremation being out of the question with the smoke issue. We wondered what to do with her belongings in the absence of next of kin. Overall, it was therapeutic, although unlike here, we didn't grow closer as a community. It did nothing to ease the tension between the factions or quell the arguments.

Freyja's disappearance was different. There was suspicion, judgment. After the first few days of concern when it was assumed she would turn up, that judgment was nearly entirely directed at me. For the millionth time since coming through the antipodean portal, I wondered where she was now. She was alive, I knew, and that was of immense relief. If only she had waited! But I fully understood why she hadn't. She had no way of knowing I would follow. It was like watching a terrible movie where the main characters keep missing each other, and you end up yelling at the screen, "Pick up the bloody *phone* and just *call!*" I understood why she hadn't wanted to go back through the portal. I shuddered just thinking about it, hearing the roaring thunder so loud I knew my head would burst. The spinning of my body in the vortex, so fast I couldn't control my limbs. First one way, then the other. I vaguely recalled the brief sensation of slowing in the middle, the eye of the storm, only to be spun the opposite way.

In one of my undergraduate science classes, we studied the Coriolis effect, that concept that cyclones spin counter-clockwise in the Northern Hemisphere but rotate clockwise in the Southern Hemisphere. When we learned about it and talked about the effects, including the direction of water down drains, I had no knowledge that one day I would experience the Coriolis effect firsthand. A human guinea pig. Freyja was right. The long way round was probably best. The problem for me was that I couldn't follow. I didn't know how to sail, nor did I have access to an ocean-worthy vessel. Freyja had grown up in a wealthy family, attended elite private schools. She had friends who belonged to exclusive sailing clubs, schools that taught sailing as part of the curriculum. My parents were a teacher and a paramedic, an entirely different world. We had led a comfortable life but certainly not one filled with exclusive clubs. She knew how to sail a yacht. Her parents had owned one. She had attended social events at the private club where they had been members since moving to Australia. Freyja had told me that her first kiss was on the beach at one of these events. Sailing to Australia from Scotland likely wasn't daunting for her. I had been on a yacht, as a passenger, a grand total of twice.

There was no pressure here for me to work. I was treated as a guest and a welcome one. It was me who felt the need to earn my keep. After my first days of exploring, my daily routine was quickly established. Waking early with the sun, breakfast with Lae and Fraser, sometimes with Isla, depending on her shifts. Isla was five months pregnant with their first child and getting uncomfortable. Despite his outgoing and effervescent personality, Fraser was a doting partner, bringing her meals, hot cups of tea, and rubbing her aching feet. Sometimes I found it overwhelming, being in such proximity to a happy expectant couple— Freyja's comment about taking our children to work still fresh in my mind.

One morning, feeling uncomfortable, I got up and started clearing the dishes. As I turned back to get the next round of plates, I caught Lae looking at me intently. I had the oddest sensation that she could see straight through me and knew exactly what I was feeling. I smiled at her, but clearly it wasn't con-vincing. She kept watching me, that same serious look on her face as I returned to wash the dishes.

After breakfasting together each day, Fraser and I went to work in the gardens. Fraser was undemanding company, always happy for a chat, and easy to get along with. He was knowledgeable, reasonable, and genuinely a decent guy. He had the respect of the vil-lage, and I liked him. From the time he found me at the stones, Fraser hadn't treated me as an outsider.

One morning, thinking of my family as I often did, I asked Fraser, "You said you were from Leurbost.

Was your family there... when...?" I trailed off, unable to finish.

Fraser shook his head. "No. I was at university in Glasgow with my brother. I was studying agricultural science. He was already there, studying law. He... wasn't chosen. No need for a lawyer here, I guess. I always teased him that lawyers were blood-sucking parasites, but I never knew that it might have contributed to..."

"Your parents?" I queried gently, subtly shifting the conversation from his brother.

"My mum died when I was seventeen. Cancer. Dad didn't cope, so he moved to Glasgow with us when we left. Said he couldn't stay here all alone. He was with Lachlan, my brother, when I left. I didn't want to go, but they insisted. Sometimes I think of all those things I said or did over the years. Had I known *this* would happen..." he trailed off quietly.

I nodded, thinking of Sorcha and all the nasty things I had said to her over the years.

"I know what you mean," I replied. "My sister. We weren't close, but I would give anything to have her back now."

Fraser inhaled, recognizing that I did indeed understand. "If Isla has a boy, we will name him Lachlan," he concluded.

CHAPTER 25

LOOKING UP AT FRASER as we dug potatoes together from raised garden boxes in the greenhouse, shook them free of dirt, and separated them into eating and seed potato piles, I paused, unsure how to start the conversation. The larger, unblemished ones could be eaten or stored. The small ones, or those with blemishes, were reserved for growing next season's potatoes.

"Fraser?"

He grunted.

"Have you ever been to Newgrange?"

Fraser looked at me. "Is that in Australia?"

"No, it is an archaeological site. In Ireland. Close to Dublin."

He scratched his head meditatively and considered for a moment. "I think I have heard of it. Never been there, though. Why?"

"I have been there once," I said slowly, "as a teenager. The site itself looked like one of the Clava Cairns, you know, the chambered cairns near Inverness?"

"Oh aye, I have been to Clava many a time. My aunt lived between there and Culloden. We used to walk her wee dogs there." Fraser looked interested now. "Beautiful place Clava is."

"Well, it is like that, but bigger. Much bigger. But unlike Clava, this one is on the top of a hill. Do you know how at Clava they are open rings, thick walls but with no roof? And there is a narrow pathway in and out? Well, this is similar. Massively bigger; you can walk in, and it is still complete and waterproof. The site had the same *feel* about it as Clava. That sense of utter stillness and tranquility. I'm not religious, not really even that spiritual, but you know how some places just have a special feel about them?"

"Aye," he drawled, but not seeing my point. "Clava is special."

"Well," I explained, "I took a tour when I was there at Newgrange. The actual cairn held about twenty people, so it was fairly big inside, much bigger than Clava. But the outside was enormous. It covered something like an acre. It had these massive curbstones around the outside with carvings on them. I don't remember what they were made of. I remember it was built over 5000 years ago, much like the stones at Callanish. I remember it being older than Stonehenge and the pyramids of Giza."

Fraser was listening, but I could see his face was wondering about my point.

"So, I was thinking... we had carvings like that, on August, in the cave. You know, the entrance to the portal?"

Fraser nodded, following my train of thought. "Freyja mentioned carvings. Celtic, she said."

"Older, I think. But the thing that struck me about Newgrange was that it was built with absolute precision."

"Precision? What do you mean?" Fraser had stopped working now and was looking at me, intrigued.

"I don't remember exactly, but there was something about the entrance being special. It was built in such a way that on the dawn of the winter solstice, and that one day only, the sun would rise, shine through a tiny window, up the main corridor and illuminate the entire tomb. It would only last for a few minutes. It was so unique that they would raffle off places to be there. Even as a teenager, it struck me that it must have taken generations of people to build this phenomenal place, that was basically a beacon to the solstice—the mid-points of the year. I remember at the time wondering how many attempts they had made at engineering it. After all, the winter solstice comes around once a year, and the sun moves, so the engineering precision had to be immense. When the average lifespan back then probably wasn't very long, that was some commitment. So, I have been thinking: what is it about these places that ancient civilizations knew they were special precisely at the solstice? Callanish, Newgrange, maybe even Stonehenge. Didn't the sunlight at the solstice fall in a certain way at Stonehenge, through the key stones?"

"Aye, I think you are right. I recall seeing that. Druid groups used to go there on the solstice. I saw it on the news a few times. So, are you saying that this place, Newgrange, is another portal? Clava and Stonehenge too?"

"I have no idea. But it is a bit strange, isn't it? Those ancient societies built these revered sites in precise locations that shone the solstice light in a certain way. Now, we know that one of them is an antipodean portal. Someone knew something."

There was silence between us as we continued to shake the dirt from the potatoes. We had quite an enormous pile now. Finally, Fraser asked, "Does that mean there are others? Like us, I mean."

"I have no idea. We were told twelve sites around the world—no idea where. But we weren't told about the antipodes. Surely that isn't a coincidence. Do you think they are all linked to archaeological sites?"

Fraser scratched his head again. "It certainly makes sense. Based on what we know, Callanish links to your island. Both had evidence of ancient civilizations. Yours, carvings in a cave. Ours the circle itself. They were marking something. That both were chosen to be ground zero sites can't be a coincidence. You have to assume that someone knew they linked and realized that eventually, we would work it out."

"Do you think Angus knew?" I asked between gritted teeth. I liked this man less the more I heard of him. The fact that he was with Freyja miles from civilization made my blood boil. Still, I knew she could take care of herself.

Fraser pondered that. "I doubt it. Had he known, he would have used it sooner. No, he asked her many questions about the passage, so I think that part came as a surprise. He knew about the other communities, how to open the dome, and kept both secret. He and Freyja undertook a lot of research, geography, history, mathematics, working out that New Zealand, Borneo, and parts of South America had many antipodal points. They also theorized that the other communities must be aligned. They were always poring over maps, trying to work out where they could be. Finally, Freyja said she was sick of reading books and theorizing. She was leaving, and he could come or not. So... they went."

"It was quite a risk, wasn't it, to leave?"

Fraser shrugged. "I guess so. They had a plan. Get to the mainland and find something bigger."

"What about drinking water?"

"They took quite a lot from here but planned to work that one out on the way. They took an engineer and two ex-military guys. I suspect they went for the adventure. Life here not being all that exciting."

Freyja was brave, but not reckless—she would find a way. But my stomach was churning as I continued to harvest potatoes in silence.

CHAPTER 26

AFTER THREE WEEKS OF working the gardens at Garynahine with Fraser, he finally convinced me to take a day off. The experiences of August still fresh in my mind, I wanted to be helpful, part of the team. Unsure what to do, I stood and looked at the horizon, wondering if I should try to locate my aunt's home. Mike had said that the dome stretched nearly as far as Stornoway. Heading toward the main road and hoping that the road signs still existed, I could envisage her house, a small cottage with a glassed conservatory at the back, overlooking the rolling green hills beyond. Images of Angela and mum sitting out there talking and laughing, drinking copious pots of tea. Steeling myself for what I might find, I picked up the pace. Goodness knows how long it would take to walk there and back.

I hadn't even made it out of town when I was stopped by a friendly-looking man, late twenties with sandy blonde hair and a wiry build. Introducing himself as Hamish, with a glint of mischief in his eye, he asked me if I would like to see something special.

Knowing that being part of the community was more important at this point than tracking ghosts and recognizing that typically I struggled with forming friendships, I readily agreed and followed him toward the main house. Everyone had a job to do, a strength that the village relied upon—hunting, raising cattle and sheep, dairy, and growing crops, and also the same technical specialists, engineers, and builders. I wasn't sure what Hamish had planned to show me, but when he led me to the stables where two saddled horses stood ready, I was surprised. I hadn't expected that. He didn't strike me as the horsey type. I tried to look interested, but secretly I was just pleased that one of the tethered horses wasn't the black spawn Hades.

He untied the two horses, already laden up with large saddlebags, and looked at me.

"You can ride, can't you?"

I smiled back bravely. "Sure," I said with a note of certainty that I didn't feel. *If you count riding a pony at the local school fete as a kid,* being the unspoken part of my answer. Despite taking horse riding lessons as a child, it was a long time ago, and unlike my sister, I had no natural affinity for horses and was no expert. But I wasn't going to admit that and humiliate myself. Covertly, I watched him mount and nearly killed myself by replicating his maneuver. I grimaced from my precarious perch on Daisy, who at least looked like a giant brown sofa. I suspected this was an evil plot, and she was a suicidal maniac who liked to gnaw on legs for breakfast, but I said nothing.

"Let's go." Hamish grinned, his grin betraying his recognition that I had no clue, but he was too polite to say so.

We rode for nearly an hour up a steep path. My butt hurt from the impact, and my thighs were cramping from clenching them to the sides of the horse, yet I appreciated the horses carried the burden. It would have taken an awful lot longer on foot. Hamish reined up under some trees and stopped, throwing his leg over and sliding off his horse like a professional as both feet hit the ground simultaneously.

Bloody show-off, I thought cynically as I tried to dismount as discreetly as possible after Hamish had turned away. I landed with a thud, which made him turn around, but I kept my balance. I was just happy not to fall on my ass in the dirt.

Hamish deftly tethered the horses and opened one of the saddlebags. He pulled out some bread and cheese as well as a brown bottle of something with a cork in it. Making ourselves comfortable, we shared the bread and cheese as well as some apples in companionable silence. Hamish uncorked the bottle and waved it under his nose, inhaling deeply. Taking a large swallow, he then handed it to me. Fortunately, I had the sense to inhale first—a mighty fine scotch whisky. Apart from the dram I had been given upon my arrival here, I hadn't had decent whisky in years. There was very little on August. We had plenty of wine and beer and made more, but there were not large quantities of spirits. I closed my eyes as I let the smoky, peaty liquid amber run into my mouth and down my throat.

"Not bad, eh?"

"This is exceptional!" I enthused, pausing for a second mouthful before I returned the bottle.

"I suspected you might not be a complete heathen. You are half Scots, I hear."

"Mum was local. From here, I mean. Dad's family emigrated to Australia when he was a child, but he was born here too, well, on Harris."

After a second mouthful and swishing it around his mouth, Hamish stood and started packing away the remains of lunch in his saddlebag.

"Come on. Let's go."

Still intrigued about where indeed we were going, I managed to mount Daisy in one wobbly attempt. She continued with the pretense of being a gentle soul and followed Hamish back to the path. Well, path was a generous term. A deer path maybe, narrow, windy, and steep.

Twenty minutes later, he reined up next to a cave, tied his horse and mine to a nearby tree, and beckoned me to follow him. I paused, unsure of what to do. The last time I had entered a cave, I ended up here, quite literally half a world away.

Hamish read my hesitation and smiled. "All good. No portals here."

My glass face had revealed my apprehension. I tried to smile but realized that it probably came out wrong.

Hamish unstrapped the panniers on either side of his horse. I copied and relieved Daisy of her burden. Carrying the heavy bags, I quickly lowered my head to focus on entering the mouth of the cave, which was relatively small and had numerous beautiful mountain cliff ferns sprouting from crevices around the entrance. Stopping to feel their textured fronds, I pondered for a moment if there was any benefit in propagating some.

Running along the floor was a small, slowly trickling spring of what was clearly mountain water.

Hamish cupped his hand to drink some, so I followed suit. It was amazing. Sweet, clear, and refreshing. Quite possibly the best water I had ever tasted. I had always thought that water tasted like, well... water. But this was something special. Again, I wondered why we were here. It was a long way to come for a drink.

Hamish walked to the back, and I could see another room beyond.

"The malting floor," he announced proudly, gesturing toward a man-made wooden floor. I could smell the distinct scent of wet fermenting barley. Emptying the bags we carried, he threw me a wooden paddle, picked up one of his own, and showed me how to turn the barley, spreading it in a thin layer across the floor to encourage germination.

"Ahh, now I get it. You brought me here for slave labor," I joked, sweating in the surprisingly warm room as Hamish turned his attention to the mash, which was over to one side. There were two short fat copper stills in the corner, shaped like the hat of a garden gnome, I noted.

Turning the barley was hard work. Grateful for the horses who had lugged the grain up here, I stripped off my donated jacket, sweating despite the chilled winter air outside. Aside from general directions on what to do next, there was little conversation. Mum had loved whisky, and we had been on tours of several distilleries over the years. I knew enough about whisky distilling to understand that this point was critical, and to mess it up would waste the grain, causing Hamish to start the entire process again.

Several hours later, it became apparent that nothing else could be done today. Hamish said he would return tomorrow. Genuinely wanting to assist, I knew Fraser needed my help in the greenhouse. Since my arrival, my knowledge in the gardens had freed up one of the other gardeners, Alex, to go hunting, another essential role here and one we didn't have on August. Deer were useful for food, but they also were a pest, getting into the gardens at night. Hunting was performed sustainably, though. The hunters never took more than was needed.

We rode back with a more relaxed air than on the way here. He had put me to the test, and I had passed. Hamish opened up about himself, leading the way for me to reciprocate. He was from Orkney but had been in Manchester at university, studying to be a doctor.

That surprised me. Even after all this time, and knowing that the people chosen for both communities were highly skilled and intelligent, I couldn't help but ask, "So, how does a doctor end up as the chief distiller?"

He chuckled at that. "Well, originally, I came here as one of the medical team until it became known that my father worked as one of the senior staff at Highland Park, a distillery just out of Kirkwall."

I nodded. My mother had loved Highland Park. I grew up seeing the beautiful intricate black label with its Viking pattern regularly. It was her evening ritual, seated in her armchair by the window, book in one hand and a small glass of whisky with two ice cubes in the other. Often, I had looked in to see her not reading at all but staring into space, the taste of the peat evoking memories, perhaps.

"One of the hunters, Rohan, discovered this cave in the year we arrived. There are quite a few of them here, you know. But when Rohan tasted the water and felt the warmth, he knew it was a great place to set up a distillery. Pure water is one of the essential parts of making whisky; the better the water, the better the whisky. When we next held a town meeting, Rohan mentioned he had discovered this cave, but without disclosing the location. It is still secret," he said as an aside. "You are one of a few people who have been here. Anyway, at that meeting, people talked about whisky and how we were worried that we might run out. I mentioned once that I used to work at Highland Park on my summer holidays to earn money for college. The community agreed that although being a doctor was great, there were several others. What they wanted, needed, was a decent whisky. As it takes nearly ten years for it to become drinkable whisky, and we don't have ten years' worth of stock.... Well, the next thing you know, I am up here turning mash and giving Ed the metalworker diagrams of how to build a pair of copper stills. Lucky we had a cooper to make some barrels as well, or we would be in trouble. He even burned them nicely on the inside. Shame we didn't have some old Madeira or sherry casks or something," Hamish mused. "Now, that would be special."

"If it is secret, why did you show me?" I asked, interested.

Hamish smiled. "First, I needed help. Second, I figured you would be gone soon and likely couldn't find your way back there, anyway!"

"A good whisky has medicinal properties, my mum used to say."

"Well, she would be right then! Whisky never complained about my bedside manner either."

Chatting about everything and nothing, we ambled back to Garynahine.

CHAPTER 27

BY THE TIME SPRING had arrived, I was well known in the community. I couldn't walk anywhere without people stopping for a chat. Unlike Melbourne, where people always had their phones in their hands and constantly looking down, here people caught your eye, smiled, and greeted you like you were an old friend. The sense of community support here was overwhelming. Everyone was prepared to assist their friends. The downside was that it was difficult to get anywhere in a hurry.

Much like a tourist, I was desperate to see some of the community outside of the village. Lae and I started planning our days off to spend together, walking, exploring, horse-riding. She was excellent company, easy to talk to, and knowledgeable, and I genuinely enjoyed spending time with her. She showed me the boundaries of the community and took me to the other stone circles at Callanish. We checked on the flocks of sheep roaming the countryside and visited families who lived in some of the old crofts, still under the dome, but who had spread out a bit to tend stock.

We saw the historical sights of the island, including a traditional blackhouse on the west coast. "I can't believe people lived in these places up to the 1960s!" I exclaimed. "They must have suffocated with peat fires inside those thick block walls."

"They had very short life spans inhaling all that smoke. Funny to think we will never smell smoke again, isn't it? Can you imagine living in that one building with all of your animals, too?"

Vague memories of smoke-filled rooms, blackened walls, and the rich smoky scent of peat smoke flooded my mind. My grandmother, despite having central heating, had loved the peat smoke of her childhood. "The smell," she said. Mum was constantly criticizing her because of Sorcha's asthma. Poor Sorcs couldn't breathe and spent most of her time here outside trying not to cough up a lung.

Leaving the blackhouse, we followed the dome's perimeter as it ran down the island's west coast, enjoying the view of the ocean, brilliant blue in the sunshine. In the mid-afternoon, we stopped at the foot of a large cylindrical stone building, high on a cliff edge. It was old and ruined at the top but remarkably well-preserved, nonetheless. Sheep grazed on the slopes amid old ruined walls and structures, oblivious to our presence.

"What on earth is that?" I gestured toward the building.

"That is Dun Carloway Broch," she announced proudly.

"Brock?" It wasn't a word I was familiar with.

"A *broch* is a cylindrical dry-stone tower. This one is Iron Age, about first century AD and likely Norse in origin."

"Seriously? First-century? It is so well preserved!"

"Come on."

Tying the horses near a lush patch of grass, we climbed the steep rocky path to reach the broch, a herd of goats grazing alongside the trail. From the road, I had expected it to be like a bell tower, a single-walled structure, but when we reached the far side, the side facing the ocean, so close to the edge of the dome, I could see that it had two parallel walls with corridors and stairs between the rounded walls. Astonished, I touched the structure. This building had been constructed thousands of years ago, yet still stood, watching the earth.

"It is quite something, isn't it," Lae said quietly from behind me.

"It really is. I can't believe I have never been here before in my trips to Lewis."

"I knew your family were from Scotland, but you never told me you had visited the Hebrides. Where are your family exactly?"

"Just south of Stornoway," I murmured, not wanting to draw attention to it.

Lae's sharp intake of breath was audible. "You have family *here*? On Lewis?"

"I do. I mean.... I did."

Lae's distress was palpable. "Why didn't you say so? I could have helped you find them!" Being so tiny, Lae looked every bit like a sad kitten. One you desperately wanted to pick up, cuddle, and keep safe. I placed a gentle hand on her arm.

"It's okay. I know they have gone. There is nothing I could have done. But I need.... closure. For my mum."

I flamed with embarrassment. I had been here for

months and was too busy enjoying myself to bother looking for my family.

To cover my discomfort, I said, "Mum's sister Angela was here, and my two cousins; they were younger than me. My grandmother passed when I was twelve, but the others...."

My voice petered out, unsure of what to say.

"Oh, Cam! *Why* didn't you say something sooner? You know I would have helped you!"

At that moment, I wanted to hug her. Such kindness and consideration for someone she had known for such a short time and was imposing in her home to boot. "That is kind, but I didn't want people to know."

"Does Fraser know?"

"Fraser is a bit distracted with impending fatherhood," I said with a smirk. "So while he knows my family is from Lewis, no, I never told him explicitly that some were still here."

Laughing, Lae said, "That is true enough. Next week then. We will go and not tell anyone. I promise."

"Thank you. Now, tell me about the broch. What else do you know about it?"

It turned out quite a lot. Lae pointed out some features, and then on the way back to the village taught me about the various archaeological theories about brochs and described some of the other brochs remaining in Scotland, mostly on remote islands.

"This part of Scotland was part of the Kingdom of the Isles, you know. I had never seen a broch before I moved here," she said, "but I had read about them. I find them fascinating." She was so calm and patient, an excellent teacher.

"How on earth do you manage with nearly forty children?" I asked, kicking Daisy so I could ride up the hill beside her, remembering how feral my primary school classes had been.

"Come tomorrow and see," she twinkled at me.

School was a four-room converted house on the edge of the village, an older home that had been cared for by its original owners. With a solid chimney and brown pebblecrete walls, it had a beautiful, established flower garden. The kind that screamed nanna. There were no gardens for beauty alone on August, and I stopped to admire the roses, rosemary, lavender, and calla lilies as I left the classroom. A garden not dissimilar to my mother's or my aunt's. Like a blow to the stomach, it hit me.

My extended family, aunts, cousins, were here. In this very vicinity, when the island had been evacuated. Did they go? Stay and perish? Did any of them survive? My face flushed with humiliation. *How could I wait so long to hunt for them? What sort of awful person am I?*

Lae saw my face but tactfully said nothing. Instead, she introduced me to the children as they arrived, aged between several months and two years. She greeted each one warmly, indicating that she knew them all well. Cheeky and chatty, I thoroughly enjoyed my morning with them, wholly distracted with reading, writing, blocks, drawing, and puzzles.

"It's okay," she whispered later when they were engrossed in activities. "We will go soon."

Almost a week later, Lae and I took two horses and set off toward Stornoway. During the week she had subtly borrowed maps and old directories to get an actual address of my aunt, using all the information I could remember. She had found the address, she told me one evening, and a map of how to get there. I nodded. I had no idea if any of dad's family remained in Harris. Even if they had, they were distant relatives. I vaguely recalled my parents discussing his cousin moving to Canada. Certainly dad, his brother, and parents had all ended up in Australia; my paternal grandparents both passed before I was born.

We set off on horseback at dawn, knowing that we had a big day ahead. Lae laughed when I told her I had originally planned to walk. As we left the village, we chatted about spring, the crops I had planted, and plans we had. She asked about my family in Australia, my parents, and my sister. Curious, she asked how they adapted to a new country. She had never left Scotland, so she wondered what traditions people took with them. Talking to her was easy, and I opened up in a way I had done with very few people. Dad and his love of the countryside and the block. My sister and her fiancé. I had her in stitches about Mum and her Scottish mannerisms, so out of place in Australia. She talked about life on Lewis, her students, her plans for the future.

As we rode, we reached the point where the main road from Garynahine forked with the primary thoroughfare to Stornoway at Achmore.

"This is where my grandmother lived," I whispered as we passed the old post office. "Just up there. My mother was raised here. She and her sister were raised by their grandparents after their own parents died in an accident. The woman I called granny was actually my great-grandmother."

"Do you want to stop?"

I shook my head. "No. The croft was sold when she passed. I helped clear out the house, the sheds. It was in fairly poor condition by then. The new owner knocked it down, but I don't think they ever rebuilt. Aunt Ange kept Mum informed."

A short distance up the road, we reached the edge of the dome, that bizarre structure that kept some in and some out. Rolling back the panel, which was sizeable, she clicked her tongue, encouraging her horse to continue through.

"How did you know how?" I asked.

Lae flushed guiltily. "I was the one who broke into Angus' house," she confessed. "We worked together for a short time. He was supposed to be a teacher here, you see. Before he decided he had better things to do. I read his notebooks. He was always scribbling in notebooks. I found a reference to opening the hatches. I figured we might need it."

"He lived alone then?"

"Yes. Well, he did. Then Freyja came, and she lived with him."

Seething rage washed over me without warning, consuming me to the point where I could barely get the words out. "She *what*? She *lived* with him?"

"Well, you live with me," Laetitia pointed out gently. "I doubt it was much more than cohabitation."

Recognizing the logic in this still did nothing to soothe my frayed temper. *Freyja had lived with that man? That soulless demon who had allowed children to die physically in sight of safety?* We continued to ride in silence, guilt finally quenching my fury. I should have been here. I knew what Freyja would say: "Guilt is a pointless emotion. You didn't do this; it wasn't your fault. You have nothing to be guilty about." But like it or not, I *felt* guilty. Guilty that I was alive, and my family was not. Guilty that I had enjoyed being here, being accepted, spending time with Laetitia and Fraser. Guilty because I hadn't found a way to get to Freyja sooner. Guilty... well, because I was happy, dammit. That last revelation took even me by surprise. *Shit. I was happy.*

I looked down at the dark mane of my horse, trying not to let Lae see my conflicting emotions. She was a master at reading me, or perhaps I just wasn't good at hiding my torment. Freyja used to tease me that every emotion showed on my face. Maybe it was true. How could I possibly be happy? Just a few months ago, I was devastated, seeking to end my life. Now I was happy, living in a strange place with strange people.

But they accept you. A small voice nagged at me. *These people have become more family to you in three months than most people on August did in three years.*

I should have tried harder to get back to Freyja, I berated myself. But then again, I reasoned, *where the hell is she?* I had no skills to pilot a boat across the ocean literally to the other end of the world, to the antipodal point of this place.

But you should have tried, my conscience nagged.

I was shaken from my emotional turmoil as we passed the sign welcoming us to Marybank, a tiny hamlet to the south-west of Stornoway where my aunt lived.

Had lived, I corrected myself mentally. There was no one here now. Outside the dome, it was silent with no sign of life. Deserted streets, filthy, rusted cars. Dead, overgrown gardens. Rubbish bins that had never been brought in, rubbish blowing around the streets. Buildings had decayed, gutters hanging off, stucco falling from walls. Windows so dirty it was impossible to see inside. But wind. Finally, there was true wind. Lifting my face to the breeze, I could feel the smell of salt on the gusts of air. Fresh and bitterly cold.

Mindful of avoiding water, we had worn water-proof jackets and pants with minimal skin showing. We had pushed the hoods off our faces as we rode, but now, once outside the shell, we pulled the hoods up, obscuring most of our faces despite the fine weather. With rubbish everywhere, we rode cautiously until we reached the address on the piece of paper Laetitia held. I stopped and looked, straining to peer past the collar on my jacket, which zipped up over my mouth. The house seemed vaguely familiar, but different. Time had passed, but that wasn't it. The colors were gone, washed out. The double fronted two-story modest house faced the street, a single garage with a white door to the side, the same brown pebblecrete walls and slate roof as the school in Garynahine. But this garden was dead. The paths were barely visible against the dirt that remained. The rambling yellow rose my aunt adored that grew around the front porch had withered and perished. Straggly brown threads were all that was left.

I dismounted Daisy and moved cautiously toward the front door. Locked. I peered through one of the front windows, but they were so dirty with several years' worth of grunge that I couldn't see anything.

Walking along the driveway, I could see the extension to the house ahead of me. My aunt had built the extension fifteen years ago when her husband, uncle Malcolm, had been in the final stages of cancer. It was a fully glassed conservatory, filled with plants, designed to capture the sun, and with views of the heather-covered hills beyond. A memory of Mum teasing Ange stirred, telling her it was a sunroom. "A conservatory was for posh people," she had taunted in a way reserved for siblings.

There was the strangest view as I walked alongside the house. The fields closest to her home were dead, brown, and lifeless. Yet the hills beyond the dome were green and full of life, a distinct divide—life and death. She would have seen it. Her world was perishing, yet the world beyond was thriving. The chosen and the abandoned.

Even after Mal passed, she loved sitting out in that space, chatting to mum. She ate her meals out here, watching the heather sway in the breeze, the storms rolling in from the sea. I had memories of sitting in that room going through boxes of my grandmother's possessions, both Mum and Auntie Ange intermittently laughing and crying as they did so, showing each other a photo, a keepsake.

Slowly, I walked around the back corner of the house. The back glass was equally packed up with soot, dirt, and grime. Using my elbow, I rubbed a patch at eye height and peered in.

Glancing around the conservatory through the small, cleaned space, I stopped short and froze. My aunt Angela was sitting in her conservatory, that glassed room she had loved, looking out to the beautiful vista beyond, surrounded by the plants she had lovingly tended, no longer green and luscious. They were brown and withered now, dead leaves littering the surrounding floor. She was wearing a dark blue winter robe covered in gray dust. Her long red hair with silver streaks, so much like my mother's, surrounded her withered, desiccated face. Her dark sunken eyes were almost gone, but still peering out across the fields. Captain Tubby, her enormous ginger cat, curled in her lap, moldering, chunks of fur fallen on her legs and onto the floor. I let out a strangled gasp as I looked through the glass and fell to my knees in what had once been her garden. Laetitia, hearing my cry, came running and held me as I collapsed into the dirt.

Midway back to Garynahine, once we were back inside the safety of the dome, I finally managed to speak.

"Were they there?"

Lae had cared for me, held back my hair as I had recovered, then left me as she entered the house, smashing a window to gain entry. Several minutes later, she had returned, helped me onto Daisy, and we had left. Not a word passed between us.

"No," she whispered. "There were no clothes in the other rooms, I checked. It looks like they... left."

"She would have sent them away. Like my mother did."

Lae nodded but said nothing.

Sneaking a look over at Lae, riding silently beside me, I wondered if she thought less of me for not visiting sooner. Without even looking over at me, she responded to my unasked question.

"Cam, you are one of the most ethical people I have ever met. When you do something, you ask, 'Is it right?' Not, 'What will *I* gain?' You feel guilty now because you took so long to come. But you needn't. You didn't know you would come to Lewis, and the three months you have been here made absolutely no difference to the outcome. The guilt you feel is not for your aunt, but for your own mother, your own family. That is a guilt we all share, every single one of us."

"Are you psychic?" I blurted, not intending to.

She laughed heartily at that. "No, but several times I have been asked if I have the sight. I spent most of my childhood alone, so I watched. Observed. I notice the little things, I guess. People think I can read them. But I can't."

"It would be kind of cool if you did have some form of psychic vision," I said. "Perhaps you could tell me what I am thinking."

"You think you are hungry?" she guessed, making me laugh.

CHAPTER 28

FOR THE FIRST TIME in weeks, I had nothing to do, no work that urgently needed to be completed. On my weekly day off for the first few months, I had either helped Hamish with the whisky or gone exploring with Lae. But now, the whisky was safely in casks, maturing. The next crop of barley hadn't yet been harvested. Hamish had returned, at least for now, to medical duties. Today, no one needed me, my time, my attention. Lae was working; one of the other teachers was sick.

I couldn't shake the feeling—the bone-deep desire to be alone, to be close to my parents, to apologize for my aunt. For not investigating sooner, even though I knew it was fruitless. Logically, I knew I couldn't have saved her. I was on August when the end had come here, but that image haunted me. Sitting there, knowing that as she died, she could see safety on the opposite side of the dome. So near, yet so unattainable. I wondered if my mother had told Ange about me, where I had gone. She wasn't supposed to, but Mum and Ange were so close, despite the distance.

They spoke every second day. I had often wondered how Mum and her sister were so close, yet Sorcha and I were not. Perhaps it was a gender thing. Maybe it was because their parents died and they only had each other. Or simply, they just got along as people.

Volunteering with the whisky had proven to be positive in several aspects. Hamish and I were on friendly terms. I learned to ride a horse without complete humiliation, but whether through time, Hamish and Fraser's validation of me, or just because I pulled my weight in the gardens and whisky distilling, I was considered a local now. I was regularly invited for meals, to visit homes, usually with Laetitia but occasionally alone. People were no longer apprehensive of me. I was embraced and welcomed in a way I had never experienced before. Everyone wanted to hear the story of the portal, and I needed to relay this hideous story over and over. They wanted to know about August, about Australia. Several had family members who had migrated to Australia over the years and asked if I had known them.

Migrants never really leave their homes, I mused. *They might move in search of a better life, but their hearts never really leave.*

Walking east out of the village, I headed toward one of the mountains that ringed it, a munro, I remember my granny calling them.

"I always thought 'Munro' was a surname," I had said when I asked to go walking up a nearby hill one day, and she laughed at me. A munro, she informed me, when she stopped chortling, was a mountain over 3000 feet. There were several hundred of them in Scotland, and they were named munroes after Sir Hugh Munro, who had surveyed and cataloged them all in the 1890s. "When I was but a wee girl," she had cackled, rolling the "r" in girl. Granny had loved teasing me, my accent, my lack of knowledge about my culture. This was usually followed by a barb at my mother for not teaching me about my heritage. While Harris and Lewis technically didn't have any munroes, the highest point being just over 2500 feet, the locals called it one.

I learned from Granny that munro bagging, basically climbing as many mountains as possible, was quite a popular pastime in Scotland. Granny had asked me what we called it in Australia. Bushwalking was the closest equivalent but didn't sound as exotic.

The narrow rocky path rose to meet me as I climbed steadily, wiping sweat from my brow. Thick tracts of heather and gorse overran the track, making the climb slow going. Despite the difference in flora around me, the ascent made me remember the bushwalking in the Australian alpine areas we had done as a family. The beautiful vista of distant gray mountains, spring flowers blooming everywhere, and straggly eucalyptus trees emerging from the rocky landscape was so similar. Fighters, despite the harsh climate and terrain.

A particularly steep and rocky patch made me focus my energy as my thighs ached from the steepness of the terrain. The path curved around the side of the mountain, clearly following a natural declivity in the landscape. As I neared the top, the view took my breath away.

Holding my breath in awe, I took in the vista. From where I stood, I had an unencumbered vantage point in all directions, taking in the sphere of rolling hills and mountains in the distance, blues, and grays. A

feeling that she knew me. We were totally at peace and just watched. Finally, a bird perched in a tree nearby squawked and broke the spell. She turned and was gone before I could even take a breath. Feeling a little shaken by this experience, I stood and looked around, searching for other woodland creatures whose home I had invaded. Finding none, I shook myself, feeling a little strange.

Bees buzzing near the base of a large spruce tree caught my attention. They were swarming over a patch of pretty blue-purple flowers, star-shaped and with a center containing nectar as evidenced by the bees humming. Not recognizing the bloom, I stopped to pick a few. Similar to bluebells, but star-shaped, more purple. I had never seen anything like them. Inspiration struck, and I dug up some bulbs as well as picking a small posy of the pretty fragile flowers, carefully tucking them away in my pack.

Drawing myself up, I turned slowly, taking in the scenery, the mountains, the green vistas, the trees, and the distant ocean views. Some of the land ended in the rocky cliff that plunged abruptly into the sea or gradual declines into white sandy beaches with waves pounding on the beach. *Why am I here? Is it a coincidence that I find myself here in the Hebrides, the very place my parents were born?* I had been here several times, visiting my grandmother, my aunt. But never had I felt like this. I tried to find a word for how it was I was feeling. Contented, yes. Happy, certainly. I stepped backward as the appropriate word floated into my head.

Home. It felt like coming home.

I exhaled audibly as the shock of my contentment hit me. Home. This was home in a way that August never had been. But here I was in a place I had visited but never spent more than a month at a time in, and yet I knew, beyond doubt, that I belonged here. I was part of the fabric of this place, a rich tapestry woven by my family history. My ancestors had hunted, fished, farmed, raised children, tended animals, built homes—lived and died here. Large numbers of them had left when times were tough, to America, Canada, New Zealand, and Australia, most never to return. They sought better lives, job opportunities, challenges and grew older, raised children, and died after becoming part of new places and new communities. But the strange thing about Scots is that their hearts always belonged here. No matter how far away they were, they still kept that small piece of themselves that was Scottish. Bagpipes, tartan, whisky, small glimpses of their previous lives may be absent, but never for-gotten. Suddenly, I realized how hard it had been for my parents to leave this place, the crisp island air, the vast green rolling hills, the vistas that took in moun-tains, heather, ocean, sky. *Is this my family legacy? Returning here?*

Absorbed in this feeling of security and being on my native soil, I slowly descended the hill, stopping by a stream cascading down the rocks. Large round boulders edged the stream and scattered throughout the small waterfall. The water was crystal blue and ice-cold, I discovered as I cupped my hands for a drink. Sweet, clear, and delicious. I dipped my hands again, and then I saw it. The branches of a tree stood in front of a small, rocky opening. I navigated my way through the stream to the cave entrance and crouched down to get inside.

A strange feeling of déjà vu washed over me as I entered the cave. The last cave I had entered alone was on August Island. At least Hamish had entered the whisky cave first. But this cave was different, had a different feel. A single room only. Small, not even the size of a bedroom. Rock lined walls and roof with a dirt floor, but no tunnels or pathways. I sat down on a rocky outcrop to rest and listened to the roar of the water rushing by at the entrance, soothed by its rhythm.

The cave provoked memories of Freyja and our sacred place on August where we had found each other and committed to each other. If this was home, then what of Freyja? She had come here, like me, by accident, but she had risked the journey back, overland, risking death by the virus, to find me. I blushed thinking of this, although no one could see me. My heart felt split in two. I could never return to August, not after what happened. But I had made a commitment to her. *What am I to do?* I could see myself making a home here, settling down, and getting older. Working the gardens with Fraser, sending my children to school. That plan was foremost in my mind, but I could think of nothing else but her face. Closing my eyes and focusing, I could see her. She was standing in front of me. Her long blonde hair was falling effortlessly down her back, emerald green eyes glistening, alive with intelligence within her beautiful, tanned face. She was smiling at me but not speaking. I started to speak, to tell her to wait, but she turned her back to me and started walking away. I called out, "Stop! Wait!"

I felt a scratching at my foot and brushed it away, too intent on the glowing hair of my love in front of me as she moved off into the sunset. She started to fade, the glow of the sun overtaking her image.

"Come back!" I called desperately. "Freyja! Come back!" The scratching became more insistent. The force of it shook me from my trance as Freyja's image disappeared. Fearing it was a rat, I hurriedly stepped back, and a high-pitched yowling filled the cave. Entirely shaken by this point, I scrabbled on my belt for my pocketknife and brandished it, ready to defend myself against whatever rodent infestation lived in this cave. Backing up toward the entrance, I was swinging the knife around wildly, looking around the cave. Nothing. I slowly exhaled, not realizing that I had been holding my breath. I heard a tiny meow and looked down to see a tiny, gray tabby kitten with large green eyes. I crouched down and tentatively held my finger out to it. The kitten sniffed my finger, then used it to push against his jawline, clearly wanting to be scratched. I carefully scratched his head, neck and under his chin, watching my hand to ensure that I could remove it in time if the cat decided to scratch or bite.

The kitten adored the attention and grew bolder in its advances. Squatting down and carefully opening my backpack to not frighten him, I unzipped the main compartment. He seemed most interested in the smell of cheese in my ham and cheese sandwich. Breaking off a small piece, I held it out to him on the end of my pointer and index fingers. He sniffed, then tucked in with such alacrity that I was stunned. Poor thing was starving. He didn't wait for me to break off the next piece. He made for the source, climbing in my backpack, foraging for food. Trying not to laugh, I attempted to take the sandwich from him but ended up wrestling him for it. Letting him win, I watched as he pulled the ham and cheese from the half-eaten sandwich and made short work of it. He licked the discarded bread, then decided against it. He returned his attention to my backpack, inspected the contents, then curled up on the jacket I had brought in case the weather turned cold, purred like a miniature chainsaw, and fell asleep.

Standing in silence watching this by-play, I realized—I had been chosen. People always said that animals chose their people, being far more emotionally intelligent than we are. With care, I picked up the backpack, adjusted it on my back, trying not to disturb the sleeping kitten, and commenced the long walk back to the village.

"It's a wee cheetie!" Laetitia was delighted at the kitten when I showed her. "Wherever did you get him?"

We sat on the bench seat outside our house where we removed outside shoes before entering. I held him up, and together we looked at him closely in the sunlight. He had beautiful markings, distinct stripes in a classic tabby formation, stunning green eyes, and a bushy striped tail with a black tip and a soft white belly.

"I found him, actually *her*," I corrected, now that I looked closely, "in a cave up the munro."

"Well, she certainly chose *you*." Laetitia laughed merrily, clearly entranced. The kitten was on my shoulders, now buzzing around my head. Her head was butting into my chin and jaw, seeking affection and making it abundantly clear that she was in charge.

Fraser nodded at us as he was walking past with Aidan, a gruff, monosyllabic man who had shown minimal interest in my arrival aside from basic formalities. They were deep in discussion about when was best to plant the barley. Well, Fraser was talking, and Aidan was grunting with agreement or disapproval; frankly, I couldn't tell. I secretly suspected that Aidan just viewed me as another mouth to feed and taking up valuable resources. We had barely exchanged more than a hello since I arrived, although he had never been actually rude.

Aidan stopped and looked straight at me. He rubbed his eyes and looked again.

"That's a Scottish Wildcat!" he pronounced, clearly in shock.

I stiffened as the kitten continued to curl herself about my head, purring. *Wildcat. Wild. Cat.*

Aidan chuckled, the first time he had ever done so in my presence, reading the sheer terror evident on my face.

"Oh, it's all right. They aren't fierce. Or that big, to be honest. A little bigger than a domestic cat, but a cat nonetheless. And she certainly likes you."

I still hadn't moved past wild... cat. *Seriously, I go for a walk and end up with a bloody wildcat. Only me.*

"Are you sure?" I asked tentatively, really hoping that he just had a warped sense of humor.

"Am I sure that it is a wildcat, or am I sure that it will be alright?"

"Both. Should I let her go?"

Aidan dropped his head to the side and pondered, watching her balanced perfectly on my shoulders and head-butting my left ear.

"I don't think you have a say in the matter, frankly. Your friend here has decided. Besides, they are very rare. They are endangered, the only native cat left in Europe if I remember rightly."

"Endangered?" I plucked the kitten from my shoulder and looked into her beautiful eyes. They had a lovely yellow fleck to them as well as a highly perceptive look.

"Aye, endangered. My brother worked at the Highland Wildlife Park in Kingussie, near Aviemore. They had a breeding program there. He would be so proud to think that they had survived." Thinking of his brother, Aidan's face lit in a gentle smile, and I handed the kitten to him, watching him gaze at her with wonder.

"Well," said Laetitia. "If she is going to be part of the village, she will need a name."

"Aye," said Aidan, scratching her under the chin. "She will be useful if you can keep her around. They are great at catching rodents and rabbits. Many don't survive their first year, taken by birds of prey usually."

The kitten had moved to Laetitia's lap beside me, and she was stroking her. Enjoying the attention, the kit was purring loudly.

"What do you name a wildcat?" I asked her.

Laetitia scratched her temple, something she did when thinking. "Well, I don't think Puss will cut it. How about Luna?"

"Luna means moon. She isn't white, though. Hmm, I'm not sure."

Fraser chipped in, "How about Minnie?"

We all looked at him in scorn. He feigned offense.

I looked to Aidan, who was still stroking the tiny kitten, watching her with awe and wonder lighting his weather-beaten, rugged face. "What was your brother's name?" I asked kindly.

"Jameson," he whispered.

"Then Jameson, she shall be," I announced. "But perhaps we shall call her Jam. Jameson is a bit of a mouthful for a cat. Besides, Australians abbreviate everything."

Remembering my second gift belatedly, I pulled out the slightly squashed blue-purple star-shaped posy and gave them shyly to Laetitia. Her face lit with delight. Fraser looked closely. "Ahh, spring squill," he said. "They grow on the coast in the machair region. Natives, you know."

"Related to bluebells?" I asked.

"Aye, both are members of the lily family. Wild garlic too."

Pulling out the bulbs, I handed them to Fraser. "Any use then?"

"Oh, most definitely. Bees love them. Great for honey."

Fraser and Aidan continued on their way, and I turned to Lae. Jam was now curling up, getting comfortable in Lae's lap as she gazed at the flowers in her hands, looking sad.

"I am sorry they are squashed. I picked them this morning for you. I just wasn't expecting to transport home a kitten as well. Next time I will try not to squash any gifts."

She looked astonished. "Did you think I was upset?"

"Well, they are a little damaged."

Tears filled her eyes. "No one has ever given me flowers before," she whispered, more emotion in her voice than I had ever heard.

"Then I will remember to bring you more," I promised. "I'll even try not to get them squashed by a wildcat next time."

Jam languorously stretched a paw, extending her tiny claws, then fell asleep.

CHAPTER 29

JAM PROVED HER CAPACITY to earn her keep quickly, and Aidan, like Laetitia and I, was besotted with her. She patrolled the grain stores and kept the mice away, whether by eating them or chasing them, I wasn't sure. I didn't care to find out. As long as I didn't find dismembered corpses or streaked entrails, I was happy. She continued to adore me and followed me like a puppy whenever I went for a walk. Initially, I was fearful that I would lose her, but she proved to have a fabulous sense of direction. Even if she bounded off into the bushes after something that had caught her attention, she always came back when I called her.

Dinners were nearly always soups and stews: some meat, lentils, barley, and root vegetables. Hearty and filling, I knew they were nutritious, and a hot meal after a long day in the cold was always welcome. After several months, I found it quite tedious. I missed the variety of foods. But I said nothing. These people had taken me in, were being gracious hosts, sharing their homes and food with me. By now, even those people initially apprehensive about me had taken me into their homes. I had met everyone in the village and was welcomed by all of them. I had no right to complain about the lack of diversity in food. There was certainly enough of it, and it was tasty enough.

You are spoiled, Mackintosh! Get over it! I mentally berated myself. I didn't mind porridge for breakfast every day. It was quick, easy, and filling. For many years, Mum had served up porridge every day for breakfast in winter. But the same stews every night were wearing a little thin. I remembered Jenny on August, her delicious pies, stir-fries, tacos and curries, even pizza and pasta. Maybe I should send for her on the next solstice? The idea of sharing Lewis with people from August shut that down hurriedly. No. This was my place. I loved it here, and I didn't want to share it with anyone.

Still lamenting the lack of available fruit a week later, I gently mentioned it to Fraser, Laetitia, and Isla, who had brought us lunch with Niamh in her arms. Fraser reached for his new daughter and looked at her with such love and tenderness that I was quite bewildered. I had never seen Fraser, this raucous man, look at anything so tenderly. After hearing me talk about raspberries, Isla sighed with exasperation, "Well, why don't you just grow some!"

"Grow some? It isn't exactly that easy."

"Why not? We have a full seed bank from the Millennium Seedbank in England. When the virus started spreading, and it became clear that this was the catastrophe that they were set up for, we were sent one-quarter of the seeds in the bank."

Fraser looked at her in surprise, then suspicion. "I never told you that. How did you know that?"

Isla shrugged. "Angus told Laetitia."

"What happened to the remaining three-quarters of the seeds?" I asked.

"No idea. He didn't say. Not sure that he knew, to be honest. I think there was some argument between the custodians about what exactly constituted an appropriate situation in which to use them," Lae admitted.

I rolled my eyes. I could all too easily imagine men in suits having that conversation.

"He said, in Sussex, they were stored in a nuclear bomb-proof multi-story underground vault. They aren't quite that well secured here," she smirked.

"Where are they?" I asked.

"I'll take you." Laetitia stood up, brushing crumbs from her lap, smiling as she saw Fraser's incredulous look that not only was his secret out, but had been for some time.

The seed vault held seeds to many varieties of trees as well as coffee plants, passionfruit vines, and a plethora of unique fruits and vegetables, some I had never heard of. There was a more extensive range than we had even on August. They were stored, if you could call it that, in a small shed that leaned at rather a precarious angle alongside the root cellars. Every day I had walked past it, pushing barrows of manure or straw, assuming it to be abandoned.

"I can't believe you have been sitting on this treasure trove for nearly three years and never planted any of it!" I exclaimed, flicking through the labels in the very robust and highly secure large case. "Don't you miss fruit? Great coffee?"

Lae smiled at my enthusiasm. "Well, we never really had anyone to teach us how," she confessed. "It isn't like mango trees grow in Scotland. And we grow coffee. It is just the roasting that we aren't sure how to do. As for me, well, I don't know how to grow anything..." she drifted off.

Scoffing, I said, "Of course you do. It isn't that hard. Everyone knows how to grow stuff."

Lae sat down on the bench next to the seed chest and smiled wryly. "I didn't grow up in the country," she confessed. "I was raised, if you can call it that, in a two-bedroom high rise council flat in a fairly undesirable part of Glasgow."

I looked at her with astonishment. Every city had low-income housing, including Australia. "Even so, you must have learned how to grow things. Everyone learns that."

She turned her head to the far wall so I couldn't see her face. "My home life wasn't exactly, let's say, ideal."

There was a tone to her voice that I couldn't interpret. Sensing there was more to this, I sat next to her on the bench and lightly placed my hand on her leg, encouraging her to continue but not wanting to ask. She exhaled and said simply, "My mother was an alcoholic who rarely left the flat. I don't know who my father was. Mum wouldn't tell me."

My hand must have tightened on her leg as she placed hers over it and unfurled my clenched fingers.

"My earliest memory was trying to make a sand-wich. I was maybe three or four. Mum had passed out on the couch again. I needed to stand on one of the dining chairs to reach the bench. She was furious at me because I made a mess, dripping jam on the bench." She tilted her head to the side, remembering. "By the time I was eight, I was independent. As long as I kept Mum in drink, she didn't care what I did."

I started to speak but didn't know what to say, and she interrupted me.

"Oh, it wasn't all that bad. I started school and discovered books. Books were an escape. Mum was often asleep by the time I got home. I had lots of opportunities to read."

Lae sat up a bit straighter then, trying to lighten the mood.

"When I was eleven, I had a wonderful teacher, Mr. Long." She smiled at the memory. "He believed in me. He convinced me to apply for a scholarship to one of the best independent schools in the country, The Glasgow Academy. We could never have afforded it. So I did, and I got it. He acted as a referee for me and even sought charitable grants to pay for my books and uniform. No one else had ever shown any interest in me before that. I was a skinny, quiet mouse from the council estates. I rarely had clean clothes or lunch. My shoes had holes. The office ladies gave me elastic bands to hold on the soles. I didn't have a winter jacket that fit me. They all came from a charity shop. I certainly didn't have the latest iPhone or iPad. But he saw *me*."

The melancholy look in her eyes indicated it was a great deal more challenging than she was letting on.

I slipped my arm around her shoulder, and she leaned into me and kept talking. "After that, I found my place. The Academy was a school where learning was valued, and the students wanted to be there, even if they didn't want to be there with the likes of *me*. I studied hard and was offered a place at a university in Edinburgh to study psychology. I was fast-tracked and had nearly finished my Masters degree when, when..." she stopped, unable to finish.

As we sat there, Lae's head neatly fitted into my shoulder.

"A psychologist?" I asked gently.

She smiled. "I was so lucky. I had someone who steered me in the right direction. I was lucky enough to get scholarships for high school and university. Sure, I never had the right clothes or had money to go to the cinema. But I had a roof over my head. I worked part-time jobs to get by, and I was so lucky. I just felt, well, that I should help children who may not be so fortunate."

I looked at her with astonishment. "I had no idea," I drawled.

She smiled wanly back at me, not sure that she should have told me. Fearful that I would judge?

"By the way, hard work is not luck. You earned that place."

"I didn't," she said simply. "Why me? There are hundreds of poor kids that deserve an education. I was so grateful when that school chose me. Me! Then the university scholarship. The same when I was chosen to come here. It all happened so fast I didn't even get a chance to go and see Mum and tell her. I was just... gone." Tears welled up in her eyes. "I loved her, despite... everything. She was my mum, and she was all I had. She struggled with her own demons. Looked for answers at the bottom of a bottle. I know she cared. She just didn't know how to show it. Didn't know how to be a mother. Part of the problem was where we lived. All day and night, we could hear people arguing, fighting. You could hear it through the walls. TVs being turned up, and then the shouting would begin. It wasn't until I moved to Edinburgh and then here that I realized that most people didn't live that way. It was all I knew for seventeen years. Mum screamed at me when I told her I was leaving to go to college. Called me awful names. Then she ignored me for the four weeks before I left. Didn't even say goodbye. I called and wrote to her and tried to visit when I could. But Edinburgh was new and exciting. I was free... and I loved it. Then when I was offered the place here, I tried to call, but she didn't answer. I never got to say goodbye."

My arms tightened around her, offering support. She was struggling. "She had cirrhosis of the liver by the time I left for university. She wouldn't have lasted long. I just hope it was fast... in the end."

I thought she had finished, but she started again. "Coming here, to the Hebrides, was the farthest I have ever traveled, you know. Since coming here, I have had so many new experiences. I had never tasted such delicious food since I came here. It has quite literally changed my life." She looked up at me, choking back tears. "I know you have lived an amazing life, been to so many wonderful places, had fantastic experiences. My insignificant life must seem so boring by comparison."

I was speechless for a moment as I stared at her in astonishment. Mum used to describe children at her school in Melbourne who had similar backgrounds. She did her best, all the staff did, but never did they consider themselves lucky. I finally found my voice.

"You are amazing," I said with genuine feeling. "Most people would have followed their parents into that life, especially with no alternative role model. Lived a life of unemployment, drugs, and alcoholism. Many more would be resentful, especially when going to school with kids with so much more. You made a conscious choice... you actually think you were *lucky*?"

"I was. I wasn't special. One teacher made a special effort to help me at a critical point in my life. That changed everything."

"He did," I agreed. "But we have all had that one exceptional teacher. He may have led you to the opportunity, but *you* did the work. Success is what you did with that opportunity. You worked hard, succeeded. Won scholarships. You *earned* it."

Lae shrugged, clearly unconvinced. "Maybe."

I hugged her. "You have found a family here."

"I have. That is why I volunteered to be the teacher. I want to nurture them, teach them, tell them things I wasn't."

"I can't imagine anyone better," I assured her. "You will be such an inspiration."

Jam had wandered into the small, rundown shed and was watching us with interest. She jumped up onto Lae's lap at this point and started purring. Lae stroked her soft gray head, and Jam head-butted her chin, encouraging more. Lae giggled and scratched behind Jam's ears. Jam closed her eyes in pleasure and curled up on Lae's lap, preparing to settle in.

"I never had a cat," she whispered. "I never had any pets."

"Well, I am happy to share her with you. I will give you a hot tip, though. No one ever really owns a cat. Cats own you. Basically, they are assholes. Driven solely by their own self-interest, they are bossy, opinionated, and determined. They seek attention when *they* want it, not when you want to give it. But when they choose you, well, you feel you are the most important person in their world. Also, I need to warn you. Jam here, she likes to attack toes!"

Laetitia's giggle reminded me of water trickling down rocks, utterly innocent but the most glorious sound in the world.

CHAPTER 30

"WHY ARE YOU SITTING here all alone in the dark? Migraine again?" Laetitia asked in a low, kind voice as she opened the front door. The light emanating from surrounding houses illuminated me where I sat in the living room. It was late spring, but it was bitterly cold outside. Fraser hadn't been at work today. It was his anniversary, two years since he had married Isla. The trigger of Fraser's anniversary had sent me downward into a spiral of despair. I had completely forgotten my own anniversary several months ago. It would have been two years together, and a year married, possibly with a child on the way. A layer of late-season snow had coated the outside of the dome, making it dark and shadowed, day and night. I could hear the muffled roaring of the wind rushing past the dome above my head, echoing in an eerie manner. It reminded me of the cave on August, dark and gloomy, and brought back memories of how I had suffered in those last months, wandering the forest, searching for evidence, Freyja's remains. Genuinely believing that she was dead. Jam adjusted herself on my lap, moving the warm spot slightly to the left. I couldn't move for fear of disturbing her.

I looked up at Lae and tried to smile through my pain. It came out as a grimace, and she looked alarmed. "Yes," I answered her question. Migraines were more frequent for me now that I knew I needed to leave again soon. Stress was one of my triggers.

She sat next to me. I could feel her warmth, her presence. "Is there anything I can get you?"

"No, I'm okay."

A massive gust of wind shook the dome, producing a buffeting sound.

I paused for a moment, trying to pluck up the courage to ask. At least with the door closed again and no internal lights, she couldn't see my face. "Can I ask you something personal?"

"Well, that depends." I could sense her looking at me as my eyes adjusted to the semi-dark room. "Go on then."

"You told me your life before here wasn't ideal. How do you get past the dark times and stop them from overwhelming you?"

Laetitia considered for a moment. I could faintly hear her lightly scratching her temple. She looked me in the eye and said with a shrug, "One good thing."

I was a little taken aback at this. Maybe Lae had misheard my question. I was asking for wisdom about dealing with melancholy, depression.

"Umm..." I started, but she continued, divining that I needed further explanation.

"Every evening after school, I used to linger, not wanting to go home. Not that I wanted to stay at school, or even that I had friends' houses to go to. I didn't. Most days, I had been taunted at school for wearing the wrong clothes, being smelly, or being the poor kid. Once a group of girls caught me stealing toilet paper because we couldn't afford it. Dirty little mouse, they called me. I waited until dark to go home so the kids wouldn't know where I lived. I was embarrassed about my home. I hung around the school or the train station. The other kids went to the mall or the arcade. I avoided those places as they required money. I just kind of hung around the school, studying until the cleaners were locking up, and then I would go home. By then, Mum was asleep and usually left me alone; she could be a bit nasty when she was drunk. School holidays were the toughest. Kids used to talk about going on holidays, going to the cinema, shopping, to visit grandparents. We never went anywhere. My mum attended nothing, a concert, parent-teacher interviews, or anything important to me.

But then, one day when I was nine, I was trying to escape a group of girls in the next year level who were trying to steal my bag and throw it in a dumpster. They said it stank, and that was where it belonged. Anyway, I slipped away from them down a side street, missed a turn, and I found myself in a part of Glasgow that I didn't know. I was wandering around the streets, just kind of taking it all in. That was when I saw this beautiful old building made of stone across the street. It had this enormous green metal dome at the top of a round room. There were pillars around the dome, like the Parthenon. Only back then I didn't know what the Parthenon was. It had massive double doors about fifteen feet high and the most fabulous stone staircase from the street to the doors, built into an alcove. I was fascinated; it looked like a castle to someone who had never seen one. I know—what a cliché, right?

Anyway, so I lurked for ages, no doubt looking terribly suspicious. Then an old lady carrying a large cloth bag walked up the steps, and I slipped up the stairs behind her, terrified the whole time that this colossal alarm would go off, alerting them to my entrance, screaming, Intruder! Intruder!"

I smiled, despite the throbbing in my head, imagining a small, scared Laetitia and a loudspeaker scaring her.

"I crept inside behind the lady, absolutely shitting myself that they would throw me out. Fortunately, she was a rather large lady in a big gray skirt, and I was quite small for my age. No one saw me. I remember thinking how lucky it was that her skirt and my uniform were the same color. She almost camouflaged me. I walked into the main foyer behind her, and then she entered the room to the left. I could see the desk she was heading toward. There were staff standing behind it, greeting her, so I bolted into the room on the right before I was spotted. I stood just inside the doorway, out of sight, and looked around. The floor had black-and-white tiles, like a chessboard, stacks, and stacks of books from floor to ceiling. High ceilings and lights hung on chains above the rows of books. More books than I had ever seen in my life. I slipped in and hid behind a stack. I could hear a group of students at the back, so I picked up a book and headed toward them, trying not to be seen. I found a room with rows of tables. There were four girls, in a different school uniform to mine, and older than me. They were laughing and working on a project, an enormous pile of books open on the table in front of them. They looked happy, and no one was bothering them. I looked at them, and I knew, at that moment, that I had found my place."

Sounding happier, she continued. "There were three lovely ladies who worked there most days. One day one of them asked me where my mother was, and I lied and said that she was in the toilet. I think she knew as she nodded and went back to placing books on the shelves, but she never asked again. I often think of that magical day when I discovered public libraries and how they changed my world. I would go there every day after school. The staff were so kind to me. Sometimes they even gave me biscuits if there had been some leftover from a meeting during the day. I spent every weekend and all of my school holidays there. That first Christmas, when they told me they would close for a few days, I cried harder than I had over anything in my life. My mother refused to sign the permission form so I could have a borrowing card. She tore it up, screaming at me, saying, why did I need to borrow books? She spent her day watching television. I had never seen her even pick up a book. Then on the last day before they closed for the break, one lady came over to where I was sitting on a blue chair, placed a brand-new library card with the name Annie Smith on it on the arm of the chair, and walked away. You know, I never thanked them, never even asked their names. I was too.... ashamed."

"I think they knew."

Lae nodded in the darkness and continued. "When I took my card and a book to the counter, I was holding back the tears. I was so scared. Then they told me I could borrow ten books. Ten! That was more books than I had owned in my entire life. I read every book I could get my hands on and then borrowed armfuls to take home. I read about fantastic places, history, art, autobiographies, and fiction. Books truly were my window into the world. The library ladies even gave me a cloth bag to carry them home, so they didn't get wet. It wasn't just a library for me. It was a refuge, a warm, dry, safe place where I felt normal. The staff called me Annie after that, like orphan Annie, I expect. I never told them my real name.

Anyway, one day I read a book, I don't even remember what it was called, only that it was a small hardcovered book, and it had a blue cover and gold lettering. It had one line in that book that jumped out and resonated with me. It said that every day, one good thing happens. You just have to be open to seeing it. I remember sitting with that page open on my lap for a long time. I remember nothing else about that book but that one line. I stewed over it. How could *my* life have good things? That day I was hungry as some girls had taken my sandwich and jumped on it, laughing hysterically, daring me to still eat it.

"Then I looked up and saw the librarian smiling at me as she put books back on the shelves, and I realized it was true! A kind word from a teacher. An unexpected smile from a stranger that makes you feel warm inside. A good grade on an assignment that you worked hard on. A beautiful rainbow after a storm. Even a snowflake. You just have to look for it. Good things are out there all the time. There are good people in the world, and I genuinely believe that you find them when you need them most. You just need to find the rainbow, find the one good thing among the storm, the crap. If you went to the tip and searched, you would find valuable things among all the rubbish.

Good things. There is always a silver lining, something positive. You just need to be able to see it."

The snow had stopped, and the moon was shining through the window, illuminating her face. Her eyes glistened with tears as she continued. "For years, I couldn't see it. I felt so sorry for myself. Why me? Poor me. Why did other kids get two parents, a warm home, new clothes, a hot dinner every night? I thought they had it easy. It took me a long time to realize that life is never easy, no matter your circumstances. It took me a long time to see what I *did* get. Independence. Resilience. Freedom. Self-sufficiency. Adaptability. Caring for people. Time. These were all good things. No, the circumstances weren't ideal. No one would say that a child raising themselves and living on bread and jam was ideal. But the skills I learned *were*."

Lae sniffed and adjusted herself on the couch. "I regret never borrowing that book. I put it back because I already had ten books borrowed. I looked for that book again and again, but I could never find it. I like to think that it was a message sent to me when I needed it the most."

I suddenly felt ashamed. Here I was, moping about Freyja when this extraordinarily positive and humble woman had lived a horrible life, and yet still had such a positive outlook that I was humiliated. I was raised by two loving parents in a stable warm home with clean new clothes, nutritious food, dental care, and a choice of schools. Supports when I needed it. Yet here I was complaining because I had lost someone who wasn't even dead.

"I'm so sorry." I cast my face down, too ashamed to make eye contact. "Here I am, dragging you down, all because I missed seeing Freyja. She is alive and well. I know that. I just... well, I just miss her."

The moon shining through the window reflected off her face. I could see Lae looking at me with such kindness and sympathy.

"It is okay to be sad. It is okay to feel *any* emotion. It just can't control who you are. You are more than this, Cam. I know they treated you badly in your village. Fraser told me. I know you didn't mean to come here; it was an accident. But you *did* come." She shrugged. "You learned what you needed to. She is alive and well, and on her way back to August to find you. The idea of going back there must be difficult. But time is a wonderful thing. I know it is a cliché, but it is a cliché because it is *true*. Time helps to heal wounds. Wounds never completely heal, but they do get better with time."

"I know. You are right. It is just that I spent six months grieving, believing her dead, only to find out that she was alive and I had missed seeing her again. It just feels, well, it feels unfair. And yes, I am frankly terrified at the idea of going back there and facing their judgment. They blamed me. They believed I killed her. How do I face them again?"

Lae's clear eyes, the color of honey, sparkled with life in the moonlight.

"You are more than this," she repeated, "and you will always have a home here." She hugged me, then quietly got up and walked into her room, firmly closing the door before I could respond.

CHAPTER 31

"DID YOU EVER THINK that the job of the people to choose the teams must have been horribly stressful?" Lae asked without warning.

Looking up from my writing, I smiled. There was a feeling of déjà vu about this conversation. We had shared this house for months now, and I knew we could discuss anything. We were very close, and I was comfortable confiding in her.

"Actually, I have. I have contemplated it quite a lot. I can't imagine what it would have been like to suspect, know even, that you were choosing some people for life, and others for death. Like an executioner."

"Exactly." Lae paused. "I've always likened it to a concentration camp. Sentencing some to live, others not. But a human being with the power to choose is just wrong—a power no person should wield over another's life. I never spoke to Angus about it, but I wondered how they chose the people they did. The selection criteria, I mean. I think of those poor people, wanting to save themselves, their friends, their own children perhaps, but being forced to follow guidelines."

"If it is any consolation, I don't think any single person would have made the decision. It would have been a team effort."

"There is some comfort in that. No one person needs to feel all the burden of guilt. But I can't fathom the sheer weight of guilt they must have felt."

Flashbacks of conversations with Freyja flitted through my mind. She hadn't felt guilty. Maybe these people hadn't either. Perhaps they just saw it as doing their job. Cautiously, I tried to explain this to Lae. She looked utterly aghast at the concept that someone wouldn't feel responsible, personally liable for the deaths of their fellow man.

"I think of all of those children who never reached their full potential."

I had no words of wisdom. I felt much the same way.

"You know..." I started, but stopped, unable to form the words.

Lae looked at me expectantly.

"I have been trying to work out why the *feel* here is so different from August."

"Feel?"

"The vibe, the dynamics of the village. I think it all comes down to the fact that on August, we co-habited. We shared facilities and infrastructure, even food, but there was always a feeling that it was every man for himself, if you know what I mean. We didn't have conflict over religion or culture. Quite the opposite. It was cohesively multicultural to the point where I didn't even think about what people's backgrounds had been before. There was true gender equality too. But there was still a divide. Ideological,

I guess you would call it. Factions. Different opinions on how society should run. Did I ever tell you that before I left, that the community on August was already split in two?"

Lae shook her head.

"It started early, a split in how we should operate. Socialist versus capitalist. Some reasoned that we should all work together. Others considered it should be a trade or barter system, hard work being rewarded. It divided us. By the time I came here, almost a third of the population had moved to Green Island. My problem was that I could see both viewpoints, and I think many others could too. I just don't feel that here. There is a genuine sense of cohesion. Everyone supports everyone else. You don't seem to have the same divisive issues that August did."

Lae nodded in understanding. "Actually, we did," she said. "In the early months, there was constant bickering and arguing, people wanting to replicate what had gone before."

"So, what changed?"

"Watching the people outside the dome die," she said simply. "Finding abandoned cottages, crofts, and farms around the countryside under the dome. Knowing that those people were moved on because of *us*. Despite the grief and anguish, or perhaps because of it, people here knew they had been given an opportunity. A gift. It brought people closer together, and we formed a true community. People look out for their neighbors, care for each other's children, share meals. We became friends."

"Even Angus?"

"Even Angus. We had no knowledge that he knew so much, then."

"I'm so sorry that you all had to witness that."

"I imagine on August it was easier, not forcibly removing people from their homes."

I considered that. "Yes," I said slowly. "In some ways, it probably was easier. Clean slate, no evidence that it was someone else's home. But it also came with no attachment to the land, no feeling of guardianship. Here, you cared for the land because it is yours. British soil, I mean. On August, we may as well have been transported to the moon. It was strange and alien. There was no kinship. No evidence of life before... well, except the carvings on the stones in the cave. But only Freyja and I knew about that. Maybe it is the essence of the place as well as the people in it. Honestly, I had never felt such a bond to land until... well, until I came here. I don't suppose you would have much knowledge of Australian indigenous people?"

Lae shook her head. "None."

"Australian indigenous people have a profound spiritual connection to the land and the water. It forms such a large part of their culture, their laws, and customs. Every aspect of their lives is connected to it. We learned about it at school, learned some of their Dreamtime stories[11]. But I never really comprehended the significance of it on a personal level. For

---

[11] In Australian Aboriginal (First People) culture, Dreamtime describes important features of Aboriginal spiritual beliefs and existence. The Dreamtime was at the beginning of time,when the land and the people were created by the Spirits. They made the rivers, streams, water holes the land, hills, rocks, plants and animals.

the first time in my life, I get it. Here. I finally feel like I have come home. This is the land I need to fight for."

Lae smiled at me. "You will always have a home here."

"I know. I can't tell you how much that means to me."

CHAPTER 32

IT WAS MID-AFTERNOON AND bitterly cold, despite being April. An odd sensation, being cold but no wind. Lae and I had been to visit Orla and Josh, a young couple who moved into an old croft a few miles down the valley so that they could run highland cattle. Everyone agreed that having the herds broken up into smaller groups to avoid potential transmission of disease was a desirable practice. No one wanted to lose all animals in one fell swoop. I had always had an obsession for highland cattle, "hairy coos," as my gran had called them, those fabulously hairy ginger-colored cows with expressive eyes and long fringes falling over their faces. As a boy, I had owned a navy t-shirt with a highland cow on it. It had been my favorite, and I had worn it obsessively until it had fallen apart. I cried when Mum threw it out, unable to get another one in those days long before online shopping. I still felt the fascination for the gorgeous beasts. I could watch them for hours.

Josh introduced me to his herd of highland cows, and I discovered they came in various colors—ginger, black, and even cream. A darling ginger cow named Delilah came over to have her face scratched. An enormous beast several times my size, she could have squashed me like a bug. Instead, she nudged up against me, demanding affection until I finally needed to climb a stone fence to get away from her. Josh stood nearby, forking feed into a metal dispenser, laughing.

"She won't give up that one," he advised.

"Please, can we not eat her?" I pleaded. "She is gorgeous."

Josh sighed. "They are good for buttermilk. It has a higher fat content, you know. But they are good for beef, too. Delilah there, she is a breeder. She will be fine for a few years yet."

Reaching over the old dry-stone fence to scratch Delilah one last time, I whispered, "You are safe, girl," before leaving Josh to find Lae, who had disappeared into the house.

Orla had given birth only a few days before to a darling girl named Lillian. Orla was besotted with her. Lillian was a sweet, placid baby with a light fuzz of hair. She stared up at me with large blue eyes. She seemed fascinated with me, and I was surprised to find that I was with her. One of the medical team had been and checked on mum and bub earlier in the week and reported them both doing well. Lae and I brought food and small homemade gifts from the village: knitted blankets, tiny socks, a beautiful multi-colored quilt, casseroles, soups, and cakes. We were quite laden with goods on our outward journey but didn't have the heart to say no to each additional person who asked us to carry the gifts.

We just smiled and said, "Yes, we will take that for you," despite wondering how on earth we would be able to carry it all. Every item was made with love and care. It occurred to me all the times I had been to a shop to buy a gift, for a birthday, or later, weddings. I had put consideration into my gifts, but I had never spent hours choosing or spinning wool or selecting fabrics, building a wooden toy with offcuts, sewing a teddy bear, or designing and making a gift with my hands. As we handed over the gifts, I finally understood what made a true present: the effort put into it, not the cost.

Handed the sleeping Lillian to hold, I sat and watched Orla and Lae put the new bedding into the cot, then unwrap the gifts. I saw Lae glance over at me several times, whether to be sure I hadn't dropped the baby or to just check I wasn't freaking out I wasn't sure. I was rather enjoying the simplicity of it, enjoying the sensation of welcoming a new human.

"How different do you think her life will be, being born here?" I asked Lae on the long walk home after a lovely dinner with lots of conversation and laughter. Josh and Orla had insisted we stay the night, but we politely declined, knowing we both had early starts in the morning. They ha kindly gifted us a parcel of the many varieties of mushrooms that Orla raised, and I enjoyed thinking about how to prepare them. The smell of cooking mushrooms rated as highly as freshly cooked bread as far as I was concerned.

It was cold and dark, but the moon was out, and the sky was brilliant with stars. Lae considered the question before responding. "I don't know," she said slowly. "Simpler, maybe. No stress of traffic, public transport, no pressure to get top grades and get into a respected university. She may never know what social media is or the internet."

"But then, in some ways, it is harder," I countered. "Limited medical care and lack of career choices. She can't exactly leave the island and go traveling, can she?"

"I guess it all depends on what you value in life," Lae responded promptly. "What do you value, Cam?"

I paused, knowing I was being put on the spot. I wasn't sure how to answer that. Lae had a manner that was direct but kind at the same time. I never knew if she was grilling me or showing concern.

"I have valued different things at different points of my life," I answered quietly. "Right now, I can't imagine anywhere I would rather be."

Lae gasped. "Look!" She grabbed my arm and pointed toward the east, past the standing stones of Callanish high on the hillside. Blue-green lights danced in the sky, an aurora in a haze just off the horizon. The purples, magentas, and scarlets followed the blues and greens and provided a spectacular backdrop to the stone circle, leaving us spellbound. Vibrant pinks, golds, and varieties of greens lit up the night sky and illuminated the stone monoliths, dark shadows cast against the colored night. We sat on a rocky outcrop and watched, scared that to speak would end the show, more spectacular than any fireworks. Never having seen the northern lights before, I had always thought that the colors would be still, but to my astonishment, they were *dancing,* flickering, moving, entrancing, and constantly changing color. The stones looked even more magical now than they did by day. Feeling her shiver beside me, but neither of us wanting to leave, I put my arm around Lae, and she snuggled into my coated shoulder as we watched, frozen by the bitter cold, yet magnetized by the spectacular vision before us.

Just when we assumed it was ending, another burst of color kept us captivated. Eventually, I looked down, intending to look at my watch. Lae sensed my action and turned her head toward me at the same moment, her lips meeting mine in the semi-dark. Instinctively, I kissed her passionately, my body remembering exactly what to do. Her lips were warm and embraced me, making me forget entirely who I was and where I was. My hand reached up to caress her hair. Recalling who it was that I was kissing arrived a fraction of a second too late. I withdrew hurriedly, awkwardly, murmuring an apology. She recoiled as if bitten by a snake, stood, and started back toward the path, not waiting for me to follow. We walked the long, dark path back to town in silence. The air between us was even more frigid than the frosty night, and I mentally berated myself for making such a foolish mistake.

How could I do this to Lae? To Freyja?

Reaching the cottage first, she went inside, leaving the door open behind her. Pausing at the doorway, I wondered if I should sleep in the greenhouse. I wasn't welcome here. The arctic air outside made up my mind. No. She had always said that I had a home here. I believed that. I would try to speak with her in the morning.

Planning to cook the mushrooms gifted to us by Orla, I found Laetitia had already left by the time I rose the next day. *Avoiding me*, I reflected sadly. We were so close, such good friends. I would hate for my time here to be marred by uncomfortable silences. Maybe I should move into the main house where I knew there were spare rooms? It was her home, after all. I was unspeakably saddened to think that I may have lost my best friend, someone who knew and understood me, someone I shared values with, and it was all my fault.

"Seriously, mate. Tell me you are joking? You can't be going through that again? Didn't you say it was like being spun in a washing machine on high speed while standing next to a loudspeaker at a rock concert, vomiting your guts out and then watching the chunks spin past you?" Fraser was incredulous at my news.

"I did," I said balefully, feeling utterly sick at the memory. "But I don't see that I have a choice."

"Choice?" Fraser snorted. "That is a cop-out. You always have a choice. You might not *like* the choices, but you have them. You can stay here. You can go back. You can go the long way around. You can wait and see if she comes back here. But you have a choice."

"True," I admitted. "Maybe I do. The fact is that I love it here, the peace, the serenity. All of you," I waved my arm, encompassing the village in front of the greenhouse in which we were working. "But I have to."

Fraser nodded, "Freyja?" he asked gently.

I sighed deeply and nodded. "We were, are, married."

The events of the night before had forced my hand. Lying awake all night after that long walk home, in silence, I knew I needed to find Freyja. I couldn't just stay here, knowing that she was out there, somewhere, searching for *me*.

"She must have been a hell of a woman."

"She is."

"Tell me."

"I have been thinking about this a lot lately. I need to find her, even if it is futile. Even if I arrive covered in my vomit, looking like the wild man of Oz. It's the right thing to do. I made a commitment. I need to see it through."

Fraser nodded, understanding. "How long until the solstice?" he asked gently.

"Six weeks."

That afternoon, as I worked, I planned what I would say to Laetitia that night. She was one of two people I had a strong connection with, and I was distraught that our friendship might now be over. The speech was all planned, word for word, rehearsed all afternoon. I roleplayed her many responses—crying, anger, silent treatment, throwing me out. I was prepared. I had rehearsed the scenarios.

Seated at the dining table, I waited for her to come in. Opening my mouth to speak, she said, "Me first," in a tone that would allow no disagreement. I acquiesced. I owed her that.

Expecting to be criticized for what happened the night before, I stiffened my spine and waited. I deserved what I got; I knew. She thought I had led her on and was furious at me. This entire situation was my stupid fault.

Lae threw her arms around me and hugged me hard. I froze, completely taken off guard and unable to react. Holding me by the shoulders, she drew back, gave me a gentle shake, and looked me in the eye.

"I heard you are leaving at the solstice?" It was a question, not judgment.

I nodded and relaxed slightly. Her knowing made things a little easier. News traveled fast here.

"Then let's spend your remaining time being the close friends we are with no unpleasantness."

That was the single option I hadn't planned for. I would never, ever understand women. "Really?" I asked, looking into her gentle caramel eyes. I couldn't help but feel this was a trick, some kind of game.

"Really," she replied with conviction. "It was my fault as much as yours. It shouldn't have happened, and I am sorry. We will not speak of it again. Now, it is your turn to cook. What are we having for dinner?"

CHAPTER 33

ARRIVING IN THE DEAD of winter, I hadn't noticed how marked the seasons were here. While there was a change between summer and winter on August, the lack of native deciduous trees made the transition less visible. Here it was like the world suddenly awoke one day. Trees showed bursts of bud and green, turning pink with blossoms. The heather was changing from green to a sea of purple, and suddenly the entire landscape had shifted. Birds and animals were active, and as a result, so was Jam, who spent longer periods away hunting. Warmer weather and longer days also made it easier to work longer hours, and I relished the idea of helping the community establish additional greenhouses before I left.

The three new greenhouses had been agreed upon and designed over winter, and much of the construction had already occurred. Initial grumbling, followed by outright objection, had taken place from the carpentry team, who felt that they had enough on their plate. But the community had been convinced by Fraser that I knew my stuff, and as I would not be here forever, they needed to build them while I was still here to supervise. So it came about that the builders were instructed to build them as a matter of priority, in the specifications that I requested, to maximize the morning and midday sun. Ten meters long by twenty meters wide. They were perfect. Despite their initial complaints, the construction team had done a fantastic job.

One had an open space inside to be dedicated to the raising of trees. Fraser and I were now busy growing everything from tropical fruits to stone fruits, raspberry canes, blackberries, blueberry bushes, a maple tree, and my babies, three mango trees—a gift for Laetitia, who had never experienced the joy of a ripe, juicy mango. All crops were clearly labeled. Occasionally I left a surprise or Easter egg for someone to find when I was gone. I hoped they would remember me fondly when I left. Time was running out; it was late May now, and I planned to travel on the summer solstice in three weeks.

Lae was reserved. I knew she was sad about my decision to go. Each day she found some way to tell me she would miss me as I would her. She had made me feel at home here, like I belonged. I would happily have stayed forever. Fraser was openly supportive of my decision, but he regularly expressed his personal opinion that he would prefer I stay.

A village meeting was held to discuss the portal and to see what use should be made of it. A small number wanted to go through, to see this island off the coast of Australia, but were reluctant when they realized it was a once in six-month trip. The other issue was that they might not get a warm welcome. I was grilled about this topic but didn't feel qualified to advise on what reception they may get. It could be welcoming; it could be hostile. I had not been part of that community for six months, and honestly, I hadn't been for several months before I traveled. I was no judge of how newcomers would be treated. We also didn't know if Angus and Freyja had made it safely to August, and if they had, how they had been received. Most were a little scared of the journey itself, especially after hearing how I had described it. There was no way I was holding back on *that* experience.

Journey made it sound like a relaxing flight or cruise. It was anything but. *The village here was far more cohesive,* I contemplated as they discussed the options. Everyone was respectful, taking the time to listen to all opinions. They were supportive, a genuine community. August had formed silos, different factions quite early. Here, everyone was on friendly terms.

The conversations around who, if anyone, would accompany me, took weeks. Eventually, it was decided that there was no rush. I should go this time and see if the community on August wanted to form a trading relationship. I was known in both places. I could act as an agent. I agreed to this. After all, I was going anyway. I could make the offer of trade, in goods and people, if August was willing.

If they even give me a chance to speak before they sacrifice me, I thought bleakly.

CHAPTER 34

ON THE 22ND OF June, the morning of the summer solstice, a small group of friends accompanied me as I made my way to the standing stones at Callanish. As we walked up the final steep incline past farmland, the sun was already well risen. The sun rose early this time of year, and I had unnecessarily prolonged my departure. These people had become friends, family in such a comparatively short time. I was at peace here, part of the fabric of the community. For the first time since I left my family in Melbourne, I had felt genuinely accepted by the people around me. A pang of sadness struck me. I was making a huge mistake. *If I am so sad about leaving, then maybe I shouldn't? How can I possibly want to go?*

As I climbed the hillside toward the major complex of stones, I could see the outlines of the other stone circles less than a kilometer away. Yet again, I wondered how many of these portals there were. How many people were doing what we were doing on this day, that came around only twice a year, where an alignment made such a miraculous trip possible?

I'd rather do this in the hold of a cargo plane, I thought grumpily as I passed an old farmhouse and walked through the gate at the end of the long avenue of standing stones, announcing the entrance to this ancient world. I stopped to admire the stones, even though I had seen them several times over the years in addition to many other visits over the past few months. I pondered the phenomenon that had brought me here. Antipodes. Two poles at opposite ends of the earth, opened and magnetized by the solstice, the midpoint of the year. Today, the stones felt different, more radiant somehow. An inner glow and a magnetic pull drew me toward them.

Maybe Angus is right, and they are magnetic lodestones. Is the magnet so much stronger when its polar opposite is directly lined up at the opposite end? I tried to recall if I had experienced this sense of magnetism when I entered the cave, our cave back on August. But I was so wracked with grief that I remembered nothing. Then I had just wanted to end the misery. Strange how six short months had changed everything.

Compared to the grotto, the Callanish complex is quite large. A central stone circle, with a giant monolith not quite at the center nearly five meters high, towers over the circle, surveying all in its realm. Five rows radiate from the center in a cross pattern, three arms of a cross in the south, east, and west, and the remaining cross arm consisting of two rows running almost parallel from the stones to the north, looking precisely like an avenue for processions.

We entered from the northern end of this avenue of standing stones, facing the circle and the largest monolith. At the foot of this monolith was the chambered cairn, the portal. Walking between the rows of enormous stones as we approached the main circle, I was humbled, and I could envision ancient worshippers carrying offerings entering from the end of the avenue as we had, facing the great circle and the prominent monolith.

A crazy thought struck me: *Should I be making an offering?* Almost as quickly, I dismissed the notion. Ancient civilizations would have had no way to explain this portal, the science behind it. They would undoubtedly have assumed a greater being, a God, had opened this for them; thus, a sacrifice was necessary to appease or thank him.

As we approached the central monolith, I cast my eye out for it. The sun was nearly directly overhead and blindingly bright as the light dispersed through the dome. I didn't want to blunder through the portal by accident. Based on Fraser's observations when I traveled on the last solstice, we were reasonably sure that the portal was open for less than a few minutes. The chambered tomb, slightly to the left of the main monolith, was squashed between the central stone and the stones to the east. It looked like it had been shoved in afterward, although thousands of years ago. Lying flat, between two giant monoliths, it would be easy to miss in the dark as it had been when I arrived six months before. But today was full light, almost midday, as it had been when Freyja had arrived.

Guarded by the monoliths, the tomb currently lay in partial shadow, but I could feel it radiating a vibrant energy, a hum so strong it was almost visible.

Soon the sun would be directly overhead, shining into the tomb, and we hoped, opening the portal. Now that I knew its purpose, I wondered if ancient settlers here had always known that this was a magical place, one that transported them to faraway places. The charged atmosphere strengthened as we approached the chambered tomb. I could feel the tiny hairs on my arms and neck rise with the electricity in the atmosphere.

Panicking suddenly, I turned to my right and headed to the east, toward Loch Roag. I took a few steps and dropped my head to my chest, exhaling heavily. I could feel my heart racing and my hands shook. I hoped no one could see my anxiety.

I can't do it. I can't face that again. They have no idea what it is like. Words fell woefully short of describing the utter terror experienced through that passage. Dark, swirling, roaring, engulfing. Every sense was exploding, and *knowing* you were about to die, actually *wishing* for it. I had experienced nightmares about that passage for weeks after the journey, and they resurfaced after I decided to go back.

Freyja. Focus on Freyja. Her face. Her smile. I took a deep breath and exhaled more loudly than I had intended. Fraser discreetly pretended not to notice that I was in turmoil and was holding a quiet conversation with Aidan about some plant species. I tried to smile at them, knowing that they were waiting for my signal. Would I stay? Would I go? No one would force me. That much was clear.

Feeling something brush against my leg, I glanced down to see Jam rubbing herself against my calves. As I picked her up, Jam butted her head affectionately under my chin, demanding love. Balancing her now significant size on my hip, I used my free hand to scratch along her face and under her chin. She purred with ecstasy, and I experienced a moment of pure contentment, and yet again questioned the sanity in what I was about to do.

Looking at the sky, I could see that the sun was now directly overhead. The electric field was fully charged, I could tell. I felt positively vibrating with the energy. I didn't know how long the portal was open, and I didn't want to wait another six months to find out.

Leaving was hard, waiting six more months—well, I likely wouldn't return at all.

"It's time," I announced with more intensity than I felt.

Handing Jam to Laetitia, who happily adapted to the change in scenery, I turned to each of them in turn. I had privately said goodbye to Fraser, Isla, and Lae last night, not wanting a public display of emotion. My guts were in turmoil. I forced myself to keep it together as I made my last farewell.

"Anyone got any travel sickness medication?" I asked, trying to ease the tension. I hated goodbyes.

"You will always have a home here," said Laetitia, seeing straight through me as usual.

"Take care of Jam, will you?"

"I promise," she said, tightening her hold on Jam and stepping back to join the others. No one wanted to fall through by accident.

Facing the horseshoe-shaped tomb, now completely illuminated and glowing orange and bronze, I stared for a moment at the stones marking the edge. *Did they once bury people here? Will this be my final resting place?* Holding my breath, I looked squarely at the massive monolith at the head buzzing with energy. Taking three purposeful steps, I walked down the slight slope between the two prominent boulders and vanished into the dark.

PART FOUR

CHAPTER 35

I SLOWLY CAME TO CONSCIOUSNESS with my legs and feet feeling hot and wet. My upper body felt like crushed jelly, the aftermath of being slammed at high speed against a brick wall. As I registered my surroundings, I saw I was lying on the hewn stairs on the edge of the springs, our springs. My legs and feet were still mostly submerged, accounting for the feeling of heat that radiated up my legs.

"Cam? Cam? Is it really you?"

Already lying on my side, I projectile vomited, barely missing his shoes. My long, dark fringe fell across my face as I rolled slightly onto my back, unable to open my eyes.

Jamie jumped back, disgusted. But concern for my welfare soon took precedence. "Cam?"

"Ugggg."

The passage was as I had recalled, but as I had known what I was doing when I stepped into the portal this time, I remembered it better. Suction first, being pulled with such force I knew that surely my skin would come off. Then the roaring started.

Roaring so loud I thought my head would burst. Spinning, escalating to the point of losing consciousness. But not quite. The spinning slowed as I reached the mid-point, only to spin the opposite way. The split second of being torn in two directions as my body tried to switch from counter-clockwise to clockwise spinning was excruciating, worse than any medieval torture device.

But I was through. I had survived. At least, I think I had.

Jamie was pulling my legs from the water. Laying in the comparative cool was reviving me somewhat. The portal had thrown my head clear of the water, or I would have drowned. Touching my tender nose, I first thought it was broken, but careful manipulation proved that it was likely bruised, but not broken. My cheekbone could easily be fractured, slamming into the stone steps with such force. I vaguely wondered how many people had drowned here over the centuries. I could feel the cave here vibrating with the same energy that the stones in Scotland had. Strange in all my visits here that I had never noticed it before. Even on my last visit. But then, I wasn't focused on magnetic fields six months ago. I was too distraught and missing Freyja.

"Frey..." I tried to say but couldn't quite form the words.

"Are you okay?" Jamie seemed genuinely concerned.

"Frey—ya." I managed to gasp through my battered and constricted chest and lungs.

"Ahh. She is alive! Can you believe it!"

I closed my eyes.

Jamie kept talking. Unable to process what he was saying, I kept my eyes closed. At one point, I thought to ask him about Jacinda, the baby, but couldn't summon the words, so I didn't.

"I can't believe it was *you* that came through. Freyja told us about the passage to Scotland, but no one was game enough to test and see if it was true. That's why I was here tonight. To see if anyone from Scotland was coming through. We talked about someone from here, traveling the other way. From here to Scotland, I mean. But the way she described it, it sounded horrifying."

"It is," I mumbled, genuinely wondering how many years each journey through that passage had deducted from my life.

"So it is all true? It sounded so... *unreal.*"

"It's all true," I muttered.

Sometime later, with Jamie supporting me—I noticed he had lost weight—I managed to walk back down the hill to the village, vertigo as bad as last time. It was slow going down the dark, steep, windy, narrow trail, even though I must have been here a hundred times in the eighteen months this had been our secret. Mine and Freyja's. It was a secret no more if Jamie was there. But why hadn't Freyja been there to greet me?

Likely the entire community knew about the cave and the hot springs. *Must be a veritable party there on a Saturday afternoon*, I thought gloomily, recalling all the intimate moments we had shared there. It was our place. Except now, it wasn't. Wracked with anxiety, I kept stopping to relieve myself. Jamie diplomatically assumed it was something to do with the vortex. I was absolutely shitting bricks at the thought of facing them all again, my accusers. They had suspected me, isolated me, and made my life a living hell. Banished me. But now they knew Freyja was alive. She was here!

We walked into the village, still moving slowly, as the world was still spinning intermittently, and not pleasantly. People lurked in the dark, evidently waiting for Jamie to come back and report. Swarms of people surrounded us as we entered the village, stunned to see me alive.

Diana was first. "Cam!!!" She pushed her way through and threw her arms around me. I held her tight. It was so wonderful to see her. Another friendly face. Jenny. She was here, too.

Heidi came over crying. "I am so sorry I ever doubted you!" She buried her head into my shoulder and sobbed. Torn between feeling sorry for her and feeling that this was a bit rich considering that I was the one who had been banished, I tentatively placed my arms around her back and murmured, "It's all okay now."

Is it? A quiet voice inside pricked me. *Will it be alright?*

The words were nearly strangling me, and I finally managed to get out, "I need to know. Where is Freyja?"

Heidi lifted her head and looked me in the eye.

"She is alive. Come on," she said between sniffs. "Let's go, and we will tell you everything."

The lights were on in the hall, waiting. Not all were here, but enough—a decent crowd. Sat down in the hall, with Diana on one side and Jamie on the other, I was asked some questions about the portal and Scotland, but I could tell they were just confirming what they already knew. Yes, Freyja had fallen into the antipodean portal, much like I had. She had ended up in Scotland, but I knew that already.

"Where is she?" I demanded. "She isn't here!"

There was lots of looking around, clearly wondering what to say. I could feel my temper rising. "Look," I said between gritted teeth. "I have just experienced the most gut-wrenchingly awful vortex of terror for the *second* time in six months. I am sick, I am exhausted, and I damned well want to know where she is!"

Heidi was the one to speak finally. "Freyja arrived here by boat about six weeks ago with four men. They said that they had come from Lewis, where you were."

I nodded.

"But, on the way, they had found other communities."

I blinked. "I'm sorry. What did you say?"

Heidi slowed her voice. "I said, they found other communities like ours."

I was speechless for a moment as I took in what she was saying.

"Freyja and Angus worked out where some likely antipodean points were. Angus said that as only a small percentage of the earth is land, plus the prevalence of ancient sites or magnetic lodestones, it wasn't too difficult to limit the options. They had found several sites on the way here, one deserted but mostly inhabited. The most fascinating one was a French island, roughly equidistant between Australia, Africa, and Antarctica, called the Kerguelen Islands. They were antipodal to a point in Saskatchewan in Canada!"

"It was a shock, let me tell you," said Jenny with a smile. "Watching a boat pull up, then watching Freyja get out, her tall willowy figure and long blonde hair rather unmistakable. Even after ten months!"

"So, where is she? Just tell me, goddammit!" My temper was at boiling point, and I was trying hard to avoid a full-scale eruption.

Diana took this one. "They left again, Cam. The last week in May."

I could feel an undercurrent in the room. Freyja's return had made quite an impact. I couldn't quite put my finger on it, but I sensed that there was something that I wasn't being told.

Phil took up the story. "We didn't believe it, you see. That's why Jamie was sent to the cave to guard the portal. Just in case. After she showed us where it was, we spent hours searching, but nothing happened. It seemed incredulous that it was a passage through the earth for just a few minutes twice a year. I've been in the springs several times in the past few weeks. Nothing happened. So we thought perhaps we should keep an eye out, just in case it was true. Then tonight, you show up! I can't believe it is true!"

"About the portal to the Hebrides? Aye, yes, it is. All true." I slumped in my chair, suddenly unable to absorb what I was being told.

Nalini, who had cared for me before, and had liked Freyja, saw me crumple and came rushing over, thinking I had fainted.

"I'm fine," I whispered. "Just exhausted."

"Come with me," she said in her best official voice. "I need to check you out."

It was a good enough excuse to leave, and I strongly suspected she was using this as a ruse to get me out, so I allowed her to steer me by the elbow out the door to the clinic. She helped me onto a bed and went through a few routine tests: blood pressure, temperature, reflexes. My blood pressure was high, but otherwise, I was fine.

"I'm not surprised," I said drily. "That trip is, well. Something else."

"So I have heard," Nalini murmured. "Well, rest now. I will make sure that you aren't disturbed."

I didn't need to be told twice. Settling myself, I closed my eyes, waiting for sleep to overtake me. Breathing in and out. Relaxing my aching muscles and trying not to focus on my throbbing nose. Fighting for sleep, my brain kept whirring, and I couldn't relax.

Hang on, that isn't right, I stewed crankily. *I am completely and utterly exhausted. Big day, long walk to the stones. Emotional departure. Awful trip. Return walk back to here. Now what? Can't I rest? What sort of sorcery is this?*

Instead of sleeping, I lay there for hours, thinking of Freyja and that trip. The one I had now done twice.

For her.

And survived.

CHAPTER 36

THE NEXT DAY, I left the clinic after breakfast. Walking toward my house, interactions were tense but polite. Aside from Heidi's public apology, more often than not, I got a gruff hello, a nod, and then less than a minute of awkward conversation. There were only so many times you could hear, "Lovely weather, isn't it?" to know that people just don't know what to say to you. Diana was the exception. Beautiful darling Diana. She was the same bubbly, cheerful friend she had always been. When I spoke with her, I couldn't believe that it had been over eight months since we had last been together. She hugged me and walked me to my cabin, where she left me to settle in. The door was open, and a couple I didn't know very well were cleaning. Someone else had moved in, and they were hurrying them out.

"I…" I faltered. I didn't quite know what to say. "Do you want me to… go?"

"No, no!" the woman chirped. "We will be done in a minute." My remaining clothes and minimal possessions were neatly stacked in two boxes in the corner of the living room.

No one wanted my stuff, I thought cynically, remembering Ilana's possessions being allocated out. Perhaps murderer's stuff was tainted.

True to their word, they were finished in a few minutes, and like whirling dervishes, they were out of the room, the door firmly closed behind them, leaving me in my now clean but strangely unfamiliar former home. The one I had shared with Freyja. Memories started flooding back. The meals we had eaten at the table. The laughter we shared on that couch. Glancing across the room, my heart sank. I couldn't walk into the bedroom. The place where we had shared our hearts, wishes, dreams, and fears with each other. Where we had kept each other warm with confessions and desires. This was a mistake. Closing my eyes, I pondered what to do next.

A gentle knock sounded at the door. Breaking my stupor, I opened the door to Jacinda, the baby in a sling at her hip, looking at me with a mixed expression on her face. I couldn't quite read it. "Jamie told me you were back," she said.

"I imagine news still travels fast," I said a little coldly.

"That it does. I was worried about you."

Looking at her face, I could see it was true. It was a look of concern. She had cared. Jamie and Diana too. They just had their own lives to lead. The ice thawed. She stepped through the door and hugged me, the baby a little squashed between us.

Drawing away, I looked at her. "I'm so sorry for leaving without telling anyone. It was... just too difficult in the end. I have always been so grateful for you and Jamie in my life, but you had a new person to focus on. You didn't need to worry about me too." While this was true, it made her a little uncomfortable. Rapidly changing the subject, I asked, "Did you see her? Freyja, I mean."

Jacinda nodded. "I did. But she wasn't here long, and I was busy with Aroha here. The first few months drag but fly by. It is an odd process, motherhood."

I smiled at the baby, a chubby black-haired girl, a mini Jacinda, her eyes wide with astonishment. "How is Aroha?"

In the way of all mothers, Jacinda launched into a dialogue about nappies, feeding, sleep patterns, and milestones. Half-listening through the fog of exhaustion and disappointment, I struggled to keep up and tried to smile in the right places. Jacinda was a natural mother, and Aroha was now her sole focus. Recognizing her cue, Aroha started to cry and thrash about, and Jacinda stood.

"She is hungry. Tired, too. I really should get her home. It is lovely to see you, Cam. Come to dinner soon?"

"I will," I agreed. I showed Jacinda to the door, and she kissed me goodbye.

"We missed you."

Closing the door, I sat down heavily. I was back, and Freyja was gone. My arms were empty, again. My head in my hands, I felt the familiar throb start behind my eyes. Closing my eyes, I willed the pain to stop.

Another knock resounded at the door, more forceful this time. "Come in," I murmured, not even bothering to get up.

Expecting Jacinda had forgotten something, I was surprised when Heidi opened the door, looking somewhat worried. "Are you okay?" she asked, recognizing that she had interrupted something.

"I guess so. It is just... well. Overwhelming."

Belatedly, I remembered my manners and waved her into the kitchen, inviting her to sit down. *They thought I was gone. It must have been an enormous relief. I wonder how long it took them to work out I was gone? Did they have a celebration? Did anyone miss me at all?*

My transparent face likely showed what I thought as Heidi cringed a little. She lowered her eyes. "We treated you terribly," she said in a low voice, so quiet I could barely hear her.

I had nothing to say to this, so I didn't reply. I sat there, waiting. To break the silence after a few long and very awkward moments, I asked, "You had something to tell me?"

Heidi was visibly relieved to change the subject. Then cringed again as she said, "I came to tell you about Freyja. We talked, after the meeting last night, after you left. We agreed that someone needed to. It may as well be me."

I nodded, encouraging her to continue.

"The boat arrived in early May. Great big luxury yacht it was. Scared us half to death when we saw it making a beeline to the cove."

"Huh? Luxury yacht? That..."

"Ahh, you wouldn't know that bit, either. So, they left Lewis and headed to Edinburgh. No sign of survivors, they said. But they found a government warehouse filled with canned food, bottled water, and a marina filled with luxury vessels. It wasn't like anyone owned them anymore, so they chose the one that best suited their needs—a superyacht Angus called it. Huge thing, like its own suburb! Called the

Selkie, it was about forty meters long with two engines, solar panels, and a large hold to store all the food and water they could collect. Plus, long-range fuel tanks, so they didn't need to keep refilling. It was amazing!" Heidi recalled. "Timber paneled living room, marble bathrooms, leather sofas in the entertainment room and the bedrooms! Heavens! They were better than a luxury hotel!"

"I get it. It was seriously swish." I was hoping she would hurry and move on.

"It really was," Heidi agreed. "Anyway, so this amazing yacht turns up one day. There are five people on board—Angus, Freyja, and three other men: Luca, Nate, and Jakob."

Nodding in agreement, I encouraged her to continue. Fraser had told me that much.

"So they had traveled to Edinburgh and then down through the North Channel to France. Nothing, at least not on the coast. But as they traveled around the coast of Spain, they found something near Gibraltar."

"Another community?" This piqued my interest.

"Not exactly. They suspected it had been, but it was deserted."

"The only thing I know about Gibraltar is something about a rock."

"Well, me too. I haven't been there. But apparently, it isn't just a rock, but a promontory made of limestone. With lots of caves and tunnels."

"Caves? I went through in a cave."

"We know. They explored and found evidence that people had been there until quite recently, as well as the remnants of the dome. They also found," Heidi paused, "quite a few human remains."

Not wanting to ask how fresh the remains were for fear of sounding morbid, I asked, "Did they find anything else?"

"Not really, but they are fairly sure there is a portal there. And that it links to somewhere on the north island of New Zealand. But not being a solstice, they didn't know for sure."

I sat up straighter at this. "So, there are more antipodean portals?"

"Wait, there is more. After they left Gibraltar, they traveled down the west African coast. That is where they discovered something really interesting."

I nodded, not wanting to interrupt the story.

"In a coastal town just north of Dakar, they found a thriving domed community. Both of African people but also French-speaking people."

"Was it a French colony?"

"Well, yes, apparently at one point. But not since the 1960s. It is an Arabic-speaking country."

"Okay, so why the French speakers?"

"That is the fascinating part. Some of the people were from New Caledonia. There is an antipodean portal from Mauritania to New Caledonia!"

Aware that my mouth was open, I consciously closed it. "You mean.... Freyja and I are not the only ones to find those things?"

"Apparently not. Freyja, Angus, and the crew stayed for a few days, restocked supplies, and learned what they could. Only one of them, Nate, spoke more than basic French. They kept going while the weather was good."

"Wow, so there definitely are more communities. And portals."

"There are. There was a third one on the Kerguelen Islands. We didn't believe them at first. When Freyja arrived by boat and told us this unbelievable story about antipodes, portals, and other communities, there was a lot of skepticism. We just thought that she had managed to find a way out of the dome and travel back to Australia, meeting these guys along the way. After all, there was no *proof*. But last night when you came through and Jamie saw it... Well, it was quite a shock to us, let me tell you! Here we thought we were the only people left on earth, only to find out that everything they said was actually true and that there are more communities, and we can travel to them!"

"It is a fascinating concept," I agreed. "The reality is slightly less attractive."

Heidi giggled. "Yes, Freyja said that too. She described the portal as 'the closest to wanting to die I have ever experienced.' She said it nearly killed her."

I shuddered. "Well, I have done it twice. I whole-heartedly agree. That is a very apt description."

"She also said that it took them some time to find us as Freyja wasn't entirely sure where we are but believed we were south of New Zealand."

I nodded. Freyja and I had discussed this privately, and I knew from Fraser that she and Angus had come to the same conclusion.

"It turns out we are on a small group of islands called the Ruapuke Islands. They were uninhabited, but we are only about fifteen kilometers from the mainland of New Zealand and thirty kilometers north-east of Stewart Island, which was inhabited, at least when the virus struck. They had planned to go there after they left here. Angus finally managed to find some maps in Edinburgh, plus a whole heap of resources to measure distance. He worked out fairly accurately where we were based on maps but also based on what Freyja had told him. He believes we are about seventy-five kilometers from the true antipodal point of Callanish, where you both ended up. While that seems a lot, he says that this is less than half a percent when you are talking roughly 20,000 kilometers apart. He was fairly confident that the magnetic pull of the caves here and the stones at Callanish was what caused the slight variation."

My mind had stuck on one point, but I was trying not to show it. *Fifteen kilometers from the mainland.* All this time, we were so close to thousands of people. Thinking of my aunt, I wasn't sure if that was a good or bad thing. The image of her sitting there, seeing the world dying, made me glad this place was uninhabited. Knowing what the Lewis community had experienced, I would never want that.

Several times when I was out with Fraser, Lae, or Hamish, walking, exploring, looking for plants or on our way to the whisky still, we had found an abandoned home. We never went inside, but each time, it was gut-wrenching and left us all in stunned silence. Kid's toys. A dog kennel. Even dead vegetable gardens or pot plants. People had *lived* there. And were now gone. Maybe it was better this way.

I tried to lighten the subject. "Does that mean you renamed the island? Back to Ruapuke, I mean."

Heidi laughed. "Well, no. It has been August Island for more than three years, so no point in changing it now. We talked about changing it for our fourth anniversary next February, but we couldn't agree on what to name it."

"What does Ruapuke mean, anyway? Surely one of the Kiwis knows."

"Two hills."

Unable to get Freyja's face out of my mind and not wanting to spend more time with Heidi than absolutely necessary, I asked, "So, where is Freyja now? Are they coming back?"

Heidi started twisting her ash blonde hair nervously around her index finger. It had grown in the time I had been away. It was longer now; she had always kept it in a short, no-nonsense bob. But now, it was long enough to tie back in a ponytail with the shorter pieces around her temples coming out of the ponytail. It was these that she was playing with.

Sensing that she was stalling, I said a little harshly, "Just tell me."

"Cam," she paused. "Freyja and Angus are.... together."

"Together?" I repeated blankly. "Of course, they are..." Then the penny dropped, and my face flamed.

"There is something else."

I blinked, unsure if I could take anything else, but looked at her with the most neutral expression I could muster.

"She is pregnant." Heidi was looking at her shoes, unable to meet my gaze. Insanely, my first thought was that I was glad she didn't see my face. My stomach tensed with the blow I had been struck. I was unable to speak.

I took a deep breath and responded as calmly as I could, "Well, I wish her all the best."

"*Nooo!*" Heidi screamed the word so loudly she startled me. "She disappeared, and we blamed you. We all blamed you. We loved her, and we thought you killed her. We were positively awful to you. Then you went, and well... it was easy, for a time. Then Freyja came back, and we realized... it was all a big mistake. You were looking for her. We loved her so much, you see."

"I see alright," I reasoned bitterly. "You loved her and not me."

Heidi saw the look of utter bleakness on my face and bravely spoke again, despite it probably being safer to run. "It isn't that. But she was just suddenly gone. We thought well.... you know what we thought."

"You couldn't work out what she saw in me. You thought she had tried to leave me, and that I killed her and hid the body. Well, I didn't. We were *happy*..." I spat coldly, trying not to lose my temper any further. I stood up. Heidi took the unspoken cue and stood to leave.

"I really am sorry, Cam. For everything." Turning to leave, she looked back at me and said, "If there is anything I can do...."

As I closed the door, I heard the echo of a lovely university friend who had terminal cancer. She told me once that people always flippantly said, "'Oh, if you need anything, just sing out.' But that was the worst part. I don't know what I need, and even if I did, I wouldn't ask for charity. How do you respond to that with, could you vacuum my house? I wanted people to say: 'Let me drive you to radiotherapy, sit with you during chemo. Let me clean your house. Walk the dog. Cook a meal.' I don't want to have to think about how people can help. I just wanted people to be there. Sit with me in the sucky times and stop asking me how I am all the time." I hadn't thought about that conversation in years, but now I knew exactly what she meant.

Over the next few days, I went through the motions, turning up for meals, smiling as I passed people in the street, making eye contact and trying to engage in conversation, but my heart wasn't in it. I tried to help in the gardens with Jamie but saw that they had replaced me. They didn't need me and were just trying to make me feel wanted. When I learned Heidi had finally taken the opportunity to slaughter our beloved Fred... I excused myself and went for a walk in the northern hills, needing to get away from people. I was so exhausted from lack of sleep that I had no energy to go far. Despite my bone-deep weariness, I lay awake on the couch at night, still unable to sleep in that bed, willing sleep to overtake me. I would even have swapped dreams of the vortex pulling me apart, bone by bone, than the feeling of sheer helplessness. Lying there, desperate for oblivion, but instead, my brain was playing scenarios over and over in my head. Seeing Freyja in our room. Seeing her in the kitchen. Seeing her with Angus, although I had never met him and didn't know what he looked like. I was sad. Angry. I hated her. I hated him. I loved her. I needed her. I had come all this way, and she didn't wait for me. I was expendable, replaceable.

By the fifth day, it became apparent that I couldn't stay here. I was no longer an Augustinian. I was an outsider. I was tolerated, but I would never be trusted.

Choices. It was six months until the next solstice. Too long. The mainland. Making plans to get to the mainland was my best choice. Heidi had said it was only fifteen kilometers, and I had a reasonable idea in which direction. When standing on the high hills at the north head, I could see land. We knew there were small islands around us, but the mainland was also to the north. A vague idea that there were decent-sized cities on New Zealand's South Island crossed my mind, but I didn't want to confirm this in the library as that could alert people I planned to leave, and I didn't want to either discuss it or deal with unwanted companions. Unsure if I could swim fifteen kilometers, I quickly shelved that plan, remembering that the virus was likely still active in the water. There was no way I could keep it out of my mouth on a swim that long. Perhaps I could make it there on a small boat and then do what Freyja had done. Find a larger boat and start exploring. Make my way to Auckland, then head out from there. The problem was, I knew absolutely nothing about building boats. Nothing. Shape, how to make it float, nothing at all. But it was fifteen kilometers. It really wasn't far. What else could I do? Canoes, rafts. Something basic, just something that floated, kept me out of the water, and something I could steer.

Acknowledging that I missed the ubiquitous Scottish breakfast of porridge, I grabbed two pieces of buttered toast from the dining room and headed to the workshops. If I could borrow some tools, maybe I could find a tree I could hollow out. Some oars and I would be on my way.

Hugh was there, a quiet New Zealander. We had little to do with each other previously, but he had always been polite and had never actively avoided me. Hugh was working on what looked to be a table when I arrived, so I stood back and watched for a bit. He managed to shape the timber with minimal effort. The wood just molded to his tools, responding to his firm but precise touch. He must have sensed me watching as he glanced up, nodded to acknowledge my presence, but kept planing the timber until it was exactly what he wanted. Then he lay the plane down, walked over, and said, "How can I help?"

Pausing for a moment, I realized the best approach here was to be out with it. I was in no mood to play games. "I'm thinking of building a boat."

His dark, bushy eyebrows raised, but he said nothing.

"I'm planning to travel across to the mainland."

He nodded, slowly and thoughtfully. "Too difficult here?" he asked kindly.

I exhaled audibly as I realized I didn't need to explain myself further. "It really is."

"When do you want to go?"

"Now. As soon as possible, I mean. I have nothing keeping me here."

Hugh looked at me directly in the eyes. He had lovely soft gray eyes with dark hair, lashes, and eyebrows—a really kind face. "Can you wait a few days?"

I looked away. I wanted to go now, but reasonably I knew that wasn't feasible. I sighed again. "Of course."

Hugh was still gazing at me intently, his face showing the inner turmoil he was experiencing. He drew himself up to his full height; he had decided. "I have been building a small rowboat," he said in his gentle Kiwi accent. "In my spare time. Not that I get much of that!" He smiled. "I am from the South Island. My family is there, were there. My sister, her three children. Two nephews and a niece. I was very close to them all. Their father died in a motorbike accident when the little one was a few weeks old. I had been there for them all their lives, like a father. Then, I up and left. At the time, I couldn't bear to see them suffer. Now I want to, well, I want to see if anyone made it. Learn what happened to them. I need to know. For the last three and a half years, I have felt so guilty. When your lady came back, and I learned we are so close...I can't just stay here and do nothing. I need to find out. I need closure."

I nodded. I knew. That had been the worst part about losing Freyja. The not-knowing.

Seeing the emotion flood my face, he looked at me calmly and said, "So you do know. If you can wait a few days, maybe three, I will come with you." Half-jokingly he added, "I'll wager you aren't much of a sailor."

I looked down at my six-foot solid frame, large hands, and long legs. "Whatever gave you that idea?" But I smiled, and he grinned.

We would get along just fine.

CHAPTER 37

THE DEAL STRUCK, WE agreed not to make it public. I had no one to tell. How could I tell Di, Jamie, or Jacinda I was leaving again? Hugh had his reasons. The community wouldn't be thrilled about losing their best carpenter—even if it was only for a few days. After all, Hugh would go back after he had reached the mainland and learned the fate of his family. The community could deal without him for a week. He was lucky New Zealand was so close. It wasn't workable for people to pop back to Australia from here. Maybe it was just as well that they were so far from their homes.

Seeing Jamie and Jacinda was easy. I visited late afternoon and was soon invited for dinner. Jacinda was vegetarian, which meant that now Jamie was as well. She made a delicious vegetarian frittata with eggs and a colorful array of vegetables. It was odd seeing produce from plants that I almost certainly planted, cared for.

The conversation was a little stilted at first. It had been more than seven months. Then, as we all relaxed, it flowed more easily. I told them about the portal, about Lewis. I spoke about Fraser and the community there, making them laugh with the story about finding Jam, the wildcat kitten. I shared my tears about finding my aunt, told them about building greenhouses and the whisky still. Jamie was particularly interested in this, his father being a Scots immigrant. I drew the still, how I remembered it, describing the lengthy process. Recognizing that I hadn't mentioned Laetitia, I considered it but realized that I didn't want them to think my loyalties weren't with Freyja. But Freyja hadn't been mentioned either. Maybe they didn't want to rub my face in it, Freyja having moved on and all. My memories of Lae were mine and mine alone.

After dessert, I thanked them profusely for dinner, excused myself, and returned to my small lonely cabin—the home I had shared but would never share again.

Diana arrived in the morning with a basket of breakfast goodies: muffins and coffee in a thermos. I hugged her warmly. It was fantastic to see her.

Diana was surprisingly still single. I probed a little, but she just replied dismissively, "Haven't met anyone." Quickly turning the conversation back to me, she asked, "Do you think you will ever get over Freyja?"

Exhaling deeply, I opened my soul. "I don't know. It is so raw, again. Like a recently healed wound has been viciously slashed open. It has been twelve months since she vanished. I was finally doing okay. Now to find out that not only is she alive, but with another man?"

Diana looked at me, sympathy in her eyes. "She is? I didn't know that part. Is that why she left again?

I just know how much you love her. But one day, you will find love again, Cam. I know it."

I doubted it but said nothing.

The village had expanded, I noted with interest. Another three smaller settlements had broken off from the principal town, several groups dissatisfied with the way things were managed. Ideological disagreements resulted in the finite resources being further divided. The old bunkhouses had been turned into duplexes now with a center wall dividing them into two decent-sized family homes, for those families who now had several children, a kitchen and bathroom at each end. I remembered the shared toilets on Lewis and smiled. So many times, I had greeted a neighbor coming out of the loo at the crack of dawn, and yet no one ever felt awkward.

It was two days until the weather conditions were best for sailing, and I spent them helping and speaking to people I knew I would never see again: Jenny, Kai, Phil, Nalini, and even Erika. Memories stirred of leaving Melbourne for the last time and visiting friends in those few days, trying to say goodbye, but not using those words of finality. It is an odd feeling, and the second time around didn't make it any easier. But I needed to leave here. I could never again be part of this community. Returning was necessary for closure, but now it was time to go. Permanently.

Hugh stashed my backpack and one of his own, along with fresh water and some food at the bow of the boat. There were three large bays on August

Island. The north-west coastline was the farthest away from the houses, the houses that had continued to spread as people had paired up and moved out. But it also meant carrying the small rowboat the most significant distance. We waited until dark and quietly carried the boat to the beach, occasionally stopping to rest. We ate in silence, looking out over the vast bay. We tried to sleep on the beach, rolled in a single blanket each. Neither of us slept well, but I must have finally drifted off as I felt Hugh shake me gently on the right shoulder. He didn't need to speak.

It was that quiet, still time before dawn. That sense that everything was still asleep. The birds hadn't yet started to wake and call. There was no rustling in the bushes. Everything was at peace. *Not like last time you left this place,* a voice pricked at me. I suppressed it. I would not think about the portal now. This would be a gentle, calm journey, not a roaring tunnel, threatening to split my head open like a melon while simultaneously tearing me limb from limb in the spinning vortex of doom.

Following my instructions on what to look for, Hugh found the triangle in the dome that could be opened, taking care to close it as we left. It was easily large enough to allow our small boat and us through. This one had the long flat base on the bottom, allowing us easier passage; the one below it was well embedded into the earth.

We pushed the boat out, then jumped in, grabbed an oar each, and started paddling as we sat next to each other on the wooden seat, wrapped as well as we could in an enormous tarpaulin to avoid getting infected water on us. I took a long look back at August, still shrouded in dark shadow as I paddled, trying to keep in time with Hugh so the tiny boat wouldn't spin.

For a time, this island had been home, a refuge. I had worked hard here, tried to be part of the community. Once, I was happy here. But those times were gone. Now... now it was just a place where there had once been memories. Memories I no longer wanted. Lifting my face to meet the new day as it rose over the horizon, reflecting its beauty in the water, I shifted my focus ahead and beyond.

Years ago, at school camp, I had learned to paddle a canoe. Not only was I no expert, I soon discovered that I couldn't tell which way was forward when in open water. Fortunately, Hugh could. Blistered, battered, and bruised, we finally made it to land. Stinging eyes from the sun, our faces sunburned and exhausted, we lay on the sandy beach, under the dead remains of scrubby salt bushes at the edge of the beach for some time, recovering our strength. It had taken over eight hours battling the tide, sometimes going with it, but mostly against. Living under the dome for so long, our skin was no longer used to direct sunlight, and we were both badly sunburned. I had forgotten how painful that could be. At times, one of us had paddled, sometimes both. Sometimes we just drifted in the general direction, hoping we weren't drifting away. Using the tarp the best we could to avoid getting water on our bodies and in our faces, it had left us sweltering and sweat-soaked.

The sun was now high in the sky, indicating that it was a little past midday. But we were here. We had paddled past tiny Dog Island. I had no idea why it was called that and being exhausted and desperate to get to the mainland, it hadn't occurred to me at the time to ask Hugh—if he even knew. The mainland was obvious when we finally saw it. Despite the desolation and ruin, buildings still lined the entrance to the bay of a tiny town called Bluff.

Bluff was a port town for cargo, judging by the warehouses and docks. But there were no boats here that met our needs. But at least it had a main road to Invercargill, which was a decent-sized place, Hugh assured me.

It didn't take long to find a mode of transport. Less than two streets inland, there was a row of houses, evidence of what had once been a small town. We found some bikes, rusted and left behind on a house doorstep. The house was in a state of disrepair. The verandah was falling at one end. The feeling was dark and sinister. We didn't go inside. They were kids' bikes judging by the size, and I spared a thought for the poor kid who had left his bike there never to be ridden again. A fresh pang of survivor's guilt made me shudder. As I was slightly taller, Hugh insisted I take the larger one, but anyone watching us would have considered it hilarious. Two grown men riding kids' bikes the thirty kilometers to Invercargill.

"We couldn't have kept looking and found a *car?*" I muttered under my breath for the hundredth time. Between our oversized, cramped legs with limited motion for pedaling and rutted roads, it was a most unpleasant experience. Add to that the fact that neither of us had ridden bikes in years, and there were many accidents, swearing, and utterances of an unmentionable nature.

The silence was overwhelming. The dead trees, plants, and lack of life was startling. There was no green anywhere, including enormous tracts of what had once been pastoral land. No living creatures, no birds singing, no insects buzzing. Dead. This was the only word I could use to describe our surroundings—dead. It felt wrong being alive in a place where absolutely nothing lived. Unlike that brief trip to my aunt's house, there was no wind here either. It was eerily still. Deserted houses lined the street as we passed, overgrown gardens brown and decayed. Trees that had died and fallen, but as they weren't blocking anyone's path, no one had bothered to move them. Children's toys outside houses, deserted cars in driveways. We couldn't bring ourselves to stop. It was apparent that we would find no one here.

Invercargill was a neatly planned city following a grid pattern, so it was straightforward to orient ourselves. As we rode down the main streets, Dee and Tay, I inwardly cringed at the blatantly Scottish names. *Should I never have left?* I had been happy there. *No*, I told myself. I needed to go, for closure. Well, I certainly had that.

Hugh and I hunted for signs of life amidst the deserted buildings, most filthy and falling into disrepair. Abandoned vehicles and rubbish lined the streets, literally piles and piles of plastic of every description, bleached of color by the sun, but still largely intact. There were bottles, bags, and piles of filthy nappies in every gutter and doorway, blocking every drain. It appeared that no one had bothered with a garbage collection in the last few months of life. What would have been the point of that? It looked, smelled, *was* a ghost town devoid of color, of life.

Traveling from August to Lewis, I had been surrounded by life, people, trees, animals, vibrant color. The marked difference here from the domed communities I had left was the *color* of death—grays, browns. I had never thought of death as having a color, but it did—muted, faded tones of brown and gray. Dirty colors. Even the piles of plastic that were once clearly brightly colored toys or bags at some point had bleached into gray. Still intact and evident in what their purpose had been, but now just littering the street. I felt sick.

*Has every city in the world ended up like this? Is Melbourne like this now? The iconic Flinders Street Station clocks—are they broken, stopped? The steps cluttered with rubbish? The Sydney Opera House—is that littered beyond access, or has it all blown into the harbor? That crystal blue water with the bridge in the background...*I squirmed as I remembered all the rubbish I had discarded in my life: plastic bags, packaging, straws. I had not given it another thought beyond putting it in a bin. With no maintenance, had the landfill rubbish just blown back into the society that had created it?

We hunted for a supermarket, keen to see what we could salvage. There had been very little tinned food left on August, and we were limited with what we could reasonably take without attracting unwanted attention. We soon found one, then another. But the same image faced us. They had been broken into by the last survivors—smashed windows, glass everywhere, and floors covered in dirt blown in by storms and never cleaned up. We entered the second one, but there was little left on the shelves.

It was funny what people consider useless when the apocalypse comes. Cleaning products mainly. Evidently, no one bothered to clean their toilet when death was staring them in the face. It isn't like your friends are coming over and judging you for it. People must have been hoarding food for months. Even pet food was gone. Memories of Merlin and giving him a final cuddle the day I left for August struck me anew. I always had a soft spot for cats. I hope his end wasn't too drawn out, too painful. I doubt Mum would have let him suffer. I turned my eyes back to the shelves, blinking away the tears of grief before Hugh saw them. Freyja had called me weak once, and the memory of that taunt still hurt. It was easy to forget the past when you were permanently busy building a society from the ground up. It wasn't so easy when the evidence was staring you in the face.

There wasn't much in the way of actual food. Some packet stuff like breakfast cereal that was out of date, but we took anyway along with powdered milk. No one had bothered taking the reusable bags from the registers, so we filled two each. A few jars and cans, baked beans, tuna, sardines, spam. Aloe vera for my now red and peeling face. While we did not need them, I noticed the almost fully stocked rows of basic spices, flour, and sugar. I found that ironic knowing how much the community missed things like cinnamon and sugar on Lewis. If only these people had known how hard it was to grow these things. But they hadn't needed them in the end. After all, cinnamon doesn't keep you alive.

Scanning the carnage of the supermarket, I looked for anything of use. It was easier to stand back and look. Besides, we didn't want to come back. The smashed jars and mess in the aisles made walking up and down challenging. My gaze saw a display of Eveready batteries that had been knocked over, empty now. Batteries had been ransacked. Dropping to my knees amid the filth and taking great care to avoid the broken glass, I looked under the shelving unit. Rewarded, I withdrew the few random packets that had been kicked under the shelving. They could be helpful. No one had even bothered to clean up the mess, and there was no point in us doing it. One of the few benefits of the virus was that it had also wiped out rodents. There was no evidence of mice, rats, or even cockroaches and silverfish. Any creature that needed water to survive had perished. *Maybe it was a good thing with cockroaches,* I pondered. I shuddered, remembering them, their creepy legs and pincers.

Hugh cleared his throat. Glancing up from my ponderings, I found him looking at me expectantly. Was I ready to go?

Nodding in acknowledgment and without speaking, we carefully stepped over the shattered glass that littered the front of the shop and left. Very few of the shops in the main street were untouched, but those that were intact were mainly clothing stores. It was food and water that people had been desperate to get in the end, fueling that longing to survive.

A few doors up, Hugh crossed the road, stopping outside a camping shop, tents, hiking boots, and a display of snow jackets in the window. What had once been an expensive women's ski jacket, a faintly diamond-patterned white with faux fur trim and gold zips, was now almost gray, with nearly a centimeter of dust on the shoulders. He looked at me and raised an eyebrow. Sighing, I nodded, resigned. We needed better gear. With no torrential rain on August, we had no truly effective raincoats. Keeping water off us would be essential if we were to avoid becoming infected. As we smashed the window with a rubbish bin that stank worse than the local tip[12] its contents used to go to, I kept looking around, expecting the police to turn up at any moment and arrest me. Foolish, I knew, but I struggled with the concept of smashing a shop window. On the fifth attempt, the window gave way, and we stood back as it shattered into a million pieces. We wrapped the blankets on our arms to clear a safe path and entered the abandoned store.

It was dark inside with no electricity, so it took our eyes some time to get used to the dimness. We found some torches and took a solid one each. Of course, I had picked up the wrong sized batteries. I mentally berated myself for not hunting harder in the supermarket, but we couldn't have known the correct size. We could get those later. Did batteries last four years? I had no idea. Whenever I needed them, I just bought them. Not an option now. We hunted behind the register and found a torch—with batteries. That was good. Even better, after a good shake, it worked. It threw off enough light to see around the smallish, but well-stocked store.

Making a beeline to the wall with a display of dusty packs, we chose a hiking backpack, each with a proper harness tailored to our size. As we were both tall, this wasn't a simple task, but we found one that was comfortable and set about filling it with a warm sleeping bag, clothes, rainwear, and boots. I couldn't shake the feeling of remorse and guilt at this blatant theft and disregard for the poor owner who had worked hard to make this business a success to pay their mortgage, feed their family, and send their kids to school. For it was a family business. Long gone now, nevertheless,

---

[12] Rubbish dump

the sense of unease remained. When they locked up the store for the last time, did they *know* it was the last time? Had they expected a miracle, and one day they would return? The neatness in the store indicated that they had indeed planned to return. Or perhaps it was just habit, cleaning up before they went home each day. My stomach was in knots, knowing that I was doing the wrong thing, despite the circumstances. Surreptitiously I wiped my sweaty palms on my pants as I thumbed a rack looking for new ones, consciously only taking what I needed, but equally feeling foolish for doing so. I could hear Freyja's voice telling me it was okay. There was no one left. No one needed this stuff. It was rotting into the ground, evidence of humanity's obsession with consumerism, but the gut-wrenching guilt at stealing remained strong, no matter how much I tried to convince my brain otherwise.

Hugh had similar qualms, indicating that he was the honorable man I suspected him of being. We didn't linger once we had changed, filled our new packs with spare clothes, sleeping bags, cooking equipment, and utensils. Still, at the last minute, I took a portable camping stove with as many additional butane cartridges as I could carry and a solar-powered lantern. I noted, without comment, that he took one also, indicating that he didn't plan to stay with me for long. I didn't know where I was going, anyway. How does one get from New Zealand to Scotland when there are no planes anymore?

It was late afternoon; the sun was setting rapidly. We wandered the streets for an hour or so, silently looking for anything of use. It didn't seem right to speak in a place of death. We found some canned food in a third ransacked supermarket, mainly sardines in oil, which I detested, and more batteries for our torches hidden behind a counter.

A memory of Mum stirred, reading me an Enid Blyton book when I was a child, *The Magic Faraway Tree*. I had loved that book and made her read it over and over. There was The Land of Take-What-You-Want and The Land of Do-As-You-Please. It felt very much like that, surreal, wandering around, being able to take anything but needing nothing at all. I wondered with a jolt if this was what it felt like to be filthy rich. Knowing that you could, at any moment, buy absolutely anything you wanted, but as a result, you didn't. I shook that idea off quickly. I had seen enough fashion spreads with $3000 jackets or ridiculously priced shoes because they bore a particular label to know that wealth was not an indication of reasonableness when it came to consumption.

Making our way back to the camping shop for the night, we opened a few cans of sardines and tinned fruit for dinner, cooked some rice on the stove, and washed it down with the single 6-pack of beer we had found in the supermarket. That was a great find. With nothing to say, we lay down and slept like the dead.

CHAPTER 38

THE THICK BLANKET OF eerie silence that muffled everything hadn't lifted by the morning. We woke when the bright sun penetrated the shop window and hit us full in the face. It just felt wrong. No traffic noise, no hum of electric lights, no birds singing. Even the usual countryside hum of insects—flies, mosquitoes—was gone. Nothing. Total and utter silence.

Not being able to face another day in awkward silence, I cracked a joke to dispel the tension. "This feels like a bad horror movie where the kids are having a sleepover with no parents. You know something bad is about to happen to them, but they are always too stupid and break the group up. Don't people know to stay together?"

Hugh grinned and followed my lead. "Or when they hear a noise, they go outside and start walking down the street, and Godzilla appears above a skyscraper. Don't you know to stay inside, you fools?!"

"Ooh, good one."

We kept up the banter about crappy movies over breakfast, cereal with powdered milk mixed with the small amount of water we had left from August.

"My friend's grandparents used powdered milk," I said between spoonfuls, trying not to gag. Disgusting, filthy stuff it was but edible nonetheless, even after nearly four years.

Hugh nodded. "Mine did too. It must have been a generational thing. All the nannas used powdered milk. I could never work out why when fresh milk was so readily available."

There was silence for a moment or two as it occurred to both of us that as there was powdered milk still in the supermarket that older people had not gone searching for food. Had the elderly perished first? I shook that thought off.

"So, where do you want to go?" I asked between mouthfuls of cornflakes. Despite the disgusting milk and the age of the food, the cornflakes were remarkably crunchy. I had forgotten how amazingly simple cornflakes were. We grew corn on August. *How hard could it be....* I caught myself. No. I wasn't going back there. I would live without cornflakes. I looked at Hugh, awaiting a reply.

Hugh looked back at me in surprise. He assumed we would part here. I tried again.

"Look, I have no plans, and I am in no rush. It is barely July. The earliest I can travel anywhere is December." *Not to mention I am not keen on going through that portal again,* being the unspoken part of that sentence. I needed to find another portal, but I was confident that Heidi had mentioned one in northern New Zealand. The one that had linked to Gibraltar, I thought she had said. It wouldn't take me that long to travel north, although finding the antip- odal point could take some time. I would need to find a better mode of transport than that bloody bike.

Hugh was an easy traveling companion, quiet, relaxed, and easy to get along with. But part of me longed to be alone. My heart still hurt from the blow Heidi had dealt. My stomach still churned thinking about it. But he had helped me, and it was my turn to help him.

"Besides," I continued, "I thought you might like a little company as you head... home." Recalling how much Lae's presence had helped that day at my aunt's house, I knew I needed to do this for him. She had managed to get me back on my horse and back through the dome before I had even realized it, my brain paralyzed with grief, playing that grotesque scene in my mind, repeatedly.

Hugh gave me an intense, leveling stare. "That would be great," he responded in a quiet voice.

"Well," I said, standing up. "It isn't like we need to do much here. No point putting out the rubbish. It isn't like a garbage truck is coming to take it away." Still, I needed to place the empty cans and rubbish in a street bin so that it didn't stink the shop out.

"It is like that joke. If a tree falls in the woods, and no one hears it, did it happen? If the shop reeks but no one is alive to smell it, does it smell?"

Hugh waved the empty can of sardines under his nose from last night's dinner. "Yes," he said firmly. "It definitely still stinks."

We had seen many cars parked in the street the previous day. Dad had taught me to hot-wire a car when we were camping in case the keys were ever lost, so I knew how to start a car. We had two concerns: flat batteries and no fuel. We broke into over ten vehicles, unable to start any of them, feeling less guilty and more frustrated as the time ticked away. We may ride our bikes at this rate. Then finally—success! We managed to start a silver Subaru only to find that it had very little fuel in it.

"Typical," Hugh muttered. He started looking for another diesel car and a pipe so we could siphon fuel from another vehicle as I kept trying to start another one. Surely, we would hit the jackpot, eventually. Then finally, another success! The second car I managed to start, a newish Peugeot, was nearly full. Was it newish? It was a new car when I had left. But it had now been, what, almost three years? *So, if cars are no longer being manufactured, does that make this still new?*

It choked and spluttered after we managed to get it started before purring into life. Remembering that the indicators and washers were on the opposite side of European cars to Japanese cars, I washed the windows. The water still worked and cleaned the screen. Flicking on the indicators as I pulled away from the curb, Hugh started roaring with laughter from the passenger seat.

"Why on earth are you indicating, mate?" he wheezed. "It isn't like anyone can see you!"

I blushed. "Habit," I muttered sheepishly, feeling foolish.

The camping shop had stocked maps, so we had taken one of the South Island. Hugh proved to be an excellent navigator and quickly and painlessly navigated me out of Invercargill. Not that it was hard exactly, with no traffic, no traffic lights, and no need to obey street signs. It made navigating a small city reasonably easy. We were soon on our way to Christchurch.

I pulled over before we arrived in the city itself and let Hugh drive. He navigated through the streets to Somerfield, a suburb to the south of the city center. With a beautiful river meandering its way through the suburbs and what was once parkland adjoining it, I imagined that once the suburb was tree-lined and green. Now it was like everywhere else, dead, dreary, and devoid of life. Again, it was the lack of color and sound that struck me. It was bizarre for the blue of the river to be the only color left.

Hugh pulled up outside a neat two-story timber house with Cape Cod windows and what had once been a manicured garden. Now it was dirty, paint flaking, and the garden was full of dead plants, brown grass, and dirt patches. A large tree with a rope swing lay across the lawn, a late fatality. We sat in the car for a moment as he looked up at the house.

"Do you want me to go first?" I asked cautiously, unsure if I was reading the situation correctly. Was he scared of what he would find, or did he just want to be alone? I always found these nuanced emotional situations so challenging to interpret. With my aunt, I hadn't hesitated to look. Dealing with the gruesome results...

Hugh took a deep breath and responded. "I'll go. I was just thinking about how different it looks."

Unsure if he meant alone, I froze. He unclicked his seatbelt, and I mine, again the feeling of stupidity washing over me. If there are no other cars and no one to save us in an accident, what is the point of seatbelts? Hugh closed the car door and purposefully walked to the front gate. He didn't look back. I took this to mean he wanted to go alone.

Watching him pause when he reached the front steps, I contemplated opening the car door. But then he took the two steps and tried to open the front door. Locked. He walked around the verandah and disappeared.

Knowing I could be here for a while, I looked for something to do, so I turned on the radio—static on every band. I tried the CD player. *Mariah Carey's Greatest Hits* showed on the screen as she hit some high notes. I turned it off again. Seriously. Even I am not that fucking desperate. Knowing that he could call out if he needed me, and as it was a fine day with no risk of rain, I went for a slow walk up the street.

Poking out of various mailboxes was yellowed, weathered junk mail rolled up, unread. Now it never would be read. *Junk mail,* I contemplated. Even then, we recognized it for what it was—junk. Catalogs. Brochures showing pages and pages of beautifully photographed items we didn't have but didn't actually need. Ridiculously priced items with an exorbitant price tag all because they had the right name, a label. Was this why our society had perished? Had we valued *stuff,* consuming and buying useless things over people, over relationships? We all knew children were starving, dying in third-world countries of preventable illnesses. We saw photos, news reports of it. Yet, we continued to place value on goods over people.

A baby catalog poking from a large brown wooden mailbox made me think of Orla on Lewis and the community helping their family, the small handmade gifts we had carried, practical and made with love. Items that would be reused for future children. Maybe there was hope. If we could get back to the fundamentals of learning the value of people over things, could we survive?

The politics on August were even more blatant this time around, especially after six months away. There was a clear divide between those who saw August as a fresh start and an opportunity not to replicate the mistakes of the past, juxtaposed with those who wanted to replicate the social order of the old world. The new break-off communities I hadn't asked about and had no idea why they had started again. A sudden longing for Lewis swept over me. Life was so much simpler there. Maybe it was the people, possibly the place. The impact of watching those outside the dome perish would undoubtedly have taken a toll. They just seemed more *grateful*. Thinking about Lewis brought back one face: Laetitia. I could see her clearly: her warm, caring honey brown eyes, her long, dark hair that glinted gold in the sun, and that gentle smile. Closing my eyes, I could see her. I needed to talk to her. I needed my friend. Suddenly, nothing in the world seemed as important as getting back, back to her.

Several houses up, I found a gardening magazine, still wrapped in plastic wrap, proving that plastic didn't biodegrade quickly, despite the misleading print on it. Tearing it open, I went back to the car to wait. I wanted to be nearby in case Hugh needed me.

I awoke to the car door opening and Hugh stonily announcing, "Let's go." It was dusk outside; I must have been asleep for hours.

Unable to ask what had happened, and he didn't want to volunteer, I just started driving. Ten minutes later, I found myself in the city center. Stopping outside the poshest looking hotel I could find, "The George," located opposite an enormous park and river, I parked and turned off the engine. While the river still flowed, the park had no life about it.

"Come on," I announced. "I have never stayed in a five-star hotel." Grabbing the solar lantern from the back seat where it had charged during the day, we made our way up the main stairs to the front door.

To our surprise, the main doors were unlocked. Jumping the desk at reception, we took two keys and walked up the stairs to the first floor. The key swipe didn't work with no electricity, but the manual keys did. We found slightly dusty but lovely large rooms with an enormous bed in each, still made up in white linen.

"I haven't slept in a king-sized bed in years!" I exclaimed with glee.

Hugh smiled ruefully, the day's events still on his mind.

"I'm tired," he said. "Big day. See you tomorrow." With that, he gave me a gentle smile, turned, and firmly closed the door.

I murmured, "Good night," and went to my room.

"Shower!" I stripped off but soon realized that although there was water, it was cold—clearly an electric hot water service. As I soaped up and began shampooing my rather long hair, uncut since Lae's help upon arrival on Lewis, it struck me that this wasn't safe. Shit. Taking great care not to get water in my face, I rinsed off quickly. I hadn't come all this way to die now. At least the towels were large, white, and fluffy, despite the light layer of dust. Shaking the excess dust, I sneezed and then dried myself vigorously to warm up.

With nothing else to do, I hopped into bed, vowing to find a bookshop tomorrow. The TV didn't work. There was no point in torturing myself in reading the menus by torchlight.

Daylight woke me, and I pottered around the room, wondering how I would get Hugh's attention. An hour went by. Accepting that he needed some alone time, I went for a walk, seeking a bookshop. I found one, completely stocked, and helped myself to an extensive selection of books. Those that I had always planned to read but had never found the time. I also found a convenience store that remarkably avoided being ransacked, most likely due to the roller shutter front that had protected the windows. After finding my way inside through the back, I stocked up on snacks and chocolate, family-sized blocks. Feeling decadent, I had not eaten chips or chocolate in years, I carried the stash up to my room. I glanced at my watch. 11am. Hugh's door was still closed.

I knocked tentatively and waited. No response. Asleep, or wanting privacy then. Maybe he had even gone for a walk alone?

Returning to my room, I chose one of the books I selected. Historical fiction, set in revolutionary war America. Propping myself up with the pillows, I settled in to read, finding that I thoroughly enjoyed it. I hadn't had leisure time to read in years. There was a library on August, Lewis too, so I always had a book on the go. But there was work to do, people to assist. One of the complex parts of a sustainable community is that you need to do everything yourself. In a consumerist one, you can just buy stuff. But on August and Lewis, it was hard work just to keep things going. Growing crops, raising animals, cooking, mending clothes, and fixing things was honest and essential work. But it was also time-consuming.

As I turned a page, I reached down to take a piece of chocolate, only to find it gone. Looking down at the block, now an empty outer wrapper and a small pile of foil, sitting next to me on the bed, for a moment, I was puzzled.

Who has eaten all the chocolate? flitted across my mind, in the next instant to realize, *Well you did, you dumbass!* Mindless eating had never been an option on either island.

Shadows were darkening the room. Looking up from my book, I could see that the sun was setting. The digital clock in the room was off, but it was late afternoon. Putting my book down, I wandered out into the hallway.

"Hugh!" I called. "Want some dinner?" I really didn't. After eating a family-sized block of chocolate after not eating chocolate for so long, I suspected I was going to puke.

No response. I pounded on the door. "Hugh! Dude! Are you alive in there?"

A sense of déjà vu washed over me, and I froze. I tried the door. Locked. I ran down the stairs, only to find the foyer in darkness. Cursing myself, I ran back to my room and grabbed the lantern. Racing back down to the lobby, I located the cleaner's keys behind reception. Grabbing key 105, Hugh's room, my heart-pounding, I bounded back up the stairs, barely noticing them. Hill climbing on Lewis had prepared me well for stairs.

As I opened the door, the smell of death hit me full in the face. I crumpled.

When I was able to stand, I picked up the crisp white note left on the desk, returned to my room, gathered my belongings, and left. Numb, I sat in the car, my head on the steering wheel, unable to process. My head was spinning, random thoughts and questions flitting through my mind. But I couldn't select one to focus on. I closed my eyes, hoping to quell the racket in my head.

Drive. One idea bubbled to the surface.

I opened my eyes and turned the key. I drove and didn't look back. I drove all night along winding coastal roads. I had no idea where or how. I could have circumnavigated the island for all I knew. My memories were jumbled, and I couldn't piece it all together. Hugh. Sam. Sorcha's face. Blood everywhere.

Near dawn, I found myself in Picton at the edge of Queen Charlotte Sound. Seeing the large boats in the marina, I drove in. Picturing Freyja and Angus, together, on a yacht, I gagged and nearly drove away, but logic took hold for just a moment. I had nowhere to go.

How do you choose a boat? It isn't like I knew the slightest thing about sailing a yacht. But I needed to get out of here. I couldn't do this again.

I wandered around the marina, unable to focus. I clambered aboard the nearest yacht, painted white and blue, and walked onto the deck. At roughly twenty meters long, it was big, but nowhere near the largest one here. There were two levels, one enclosed, and a large open deck above. There were several white timber chairs on the deck, all overturned but not broken. Banquette-style seating lined the edges. A large, somewhat stained shade sail, originally white, but now a dirty beige covered most of the deck, securely tied to the rails. That was a good thing with my skin. My face was still in pain after paddling in the full sun two days before. I could see the wheel and instruments at the front of the yacht. I meandered through, mindlessly, until I found the stairs leading to the lower level.

A large semi-circle white leather sofa faced a wooden table immediately past the bottom of the footwell with the small kitchen galley beyond. There was a television on the wall. I glanced through the kitchen and turned back toward the stairwell. Past the stairs to the upper deck, a few steps were going down. At the end, I could see three doors. Opening the one immediately in front of me, I found a large bedroom with an enormous round bed.

How do you even get sheets for a round bed? I thought absently.

A bathroom with spa, shower, and toilet led off this bedroom and a large walk-in wardrobe. I snorted, thinking of the backpack in the Peugeot with my sleeping bag and a change of clothes from Invercargill. I glanced out of the small window in the bedroom and could see the red hatchback in the distance, still parked on the dock, keys in the ignition.

After all, who was going to steal it?

On either side of the master bedroom were two smaller bedrooms, one single and one twin, each with a tiny en-suite. Judging by the prints on the walls, they were children's rooms, something that disconcerted me. Children would never travel on this boat again. As I walked back into the main living space, I saw another control panel, this one with the main screen and lots of buttons and knobs facing a wide arc of windows, giving me an unobstructed view in front of the boat. Good, so I could see where I was going. I looked back at the immensely complicated control panel. I had no idea what any of them did. A glance to my right revealed a shelf with books and joy! Instruction manuals. Let's hope there were GPS or autopilot controls, or I could end up in Antarctica. Or worse, back on August Island. It struck me: how do I tell anyone that Hugh is dead? Would they blame me again?

I shook my head to dispel this notion. No. He had left a note in his workshop. They knew he had gone to look for his family. As for me, well. Would they really care? Feeling for the note Hugh had left me, I felt it clearly in my pocket. Unread. Time for that later.

Picking up the radio receiver, it looked much like the CB radio my dad kept in his car for country driving. I fiddled with a few knobs. Dead. Not even static. Well, I had better not get into any trouble then. Returning to the car to unload my gear, I glanced at the keys in the ignition. Having second thoughts about a potentially long sea voyage, I hopped back into the driver's seat and headed into town. I should try to stock up on food. I didn't know how long I could be at sea.

Picton was a small town, but big enough. I filled a bag with the few long-life goods remaining in the supermarket. My conscience pricked me as I broke into a large, clearly expensive waterfront home, where insanely I discovered a supply of bottled water and an enormous stash of long-life food—cans, packets, and containers of every type of foodstuff imaginable. Rich people who had stockpiled water, food, and toilet paper, letting their poorer neighbors miss out. Regardless, it hadn't saved them. I loaded the boot of the Peugeot using reusable bags from the supermarket, needing to make several trips. The ship's galley was tiny for such a large vessel, and I ended up storing most of it in one of the spare bedrooms. It wasn't like I was expecting guests. Wandering around Picton, I had also managed to get toiletries, books, and some more clothes. I accepted I was alone. No one was looking for me. No one was here. It could take me months to sail back to Scotland, so I may as well stock up the best I could to avoid needing to search again later.

After several frustrating attempts, I finally managed to fill the yacht. 6000 liters. My stomach lurched. My old car at home took sixty-five. I didn't want to think about what that would cost. Let's just hope it got me a long way. But not far enough, I suspected. Sitting to read the manual and unable to focus, I struggled to take it in.

Shadows fell across the page, and I looked up to realize it was likely early evening. Being early July, the sun set early, and I would soon run out of light. From the manual, I now knew enough to turn the power on. I tentatively pushed a few buttons and waited. Nothing. I tried again. Cursing, I tried a third time. Fourth.

On my eighth attempt, the motor roared into life. Lights came on, and so did the television. I nearly stained my pants when I heard the roaring static noise behind me. Scrabbling around to find the remote control and turn it off, I noticed the racks of Blu-ray movies, everything from action to animated kids' films.

Finally moving, I did my best to navigate. Navigation was not a strength of mine. I had been beyond thrilled when both my parents, after years of fighting technology, had upgraded to a GPS in their car, and I no longer had to sit in the passenger seat with a street directory on my lap. Dad had still insisted on reviewing the route on the map first, then following the GPS. He never trusted it straight away. I was lost without a GPS, even when I suspected it didn't take me to my destination using the most direct route. Setting a course roughly south, I knew I would need to skirt the southern island of New Zealand before moving west toward Africa's southern coast.

Lae's words, "You will always have a home here," rang in my ears. I prayed that this was still true. This route should take me back via Christchurch, and I could refuel and source anything else I needed before making the long ocean voyage. Goodness knows how many months I could be at sea, alone. The aloneness didn't bother me. Being alone differs from being lonely, although I wished I had Jam or Merlin along with me. Cats are splendid company. They listen and happily sit with you for companionship but demand little of you: food, affection, the odd kind word. Cats, unlike dogs, are more independent. An image of Jam curled on Lae's lap on the couch in the home we had shared made me halt. Jam and Laetitia. I desperately needed to get back to them.

It took me a day of learning to navigate my way to Christchurch, but I was in no rush. I would be on this vessel for months. I may as well learn how to work the equipment. Being in Christchurch again gave me a sick feeling, and I touched the note from Hugh, still unread in my pocket. As I rounded the tight peninsula at Southshore, I could see the snow-capped mountain range that framed the city of Christchurch ahead of me. The mountains were still and beautiful. The city skyline was still there but silent. No traffic, no birds. Just stillness. The waves moved, the wind blew, crackling the leaves on the dead trees and bushes, those that were still standing. Trees had fallen because of the dried-out earth and formed layers of moldering death. I shuddered. I gently moored the *Sea Witch* into the harbor, banging her slightly harder against the dock than an experienced yachter would have done, and dropped the anchor.

My heart was racing, and my palms were sweating. Step one—complete. Not perfect, but okay.

I dropped myself with a sigh into one of the chairs on the top deck, watching the sunset over the cathedral. The gray roof shone in a range of orange, gold, and dark red until finally, it too fell into shadow. Digging the note out of my pocket, written on crisp white hotel stationery, I tore open the envelope and read.

> *Campbell,*
>
> *Now that I am sitting here with pen and paper, I don't really know what to say. It isn't like I have written a note like this before. Okay, that is a totally dumb thing to say. Of course, I haven't. It isn't like we know each other all that well, but I feel like I owe you an explanation... of sorts.*
>
> *Let me start at the end, in case I forget. There is never an easy way to say goodbye. So I will start with that. Goodbye, and thank you.*

Thank you for coming with me, being with me. I appreciate it more than I can say.

You are no doubt wondering why. Why did I wait all this time, travel all this way, and want to go now? It is simple. I made a promise. When their father died, I promised I would take care of them. But I let them down, all of them. In the end, it was my sister, Jenna, who took matters into her own hands. I found them curled up in Jen's bed, her arms still around them. Little Adeline still had her favourite teddy clutched to her chest. It looked like a peaceful end. Jenna was a nurse, and she planned it this way. But they didn't suffer. They were together and happy. That is all any of us can ask... in the end. But know that I, too, am at peace. This is what I want, to be with my family. This is where I should always have been. I should never have left them, and now I am returned.

H

Tears were streaming down my face as I read, and I didn't even bother to wipe them away. I got it. Completely. If that had been my parents, sister in that house, I doubt I would have had the strength to leave. Finding my aunt and her cat was one thing. My parents and sister would have been something else. Unable to leave the boat, I wandered down to the bedroom and slept.

The following day, I woke with the sun streaming through the window to my right, east clearly. I grabbed some dry crackers and headed up on deck. Watching the sunrise over the city, beautifully laid out in front of me, I saw the sun hit the mountain peaks and rose above the snow-caps, changing the colors of the snow as the sunrise glowed on the white crystalline surface.

Much of the morning I spent in inner turmoil, knowing that I needed to seek supplies but crippled with anxiety for Hugh and my inability to save him. I roamed the deck, picking things up and putting them down. I walked up and down the stairs, hunting, searching, but for what—I didn't know. Finally, physically exhausted, I lay on the couch, unable to process. Unable to do anything. Closing my eyes was worse. I could see Hugh lying on top of that bed with its dusty white sheets still perfectly made. He was propped up against the pillows, his long black hair spilled out over them. He looked calm, at peace. Not how Sam had looked. Sam had looked distressed, shocked, when Sorcha and I had found him. Lying in a bath filled with his own blood. Hugh had looked... at ease.

"I'm sorry, Sam," I whispered aloud, staring off over the horizon, feeling rather foolish. It wasn't like anyone could hear me. I repeated it, more loudly and felt better for it.

"I am so sorry. You wanted to play golf that day, but I had an exam. I put it off. You pushed it, and I could tell you wanted to talk to me, but I thought it could wait until tomorrow. I didn't know. I didn't know that tomorrow wouldn't come. I would do anything to change that decision. Maybe if I had made time on that day... maybe you would still be here?" I stopped.

Would he still be here? Would he and Sorcha have been married that following weekend, had kids, and settled down? Would those children have perished in the same cruel way that so many others had? Suffering, writhing in pain? No fresh water, not enough pain killers to go around? Had Jenna got it right? Choosing when and where and ensuring that they were surrounded by the people who loved them? And Hugh. Choosing to go the same way. Maybe that is all any of us can hope for in the end.

CHAPTER 39

I DON'T RECALL LIFTING THE anchor or starting the engine. I just sensed the gentle motion gradually increase until I was drifting, surrounded by water. Looking out of the window, I lay down again. Gently drifting, floating.

The next few days passed in a fog, sipping intermittently at the bottle of Valkyrie, an expensive single malt whisky I found in the yacht's liquor cabinet. *I wish my mother had been alive to try this*, I thought in an alcohol-fueled haze. Mum, dad, Sorcha. They were constantly on my mind, seeing them everywhere I looked. *It isn't like anyone would miss this now*, I thought as I reached for the next bottle in the cupboard. We save things for special occasions. Only those occasions may never come. My grandmother with her good china. Mum having special occasion dresses. But really, what was the point? We save things but never enjoy them. I wondered if Hugh had ever saved something, tools perhaps, just because they were special? Fat lot of good they did him now. Some people, like Laetitia, had nothing at all. Did she feel the same way? That certain items were categorized as special and therefore rarely used? The longing to ask her pierced my chest. My mind drifted, and I could see Laetitia, her gentle, kind face gently pulsating in and out of my sight. Fuzzy, then distinct. I blinked, trying to focus, trying to hear what she had to say. Straining. I could see her mouth moving, but I couldn't hear her.

"I'm sorry I left you," I said as my body convulsed and I was thrown to the floor.

The reality hit me with a jolt. What I had in those six months with Laetitia was beyond friendship. What I had with Lae was a true *partnership*. Sharing a life with someone. Partnership is a sense of truth, of belonging: knowing that someone else has your back, and you have theirs; being able to tell someone your deepest secrets, dreams; sharing your fears and knowing they won't judge—things you barely want to raise to your own consciousness by thinking about, yet you feel safe telling someone else so they can keep your secret safe too. Love is... a partnership. Love is knowing that you are complete as part of a whole.

Startled awake, I found myself lying on the floor of the living room, having been thrown from the couch. Laetitia's face slowly faded. I blinked and tried to focus my eyes. Slowly I stood, holding onto the sofa for support. With a start, I realized that for the first time in several days, I wasn't moving. The yacht was still. Before I could go upstairs, I had two emergencies. I was immensely thirsty, and I desperately needed to piss. I staggered off to the bathroom to deal with the latter emergency first. Then water.

Too scared to drink from the taps, I fossicked in the spare bedroom for a six-pack of the bottled water I had found in the house in Picton. Fumbling, I cut one open and drank thirstily, drops spilling down my chin. Another. A third. The water tasted slightly off, but I was so desperately thirsty that I didn't care. As I placed the third empty bottle on the bench, I heard it. A voice. A man's voice. Calling. Some distance away, but getting louder.

Fuck, fuck, fuck. I've bloody arrived back at August!

Staggering to the control panel, I wondered how long it would take to work out reverse.

I could hear several voices now, men and women, scared? Excited maybe? Angry? No, not angry.

I crept to the window closest to the voices and peeked. A large group of people on the beach about twenty-five meters away. The trees behind them were green and swaying. Green. The trees were alive! *I was back on August.* I panicked, thinking of Hugh's note. Patting my pocket to find it, but it was gone. *Shit. They would hang me for sure this time. Okay, Campbell, think. I was still afloat, but stuck. The dome. I must be on the outside of the dome. Maybe I had some time. How do I free the boat and get away? Was I badly stuck? Had I run aground on a rock? Wedged on a sandbar?*

The men were taking shoes off, clearly intent on paddling out to the yacht. They were still calling, but the wind was traveling in the wrong direction. I could hear the wind rustling the leaves. I could hear their voices, but I couldn't make out the actual words. Peeking again, it struck me. This island was mountainous. I hadn't seen it straight away as I had only seen August from the air once as I had arrived those three long years ago, and from the sea as I was leaving, but that was in the dim early dawn light. The coastline was different. There were stacks and rocks along the coastline. This wasn't August. I was somewhere else. Those people were strangers. But they were alive. There was a geodesic dome in place.

Unsure if this was positive or not, I returned to the control panel and tried to start the engine. It whirred and spun but didn't start. Shit. I tried again. Nothing. *Faaaaaaark*!

I crept back to the window. They had heard the motor spinning and were now looking panicked. Now they *knew* someone was here. What if they had weapons? We didn't on August. But that meant nothing. Taking more time, I looked closer at the topography. I was definitely not on August. That was certain. I couldn't make out features, but I was reasonably sure I didn't know those people. *Where in the bloody hell am I?*

My brain was racing. Options. One, try to escape. Well, that would require a working boat, and evidently, I didn't have the skills to make that happen anytime soon. Two, swimming, was out of the question. If they didn't catch me, I would be infected or drown. Three, surrender and hope for the best.

Making my way onto the deck slowly, maneuvering myself slowly, so I was in full view, hands outstretched in what I hoped was the universal indication of unarmed, had the desired response. They saw me, and there was a collective gasp. Of fear? Excitement? I couldn't tell.

Cautiously I made my way to the edge of the railing and called, "Ahoy there!"

More murmurings. *Do they not speak English?*

I tried again. "Bonjour! Hola! Buongiorno? Konnichiwa!" Okay, I was rapidly running out of languages to greet in.

A woman with long black hair in a loose ponytail leaned forward, ever so slightly. A look of puzzlement on her face as she squinted at me.

"Cam?" she mouthed tentatively.

The look of amazement must have given her the answer she needed. I was utterly blown away. *How did this woman know my name?*

The group on the beach was talking excitedly now. The woman who had spoken my name was animatedly explaining something, but she was side on, and I couldn't see her face. All I could see was her using her hands to explain something. It was evidently safe, so I slowly lowered the ladder and climbed down. The water was shallow here, and immediately I saw the problem. The *Sea Witch* was firmly stuck on a sandbar. Then I realized I *was* on the outside of the dome. The light was shining in such a way that I couldn't see it, as I was right on top of it. That explained why they sounded so muffled. Looking around for an escape hatch, I tested panel after panel. One man shouted something and pointed to my left. I tried that one and stepped through. Closing it carefully behind me, I half walked, half paddled to the beach, keeping my head out of the water despite my raging hangover. Holding my breath, I approached the waiting group. Had everyone known about the escape panels except us?

The woman who had called to me stepped forward. I looked at her dirty jeans, clearly several years old, and dark faded t-shirt. Her hair was very long, dried from the weather, and tied back in a long ponytail. But her face. I knew that face. I grasped for the name.

"Callie?" I ventured.

"It *is* you!" She squealed and threw herself at me. "How did you get here?"

I withdrew slightly and shrugged, waving an arm encompassing the yacht.

"Have you been sailing all this time?"

I found my voice, rusty from disuse. "No. I came from an island. With a dome."

Everyone started talking at this, firing questions, grabbing at me, and making such a racket that I couldn't take any of it in. I placed my hands over my ears to block the din.

An arm crept around mine and pulled me away from the noise. Then she turned and bellowed, "*Shut up*!!"

They all stopped and stared. "Come on!" she exclaimed. "Give the poor guy a chance! Are you alone?"

I nodded. Alone.

"Can you walk?"

Waking with the gait of a person who has been aboard an ocean vessel for days, drunk, but with a bit of support, yes, I could walk. I nodded again.

The group led the way, Callie and I bringing up the rear. I could tell that she was positively busting to ask me a million questions but restrained herself. It evidently wasn't far. It wasn't. Just over a kilometer inland along a well-worn sandy path with scrubby bushes at the edges, we came into a clearing. I looked up to see the village. I stopped and gasped when I saw it. An identical replica of the community on August greeted me. The same houses, cabins, shared spaces. Built using the same template, same materials, the same layout. My head started to spin. Feeling around behind me, I sat on a tree stump before I fell and stared.

"It is... the *same,*" was all I could manage.

The thoughts came hard and fast, so fast that I couldn't deal with the first one before the next overlapped it. *We weren't alone. More villages. More islands. How many? Who else was alive?*

I put my head in my hands.

Callie propped next to me. There wasn't quite enough room to sit. Just rest slightly on the stump edge.

"When I got here, and you weren't here, I just assumed that you hadn't made the cut," she said quietly.

"So did I," I admitted. "I didn't know anyone in my community. I just didn't know that there were... *others*."

"Did you not know there were several communities?"

I looked up at her, rubbing my eyes. "I did," I responded slowly. "We were told twelve, spread out across the world. But I didn't know it would be so close, and so... exactly... the... same!" I finally managed to say.

Now it was her turn to look shocked. "What do you mean by the same?"

"I mean... Exactly. The. Same. The island I was on, with 300 people. Not that far away, I'm assuming. It looks exactly like this one. Right down to the windows."

Callie started to slip off the stump, so I adjusted my weight to one butt cheek so she could sit better.

"We also knew there were eleven other communities, but we believed they were in different places around the world." She looked at me strangely. "Are you saying that you were... nearby?"

"Well, not next door, but geographically speaking— yes. We were on an island just off the southern island of New Zealand."

Her face paled at this. "That is where we think *we* are."

"You are," I assured her.

"Quite a few of our group are New Zealanders. They were fairly certain that we are on an island called Campbell Island. So much so that we called it Bellcamp Island."

I looked at her, puzzled.

"Camp–bell. Bell–camp," she explained with a twinkle in her eye. "Our lives were turned upside down, so we mixed up the name too."

I groaned. "Well, it is better than ours. August Island, we called it."

"Why August?" She wrinkled her nose. "We went in February. Didn't you?"

Sighing, I explained. "August Island. Halfway between Easter Island and Christmas Island."

Callie laughed hysterically at that. "Typical Aussies," she wheezed. "Making a joke out of anything. If you are up to it, let's go. Everyone will want to hear this too."

Ten minutes later, seated in a hall unsettlingly identical to that on August Island, complete with the same chairs and furniture, I introduced myself. I started with a statement about it all being true, but being hard to believe. An hour later, I was finishing with how I had sailed from Christchurch. I told them nearly everything. Freyja, the dome, Angus, the portal. What I found in New Zealand. The yacht. I left out the part about Hugh and how I had ended up here. They didn't need to know that.

They had all sat enthralled as I spoke, and now the noise started up again.

"Look," I said, interpreting the chatter as disbelief. "I know it is all hard to take in. But I assure you it is true. If I could prove it, I would." I spoke again, but the din was so loud by this point that I couldn't continue. No one would have heard me, anyway. I wondered if they had cells here, a jail in which to keep mentally unstable people.

A man, clearly a leader of some sort, stood up and held up his hands to quiet everyone. The chatter subsided with the odd comment muttered in the back.

"Campbell." It wasn't a question, but I nodded anyway. "I'm Blake." Apprehensively, I looked at him as he paused.

"I can't tell you how wonderful it is to meet you and hear your... (pause)... rather fantastic story."

"It is all true," I protested.

He raised his hand to stop me and continued.

Here it comes, I thought bleakly. *The part where they label me a raving nutter and throw me off the island.*

Everyone fell quiet again.

"About two years ago, four strangers came here—a hunting party. From Ireland," he continued. "From Newgrange, Ireland, to be precise."

My jaw dropped. I had been right.

He smiled at me. "We have been wondering if there were other passages, and you have just confirmed it."

My face lit with excitement. "Newgrange? I have been there! Not recently, of course. Is that your antipodal point?"

He nodded. "It is. Campbell Island is roughly antipodal to Newgrange, Ireland. Not precise though, the actual antipodal point is nearer to Limerick, which is slightly farther south. But like your cave and the stones at Callanish, these ancient sites seem to mark the entrance point."

Excitedly I added, "We think it has something to do with magnets."

"Well, we know it does."

I blinked. "Know? How?"

"Well, when we first found the travelers, it was our summer solstice. They came through by accident, much like you and your friend. They were hunting for food; it had been a tough winter for them. They were caught out in the freezing cold on the winter solstice night and stepped into the chambered tomb at Newgrange to warm up and ended up here. But now we have regular traveling parties on the solstice and the equinox."

"How often do the traveling…" I stopped mid-sentence. I was just about to ask about the traveling parties, but the other words in his comment registered.

"Did you just say equinox?"

Blake grinned. "I did. We worked out that not only is the passage open on the solstice, but with a large magnet, we can also manually open it on the equinox."

"But the spring equinox is…"

"Just over nine weeks away," he finished for me.

I sat with my mouth open. There were smiles around the room. A large number, seeing Blake gear up for an extended conversation, quietly got up and left the room.

"I should warn you," Blake continued. "The journey on the equinox is not as smooth as that on the solstice."

"Smooth?" I asked in angry disbelief. "Smooth? I don't know what you have been told, but I can assure you that it is the most disturbingly agonizing nausea-inducing spew fest of a torture ride I have ever experienced in my life!"

Blake laughed so hard he had to hold his sides at my description.

"So you have done it. I have too. And I am telling you, the equinox is worse. Slightly longer too," Blake added.

Longer. My face had turned the color of puce, feeling like I was going to vomit, not aided by my dehydrated, hungover state.

"How much longer?" I asked tentatively. I was desperate to get back to Laetitia but unsure if I would survive another passage. Three times in nine months?

"Honestly, we are still trying to work it all out. We have a team, both here and in Ireland, who are trying to work out the dynamics of the portal. It would be fantastic if it were open all the time."

"Fantastic for whom?" I muttered.

"Well, trade for one! But I take your point."

Still, he had piqued my interest. "What have you worked out?"

"Process of elimination. We know the portal is only open for a few minutes at the mid-point of the mid-days of the year. So, winter and summer solstice and the very middle point of those days only. At the point of origin where it is the summer solstice, it is the mid-point of the day when the sun is at its zenith. So, the precise mid-point of the longest day of the year. At the other end, where it is the winter solstice, it is the mid-point of the longest night."

Blake reminded me of Phil, intelligent, highly enthusiastic, but unable to get to the point succinctly—loved showing off his superior intellect but not in a nasty way. Today, I was in no rush and keen to learn what I could.

"Okay, I get that. But there is what, ten- or eleven-hours' time difference between here and Ireland? So, how does that work?"

Blake looked at me with admiration. "Good question. We asked it too. Then we worked out that the mid-point of the day doesn't correlate with the more modern concept of telling time. The current system was invented in 1847, you know, Greenwich Mean Time and all that."

I nodded. I learned that at school but couldn't recall all the details. Blake read my hesitancy, and with enthusiasm, supplied the missing facts.

"All ancient cultures had a capacity for keeping time: Ancient Incas, Egyptians, Greeks, even Native American tribes. But in modern times, the keeping of time is fairly arbitrary. We track years, months, days. Let's not worry too much about hours, minutes, and seconds right now. A month, derived from the word moon, by the way, was supposed to track the time it took for the moon to go from new to full and back to new, and this is about twenty-eight days. This is why most ancient civilizations used the moon for their calendars. But conflictingly, a year—the point from the summer solstice to summer solstice, is roughly 365 days. So the solstice is a measurement of the sun, and months were a measure of the moon. But full moons rarely fall on the solstice."

"That is interesting," I said. "I didn't know that about full moons and the solstice. I just assumed that full moons fell on the solstice. What about leap years then?"

"That is another problem. The year is not exactly 365 days long, but has another six extra hours, hence the leap years to correct for this, but this correction didn't happen until much later."

I was feeling bamboozled. People had drifted away. The hall was emptying rapidly, and Blake was settling in for a long chat.

"Alright, so we have the 365-day calendar, and the Babylonians divided it into twelve months of thirty days, and that is who we inherited it from, incidentally. There were five extra days that some cultures considered bad luck. The custom to start the year in January came from the Romans with that month dedicated to their god Janus. Janus is a god with two faces, one staring at the future, the second at the past. The months vary in length because the Roman emperors wanted the months named after themselves, and to be longer, which was considered good luck. That is why August and July have thirty-one days. Those were taken from February; other months grew to thirty-one days to make those five extra days disappear."

I was trying to absorb this, but as I didn't speak, Blake took it as an invitation to continue. He was enjoying himself. Goodness, he reminded me of Phil. I would love to introduce them. No one else would stand a chance of getting a word in. Another glance around the room showed that Blake, Callie, and I were the only people left. Everyone else had seen the potential for Blake to talk for hours and had slipped out. Callie was paying no attention to Blake and only here waiting for me. I wondered whether I should wrap this up.

"The week was a later invention. Some cultures used five days in a week, or eight or even ten, but eventually, the seven-day week took hold because we had seven heavenly bodies visible to the naked eye. In English, we kept Sun-Day and Moon-Day, but changed the remaining five to align with Anglo-Saxon gods.

Tuesday comes from Tiu, the Anglo-Saxon name for Tyr, the Norse god of war. Tyr was one of the sons of Odin, or Woden, the supreme god after whom Wednesday is named. Similarly, Thursday originates from Thor, the god of thunder. Friday is derived from Frigga, the wife of Odin, representing love and beauty. Saturday comes from Saturn, the ancient Roman god of fun and feasting."

"Okay, that is all really interesting," I said, aware that I wasn't really here for a history lesson, and we had deviated somewhat from the crucial point.

"Sorry," Blake replied sincerely. "While I am an engineer, one of my degrees was in philosophy. Can you tell?"

I could. But smiled, nonetheless. It was interesting. Just not now.

Blake was speaking again. "Back to when the portals are open. We think they are older than any of those concepts of time. The one thing I didn't mention is the time zones."

I started to object but closed my mouth. What did it hurt to indulge him? There were nine weeks until I could go anywhere. Callie smirked at me over his head.

"It took a long time for the world to agree on the concept of time zones, the late 1800s. And it was becoming an issue, mainly because of the capacity to travel more rapidly. People recognized it couldn't be noon simultaneously in different places around the world, but it was also a local problem. When people traveled by train, and different places set their clocks differently, it was hard to keep track. Greenwich Observatory in England had a reputation for being reliable and accurate, so many people informally used Greenwich as the prime meridian, basically the standard from which variations were derived. Eventually, it was agreed. Every place on Earth was measured in terms of its distance east or west of the prime meridian or zero degrees longitude in Greenwich, London. We know the earth is round or 360 degrees. Therefore, every fifteen degrees longitude, there would be a new time zone to accommodate a 24-hour day, 360 divided by 15 is 24 hours."

I must have made a noise, as Blake paused and looked at me. "All good so far? So you would think that being 24 hours in the day, there would be 24 time zones, right? Well, no. When we left Australia, there were thirty-seven different time zones in use, some differing by half an hour, some using daylight savings, and some not. Then there is a second problem. Because of Earth's uneven speed in its elliptical orbit and its axial tilt, noon, or 12 o'clock, Greenwich Mean Time is rarely the exact moment the sun crosses the Greenwich meridian and reaches its highest point in the sky there. This event may occur up to sixteen minutes before or after."

My head was spinning by this time, trying to derive the actual point. Screwing my face up, I tried to process what Blake was telling me.

Seeing my confusion, he summarized. "So here is what we know. Our concept of clock time has no impact on the portals. The moon cycles have no impact on the portals. The only thing that appears to open them is the mid-point on the mid-day of the year as determined by the *sun*. Full moons, time zones, calendars all have no bearing on whether the antipodean portal is open. So it is a mistake to track the portal by anything other than the sun," he finished.

My mouth dropped open. "I don't know why you couldn't just have said that to begin with."

Callie and Blake laughed at my frustration. Blake managed to gasp, "What is the fun in that?"

Over the following weeks, I learned the Bellcampians knew an awful lot about how the antipodal portals worked, including some likely locations for more settlements. Blake was particularly interested in equatorial countries like Indonesia and Kiribati, which he was reasonably sure would have access to each other at the equinoxes and not the solstices like those on a more north/south access. His fundamental theory was that the portals were usually on islands, and Kiribati was very close to being an antipode to an island off the west coast of Africa called Sao Tome and Principe.

"How is it that people weren't popping through them all the time?" I asked Blake one day when he came to visit me in the gardens. "I mean, people visit Newgrange and Callanish every day, so how was it that someone there at the midpoint of the summer solstice didn't just disappear?"

"That is something we have wondered ourselves," Blake admitted as he took a seat and watched me. "People would have gone missing, others would have noticed, and it would have been widely reported and eventually proven. But can you imagine what would happen if it was common knowledge that such portals existed? People would line up for free travel every solstice, and as we know, the window of opportunity is only open for a few minutes. Can you imagine the chaos? What would happen if someone died en route? Governments would never take responsibility, plus all the immigration and quarantine issues. I have a colleague in Newgrange, Kevin is his name. He knows a lot more and is researching this topic now. My feeling, but I have no proof yet, is that it was deliberately deactivated."

I paused, leaning on the shovel. "Do you have any idea how?"

"I do, actually."

Groaning, and recognizing I was in for another lecture, I said, "Dare I ask?"

"I'm not sure how they would have done it on this scale, but it is possible to demagnetize magnets. It is also possible to re-magnetize them. So, the logical answer is that the lodestones were demagnetized years ago."

"Only to be re-magnetized when the domes were put in place?"

"Exactly. They had to have known that a community of knowledgeable people would work it out. It is genius. Then communities can connect and ensure the survival of people, while staying within their secure biospheres."

"Like your cave on August Island, the cave on Bellcamp Island is lined with lodestones, naturally occurring magnets. One of our scientists came up with the idea of further magnetizing them to see if we could open them at alternate times. The only way we could do that was to hit them with a gigantic bolt of electricity, like lightning. So that is what we did," Callie finished. She had been sitting quietly at the edge of the garden, listening to Blake explain the dynamics of the portals.

"Harness lightning? How did you do that?"

"We worked out how to attach a lightning rod to the top of the dome, waited for a lightning storm, and charged a battery. On the equinox, we directed it to the lodestones. It doesn't always work, you know," she warned. "It isn't like you can predict where lightning will strike. But we have had them up there for nearly two years. Only once in that time have they not been charged sufficiently to open the portal. Both ends need to do it too," she explained. "They get violent storms in Ireland, though, so they don't seem to have the problems we have charging them."

"What happened the time it didn't work?"

"Nothing our end. It was like a normal day, a non-equinox day," Callie admitted.

"And the opposite end?"

"They managed to travel a short distance into the portal, presumably as their end was charged by the battery, but they were then thrown out again. With quite some force, we understand. The poor guy that went first was thrown so far back out he broke both legs. The second person landed on the first, breaking his fall somewhat. So, now we test with a box or cask."

I looked at her with amazement, giving up all pretense of working now.

"Trade?"

"Absolutely. They keep us in wool, whisky, and potatoes. We do well in fruit, coffee, and vegetables. Among other things." She dimpled. "We have quite a few mixed-community children now, including my own, which I suspect was the entire point of re-magnetizing them."

"You said that the Irish traveler broke his legs?"

"He did. So they set up a protected area after that. Unlike Newgrange, there are no rocks here."

"Ahh, that makes sense. The first traveler from August hit her head on a rock and was in a bad way for weeks."

"Well, I can assure you we take precautions. On an unrelated note," Blake asked, a glint in his eye. "What do you plan to do with your vessel over there?" He gestured toward the *Sea Witch,* still wedged firmly on the sandbank from several weeks before, glistening white in the sunshine.

"I hadn't considered it. Why? Do you want it?"

"I do. I really do." The enthusiasm in his voice was bubbling over.

"It isn't really mine..." I considered, "but as the owners have no doubt... died," I coughed, "I can't imagine they will mind either. What do you plan to do with it?"

"Explore," he responded, as though it were the most natural thing in the world. "Look for new places, people."

I nodded. "I had contemplated that, but well, I am just one man."

And you really just want to get home, a small voice in my head said.

Bellcamp was a fascinating place. Without the factions that had divided us on August, the community seemed to have worked out the right mix of collegiality and independence. There was a robust barter system in place. People took responsibility for their own products and grew what they needed. The excess was traded for goods such as eggs, vegetables, and grain, or for services such as carpentry, pottery, and cooking. Services needed by the collective, such as community facilities, engineering, and medicine, were paid for out of a village levy.

Ahh, tax, I reasoned. *It never takes long.* My observation over the past weeks was that mostly, it worked well. Individuals set their price, and the market would work out if it were reasonable. One morning over breakfast, I was told the story of a lady here who had tried to sell crockery at an astronomical price a few years ago. Admittedly her product was of excellent quality and highly valued, yet people objected to her prices. The result was new people hurriedly setting up underground kilns and selling pottery, undercutting her significantly.

"Market forces." Callie grinned.

The weeks passed painfully slowly. Like all situations when you are counting down toward a goal, minutes feel like hours. Most days, I followed a similar routine to one I had followed on August and Lewis. Breakfast, gardening. Dinner with Callie and her partner, Tadhg, or in the dining room. People were friendly, invited me for meals, for a chat. Despite enjoying it all, deep down, I was desperate to get back to Lewis.

On the morning of the spring equinox, I couldn't sit still. Eventually, I offered to dig some vegetable beds for Callie and Tadhg, both engineers. With two young children, they had limited spare time. By late afternoon, I was physically shattered.

Maybe I could fall asleep through the portal? I pondered absently.

Wishful thinking, the other part of me said.

Callie had arranged for a friend to watch their children as we set off, not wanting to miss the brief window of opportunity. Three Irish travelers were returning to Ireland, and four Bellcamp residents were heading through for the first time. The Bellcampians looked excited. The three Irish, two men and a woman, and I looked far more apprehensive. We knew what to expect and were not looking forward to it at all. Just once more. I closed my eyes and repeated the mantra. *Just once more.*

I was the fourth to go through. I watched Dermot, Sean, and Aoife go through. Twenty seconds between travelers. No one knew how long it was open for. A few minutes at most. I hugged Callie and wished her all the best.

"We will see each other soon," she asserted.

As much as I wanted this to be true, as I stepped into the void, part of me fervently wished never to travel again.

CHAPTER 40

FRASER FORCIBLY PUSHED HIS way through the crowd, a beaming grin lighting his rugged face.

"You came back! Great to see you, man!" he exclaimed. He held me by the shoulders, paused, then hugged me quickly and fiercely.

"It is barely October! We expected you would come back through the stones. Could you not wait to see me then?" he asked teasingly.

I hugged him back. It was fantastic to be here. I could feel the smile emanating from my weary face. People were smiling back at me, genuinely pleased to see me. The villagers took turns to give me a quick hug, a handshake, or a friendly smile. I was quite overwhelmed with emotion and a little embarrassed, being the center of so much attention. As I looked around the rapidly increasing crowd, I was certain. *This* was my forever place. A small, warm hand slipped into mine. I looked down to see Laetitia's glowing face and beautiful brown eyes smiling up into mine.

"I've missed you," I said fervently.

"Let's go home," she said with a knowing smile.

Oblivious to the crowds, I gathered her in and kissed her. We had no need for oxygen as the bubble over us descended. After all the pain and heartbreak, travel and hardship, we were together now, and that was all that mattered.

BOOK CLUB QUESTIONS

1. Project Hemisphere is a book about choices. If you had been selected to travel to one of the domed communities, would you go?

2. Who do you think had it tougher, those who left, or those who remained?

3. Cam and Freyja's first argument is about survivor guilt. While each candidate was chosen for their skill, would you feel guilt that you were chosen or recognize that you were the best candidate for the job?

4. When August Island splits on ideological grounds, which community would you choose? The main community where all work is done for the cooperative and shared equally, or Green Island, set up along capitalist lines? Later, Cam travels to Lewis, another cooperative, and Bellcamp Island where a barter system and community tax forms the economic system. What works best?

5. Do you agree with the decision to not encourage religion in the new community on August? Why or why not?

6. How was the community on Lewis different to that on August?

7. Antipodes are two places at opposite points of the earth, and the concept goes back hundreds of years. Where would you like to have ended up if you entered the portal?

8. Cam struggles with anxiety. Does this make him a more likeable or realistic character?

9. Economist Thomas Malthus, in 1798, describes the theory that a population will always grow faster than its capacity to feed itself, and unless the population is kept in check, it will never achieve happiness. Do you agree?

10. Why did Cam leave the August community after being suspected of Freyja's murder? What would you have done?

11. What would you miss the most about the old world?

12. Why did Hugh take his own life after returning home to New Zealand?

13. Cam feels guilty breaking into the shops in New Zealand and taking items. Why?

14. Which character do you most resonate with? Why?

15. This series poses the question, "if the world as we knew it ended, would we replicate the mistakes of the past?" Is it the human condition to repeat the mistakes of our ancestors?

AUTHOR BIO

T.S. SIMONS IS AN Australian author of Scottish heritage. Living in the alpine region of Australia, she believes in the values of sustainability and community in a world where we place greater value on possessions than people. The Antipodes series addresses the question—if we gave young people the opportunity to start over, would we replicate the mistakes of the past?

She holds Bachelor and Masters degrees from Monash University, and enjoys strong coffee, travelling, mythology and snow skiing, while attempting to live as sustainably as possible. She is owned by two rather bossy standard schnauzers and two rescue cats who co-manage her household.

The Antipodes series includes Project Hemisphere, The Space Between, Infinity, Circle of Protection, and Sessrúmnir. She is now working on a related series, The Latitude Series

4 Horsemen Publications

Fantasy, SciFi, & Paranormal Romance

Beau Lake
The Beast Beside Me
The Beast Within Me
Taming the Beast: Novella
The Beast After Me
Charming the Beast: Novella
The Beast Like Me
An Eye for Emeralds
Swimming in Sapphires
Pining for Pearls

D. Lambert
To Walk into the Sands
Rydan
Celebrant
Northlander
Esparan
King
Traitor
His Last Name

J.M. Paquette
Klauden's Ring
Solyn's Body
The Inbetween
Hannah's Heart
Call Me Forth
Invite Me In

Lyra R. Saenz
Prelude

Falsetto in the Woods: Novella
Ragtime Swing
Sonata
Song of the Sea
The Devil's Trill
Bercuese
To Heal a Songbird
Ghost March
Nocturne

T.S. Simons
Project Hemisphere
The Space Between
Infinity
Circle of Protection
Sessrúmnir

Valerie Willis
Cedric: The Demonic Knight
Romasanta: Father of Werewolves
The Oracle: Keeper of the Gaea's Gate
Artemis: Eye of Gaea
King Incubus: A New Reign

V.C. Willis
Prince's Priest
Priest's Assassin

4HorsemenPublications.com